Darkrise

M.L. Spencer

Stoneguard Publications

DARKRISE

STONEGUARD PUBLICATIONS

Cover by Claudia McKinney and Teresa Yeh
phatpuppyart.com
Edited by Morgan Smith

ISBN: 978-0-9997825-0-7

Printed in the United States of America

The Southern Continent

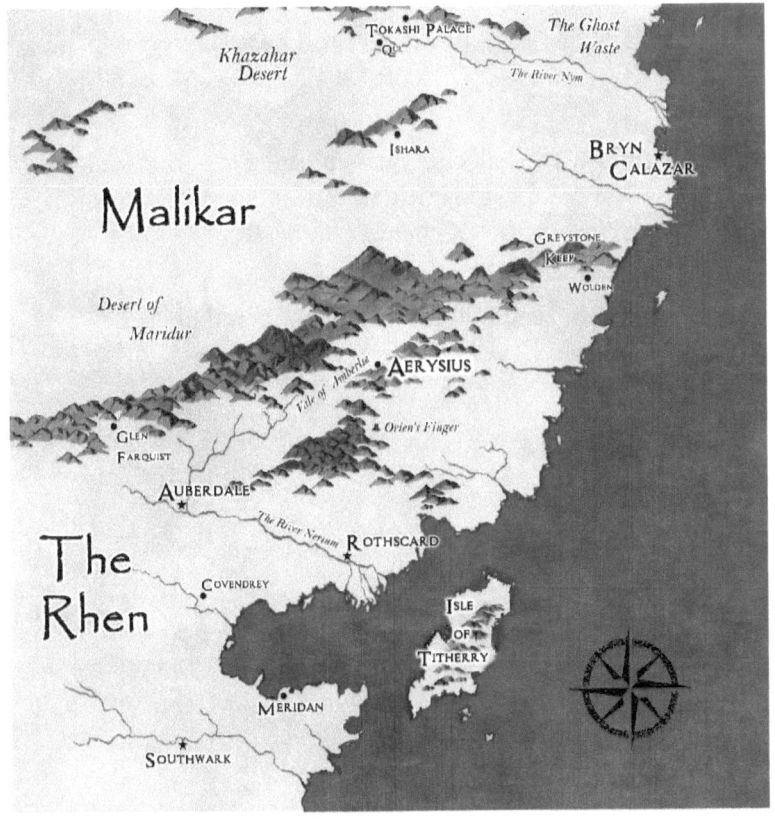

Praise for Darkrise

"One of the best fantasy stories I've read this decade."
BookNest

"Betrayal, lies and destruction follow across every page."
Grimdark Magazine

"I don't believe I shall ever read another story that will test the moral compass in such a beautifully epic fashion."
Goodreads Review

"Another incredible book in an incredible series."
Amazon Customer

DARKRISE

M.L. Spencer

THE RHENWARS SAGA

Darkstorm (Prequel)
Darkmage
Darklands
Darkrise

Chapter One
Darkening Dawn

Pass of Lor-Gamorth, The Front

There's a kind of promise the dark makes. Kyel Archer thought he remembered it well enough.

He stared up at the ink-black slopes of the Shadowspears, at the ghostly lights that flickered in the clouds. His memories of this place were vivid with shadow. The darkness whispered at him from the gullies and ridges, echoed off the high mountain passes. Unfurled before him in the storm-tossed sky. Its vast emptiness raked dread into his heart, feeding his soul with trepidation.

The dark that encased the Shadowspears promised only a legacy of sorrow. After a thousand years of conflict, that was all it had to give.

He glanced at the gray-cloaked sentries warding the long stair ahead. It was not the same stair he remembered, just as Greystone Keep wasn't the same fortress. It had evolved. The Pass of Lor-Gamorth had changed a great deal in the past two years.

Below, he could make out the ruins of the old keep, now just a shattered and scorched foundation. The new stronghold lay farther up the ridge, perched high on the cliff. The new keep made better use of the natural defenses of the slopes, half-built and half-carved out of the mountainside itself.

The steps to the keep were narrow, zig-zagging up the ridge. Kyel felt short of breath before their party was even halfway up; he wasn't used to the elevation. Or the exercise. At his side, a weary Cadmus panted and gasped, grappling his considerable weight up the treacherous stair. Kyel felt sorry for the cleric. Cadmus hadn't journeyed a step outside the Valley of the Gods in decades.

It took their party long minutes to gain the entrance of the fortress: a narrow arch formed from hewn granite that opened into darkness. A tunnel leading straight back into the heart of the mountain itself.

Kyel stopped to catch his breath, craning his neck to glance up. Far overhead, a high curtain wall skirted the summit of the ridge. There were no stairs that could be seen; the keep's entrance must be buried somewhere deep within the rock. Kyel was impressed. Whoever had designed this new stronghold had intended it to be impregnable.

He continued onward with Cadmus at his side, a small group of uniformed soldiers treading behind them. The Conclave had seen fit to provide him with five Guild blademasters to form his personal retinue, as deadly an honor guard as a man could wish for. Unfortunately, the swordsmen were a necessity.

Kyel was, after all, the last surviving mage left in all the Rhen.

He'd sworn a vow to serve his land and his people. He'd sworn another vow never to inflict harm upon a living thing. Those two oaths, each contradictory, nagged at Kyel every moment of every day. He could feel the oppression of their conflicting doctrine dragging him down, like iron counterweights dangling from his wrists.

Within the tunnel, the dark descended with its promise of sorrow. Vibrant torchlight labored in vain to constrain the shadows, forming orange pools of flickering light. The flames did little more than illuminate the path beneath their feet. Kyel walked with his head bowed, hands clasped in front of him.

The tunnel ended at a portcullis. They waited as soldiers labored to raise the iron grate, heaving on long chains suspended from a mechanism overhead. On the other side, a stairway veered upward, angling steeply.

"Avoid the wood. Walk only on stone," cautioned a Greystone sentry.

Kyel nodded his understanding. Behind them, the portcullis lowered with the clattering whirl of chains racing through systems of pulleys. The stairs were made of steps arranged in alternating patterns of wood and stone. Kyel obeyed the sentry's instructions, avoiding the boards and stepping only on the granite-hewn stairs. He didn't know for certain what would happen if he missed a step, but it wasn't difficult to imagine. Kyel had no wish to plummet to his death.

The stairs emerged into a wide courtyard surrounded by crenelated towers and soaring palisades. The keep itself loomed before them, its imposing stone ending abruptly in a jagged array of blocks. The main fortress was left unfinished, Kyel realized with dismay.

"Bloody hell," he muttered under his breath, staring at the structure. It reminded him too much of the old Greystone Keep, with its crumbling rear wall and caved-in roof. The sight of the incomplete stronghold made his stomach clench in apprehension.

"Great Master."

He turned to face the soldier who acted as his guide. The young man carried a hornbow slung across his back, a quiver strapped to his leg. Probably a conscript, Kyel presumed.

"This way."

He motioned the young soldier forward, falling in behind. His gray-cloaked escort led them across the bailey to the castle's upper ward. From there, they proceeded through a series of hallways to a rather unremarkable door on the second floor of the tower. The soldier he followed knocked twice.

The door opened immediately.

"Your men will need to wait outside," the soldier said.

Kyel nodded, signaling his guards. Then, gathering his courage, he stepped into the room.

The first thing he saw was Traver's narrow face, now covered by a wiry growth of whiskers. No longer lanky, Traver had the hardened body of an infantryman. Kyel's mouth dropped open; he almost didn't recognize his old friend. Before he knew what was happening, Traver crossed the room in two large strides and scooped Kyel up in his arms, hefting him off his feet.

"You damnable fool!" Traver exclaimed, giving Kyel one last squeeze before setting him down again. "You've no idea how worried I've been!" He grinned wryly, a shaggy lock of auburn hair falling into his face. He flipped it back with a toss of his head.

"I'm fine, Traver. Really." Kyel made a half-hearted attempt at a smile. It was difficult. He was glad to see his old friend. But the sight of Traver was accompanied by a pang of sadness. He felt suddenly homesick. "How've you been?"

"Well enough." Traver grinned and raised his left hand, wiggling the three fingers he had left. "Except for this. But I rather think I'm better with half a hand than most men are with a whole one. Forces me to use my head."

The other man in the room shifted his weight conspicuously over his feet. Kyel turned toward the imposing form of Devlin Craig. Craig's straw-gold hair was pulled back from his face, which was covered in what looked like a week's growth of stubble. He wore a quilted gambeson that hung to his knees, an enormous sword strapped across his back. Kyel extended his hand, smiling at his former commanding officer.

"Force Commander Craig."

"Archer." Craig nodded curtly. His gaze travelled over Kyel, lingering for a moment on the black cloak that fell from his shoulders. His face conveyed a look of profound skepticism. He took a step forward and accepted Kyel's handshake with a firm, double-fisted clasp.

"Thanks for coming. We've got a problem." His voice was low and gruff. Kyel could see the tension in his eyes.

"I know."

Craig shook his head. "No. I don't think you do."

Kyel frowned, uncertain what the soldier was alluding to.

"Come with me." Craig tossed his head, already moving past him.

Kyel fell in behind, following Craig's burly form as the man strode through the doorway, moving toward a flight of stairs. Kyel mounted the steps after him, jogging to keep up. He walked beside the commander up a spiraling staircase that ascended into the reaches of the unfinished tower.

He trailed his hand along the wall as he climbed, at once taken back in time to the old Greystone Keep of his memory. The old fortress had a very similar stair that had led to Garret Proctor's quarters at the top. This new tower preserved much of the same character, down to the arrow slits that followed the rising curve. Only, this tower ended halfway up. Kyel gasped as he realized he was standing on the last stair with one foot already lifted off. One more step would have sent him over.

Kyel flailed his arms, groping to catch himself on the unfinished wall at his side. Craig's hand shot out and caught him by the scruff of his cloak, clenching a fistful of fabric. He jerked him roughly backward. Kyel dropped to his knees as the world surged beneath him.

"Watch your step."

He rose, trying to catch his balance and his breath. Then, leaning over, he looked down over the unfinished portion of the wall. The view below was harrowing.

Kyel's vision swam as his stomach dropped right out of him. His palms broke into a sweat, toes curling in his boots. His eyes traced down the length of the tower, past the curtain wall and parapets, all the way down the side of the mountain. Before him rolled the sprawling black peaks of the Shadowspears stabbing out of a murky bank of fog. If it weren't for the fog, he might have been able to see all the way down to the bottom of the pass. Perhaps all the way out into the Black Lands themselves.

"Look."

Craig raised his arm, pointing out across the foggy sea below. Kyel tried to make out what the commander was trying to indicate, but there was nothing to see. Just thick, blanketing mist that extended like an ocean to the distant horizon.

Then the mist parted.

Kyel saw what the fog had been obscuring. Black, sinister forms arranged in geometric patterns extended across the dark plain ahead, no natural design. Fires glowed in the distance: thousands, perhaps tens of thousands. So many. Strangest of all, a set of dark, parallel lines, curving away toward the north.

"Mother of the gods," Kyel whispered. "What is all that?"

"That," Craig responded, lowering his hand, "is the Sixth Invasion. So far, they're eighty thousand strong, with more arriving each day."

Kyel's jaw sagged as he looked out across the fog. Below, cold fingers of mist trailed together to conceal the staging army. He turned away from the site, not wanting to see more. He looked down at the stone in front of his boots, instead. His heart beat furiously, tumbling within his chest. His nerves were cold. Numb. He felt unable to conjure an emotion.

This is what Darien must have felt like.

Kyel swallowed, slowly shaking his head as he worked his fingers together. He dug into the skin of his hand with a nail, finding the pain somewhat helpful. It gave him something else to focus on. Not that distraction was the answer. It wasn't. There was no answer to the size of the army gathering beneath the fog below.

"What do you expect of me?" Kyel asked, his words trembling under his breath. "What do you think I can do against that?"

Craig stared at him, his face impassive. Then he reached out and snatched Kyel's wrist. The burly man raked back his white cotton shirtsleeve, exposing the intricate markings of the chain engraved into Kyel's wrist. The mark of the Oath of Harmony.

"By my best guess, you've got less than a month to figure it out."

Craig dropped Kyel's arm with a final glare and stormed away, his long strides carrying him quickly down the steps. Kyel rushed after him to catch up. He was too stunned to protest and too appalled to think clearly. At the bottom of the steps, he almost ran headlong into Craig's back.

The force commander turned toward him with a harsh expression, considering him wordlessly, as if he were sizing up a piece of meat. Kyel could do nothing but stare right back. He knew fear was etched into his face, but there was nothing he could do about it. He didn't bother to try to hide it. He knew he had every right to be afraid.

Devlin Craig scowled and brought a hand up to rub his eyes. When he looked back again at Kyel, his expression was softer but even more unsettling. It spoke volumes of regret.

"I'm sorry, Archer. I wouldn't be doing this if I had any other choice. But I don't. I promised myself years ago that I'd never do to you what Proctor did to Darien. But when all's said and done, it comes down to this: you're just another asset. No more, no less. Like all the rest of us here. And with the size of that army down there, I'm going to have to exploit every asset I can get my hands on."

Kyel's throat tightened, hearing that. Now he knew how Darien must have felt, staring down at such a similar scene. Knowing that all he could give would never be enough. Knowing that he was defeated even before he began. And knowing that every man in the keep would be looking to him, seeing him as their one desperate chance to even the odds.

Kyel's shoulders slumped. He felt vaguely sick to his stomach. But he forced himself to gather his courage and look the commander straight in the eyes. "I'll do all that I can. Anything you ask. Anything in my power. *But I will not break Oath.* That is where I draw the line. Do we have an understanding?"

Devlin Craig's eyes wandered over Kyel's face for a long, silent moment. At last, he nodded. "I won't ask that of you. You have my word: that is the one thing I won't do."

Kyel stared back hard, searching the commander's face. There was nothing in Craig's gaze that gave him reason to doubt the man's sincerity. Devlin Craig had remained loyal to Darien's commitment to his Oath, standing by his decision even in the face of calamity.

"Now. There's something else you need to see." Craig turned on heel, beckoning Kyel to his side. The young mage had to move quickly, working hard to keep pace with the man's long strides. Craig spoke without looking at him as they crossed Greystone's bailey past roving groups of cloaked men.

"Two days ago, one of our patrols stumbled across a woman who escaped the Enemy. She's not one of theirs…She's one of ours. She's the only person ever to walk back out of the Black Lands after walking into them. I'd like to get some information out of her. The only problem is, there's not much of her left. I'm hoping you can help. At least heal her up enough to answer a few questions."

Healing wasn't Kyel's strong suit. Especially if this woman was as badly injured as Craig made her out to be. "I'll see what I can do."

He followed Craig toward a long building that looked like a barracks. Craig led him to one of the wooden doors and, nodding at the man who guarded it, stood back as the door swung open. The ceiling inside was low; Kyel had to duck as he entered. Inside, he groped through the dense shadows. When his gaze fell on the form of a woman on the floor, he froze.

She was lying on her side, her hands clenched before her face. Her fingers were contorted, wrapped in stained rags that seeped blood and pus through the fibers. Kyel could smell the stench of her wounds. It turned his stomach: a putrid, sick-sweet odor.

"She's rotting," he whispered, looking at Craig.

The commander nodded. "Aye. I'll get some of my men to carry her out of the node. I want you to see what you can do with her."

Kyel doubted he could do anything. On the floor, the woman moaned and thrashed. He didn't have any idea what to do about this kind of injury. He'd never dealt with anything so severe on his own. Kneeling, he reached out to lift the fabric that obscured her face.

He flinched back with a gasp.

Kyel tried hard not to wretch. Beside him, Craig dropped to one knee, laying a steadying hand on his shoulder. "What is it?"

Kyel's tongue didn't want to work. He brought a hand up to his mouth, choking on horror.

"Gods' mercy," he whispered. *"It's Meiran."*

Chapter Two
In Darkness, There is Light

The Khazahar Desert, The Black Lands

Soft ribbons of magelight filtered down from the sky, unfurling in gentle, amber strands. Warm rays fell on Darien's skin, delivering comfort like a summer day. A breeze stirred, moving the tall grass of the pasture, rustling the leaves overhead. The entire world was awash with roiling swirls of orange and gold.

He sat beside Azár under the sprawling branches of an oak, one knee drawn up against his chest. His attention was captivated by a chestnut horse that loped in slow circles, roaming the confines of its enclosure. The stallion tossed its head and bucked, muscles rippling beneath its coat. With a snort, the animal bolted in the opposite direction, turning only when it reached the fence line. It moved in easy circles around the pen, the sound of its hoofbeats marking time to the wind. Darien watched, enthralled by such display of power tempered by grace.

A soft breeze chased his hair. If he closed his eyes, he could imagine that he was someplace far away. If he tried very hard, he could almost imagine he was home.

To the woman sitting beside him, he asked, "What would you do if you woke up one morning and realized that everything you believed was all just a lie? That everything you thought was right was actually wrong? Would you think you'd gone insane?"

The question had been rhetorical; he was surprised when she answered.

"I'd thank the gods for opening my eyes."

Her words came from a startling perspective. Darien turned to look at her as if seeing her for the first time. What he saw surprised him. When he looked into Azár's face, he saw beauty. Wild, untamed grace like the kind on display in the paddock before them. Despite the golden warmth of the magelight, Darien felt abruptly cold.

"I don't know what to believe anymore," he confessed.

Azár scooted toward him and brought a hand up to touch his face. She leaned forward, staring into his eyes. "Then believe in me."

Darien bowed his head. The cold settled further into his bones, became a disturbing sensation. It took him a moment to recognize it as fear. It numbed him. Paralyzed him. The feel of her touch was too much, too soon. Too raw. He didn't want anything to do with it.

He felt her soft lips against his, questioning.

The fear welled into panic. He broke off the kiss, wrenching his face away. "I can't do this."

"Then don't." Azár shrugged, pulling away.

Darien collapsed back against the tree, dazing up at the silhouette of oak leaves twirling against a background of golden light. Confusion nettled him, a violent storm of conflicting emotions.

"I am your Lightweaver," Azár said. "That is all I need to be."

He considered her face, marveling at her pride. Azár had remained by his side after Meiran's betrayal. She'd tended him when he was at his most vulnerable, helped him find his way back to himself. In so many ways, she'd proven her loyalty. In all the world, she was the one person he knew he could trust.

He should be able to feel something for her. Anything. Conjure some scrap of emotion. But he couldn't.

The fear subsided. It was replaced by anger: anger at Meiran. He hadn't deserved what Meiran had done to him. She'd robbed him of everything he had, all that he was, everything he had ever been. Left him hollow and ugly inside.

"You should marry me," Azár said.

Her words knocked the wind out of him.

He couldn't move. He felt dizzy. Stricken. He went stiff, gazing unblinking into her face. She looked wild, beautiful. Terrifying.

"Why?" he gasped. He couldn't understand. "Why would you wish to marry a demon?"

She scoffed. "You were not always a demon. Once, you were a man."

"I'm not that man anymore." He scowled. "The truth is, I don't know what I am."

She raised her chin, defiant. "I know what you are, Darien Lauchlin; it was I who summoned you…and now you must do as I ask. That is the rule, is it not?" Her smile was mischievous.

But Darien shook his head. "You only get one request. One. And you've used it up already. I'm pledged to deliver your people. That's the end of it."

Azár raised her eyebrows, a confident smirk on her face. "And how are you going to deliver my people if they refuse to follow you?"

Darien frowned, suddenly concerned. He didn't know where she was heading with this. It was a new direction. Azár could be unpredictable, but she was always honest.

"I have the Tanisar corps behind me," he reminded her.

Azár shrugged, standing, and paced away a few steps. Then she turned back to face him. The cotton skirt she was wearing rippled around her knees. "You will need more than just the Tanisars. You must have the support of all the tribes of the Khazahar. But they will never follow you—not without blood ties to the clans. If you marry me, then my clan would claim your blood as their blood. It has been done before."

At last, Darien understood what she was trying to do. She was trying to help him achieve the goals she'd set out for him. Azár had sought to motivate him emotionally. But when that failed, she'd resorted to winning him over with logic.

He stood up, shaking his head. "I can't give you what you want, Azár."

She chortled at his words. Her eyes traced over him, moving down his body. All the way to his feet.

"Always so arrogant. What makes you think you have any idea what I want?"

Darien could only guess. The woman never ceased to confound him; every time he thought he had her figured out, she delighted in proving him wrong. It was a favorite game of hers.

He said, "I assume you'd want a husband who has the capacity to love you back?"

Azár spread her hands. "Love is not important. What I desire is a husband I can trust. And I trust you."

Darien stared into her eyes, probing her intent. He had to make certain she felt as little for him as he did for her. In Azár's brown eyes, he found only sincerity.

"I'll think on it," he said at last.

She smiled, pausing as she turned away. "Think on it well. The future of the Khazahar rides on your decision. We need you to be more than just a Sentinel. We need you to be an overlord."

Darien sent his horse away from the lightfields at a trot, guiding the red stallion with the pressure of his legs. He gave a quick glance back over his shoulder, wanting one last sight of Azár. But the darkness fell like a shroud around him, cutting off all sight of her. He turned back to the road ahead, concentrating on the rhythmic sound of hoofbeats.

Sayeed rode at his side on a mare that was the same delicate breed as Darien's own mount. Both horses were of similar color, without one mark of white despoiling their red coats. Darien rode without a saddle, just a richly embroidered blanket beneath him. Blue tassels swayed from his horse's bridle, which jingled with the sound of tinkling beads.

Sayeed said, "Your Lightweaver does not seem happy."

Darien shrugged. "She wants to marry me." He didn't know why. It was all so confusing. He reached a hand up and rubbed the back of his neck, avoiding Sayeed's look of speculation.

The Zakai officer grunted, a small grin forming on his lips. "May you have more luck with this woman than you had with the last."

Darien clamped his lips closed to hold back the retort he wanted to let fly. The old anger flared. He closed his eyes against images of Meiran. Meiran, the mother of his child. The woman who'd wanted him dead. His chest still tightened every time he thought about her.

"I am sorry," Sayeed said. "I didn't mean to offend."

"You didn't offend."

Darien rode in silence, listening to the hypnotic rhythm of hoofbeats. He cleared his mind, throwing a shield up between himself and the violent energies of the vortex that closed over them. It was a long ride back to Tokashi Palace from the lightfields. Already, he missed the golden warmth of Azár's magelight. And he missed her company, he had to admit.

Sayeed said, "I am indeed sorry. May the gods bless your union, and may the both of you know happiness."

Darien glared at him. "I haven't decided yet."

A long gap of silence passed with only the constant jingle of tack. Darien felt foolish; he hadn't meant to snap at the officer. Like Azár, Sayeed had been nothing but loyal. He was Darien's staunchest supporter, his closest friend. He deserved better treatment.

"She says the tribes of the Khazahar will not follow me," Darien said. "Not without blood ties to the clans. Is she right?"

Sitting up straighter on his horse, Sayeed appeared to be considering. At last he shrugged. "Your Lightweaver is correct. The Tanisars are bound by oath and duty to follow you. But the tribes care only about blood-bond."

"What is blood-bond?" Darien had never heard of the term. Whatever it was, it sounded ominous.

Sayeed explained, "All the kinfolk of a tribe share the same common blood. It flows through all their veins, every last person. 'The blood of the son is the blood of the father,' it is said. Blood-bond is what binds a people together in obligation and duty."

Darien considered Sayeed's words, his mind mulling over the ramifications. The concept was altogether foreign to him. The politics of the Rhen had nothing to do with blood or kinship. Alliances and feudal allegiance went much further in inspiring loyalty. And though Sayeed's concept of blood-bond explained a lot, it still didn't account for everything. A marriage to Azár might bind him by blood to a single tribe, but he failed to see how that would advance his cause much. The other tribes would have no obligation to follow him.

"I don't understand. The prime warden proclaimed me Overlord of the Khazahar. Shouldn't that be enough?"

Sayeed spread his hands. "Zavier Renquist pronounced you overlord, but that title is all but empty unless you can unite the Khazahar behind you."

Darien frowned. "Would the tribes follow a man of foreign blood?"

"No."

He rode in silence, ruminating on the information. Overhead, sinister clouds raced across the ever-black sky. In the distance, the jagged spikes of a mountain range stood backlit by flickering cloud-light. It was damn cold. The kind of cold that seeped under the skin, burrowing all the way to the bone. It seemed years since he'd last felt sunlight on his skin.

A thought occurred to him. "One of my ancestors was Omeyan. Could I claim that as my clan?"

Sayeed flashed him a startled look. "There are no Omeyans left in all the world. The Omeyan Jenn perished during the time of Desecration."

Darien shrugged; it was just a thought. "It's a distant relation," he admitted.

"Very distant." Sayeed maintained a stiff look of concern. "And yet…if you can prove your lineage…" His face brightened. "Can you name all of your ancestors, all the way back to this ancient Omeyan?"

Darien thought about it. At last he nodded. "Aye. I think I can. The lineage of my family is well-known to me."

Indeed, he had been made to memorize his entire pedigree, both his father's side and his mother's. Both bloodlines figured prominently in the history of Aerysius. His father's line had produced several prime wardens and many famous Sentinels. His mother's ancestors had been just as esteemed, her line extending back even further into the records.

"You must write down your family's lineage and present it to the elders. Only then might your claim be considered." Sayeed looked at Darien with a pensive expression. "Never has a perished tribe been restored to us. I truly hope this thing can be done. It would be a great blessing to all the clans. When we arrive back at the palace, I will make arrangements."

"I'd be grateful." Darien smiled his appreciation. He'd come to lean heavily on Sayeed in the months since his arrival at Tokashi Palace. He'd let the man into his confidence, closer than anyone.

Anyone but Azár.

They rode in silence across the darkness of the wastes, clouds surging toward them from the bleak horizon. Hours passed with only the clip-clop of hoofbeats to mark the slow passage of time. Eventually a long lake appeared in front of them, its water's dark and opaque. Darien gazed into the lake's black depths. Somewhere down there, beneath the waters, lay the ruins of ancient Vintgar and the Circle of Convergence it contained, now drowned beneath the lake.

They crossed a long bridge, arriving finally at an enormous fortress pressed up against the hillside. Tokashi Palace was like a continuation of the mountain itself, towers spiking like teeth into the air, looming over the dark valley and the lake. The lights from hundreds of windows made the fortress gleam like a night sky full of stars. The two men rode through the arching gate into the courtyard, drawing their horses up as soldiers bowed and backed away, pressing their bodies up against the walls.

Darien acknowledged the Tanisars with a stiff nod as he dismounted. He swept his gaze around the courtyard, wary. Even after all the months he'd spent at the palace, the behavior of these people still made him tense. The soldiers stood still like statues along the walls, unflinching. Even the servants seemed frozen in their positions, heads bowed, hands clasped. There was no sound in the courtyard, not even the rustle of fabric. It was the totality of silence that unsettled him most.

Darien looked around, sweeping his gaze over dozens of men who had sworn to serve him with their lives. Or with their deaths. He took note of their conduct with solemn respect. He had never known a better fighting force. Certainly, nothing in the Rhen could equal the discipline of the Tanisars.

He set out across the courtyard with Sayeed, leading his mount into the depths of the fortress. Servants bowed and backed away from his approach, lowering their gaze respectfully. Darien walked past each of them without acknowledgement. He was used to the treatment now. At first, just walking the corridors had been difficult for him. He had never felt so self-conscious. It was surprising what one could grow accustomed to.

Looking ahead, he saw a small group of officials clustered in front of the entrance to the Residence, awaiting his arrival. They formed a small clot outside the grilled gate that separated his living space from the rest of the fortress. The men turned toward him, forming a line and bowing in unison.

"Blessings upon you, Darien Nach'tier, if I could have just a moment of your time?"

"*Ranu kadreesh,* Lord, five minutes is all I need!"

"Overlord, I have just one question!"

"*Back away!*" Sayeed bellowed, startling the horses.

The officials bowed and scrambled aside to clear a path to the doorway. Fear radiated from their bodies, so sharp he could almost smell it. They hated him; he could see it in their eyes. But they were too terrified to do anything about it.

"I'll meet with all of you after *domadh,*" Darien assured them, raising his hand.

The doors to the Residence swept open before them. Darien led his stallion into the corridor beyond, Sayeed following with his own mount as the grilled doors were bolted behind.

Inside the Residence, the character of the fortress changed drastically. They moved through a wide hallway illuminated by gilt lanterns. The walls and floor were tiled in sprawling geometric patterns of red and blue, broken by draped folds of colored cloth. Scalloped columns lined the passage, wrapped with scrolling inlay. Darien moved under the warm light of countless lanterns, pausing at the first wide doorway they came to. There, he offered his horse to a servant waiting at the entrance.

The boy took the stallion's reins, conspicuously avoiding eye contact. Another took the reins of Sayeed's mount. Darien waited for the Zakai officer to retrieve their packs and then turned toward his own bedchamber, just across the corridor from the stable.

He lingered as Sayeed opened the door and entered first, taking his time about inspecting the interior of the room. Only when the officer gave a nod did Darien enter behind him. The chamber was large, an enormous canopied bed the focal point of the room. There was also a hearth recessed into an alcove on the far wall. Only a few items of furniture were scattered about: two wooden chairs and a small writing desk. Silken fabric hung from the walls and the bed's canopy, echoing the colorful patterns of the rugs.

From the corner of the room emerged a living shadow that approached with gleaming eyes. Darien smiled, moving forward to greet his pet. He'd left the demon-hound behind intentionally; the horses didn't care for the scent of damnation. He ran his hand through the beast's thick fur, tugging one ear affectionately. The thanacryst purred at the attention, managing to seem both dreadful and content.

"Will that be all, Lord?" Sayeed still lingered in the doorway, his face expectant.

Darien turned toward him with a nod. "That's all, Sayeed. Thank you for your company."

The officer bowed and backed away, pulling the door closed behind him.

Darien stared at the door for a long moment before turning away. He gave the thanacryst one last scratch, then moved to the writing desk in the corner. He slouched down into the chair, drawing in a deep breath. He smelled of horse. It was a scent he was rather fond of. It mingled nostalgically with the fragrant incense that permeated the chamber.

With a whimsical smile, Darien picked up an *elam* from the desk, a writing instrument made from a hollow reed, its tip carved to a tapering point. He held the *elam* in his left hand, pausing a moment in reflection. Then he unstoppered a pot of ink that smelled of soot, giving it a quick stir before dipping the tip of the *elam*.

At the top of a page, he inscribed his own name in bold calligraphy. Below, he wrote the names of both his mother and his father. Upon second thought, he crossed out his father's name. He was descended from the Omeyans on his mother's side; his father's lineage was not important in this context. Under his mother's name he wrote out his maternal grandfather's name and title. He kept scribing, one name after another, moving slowly down the parchment as the tapers on the desk burned lower. About halfway through the list he paused, using a blade to sharpen the dulling tip of the *elam*.

Minutes passed. At last, Darien finally scribed the last name of his lineage:

Braden son of Marthax,
Omeyan Clan of the Dur ul-Jenn

Darien gazed at his ancestor's name for a long moment. Then he set the *elam* down on the writing desk, stoppering the ink pot.

He rose then, strolling toward an ornate chest pushed up against the wall. There, he knelt and lifted the lid. He stared into the depths of the chest for a moment before finally removing the first item that caught his eye. Holding it up, Darien felt his face burn with anger as he gazed down at the silver pendant that had once been Meiran's. He squeezed his fingers closed around it. Reluctantly, Darien placed the necklace back in the chest. Then he withdrew the other items left behind by Quinlan Reis.

He stood up, holding the Omeyan warbelt in one hand and a scroll of parchment in the other. Quin had left both items behind in Qul. Darien unrolled the scroll, his eyes scanning quickly over the page.

This belt is yours by rights. It belonged to your ancestor, Braden son of Marthax, Warlord of the Omeyan Clan of the Dur ul-Jenn. It is the last of its kind in the world, just as you and I are the last of our kind. Wear it with pride in memory of my brother.

~Quin

Darien stared down at the worn leather in his hands, his eyes roving over the golden buckle that depicted the image of a horse bent backwards at an impossible angle. The belt itself was decorated with many hooks and thongs, from which an assortment of implements could be hung.

Before, he had lacked the conviction to put it on.

Now, Darien lowered the scroll and drew the belt around his waist, fastening it securely with the gold buckle. He stared down at himself, at the black wrap he wore about his hips tied with gold tassels. The warbelt complemented the wrap, adding a martial quality to the ensemble. Rubbing the weeks' worth of stubble on his chin, Darien wondered if any of his old friends would recognize him if they saw him. He didn't think he looked much like a man of the Rhen any longer. He'd been away too long.

His eyes found the demon-hound slumbering in a corner by the hearth. He made his way to the bed, fingers working at the buttons of his shirt. He let the soft fabric fall to the floor and sat down on the edge of the bed, leaning forward.

The thanacryst startled awake, raising its head. A low, menacing growl rumbled deep in its throat. The hound's green eyes narrowed to slits, its attention rapt upon the door.

Darien looked up, his body stiffening.

There was no knock. The door burst open, admitting Sayeed. Darien opened his mouth, but then he saw the look on the officer's face.

"Sorry to disturb you, Lord," the man blurted, his face pale. He lowered his head to stare intensely at the ground. "You have a visitor…"

Before Darien could react, another man strode into the bedchamber.

Darien froze. He'd been expecting this for some time. He was just surprised it had taken them so long. His eyes locked on Sayeed's. "You may go."

The officer bowed formally before backing out of the room. He pulled the door closed behind him.

Darien raised his eyes to Byron Connel. With his hand, he indicated the nearest chair. "Please. Have a seat."

But the ancient Battlemage shook his head. Connel's face was as hard as chiseled stone. "I didn't come for conversation. I'm here to formally charge you with the murder of Nashir Arman."

Chapter Three
An Orlian Knot

Ishara, The Black Lands

Quinlan Reis scowled as he stalked toward the town center of Ishara. The air was damnably cold, made worse by a penetrating mist that clung close to the ground. It had rained earlier, and the streets oozed with muck. Quin trudged through mud that stuck to the bottom of his shoes, making suctioning noises as he walked. Every scrap of clothing he wore was soaked through. He shivered and rubbed his hands together for warmth, which didn't do much good; his gloves were just as saturated as the rest of him.

He was miserable. For some reason, luck just never seemed to be on his side. It avoided him completely, like a discarded lover. He'd thought that swearing his soul to the God of Chaos would have improved his lot. Occult intervention or something of the sort. But no; even Xerys had no patience for him, it seemed. He'd used the transfer portal system to journey as far south as Meridan in the Rhen. But that was as far as the crippled system went. Without the Aerysius hub, it was impossible to transfer directly to the Isle of Titherry. Which left Quin with only two options: abandon his quest or hire a ship.

He wasn't about to hire a ship. So he'd given up.

Quin had returned to the Black Lands to bide his time. He had no plans for going forward. His strategy was recklessly simple: avoid Renquist. He didn't wish to be taken to task for the murder of Sareen, even though he knew he had it coming. Other than making himself as inconspicuous as possible, he had nothing on his plate. Which surprisingly left him with a scarcity of options.

Up ahead, the sounds of commotion came from the square around Ishara's temple. Quin's first inclination was to turn down the next alley and disappear into the shadows of the night; his last visit to the temple had left visible scars. But curiosity got the better of him. Instead of doing the sensible thing, Quin set his feet in the direction of the town's ziggurat.

The streets of Ishara were deserted. Ramshackle households bordered the avenues, surrounded by mud-brick walls. Clouds of soot belched from stone chimneys, thickening the air with oily grit. Quin reached into his pocket and pulled out a scarf, holding it over his mouth to make it easier to breathe. He despised the filth that polluted the air, even though he knew the burning of coal was necessary. After all, it had been his own actions that had created the situation.

What he found at the center of town was a now-familiar sight: scores of people surrounding the base of the temple, waving and shouting, jostling each other as they vied for a better view. Some held flaming torches; others brandished weapons in the air. It was a scene of civil chaos and disorder that seemed to be the hallmark of the Black Lands. Just the same as the last time he'd passed through this wretched town—a town all the gods, save one, had abandoned.

A few people on the margin of the crowd turned to mark Quin's passage. Seeing the red mist that trailed at his feet, the eyes of the villagers widened in recognition. Their jostling ceased, their gazes lowering to the ground. A few men fell to their knees, bowing low at Quin's approach. It was like a wave that passed through the crowd, starting at the back and rippling toward the front, leaving only a lingering silence in its wake. A path opened up before him as the crowd drew back, yielding an approach to the temple steps.

Most of Ishara's citizens already knew his face. But even more familiar was the color of his magelight. No one moved to confront him as Quinlan Reis mounted the ramp of steps that led to the topmost terrace of the ziggurat. Above, a group of men dressed in crimson robes waited to receive him. The square was motionless; the frothing turmoil had stilled.

As he crested the top of the steps, anxiety spread like a toxin through Quin's body, awakening every nerve. He tried to shrug it off. Maybe it was just the memory of the beating he'd taken at the hands of these same men, when he'd entered Ishara with Meiran. But it seemed to be more than just that. Something much more pressing.

For some reason he couldn't explain, Quin felt a haunting sense of urgency.

He paused to consider the crowd of men gathered at the top of the terrace. He let his gaze sweep over them, lingering on each face in turn. The men in red cloth were priests of Xerys. They were assembled in two tight clusters on either side of the stairs. It seemed they had amassed quite an impressive stack of coal bricks in the center of a raised platform. Sprigs of herbs and flowers had been laid over the pile the coal, along with the branches of fruit trees. As though the priests had assembled the makings of a spectacular feast.

Only, it wasn't an animal they were preparing to roast.

Quin's eyes fell upon the focus of the priests' attentions, his throat going tight.

This wasn't a feast. It was a cremation.

Before the mounded stack of coal lay the body of a dead woman. At least he assumed she was dead, judging by the amount of blood still leaking from the carcass. The strange thing was, it all looked so very *recent*. As if she'd been beaten to death right there, at the top of the temple steps. She hadn't died somewhere else, her body dragged here for a funeral pyre. Blood was everywhere, splattered across the gray stone of the temple.

Quin's stomach clenched in anger. He took a step forward, his eyes falling on the dead woman's outstretched arm. The skin of the arm was papery white, a bright contrast to the puddles of blood pooled on the stone.

Then Quin saw the scars on that pale wrist. And he knew.

Not a cremation. An immolation.

The woman wasn't dead.

He tugged hard at the Onslaught, filling his gaunt body with all the power of hell he could muster, all the vile energy he could withstand. A terrible green light suffused his flesh, surrounding his body like an insidious aura. The priests of Xerys backed away, eyes filled with awe and fear. Quin trudged forward, glowering at them from beneath the shadow of his hat.

"I'll take it from here." He spoke softly, dangerously. It was a tone he hadn't used in years.

The priests did not argue.

Quin knelt down beside the bloodied form of the woman. He lay a hand on her forehead and closed his eyes. Anger flowed into him along with knowledge. The young woman at his feet had been beaten within an inch of her life. The priests had cruelly left her that narrow inch. They were going to use it to feed her soul to their vengeful god. Which was, of course, his own vengeful god. Quin didn't stop to consider the ramifications of that fact. He just acted.

He flooded the woman's body with healing energies, working quickly but efficiently to repair the damage she had sustained. Then he lifted her dead weight into his arms. The temple priests made no attempt to deny him. They knew better.

Carrying the unconscious woman, Quin turned and made his way down the long flight of steps. When he reached the level of the street, the parted crowd drew back from him even further, looks of fear on the face of every person gathered in the square.

Quin said nothing as he strode back through Ishara's empty streets, the unconscious woman in his arms. He kept walking until he reached the town gate. Even then, he didn't stop. He walked straight out into the thick nothingness of the waste. He didn't look back. He didn't pause. He just kept walking.

The woman slept for two days.

Quin had built a campsite beside the hill that housed Ishara's transfer portal, tucked away in a deep recess in the cliffside. There, he'd built a small fire, just enough to take the edge off the chill. He would have preferred to camp inside the portal chamber itself, but he didn't dare take the risk. He still didn't know if

Renquist had figured out his involvement in Sareen's death. Quin reckoned it was probably a good bet he had.

He hunkered down beside the fire, rubbing his hands together. He shot a glance at the woman sleeping next to him against the cliff face. She was hardly old enough to be called a woman. And cleaned up, she was rather quite lovely. She slept with her lips parted, infinite volumes of dark auburn hair surrounding her face. Quin leaned forward, reaching out to adjust the blanket he'd thrown over her.

She moaned, tossing a bit in her sleep.

Quin's eyes fell on the scar on the woman's wrist. Her right wrist. He stared hard at that cherry-red marking, unable to take his eyes off it. It was dreadful, distinctive in its pattern. He'd seen such scars before. And he knew well what they signified. It was hard, but he finally managed to look away.

Only to find her staring up at him, wide awake.

The woman's eyes were fierce and bright with fear. She thrashed, scooting away from him as far as the rock behind her would allow. She sat there in a tight ball, hands raised defensively as if trying to ward him off.

Quin shot up a hand. "Relax. You're safe. I won't hurt you...I think."

The woman glared at him, eyes full of spite and accusation. "Who are you?"

Her voice was melodic and rich, thickly accented. Moving deliberately slow, Quin removed his hat. Tucking it against his chest, he said, "Grand Master Quinlan Reis of the Order of Arcanists, at your service. I deduce you must be Naia."

Her eyes narrowed. "How do you know my name?"

Quin smiled wanly. "Process of elimination. There are not so many mages left in the Rhen. You're not Kyel, obviously. And you're not Meiran—thank all the gods!"

Her eyes narrowed even more. "What did you do to Meiran?"

Quin chortled, thrusting his hat back atop his head. "*Do* to her? Why, absolutely nothing that she didn't agree to in advance. On the contrary; despite my rather blemished reputation, I can make for rousing company. Really. It's true, so you don't have to look at me like that. You just might hurt my feelings."

Naia sat up, glaring her ire at him. "I have no desire for your wretched company, and I couldn't care less about your feelings. Take me to Darien Lauchlin. *Immediately.*"

Quin couldn't help but laugh. "I'm sorry, darling, but Darien isn't in the mood for any more visits from former sweethearts. He only narrowly survived the last one."

The expression on Naia's face transformed, her ire replaced by a look of concern. "What happened?"

Quin shrugged, thinking the answer should be obvious. "Meiran did her damnedest to send his soul back to the netherworld. Fortunately for Darien, I deigned to intervene."

The woman's eyes widened. She had beautiful eyes. They were wide and dark, radiant with the spark of the gift within her.

Quin said, "As you can imagine, after that, I won't be letting you anywhere near him."

Naia fixed him with a look of disdain. "Then what are you going to do to me?"

"That depends." Quin picked up a thin metal rod, using it to prod at the graying coals of the fire. "By the look of your arm, I gather you've been forced to make some rather difficult choices lately. Dare I ask?"

The woman looked away. She folded her arms, refusing to answer.

Quin cracked a grin. "I seem to have the same effect on every woman I meet. They all end up speechless and appalled."

Naia's eyes widened in shock before they narrowed to smoldering, slivered coals.

"I killed Sareen," she growled, leaning back against the rock wall.

"No. *I* killed Sareen," Quin differed astutely.

"I killed her again."

Quin frowned in consternation. He couldn't believe the woman was actually arguing with him over this. She was turning out to be nearly as infuriating as Meiran. He was starting to get a feel for the kind of woman Darien was drawn to. Come to think of it, the man really did seem to have a penchant for abuse.

Quin reached up to scratch the side of his face. "This is turning into quite the Orlian knot. Perhaps we should start over. I killed Sareen the night I left Rothscard with Meiran."

He waited for Naia to supply her part in the tale. When it became obvious that she wasn't going to, he raised his hand in a beckoning gesture. "It's your turn. That's the way this works, you see. I talk. Then you talk. We take turns."

Naia scowled in distaste. But at last she favored him with an explanation. "Kyel and I found Sareen dead. We wished to question her. We wanted to find out where you had taken Meiran. So we did what we could to preserve her body and then later brought her back to life. She tried to kill Kyel…and so I acted. Without thinking, obviously."

Quin stared at her for a moment with eyebrows raised, mouth hanging slack. He waited for her to elaborate. When she didn't, he reached up and rubbed his tired eyes.

"You do realize that nothing you're saying makes any type of reasonable sense?"

"I *am* making reasonable sense!" Naia snapped. "You're just too *unreasonable* to understand it!"

Quin smiled acidly. "So…it seems you're not as shy and timid as you would lead me to believe. Which is fine; I can fight fire with fire. I *am* a demon, you know." Seeing her expression, he continued in a blander tone, "Perhaps we should back up a bit. Retrace our steps. First, what in the world could possess you to want to question a dead woman?"

Naia wriggled into a more comfortable position, scooting forward to warm her hands over the fire. She glanced up at him through a lock of spiraling hair, obviously still ruffled. "We had no idea what happened to Meiran. All we knew was that you'd taken her. We thought Sareen might have that information. And we had reason to suspect she would be willing to help us…Since you were the cause of her death, after all."

"And you just spontaneously decided to reanimate a corpse?" Quin supplied a weak grin. "And how, may I ask, did you accomplish this?"

Naia didn't answer. She sat staring down at her hands, warming her fingers over the flames as though she hadn't heard him.

"So, it's to be the silent treatment?" Quin sighed, resigned. "I seem to receive that from most women I encounter. I don't have the faintest notion why." He sagged back with a yawn. "All right, then. Let's change the subject. Assuming that you did somehow manage to wake the dead, what did Sareen have to say?"

Naia glanced at him. "She told me you killed her. And she said I was valuable…and that Kyel was not."

Quin sucked in a cheek. "How uniquely disturbing. I fear I'm starting to believe you. So, Sareen tried to kill Kyel, and you killed Sareen, which voided your Oath of Harmony…And then you somehow ended up here beside a pile of coal bricks. But that still doesn't explain how you fled the Rhen."

Naia looked down again at the fire without answering. Which was really too bad; out of all the questions he'd asked her, that was the one Quin wanted answered most. He sighed and tossed his hat down in his lap.

"Well, my dear, it seems I have no choice but to lay it all out for you. Let me tell you a bit about my situation. And what you can do to help." Leaning forward, he made sure his eyes captured her attention. "If I don't find a way to end this darkness, there's going to be a war. And not just any war. A war unlike anything we've ever seen in all of history. The land will run with rivers of blood and the fallen will outnumber the living."

He waited, watching her eyes as the information seeped through her skin.

He continued, "I need to journey to the Isle of Titherry to use Athera's Crescent. You came along at just the right time, you see. I could really use your help…Especially if your talents are as exceptional as they seem."

She glared back at him through thick lashes. A hand came up, fingering a crease in her blue gown. She asked, "What makes you think I'd want to help you?"

"Because I believe I've found a way to lift the curse over the Black Lands, which would stop this war before it starts." Quin's smile waxed exultant. He offered his hand to Naia, open and inviting. "Care to help?"

Chapter Four
The Darkness Within

Tokashi Palace, The Black Lands

Byron Connel asked, "Do you deny killing Nashir?"

Darien took a deep breath. "No."

There was no use denying it. Another Servant had died by his hand. It wouldn't do any good to lie about it. He didn't want to give Connel any reason to doubt his word; there were far more pressing things he needed to keep hidden.

The Battlemage shifted his weight over his feet, his expression grave. The indigo robe he wore swayed with his motion. "Very well. Do you have anything to say in your defense?"

Darien said, "He moved against me. I was left with no choice."

Connel took a menacing step toward him, eyes full of skepticism. He set his gloved hand on the leather-wrapped haft of his weapon, a silver morning star that was a powerful talisman. "How did he move against you?"

"He tortured me. He wanted me to deny our Master." Darien's voice was matter-of-fact. He made no attempt to elaborate; there was no reason to.

Connel's expression remained doubtful. "Why would Nashir do that?"

Darien shrugged. His hand went to the buckle of the warbelt at his waist, his fingers tracing over the raised image of the horse. "Revenge. He intended to banish my soul for killing Arden."

Connel's grip on Thar'gon's haft relaxed slightly. His frown remained dangerous. He ran his hand back through a thick mane of red hair. "What did you do with Nashir's corpse?"

"I disposed of it."

"How? Where did you dispose of it?"

"Come. I'll take you to him." Darien extended his hand toward the chamber's entrance. He waited, eyes fixed on Connel's glare.

At last, the Battlemage relented and strode to the door. Darien fell in at his side, matching his pace. He led the big man into the hallway, turning in the direction of the stable. Sayeed was there, lingering along the side of the hallway. He stood rigid as stone, staring straight ahead into nothing.

Connel made no attempt at conversation as Darien led him into the stairwell that accessed Tokashi's warren of subterranean dungeons. Spiraling steps took them downward, away from the warmth of the Residence, into the frozen heart of the glacier that consumed the lower levels of the fortress. The air grew colder the further they went. The walls of the stairwell darkened, became moist with condensation. A pool of chill air greeted them as they reached the bottom of the steps.

There, Darien opened a large metal door that led into the bowels of the dungeon. A gush of frigid air rushed past them, along with a wash of eerie blue light. Darien stepped into the ice-carved passage then turned back, waiting for Connel. The Battlemage looked around, planting the palm of his hand against the slick wall of ice.

"He kept me here," Darien explained as he strode forward into the depths of the ice warren. "They locked me up and kept me near death. Then they dragged me there."

Darien pointed, indicating an iron door straight ahead at the end of the hall. He made no move toward it. He had no desire to look within; he didn't wish to confront the nightmares that door unlocked. His memories of the chamber beyond were riddled with holes. Some things he remembered luridly well, like the feel of the dust-filled rag in his mouth and the ghastly sounds of Meiran's screams. The clicking noise of the mechanism. Other things he couldn't remember at all. He had no recollection of how he'd come by the gut wound that had almost killed him. He had no idea how he'd survived.

He stepped aside and waited for Byron Connel to work the latch. The Battlemage regarded him with a long, searching gaze. Then, one hand on his weapon, he opened the door and stepped into the dark chamber within. He walked forward a few paces then stopped, stark-still.

Darien followed grudgingly. He moved to the side, standing with his back against the jagged rock wall. Above, rusted chains and hooks dangled from the ceiling. Mechanical devices with winches and gears, cogs and screws, had been placed all around the edge of the room. A long, narrow table equipped with leather straps stood on the far end of the chamber, its surface stained dark with blood. The scene was gruesome, appalling. Darien's gaze avoided all of it, remaining instead on the one object in the room that overshadowed all the rest.

A living nightmare hovered in the center of the chamber, rotating slowly, its silhouette form orienting toward them.

Darien stared at the necrator, repulsed by his own reaction to the thing. He should be frozen in fear, terrified beyond capacity to act.

Instead, Darien felt nothing.

This monster was his own creation. He had willed it into existence from the scorched fabric of Nashir's soul, granting it life by feeding it death. Only, he had no recollection of doing so.

Connel turned to look back at him. His mouth hung slack. Revulsion and disbelief glassed his eyes. "You did this?"

"Aye." Darien nodded once. He stared fixedly at the necrator. He didn't trust it. Even though he was well beyond the creature's influence, he loathed it utterly.

"Can you command it?"

The question took Darien by surprise; he hadn't thought of that. "I don't know," he admitted.

"Try."

Darien looked down at the floor. To where a dark brown stain mottled the stone near his feet.

"Visea," he whispered.

Immediately, the necrator in front of him melted into the ground. It was gone, as if absorbed by the porous stone. Byron Connel turned to gape at him, his expression full of dismay. His hand clutched his spiked weapon tight against his chest.

"Bring it back," he whispered.

Darien closed his eyes and willed the necrator back into existence. When he looked up again, the shadow was back, hovering, crystalline-black and sinister. Silently awaiting his command.

Connel stared long and hard at the abomination. Finally, he dropped his chin to his chest, shoulders sagging. "What you have done…" He sighed heavily. "If I didn't know Nashir so well, your soul would be halfway to hell right now. But fortunately for you, I did know Nashir. I know what he was capable of. And now I know what you're capable of."

He glared at Darien significantly.

Darien nodded, internalizing the threat.

Connel dropped his hand, strapping Thar'gon back to his belt. He was trembling in either rage or fear; Darien couldn't tell which. The look on Connel's face was impossible to read.

The Battlemage said, "You're absolved of the murder of Nashir Arman. But make no mistake: I will never turn my back on you. Ever." Connel glanced at the necrator. "Get rid of it."

Darien obeyed, watching as the malevolent shadow melted away. He turned, walking back through the doorway. In the corridor outside, he waited for Connel to emerge. The door closed behind them with an echoing *thud*.

Byron Connel said nothing the entire long climb back up to the level of the palace. As they moved out of the cold stairwell, he stopped beside a servant standing to one side, rigid enough to appear painted on the wall.

"Bring wine," Connel ordered. "And plenty of it."

The servant bowed, backing away, then hurried off in the direction of the kitchens.

Darien led Connel back to his own chamber, offering the man a cushion by the hearth. He sat down across from him, eyes darting to the thanacryst across the room. The demon-dog was curled up in the corner by the door, staring at them with disinterest.

The servant returned with a decanter of wine and cups arranged on a silver tray, which he set down on the floor between them. Without uttering a word, the man bowed and backed out of the room, closing the door in his wake.

Darien waited for Connel to serve himself before pouring his own cup of wine. He raised the cup to his lips, breathing in the sweet scent of the grapes. Then he threw his head back, draining half the cup in one swallow. The wine was harsher than it smelled. It burned his throat going down.

"Quin and Sareen have vanished." Connel set his cup down on the floor at his side. His eyes locked on Darien. "Do you have any knowledge of their whereabouts?"

Darien took another swallow, finishing the remainder of the wine in his cup. He wiped his mouth dry on his shirtsleeve. He answered truthfully, "I've no idea where they could be."

He'd had no word from Quin. Darien assumed the man must be halfway to Titherry by now, but he had no way of knowing for certain. In this case, he was grateful for his ignorance.

"We have reason to suspect the temples are aligning against us," Connel said as Darien poured himself more wine. "The disappearance of two of our own is disconcerting. And now with Nashir…"

His voice trailed off. He took a heavy sip from his cup. "We're down to only five of our former number." Connel regarded Darien with a frank expression. "I'll be relying on you as a Battlemage. You're my second-in-command, now."

Darien looked away, gazing intently into the fire. The oversized hearth burned bricks of coal instead of logs. The coals glowed orange, silvering at the edges. The smell was acrid, mingling with the floral scent of incense that permeated the room. It was not a pleasant combination.

Connel grumbled, "We're running out of mages, and we're running out of time. The southern population centers are already mobilizing. Renquist wants the entire Khazahar ready to deploy within a week."

Darien glanced up. "A week isn't enough time to prepare an invasion."

"This isn't an invasion," Connel corrected him. "It's an evacuation. We're emptying all the Black Lands." He downed the remainder of his wine and set the empty cup on the floor, holding Darien's gaze the entire time. Watching his reaction to the news.

Darien shook his head, unable to contain his surprise. Everything was happening so much quicker than he'd expected. Which complicated his plans. He'd hoped that Quin would find a way to break the curse, to release Malikar's skies from the grip of darkness. Evacuating the entire population into the Rhen was a nightmare situation that Darien hoped they could avoid. He still had faith in Quin.

He insisted, "I need more time."

"Time is the one thing you don't have. Travel alone to the staging area will take you a minimum of three weeks."

Darien felt hampered at every turn. He needed a way out, a change of direction. A jarring thought occurred to him. "Isn't there a transfer portal nearby?"

"Under the lake." Connel poured himself a fresh cup of wine. "How deep can you swim?"

Darien scowled, not appreciating the sarcasm. He lowered his cup, leaning back against the wall beside the hearth. The warmth of the fire felt good despite the noxious smell of coal. He could feel the effects of the alcohol on his mind, smoothing his tattered nerves. He felt suddenly weary.

Connel leaned forward and clapped Darien on the shoulder. Then he climbed to his feet. "I'll have your man find me a room with a bed in it. Report to me after *thalath*. We'll begin your education."

Darien followed Connel to his feet. The Battlemage extended his hand, palm outstretched. Darien accepted the gesture, noting the hesitance in Connel's grip. There was a void of trust there he'd have to work hard to bridge.

Connel turned away. But instead of making his way to the

door, he wandered instead toward the writing desk in the corner of the room. Darien stiffened, remembering the catalogue of his ancestry he'd left there in plain view. The list that ended with the name Braden Reis.

He did not want Connel to discover his relationship to Quin Reis.

The red-haired mage picked up the parchment from the desk, raising it up before his face. His eyes scanned over the long list of names, starting from the top. But he broke off not even halfway down, his eyes flicking back to Darien.

"What's this?"

"My family lineage," Darien answered stiffly. It was hard to keep the anxiety out of his voice.

Connel set the parchment back down on the desk. "What inspired you to write this all out?"

Darien shrugged. "Sometimes I fear I'm starting to lose myself." That, at least, was sincerest truth.

Connel nodded. He strode toward the door, clapping Darien on the back as he passed by. "You can't lose something you never had, Darien. Get some sleep."

He strode out the door, shutting it behind him as he left.

Darien sank down on the edge of the bed. He leaned forward, cupping his head in his hands. His stomach felt ill. He could feel the effects of the alcohol draining out of him like blood leaking from his veins. The warmth of the wine was replaced by stone-cold fear.

The next time he saw Connel was early afternoon.

The Battlemage had assembled a small party of Tanisars, men who would normally follow only Darien's command. But in the shadow of Connel's presence, it seemed he'd been outranked. They rode out from the palace on the few mounts they had. Past the dark lake, beyond the denuded foothills to the south. Out from under the oppressive energies of the vortex that swirled around Tokashi Palace.

Connel didn't speak a word to Darien the entire ride. The

Battlemage remained encased in the cold grip of silence, his intractable stare scouring the landscape. Sayeed trailed behind on his own mount, a quiver of spears hanging from his shoulder. His mare dragged an empty travois that raked a trail behind them that looked like dual claw marks in the sand.

Darien wondered about the travois, speculating why it was necessary. He almost asked. But then he stopped himself, reckoning that he probably didn't want to know the answer. He didn't know where they were riding or what to expect; Connel wouldn't tell him. But by the long looks on the faces of the men, he had a feeling it wasn't going to be pleasant.

Connel angled his horse off the road, guiding his courser down a path that led to an opening in the cliff wall just ahead. At first it seemed just an indentation in the rock. But to Darien's surprise, it turned out to be the entrance to a slender canyon that parted the cliff face.

Connel reined in and climbed down from his horse. Darien followed him to the ground, leading his mount forward to examine the opening. The walls to either side had been carved in bas-relief. Twin images depicting winged horses with hawk-like faces stood like a pair of ancient sentries on either side. The gate they created was daunting, striking in every detail. Running his hand over one of the sentinels, Darien could feel every rippling muscle, the barbs of the feathers that decorated the wings.

They led the horses on foot through the opening between the stone guardians. The walls of the crevice beyond were tall and steep, smooth like fire-polished glass. The path they tread had been a streambed; now dry. The water had eroded the rocks, forming the narrow passage. Darien could make out different layers of sediment, some ruddy, others more golden in hue. The splendor of the cliffs had been diminished by the Desecration but not permanently undone.

"What is this place?"

Connel glanced back at him but said nothing.

It was Sayeed who answered. "This is an ancient place that is held to be sacred by all the tribes of the Khazahar. There is a spring hidden deep within that seeps water blessed by the gods. It is said that drinking from this well cleanses the heart of all fear. Men come here to drink their fear before going into battle. It is tradition."

Darien nodded even as he dismissed the man's claim. The culture of superstition ran deep in Malikar's bloodlines.

The canyon curved sharply then ran straight ahead for some distance. Looking ahead, Darien saw that soldiers had been stationed every so often at intervals along the passage. Each man stood alone beside a small campfire.

Connel stopped and handed the reins of his horse to a soldier. With a gesture, he instructed Darien to do the same. As Sayeed relieved him of his horse, Darien saw a trace of sadness in the man's dark eyes.

"May the gods lend you courage, my friend," Sayeed whispered. "Drink your fear."

Darien turned to Byron Connel in alarm. "What is this? What's going on?"

Connel untied the spiked silver weapon from his belt, wielding it like a club. His red-bearded face was full of arrogance and ice.

"It is called the Rakkah," he said. "The final test of a Battlemage. You are well-schooled in defensive tactics, but that's only half the equation. Now you need to learn how to kill. Above all else, you must fortify your resolve."

He motioned ahead at the line of men stretched out along the walls of the canyon.

Darien felt ice-cold dismay as understanding hit him in the face.

"You want me to kill *all these men?*"

The Battlemage nodded. "I need you combat-effective."

Darien paced away a few steps, eyes studying the first man in the long, drawn-out line. The man was a soldier, a Tanisar by the uniform. He stood at attention beside his small fire, face untroubled by emotion. He had the look of a man resigned to duty and fate.

Darien spun away, feeling sickened. "Who are they?" he

demanded. "What have these men done to deserve death?"

Byron Connel moved to stand in front of him. He was taller than Darien, his face set in harsh, uncompromising lines. "They are Tanisars. Soldiers who volunteered for this duty. Men who desire only to serve you."

That explanation sickened Darien even more. His throat clenched in revulsion. "Why would they volunteer for this?"

"Because I asked them to. There is much *sharaq* in such a death. They know they lay down their lives to help prepare the greatest weapon Malikar has ever known. The selfsame weapon that will deliver their families from the curse of darkness."

Darien shook his head, backing away from Connel. "I'm not a weapon," he whispered.

The Battlemage narrowed his eyes. "After today, you will be. You will be the most fearsome weapon our world has ever known. Never before has there existed an eighth-tier Battlemage trained in offensive tactics and capable of wielding the power of the Onslaught. After today, you will be indomitable. No mortal force will be able to stop us."

Darien shuddered, sickened with disgust. "I will not murder these men."

"Yes, you will," Connel said gruffly. "This is the Rakkah. The final trial of an apprentice Battlemage. You must pass the Rakkah to earn admittance into our order. The price of failure is death. There is no going back. There's no halfway. The Rakkah has already begun."

"I won't do it." Darien turned his back on Connel and began stalking away.

The hand of the gods reached down from the sky and slapped him off his feet, hurling him hard against the face of the cliff. Darien slumped to the ground, where he lay stunned, gazing up at the ink-black sky, slowly blinking. The taste of blood filled his mouth. His vision went from white to red.

Connel reached down and hauled him to his feet. He wielded his spiked talisman in his right hand, bracing Darien upright with his left. Darien staggered, reeling. He couldn't seem to focus on the man's face. Pulling at the magic field, he struggled to heal his injuries. The world went dark, and he wilted to the ground.

Pain flared inside, tearing him wide awake.

"Be warned," Connel growled into Darien's face, leaning over him menacingly. "The next blow will be a killing strike." He motioned to the first man behind him. "*Stand up!* You bring dishonor to Sinan."

Darien rolled over, pushing himself weakly to his knees.

"Who's Sinan?" he asked, still half-dazed by the talisman's magical strike. He staggered to his feet, taking a limping step ahead. He brought a hand up to his face, smearing a trail of blood that trickled from his nostril.

"Sinan is the soldier whose duty it is to teach you the *hijaz* attack."

Darien glanced at the young Tanisar by his lonely campfire. "I don't understand. How can that boy teach me anything?"

"Ask him."

Darien didn't want to ask. He swallowed against a knot of despair in his throat, feeling the last of his resistance crumbling away. He knew when he was beaten. There was no use in putting up a fight; with Thar'gon in his hand, Connel was far too powerful.

Heart pounding in his chest, Darien walked toward the first man in line.

He regarded the soldier before him: a young man with dark, shoulder-length hair and a prominent nose. There was no trace of struggle nor sadness in the soldier's eyes; only a calm, determined strength. The man dipped his head in greeting.

"Lord, I am Sinan son of Semal. It is my honor to teach you the attack known as *hijaz*. It is a very complex attack to master, I am told, so you must pay very careful attention."

Darien blinked, gazing deeply into Sinan's dark eyes. The young man was rattling off a prepared statement, something he'd been made to memorize. It had the distinctive formula of a ritualized speech.

"The *hijaz*, if performed correctly, will cause the body of a victim to explode. This is a very effective tactic for spreading fear to demoralize your enemy. Darien Nach'tier, please allow me the honor of teaching you the *hijaz* attack."

Darien swallowed, his mouth filling with the sour taste of acid. He brought his hands up, gripping the man's shoulders. "Your name is Sinan son of Semal?"

The soldier nodded. "It is, Lord."

Darien closed his eyes, clenching his teeth against the ache of horror.

"I don't want you to teach me this, Sinan."

The young man regarded him with an expression akin to sympathy. "I am sorry, Lord. It is my duty."

Darien released Sinan's shoulders, glaring his hatred back at Connel.

"Don't make me do this."

The Battlemage stepped forward, taking Darien's hand in his. "Feel through me."

There was absolutely no emotion in his voice. Darien could feel his hand shaking in Connel's grip. His whole arm trembled. He closed his eyes, opening himself to Connel's link. Instantly, he felt inside of Sinan. He could feel the pressure of the young man's blood as if feeling his own veins. It pulsed and throbbed, swelling in volume with every heartbeat.

"Please. *Don't.*"

He could feel what Connel was doing with his mind. Increasing the pressure of the blood against Sinan's arteries, at the same time applying a counterpressure that kept the system in balance. He could hear Sinan groaning as the pain became unbearable.

"Do you feel it?" Connel asked.

Darien grimaced. He felt it. It was awful. He could feel Sinan's blood on the verge of boiling. The soldier in front of him collapsed to his knees, throwing his head back as he moaned in tortured anguish.

"Do you feel it?"

Darien nodded, clenching his teeth. *"Aye."*

"Then finish it."

"I can't," Darien gasped, shaking in revulsion.

Byron Connel leaned forward and growled in his face, "Don't let him suffer!"

Darien stroked Sinan's body with his mind. He released the counterpressure Connel had applied to contain the man's raging blood.

Sinan exploded in a showering rain of gore.

Darien shielded his face with his hands. He stood there shaking, hands trembling over his face, unable to bring himself to open his eyes. He felt Connel's hand on his neck, grabbing him by the fabric of his shirt, hauling him forward. Darien's stomach wrenched. He swallowed against the taste of vomit in his mouth.

Connel's harsh grip jerked him to a halt.

"Lord, I am Alton son of Orhan."

Darien opened his eyes. He stood in front of the next soldier in the line. This man was slightly older than Sinan had been, slightly taller. A fine mist of blood covered one side of his face. His forehead had broken out in a sheen of perspiration despite the chill of the air.

Darien stared at Alton son of Orhan.

"It is my honor to teach you the attack known as *nebiza*. If performed correctly, the *nebiza* causes the nerves of your opponent to quit functioning. This is a very effective tactic for stopping the hearts of many warriors at once. Darien Nach'tier, please allow me the honor of teaching you the *nebiza* attack."

Darien groped for strength, his breath shuddering in his throat. He stepped forward, gripping Alton's shoulders with his hands.

"Your name is Alton son of Orhan?" He wanted to make sure he had it right.

Sinan son of Semal. Alton son of Orhan.

He would remember those names. He swore right then and there he would never forget them.

"It is, Lord."

Darien bowed his head. "You honor me, Alton."

"The honor is mine, Lord."

Darien pulled back, glaring at Byron Connel. The Battlemage

took his hand. Again, Darien found his consciousness fed through Connel into the soldier standing in front of him. He could feel the man's nerves at work, regulating the pace of Alton's heartbeat. A subtle change in those impulses could stop that instantly.

"Do you feel it?" Connel whispered.

"Aye."

"Then finish it."

Darien sagged, groaning. He didn't want to kill Alton son of Orhan. He admired the gentle depths in the man's dark eyes.

"Forgive me."

With a wrench of Darien's mind, Alton's heart seized in his chest, his body crumbling to the blackened earth. Darien stared down at him, drowning in self-loathing.

Connel guided him forward to the next man in line.

"Lord, I am Devrim son of Enver. It is my honor to teach you the attack known as *ruhk*. If performed correctly, the *ruhk* will cause the flesh of your opponent to catch fire. This is a very effective tactic for causing a terrible, excruciating death. Darien Nach'tier, please allow me the honor of teaching you the *ruhk* attack."

Darien leaned forward, gripping the man's shoulders in his hands. He stared into the depths of the young man's eyes.

"Your name is Devrim son of Enver?"

"It is, Lord."

Sinan son of Semal. Alton son of Orhan. Devrim son of Enver.

"You honor me, Devrim."

"The honor is mine, Lord."

Darien offered his hand to Byron Connel. Instantly, he was transported deep inside Devrim, feeling the warmth of the young man's core. He could feel the source of that heat. He understood how to change it. Such a subtle difference. But if done in every tissue of the body altogether at once…

"Do you feel it?"

"Aye."

"Then finish it."

Darien squeezed his eyes shut, trembling as Devrim burned.

The soldier's screams were appalling. They went on for a very long time.

He felt Connel's hand on his back. He walked forward, swallowing his emotions, stoppering them up inside. He raked his shirtsleeve across his eyes, wiping away his humanity.

Darien approached the next man in line.

"Lord, I am Serkan son of Arsil…"

Chapter Five
A Sentinel's Duty

Pass of Lor-Gamorth, The Front

Kyel staggered as the magic field surged back into his mind. The relief was so intense that it wrenched a gasp from his lips. He swayed over his feet, relishing the field's sweet comfort. He stood there for a moment savoring the pulse, a feeling of contentment unlike any other. The magic field had been denied him ever since his arrival at Greystone Keep. The fortress had been constructed within the protective confines of a node. He understood the necessity, but the field's absence ate at Kyel every second he was away from it.

His hands tightened reflexively on the wrapped bundle he lugged in his arms. A crackling noise issued from beneath the layers of cloth, a sound no human body should ever make. He took one last step just to make certain the field was at full strength. Then he lowered Meiran to the dirt as Traver wrestled with her legs. Gusts of wind whipped at their backs, cold and punishing. Traver righted himself and took a step back, staggering. He held his hand up in front of him, flexing the three fingers he had left. Then he grimaced, wincing back and covering his mouth with his cloak.

"Gods' mercy, she stinks!"

Kyel nodded, his eyes watering as he held a cloth up over his own face. His stomach lurched, threatening to spill its contents into the dirt at his feet. "It's the rot."

They'd shrouded Meiran in thick folds of cloth, which covered the raised blisters that oozed gore over her blackened flesh. But there was nothing they could do about the stench. It was terrible, much worse than the smell of decay. Whatever disease had hold of her, it was consuming her entirely.

"Is there anything you can do?" Traver was pale, his eyes watering. He looked a bit green. The captain had handled enough corpses in his career that he should be used to the stench of decay. Maybe it was different when the victim was still alive.

Kyel looked back up the hill in the direction of the keep. The path they'd taken down the ridge was empty; no one had followed them. Kyel felt relieved—he was glad to be free of Cadmus and the retinue of guards that followed him everywhere he went. Thanks to Traver, they'd managed to slip out of the fortress unaccompanied.

He turned his attention back to Meiran. "I don't know if I can cure this," he admitted, dropping to a crouch at her side. She looked asleep. But Kyel knew better; it wasn't sleep that was taking her. The way he figured it, Meiran didn't have much time left.

He swallowed the lump in his throat and went right to work. Using his knife, Kyel sawed through the cloth wrappings to expose the blackened flesh beneath. He drew back away from the smell that spilled out. Meiran's bloated form was barely recognizable as human. Viscous fluids streamed from cracks and large blisters in her flesh. Her limbs were deformed, fingers and toes withered and rotten. Kyel fought the urge to retch, clamping his teeth together.

"What happened to her?" Traver gasped.

"I don't know. And I don't have time to speculate. Do me a favor and just stand back."

A flare of lightning stabbed the mountainside nearby, followed by a deafening peal of thunder. For a split-second, the Pass of Lor-Gamorth lit up bright as day. Then the darkness came crashing back down on top of them. A gust of wind tore at Kyel's cloak, rippling it out behind him.

Kyel set his hands on Meiran's shoulders, holding his breath against the stench. As his fingers caressed her skin, something inside made a crunching noise. His stomach twisted. He closed his eyes and reached within, grappling with the power that sustained him. The magic field flooded into him, coursing through his hands into Meiran's corrupt tissues. He reached inside her, probing the full extent of her ruin.

"Oh, gods," he gasped, pulling back. Vomit surged into his mouth. He swallowed it back down again. Steeling himself, Kyel sent a desperate flood of healing energies into Meiran's failing body. It didn't go very far; it was like pounding a fist against a stone wall. He drew back with a cry of frustration.

"What is it?" Traver called over the rising wind.

Kyel was unable to answer. He was too horrified. He stood there numb, shaking his head as precious seconds ticked by.

"She's more dead than alive..." he finally managed to whisper. "I can't..." He gaped at Traver, shrugging helplessly. Another bolt of lightning splintered the air.

Kyel glanced around, at last recognizing where they were. It was the same spot where, two years before, Devlin Craig had saved Darien's life after Arden Hannah had tried to roast him over a bonfire. Craig had carried Darien out of the node and dumped him down in this same place. He'd worked on him until Darien drew breath again.

Craig hadn't given up on Darien.

Kyel knew he couldn't give up on Meiran.

Closing his eyes, Kyel knelt and placed his hands on her rotting flesh, using the magic field to probe deep inside her. He needed to make sense of the damage, at least get an idea of where to begin. It was like healing a corpse; most of her was already more dead than alive. He seared the toxins from her blood first, then set about burning away corrupted flesh. Beneath his fingers, new skin wove together, tightening, squirming into place. He invaded her core, restoring blood to organs starved for air. The whole process took only minutes, but to Kyel it seemed like hours. The infected flesh sloughed away, revealing fresh pink skin underneath.

Meiran lurched, drawing in a sharp gasp. Her chest heaved, her back arching. Then she collapsed in a fit of coughing before going limp again. Kyel put his ear to her chest, listening to the faint sound of her heartbeat.

"Is she healed?" Traver shouted over the wind.

Kyel pulled back, watching the rhythm of Meiran's chest, not trusting it.

"She's alive," he said in wonder, only half-believing himself.

Devlin Craig picked up a roasted fowl and held it up to his mouth, tearing off a long strip of meat. He chewed noisily then swallowed, chasing it down with a swig of mead. "Did she say anything at all?"

Kyel shook his head, gazing down at the blackened hen on his own plate. The cooks had done a number on the small bird. It reminded him too much of what Meiran's skin had looked like. He didn't think he could eat it. He nudged the plate away a fraction, taking a sip from his cup, instead.

"No." He shook his head. "She hasn't awakened yet. Where exactly did you find her?"

Craig tore off another strip of charred meat with his teeth. He chewed with his mouth open, smacking the food around noisily. "Sentries found her lying in the riverbed. She'd been peppered with arrows and left for dead."

Kyel tugged at a bird wing, twisting it between his thumb and forefinger. The joint separated, coming apart. He picked it up and sucked the flesh off the bone, closing his eyes as he tasted the fatty juices. Despite being charred, the hen wasn't as bad as it looked. It was far better fare than he'd been treated to during his last stay at Greystone Keep. Apparently, the Southern kingdoms now took the Enemy threat more seriously.

"That's not like them, is it?" he mused as he chewed. "To leave a mage just lying about on the ground like that? I mean, why didn't they burn her like all the others?"

"Don't know." Craig plucked a bone out from between his teeth and tossed it down on the board. "Maybe they didn't know she was a mage."

Kyel wondered at that. The chains on Meiran's wrists were conspicuous. But perhaps they hadn't been evident with all the rot.

Craig wiped his mouth on the padded sleeve of his gambeson. "How is she?"

"She'll be unconscious for a few days, I suspect. We won't know for sure until she wakes up. The arrows were poisoned. I did my best, but there's no way of knowing if I got it all. If I didn't, the rot will set right in again."

Craig tossed the bird carcass down on his plate, fixing Kyel with a smoldering glare. His wheat-colored hair fell in disarray about his shoulders, his beard matted with greasy juices. He looked a lot older than Kyel remembered.

Craig nodded at the charred hen on Kyel's plate. "You about done with that? There's some reports I'd like you to take a look at."

Kyel hesitated, seeing the commander's expression. There was something there that he didn't like. He pushed his plate back. He felt suddenly on edge. "What kinds of reports?"

Craig stood up from the table, casting down the napkin he hadn't used. "The Enemy's been redistributing forces along their perimeter. They're splitting their assets."

Kyel glanced up at the man's looming hulk. He dabbed at his mouth with his own napkin before setting it down. His mind fumbled with the information. "I don't know what that means," he admitted finally, a little embarrassed. "Am I supposed to?"

"Aye. You're supposed to." Craig planted his big hands firmly on his hips, glowering down at him. "The problem is, you don't. It's high time you learn to actually *be* a Sentinel instead of just strutting around calling yourself one."

Kyel blinked, the sting of the insult coloring his cheeks.

Craig turned away and walked back across the room to another table with maps and charts layered over its surface. A larger map hung from the wall, a replica of the one that had been mounted in the tower of the old keep. Kyel felt drawn to the map, feeling suddenly sentimental. He reached up, running a hand over the vellum's soft texture.

Craig rapped his knuckles on the table to get his attention.

"Look, Archer. There's some things we need to get settled between us. There's going to be a battle here in a matter of weeks, possibly days. I'm supposed to be able to rely on you. But I can't. As far as I'm concerned, you only know enough to be dangerous."

Hearing that, Kyel hung his head. He knew he wasn't the Sentinel that Darien had intended him to be. But he'd been trying his hardest to make himself more effective. In the past few months, he'd spent every spare moment with a book in his hands. But learning was proving to be all but impossible without a master to guide him. "I can give you my best," he said. "That's all I can do."

"It's not enough," Craig snapped. "You're the only Sentinel we have. And I need you to do your gods-damned duty. What do you know of siege warfare?"

Kyel stared hard at the floor. "Not enough."

"Then welcome to your first day of training." Craig planted two fingers squarely on one of the maps laid out on the table. "This is their primary staging area, right here, at the base of Orguleth." He punctuated each syllable with a tap of his fingers. "They're well-entrenched and sustained by robust supply lines. More forces arrive by the hour. Soon they're going to reach a point where they'll have to either disband or advance. They can't just sit there forever.

"The way I see it, they'll deploy an advance force consisting mostly of foot soldiers…"

Kyel stared at the map as the man's words droned on into meaningless noise. He tried to pay attention. But all he could focus on was the image in his head of the mounded piles of corpses he'd been forced to walk through after his last battle in the pass. Kyel remembered it well, the wails and moans of the fallen, the stiffening limbs, the spreading rivulets of blood. The smell of the aftermath. He'd witnessed the personal hell Darien had gone through trying to heal the injured. That battle had changed him; after that, his eyes had remained forever haunted. Darien had never recovered from that day.

Kyel bowed his head in resignation. He didn't want that kind of future for himself.

He didn't think he could handle it.

When he went to bed that night, Kyel's sleep was fitful. He snapped awake drenched in sweat, consumed by a terrible sense of foreboding. He sat bolt upright, throwing off the covers. Gazing blearily into the darkness of his quarters, he tried to make sense of the shadows. He scanned the corners of the room, his heart and mind racing.

He remembered having a nightmare. Only, this nightmare had felt real.

Kyel rolled out of bed and reached for a ceramic jug set out by his bedside. He brought the jug up to his lips, gulping a mouthful of stale water as sweat trickled down his face. An eerie feeling of apprehension slid down his spine as he set the water jug back down.

A shadow lurched toward him from the corner.

Kyel flinched back, bringing his hands up and gasping, "Who's there?"

The shadow fell across him. Kyel sagged in relief, breathing an audible sigh. For a moment, he couldn't move, just stood staring into the familiar face revealed by a streak of light slanting in from the window. It took him a moment to compose himself enough to smile.

"Meiran," he whispered. "Thank the gods."

The woman nodded. Then she collapsed into his arms, sobbing wretchedly as she clung to his shoulders.

Chapter Six
The Whim of the Gods

Tokashi Palace, The Black Lands

Darien let the blood-soaked wrap fall from his hips, stepping naked into the gray-tiled bath. The air was warm and heavy with humidity. He moved forward through a thick mist of steam, feeling heat radiating up into his feet through the tiles of the floor.

Blood leaked from his body at every step, pattering in dark droplets that mixed with beads of water already on the ground. It ran in crimson streams toward the drains.

He reached the far wall and groped at a gilt handle protruding from the surface. Immediately, a shower of warm water flowed from a spout set high above, falling in soothing droplets about his shoulders. Darien leaned forward, resting his forehead against the tile, arms pressed against the wall. He closed his eyes and let the warm water course over his skin. He could feel the crusted blood softening, releasing from his body. Gently washing away.

None of the blood was his own.

Sinan son of Semal. Alton son of Orhan. Devrim son of Enver. Serkan son of Arsil…

His lips moved without words, forming names without sound, a droning litany in his head. Darien kept his eyes squeezed closed, head bowed under the steady stream of the water. The blood of innocents ran in streams across the floor, collecting in shallow puddles around the drains.

The walls of the bath wept garish streaks of red.

He stayed there for minutes in the water, shivering despite the warmth of the steam.

At last, he turned around. Darien pressed his back against the tiles and let his body slide down the wall to the floor. He leaned forward, cradling his head against his knees.

He sat there for a long time, grimly contemplating death.

It wouldn't take much to rend his tattered soul and scatter what was left of him on the winds of Oblivion. Just three simple words:

I deny Xerys.

If he could say it in his mind, then he could say it out loud. It shouldn't be very difficult.

Sinan son of Semal, Alton son of Orhan…

Darien clutched his head, shoulders trembling. He gripped his fingers into fists.

"I…deny…"

The words collapsed, his intent imploding in his mouth. He lacked the conviction to say the words that would end him. He threw his head back, letting the water from the spout drizzle miserably over his face. It felt almost like rain. But bitter, like hot, salted tears.

Eventually, Darien wandered out of the bath. He bent down and picked up the black wrap he'd discarded earlier, holding the stiffened fabric in his hand. With just one thought it was clean and unsoiled, supple, as if no stain had ever corrupted it. He wound the fabric around his hips, knotting it in place.

With a knock, the chamber door shuddered open.

Sayeed appeared, his face rigid with concern. He held a bottle of wine in one hand, a cup in the other.

"Better bring more," Darien muttered. He trudged forward, relieving Sayeed of the bottle but not the cup. He unstoppered the wine and took a long pull from the bottle. The Zakai officer bowed and left. Darien settled down onto a cushion, leaning back against the wall. He knocked another mouthful back then upended the bottle, draining its contents down his throat. He set the spent container down on the floor then stared vacantly into the fire dancing in the hearth.

Darien was relieved when Sayeed returned quickly.

He hoped that, with enough wine, he could work up the nerve to cast his soul to the winds.

Darien awoke on the floor in a jumbled collection of bottles, his head throbbing in time to every heartbeat. He lay on his side, staring at a blurry, overturned bottle in front of his face. His fingers twitched. With a scowl, he wrenched himself upright, his vision fading before sharpening.

The door to his bedchamber boomed three times, jolting on its hinges. Someone outside was growing impatient. The insistent knocks had woken him from his stupor.

He shoved himself to his feet, staggering across the floor. Darien opened the chamber door and stood there regarding Byron Connel in silent contempt. He stepped back enough to admit the darkmage into his quarters.

Connel paused, shaking his head at the array of bottles scattered about the room.

"I hope it was worth it."

Darien ignored him. He walked away, casting his graceless body back down on the mat. He focused his stare on the wall behind Connel, his fingers caressing a soft tassel that hung at his side.

Connel dropped to a crouch in front of him. Hands on his knees, he peered intently into Darien's face.

"Yesterday, I forged you into a weapon. I neglected to explain how much that would cost you. You see, weapons don't feel. They don't wrestle with indecision or grope for understanding. They have but one purpose: they simply kill. They don't regret. They never hesitate. And they're never to blame for what they do."

Darien's stare remained fixed on the wall as Connel's words crawled under his skin, worming their way into his brain. He understood very well what the man was trying to say. He had an acute appreciation of what he'd become. And all that he'd lost.

Connel reached out and clapped Darien on the shoulder. Then he pushed himself erect. "I'm leaving. Rally the Tanisars. I'll expect you at the staging area in one month's time." He stared down at Darien for a moment, awaiting a response. When none was forthcoming, the Battlemage simply shrugged.

"May you know the peace and blessings of the gods."

With that, he turned toward the door.

"Who's to blame?"

Connel stopped. He turned back around.

Darien finally looked up at him, resentment seething in his eyes. "You said a weapon is never to blame. If not the weapon, then who?"

The Battlemage reached into a pocket of his robe and withdrew a folded pair of gloves. He worked his hand into one, flexing his fingers to stretch the fabric. "No man has the authority or power to determine another man's fate. All lives are lived at the mercy and whim of the gods. They alone are to blame."

He turned away, tugging the other glove on over his wrist.

Darien lowered his stare back to the hearth. "Then damn all the gods. And damn you, too."

Connel nodded. "Take care, Darien," he said as he left.

Darien waited only long enough to be certain the man was well and truly gone. Then he scooped up his sword and shirt and thrust open the chamber door. He strode across the empty hallway and tugged open the door of the stable. There, the strong scent of horse filled his nostrils.

From the other side of the dim room came a welcoming nicker.

Darien moved forward, his hand reaching up to stroke his stallion's soft neck. It didn't take him a minute to slip a bridle on over the horse's head and laid a blanket over its back. Thrusting open the stable door, he led the animal into the hallway.

He mounted swiftly and rode at a trot through the corridors of the palace, the echoing sounds of hoofbeats ringing off the walls. Tanisars and servants scattered out of his way, dodging back to let him pass. Darien rode out the gate into the night, urging the stallion forward at a gallop.

He found Azár in the lightfields. She looked up at his approach, confusion pinching her face.

"Darien?"

He dropped his horse's reins, trudging stiffly toward her through the grass of the meadow. Azár held her ground, face frozen in concern as her eyes tracked his motion. Her stare delved into him, searching. Her mouth twisted in compassion.

"Come here," she whispered.

Darien crushed her against his chest. His lips moved over her, desperate, scouring her face. His shaking hands groped behind her back.

He lifted Azár in his arms then bent to spread her out on the grass. He collapsed on top of her, the strength of his need rendering every motion frantic. His lips found hers, furious, ravaging. He slid his hands under her shirt, forcing back the thick fabric and exposing the soft flesh of her middle. His hips bore down against hers.

He was desperate.

Desperate to feel something beautiful again.

He parted her legs with a knee, fumbling with the drawstring of his trousers.

"*Stop.*" It was the faintest, saddest sound.

Darien froze.

"Please," Azár whispered. "*Stop touching me.*"

Panic infused her voice, so much that it made him sick.

Darien rolled off her, sitting up. He clutched his head in his hands, his body quivering.

"Look at me."

Azár wrenched Darien's face toward her. He kept his eyes lowered; he was too ashamed to look at her.

"If you ever touch me like that again, I'll kill you."

He forced a nod. Then he lurched to his feet and staggered away.

Chapter Seven
The Semantics of Servitude

Ishara, The Black Lands

Quin hovered over the kettle, bringing the spoon up to his lips for a taste. The fragrance of the stew filled his nostrils with warmth, bringing a whimsical smile to his lips. The sweet blend of seasonings tingled on his tongue, transporting him back in time with a nostalgic flood of aching sentiments. The smell reminded him of home. Not any recent home, but the Bryn Calazar he remembered. The city had been filled which such rich flavors, sweet fragrances and incense.

Now, all lost.

Lost in time. But not in memory.

The smile slipped from Quin's face. The taste of his cooking was another unsubtle reminder of his damnation.

"What is it?"

"Mujaz." Quin's voice was hollow with melancholy. "A stew made from dried fruits and seasonings." Noticing the dubious expression on her face, he added, "You eat it."

He dipped the spoon into the kettle then offered it across to her. Naia stared at the spoon for a moment, finally guiding it into her mouth. She closed her eyes as if savoring the taste. Then she crinkled her nose, wincing as if in pain.

"Strong," she complained. "What do you do, carry spices around in your pockets?"

"In fact, I do." Quin reached into his pack, extracting a rolled satchel that he opened in front of her. One by one, he began pulling out an assortment of small cloth sacks tied with drawstrings, laying them out on the ground between them. "In

Malikar, spices are rare and highly prized. They are used in place of currency."

Naia reached out and grasped one of the small sacks in her hand. She brought it up to her nose, sniffing. "This is familiar."

"Cumin," Quin said. "It aids digestion."

She looked up at him with interest in her eyes. "How do you know which spice it is?"

He pointed a finger, indicating the color of the braided drawstring. "Each spice is associated with a particular pattern of braid. It's an ancient system that's survived since before my time."

Naia set the small sack down and picked up another, giving it a whiff. "Cinnamon. This is used in the preparation of bodies for funeral. I would never have imagined seasoning food with it."

"Cinnamon has extraordinary value." Quin plucked the sack out of her hand. "It's used to prevent food from spoiling, but it also has medicinal properties. It can treat festering wounds."

Naia frowned. "Don't your mages tend to the injured?"

"No." Quin raked the packets toward him and stuffed them back into the woven satchel. "If there's one thing in Malikar more precious than spice, it's mage-power. Next to light, that's the most limited resource."

Naia nodded, seeming to understand.

Quin served up a bowl of stew for her, thrusting it into her hands. "Enjoy your *mujaz*. Tonight, we feast like royalty."

She lifted the bowl with both hands and tasted the mixture, making a face.

Quin plunked the spoon back into the pot. Under his breath, he muttered, "I sometimes forget how much you people eschew anything that stimulates the senses or even reason."

Naia stared at him over the brim of her bowl. "What is that supposed to mean?"

"Nothing, really." Quin shrugged, serving himself a portion. "Just that you Southern folk seem to lead a very drab existence devoid of any substance. Now, eat your stew or go hungry."

He raised his bowl to his lips, drinking the sweet nostalgia delivered by the taste.

Looking defiant, Naia raised her own bowl and ate without further complaint.

When the meal was finished, Naia sat in silence while Quin went about the business of cleaning up their little camp. He could feel her eyes on him, tracking his every motion as he scrubbed out the cook pot with blackened sand and added coal to the fire. At first, he tried to ignore her looks. When the work was finished, he relaxed back against the cliff wall and tried using the brim of his hat as a shield against her stare. He focused his eyes and thoughts on the flickering of the campfire. It didn't help; he could still feel her there.

At last, when he could stand the attention no longer, he pushed back the brim of his hat, demanding, *"What?"*

The infernal woman continued to glare at him. "You lied to me."

Quin frowned, not understanding at first. It took him a moment to figure out what she was getting at. Even then, he disagreed. "No. I didn't."

"You told me you knew how to lift the curse over the Black Lands." Her eyes lingered on his face, accusing. "That was a lie."

He wondered what had given him away. Quin scowled, not wanting to be cornered into elaborating. "I told you I'd found *a way* to lift the curse. I didn't say that I knew *exactly* how to go about it."

Naia raised her eyebrows, scoffing at his explanation. "Semantics. Be more specific."

Quin grimaced, bringing a hand up to scratch his chin. "I can't."

"Why not?"

He sat upright, pulling his knees up against his chest and sweeping the hat off his head. This was exactly the conversation he'd been hoping to avoid. "All right, if you insist. But first, we must talk about the ground rules I have to live by." He took a deep breath, sorting through his thoughts. Trying to figure out how much to tell her. And how much to keep hidden.

"First of all, I'm a Servant of Xerys," he said finally. "That means I'm compelled to act with my Master's objectives always in mind. The moment my own interests lead me astray, I risk losing my Master's support. If I stray too far from my path then, why, my soul will be erased"—he snapped his fingers—"like that. Unmade and consigned to Oblivion. Understand? I walk a very treacherous and narrow path.

"My Master's purpose is to protect the magic field. Which can't happen if what I suspect about the curse is correct. So…I really can't divulge any information that would jeopardize my mission. That would conflict with my nature, and I'd find myself unmade rather rapidly and painfully."

The woman gazed at him with a healthy dose of skepticism. "So you can't tell me anything? Isn't that rather convenient?"

"Actually, I find it rather *in*convenient," Quin countered. "Believe me, I'd love to avoid the verbal sparring and skip right to the part where we agree to help each other. All I can tell you is this: if there is a way to lift the curse—which I believe there is—we can find it by using Athera's Crescent. And then, after the magic field is stabilized…why, then, my services will no longer be required by my Master. And I'll be at liberty to act."

"After this Reversal of the magic field you keep insisting is coming," Naia elaborated. Her eyes grew cold. "After we're all dead, you mean."

"Yes." Quin nodded. "After *you're* dead, rather. I'm already dead—which, in this case, works out serendipitously."

At least she'd listened to him when he'd told her about the Reversal. Unlike Meiran, Naia seemed to have a good appreciation for the threat it posed. Not just to magekind, but to all the rest of the world. He studied the woman's face, watching the flickering expressions that played across it.

When her eyes met his again, the icy fire was gone. "I believe you," Naia said finally. "Darien trusts you, so that tells me a lot. I suppose I'll have to trust you also. In all honesty, you've given me no reason not to."

Quin blinked. He had anticipated much more of a fight. This was almost too easy.

To his shock, a small smile brightened Naia's face. "I understand why you killed Sareen," she said. "You're not like her at all."

"No," Quin agreed with a wry smile of his own. "I'm not. Not that Sareen was entirely bad. Our objectives were just…incompatible. It was my intent to reunite Meiran and Darien simply because it was the right thing to do. Sareen wanted to use Meiran to control him. I believe you'll find, if you ever get a chance to meet the other Servants, that not all demons are evil. We're all just damned. There is a distinction, you know."

"I believe that I see it," Naia whispered. She dropped her gaze to the ground, looking suddenly saddened. Quin thought he could guess the reason why.

He adjusted his posture, slouching further down against the rock and draping an elbow over one knee. So far, Naia was proving to be a much more reasonable companion than Meiran had. Of course, the scar on her wrist spoke volumes for her character. As far as Quin was concerned, that ugly, puckered welt was far more virtuous than Meiran's unbroken chain. It was a bold declaration of freedom.

He pushed his hat back, cocking his head. "I need to know how you escaped the Rhen," he said in as gentle a tone as he could muster. "We're going to have to travel to the Isle of Titherry, and we don't have time to take a ship. If you've found a transfer portal south of Rothscard, then I need to know about it."

Naia stared at him hard, brow knitting in confusion. "Transfer portal? What is that?"

Quin managed a smirk. "Not a transfer portal, then. Look, darling, why don't you just tell me how you got here?"

Naia's face turned toward the fire, her eyes distant in thought. Her hand came up to tuck a lock of soft auburn hair behind her ear. She glanced away. And then her gaze snapped back to him.

"I came to the Black Lands through the Catacombs of Death," she admitted.

Quin blinked. And blinked again. Never in a thousand years would he have thought to use Death's Catacombs for that purpose.

"Truly?" He sat fully erect, his interest piqued. "Well, don't stop there. Pray continue…"

Chapter Eight
Come the Monster

The Khazahar Desert, The Black Lands

Darien staggered away from the lightfields and wandered alone into the dark turmoil of the waste. He lumbered northward, following the snaking line of the river. He wasn't particularly aware of where he was going. He didn't care. His feet carried him forward, so the rest of him followed. His thoughts swam across his vision like the swirling colors in the clouds.

He didn't understand. Didn't try to understand. Didn't care. Nothing mattered.

I am a monster.

The image of Sinan exploding in a showering mist of blood made him flinch.

From his memories, an avalanche of fire poured forth to vaporize armies.

Naia stared at him through her veil, hurt collecting in her eyes.

Azár's firm legs spread out beneath him in the grass.

Darien brought his hands up to cover his face as his feet stumbled over rocks. All around him, the wild flux of the magic field surged with fury. The vicious energies sawed at his head, raked at his brain. The violence of the field became uncomfortable. He ignored it for as long as he could. Until the pain demanded his attention.

Darien stopped, blinking dumbly at the river that had appeared in front of him. He turned slowly where he stood, eyes taking in the landmarks all around him. He could feel his stomach loosening as he realized where he was. And what he'd almost done.

He'd stumbled into a vortex without shielding himself from it.

He slammed up a barrier in his mind to protect him from the wailing torrent of energy. Trembling in dismay, he continued on toward the river. He walked with no particular destination in mind. Away from the lightfields. Away from Azár. Away from his past. He could feel the vortex raging against his shield, suffocating in its fury. He didn't care.

Let it rage.

The river beside him became a whitewater. And then a blackwater.

Darien stopped, gazing out at a solid wall of rock that bent the river in its course. He looked up. And up, craning his neck. The wall of debris stretched across the great expanse of the gorge. It blocked the passage of the river, diverting it from its channel. He could see where the canyon ahead forked. Another riverbed, long dry, veered away to the west, into the vast expanse of shadowlands beyond.

Darien's mind snapped suddenly into focus.

The wall of rock was the source of the black lake that lapped at Tokashi's gates. It must have fallen from the mountainside, damming the gorge and redirecting the river from its path. If he could move the rubble, then the lake behind it would drain…which would uncover the transfer portal lost beneath it.

Only, such an act was impossible beneath the fury of the vortex.

Darien paced forward, eyes scanning the massive wall of debris in front of him. The entire side of the mountain had collapsed into the canyon. The obstruction stood hundreds of feet high, an enormous dam made of black earth and chunks of stone.

When he had attacked Nashir in the dungeon, Darien had drawn on the power of the Onslaught within the same vortex. The difference was, his mind had been protected by the dampening effect of Quin's sword, which was a powerful magical talisman. But here, his mind wouldn't be protected. One slip, and the raw fury of the vortex would end him instantly.

Perhaps he could keep his mind shielded while drawing on the

Onslaught. It might be possible. It might also send his soul screaming back to hell.

Darien stared down into the gorge, contemplating the rocky dam, weighing his options. Long minutes wore by. A breeze came up, ruffling his hair. A cold sweat broke out all over his body. At last he made his decision.

He had nothing better to waste his death on.

He searched the canyon around him and found a trail that cut up along the wall of rock. Seeking higher ground, Darien took the trail up the rock face of the cliff. As he walked, he allowed his mind to wander, unfocused and adrift. Eventually he reached a plateau that overlooked the canyon and the lake. It was much cooler at that altitude. Overhead, clouds raced in dark streaks across the sky. Lightning flickered in the east, jagged forks stabbing down at the desert.

His skin crawled; he could sense the hostility of the vortex that surrounded him.

Darien tilted his head back, closing his eyes, and spread his arms out at his sides. He fixed his attention inward, at the shield he'd thrown up to block his mind from the vortex. He focused on that shield, reinforcing it with every effort of will he could muster. Then, dividing his attention, he opened a window to the Onslaught. Darien grimaced, feeling the strain of concentration. It felt as though his mind were being pulled in two different directions at once.

At first there was nothing. Then, ever so slowly, the Onslaught began leaking into him. When it started, it was just a trickle; not enough to do anything with. Darien willed himself to relax, to open up. Tried to open one part of himself wider while keeping another part walled off. Clenching his jaw, he reached out and took hold of the Hellpower, drawing it greedily from its source.

Scorching fire lanced into him, searing down every nerve of his body.

Darien screamed and fell to the rocks. He lay there moaning, writhing, gasping for breath through bubbling froth in his throat. His sight went black and then red as his eyes filled with tears of blood.

Mercifully, the pain didn't last long.

Darien's mind was swiftly overcome.

When he awoke, Naia was somehow sitting at his side, her dark eyes obscured by the sheer fabric of her veil. She reached down and tenderly stroked his face, her touch a soothing grace. Darien relaxed a little, savoring the feel of her. He couldn't remember why she was there.

"What is my name?"

Naia…

But that wasn't right. He struggled, wrestling for clarity through a fog of pain.

"Azár…"

The image of her face receded into darkness. Then someone was shaking him. The pain in his head exploded into agony, threatening to drag him back under.

"No!" Azár gasped. "Stay awake!"

She smeared the blood from his eyes, her fingers trailing down to cup his head. Darien drew in a deep, choking breath that rattled in his throat. It wasn't enough. Azár wrapped her arms around him, leveraging him up until he was staring into her face. Her forehead touched his, her hair swaying forward to veil them both.

She was panting, eyes wide and full of panic. "Were you attacked?"

Darien struggled to remember. All he could do was lay there gulping mouthfuls of gurgling air. Every muscle ached. His head felt like it had been smashed with an iron maul.

"No…" he finally whispered. "Not attacked. I tried to use the Onslaught…"

Azár's mouth fell open, her face aghast. "Why? Why would you try to destroy yourself?"

Was that what he'd intended? Darien struggled, unable to recollect his purpose. The fog in his brain weighed down at him, dragged him back toward unconsciousness.

"What does it matter?" He let his eyelids slide closed. The pain eased. He was drifting away.

A ringing slap startled him awake. He cried out, cringing as Azár clawed at his hair, wrenching him up off the ground.

"Listen to me!" she raged, spittle flying from her lips. "Until my people are free, *I do not release you from your duty!* I didn't raise you from hell just to have you die a coward's death! Take hold of your nerves!"

Her anger cleaved right through the fog that shrouded his mind. Darien struggled, fighting to sit up. He only got halfway there before a surge of nausea made him fall flat on his back again. He stared up at Azár, blinking miserably.

"I was trying to drain the lake," he explained. "Underneath, there's a transfer portal. I need it."

"Why?" she demanded, leaning over him. "Why must you risk death to find this thing?"

Darien sat up, swallowing back nausea. "Because we could transfer our people directly to the staging area. It would save hundreds of lives that might be lost travelling across the desert. And we can use it as a supply line, so we won't need a baggage train to cross the waste."

He looked up into her face. To his surprise, she seemed more shocked than appalled.

She said, "You exposed your mind to the vortex. How is that possible? You should be dead."

Darien brought a hand up to rub his temple. Even his scalp was sore to the touch. "I'm a demon," he reminded Azár. "I used the Onslaught, not the magic field. Like I did with Nashir."

Azár folded her arms across her chest, looking defiant. "With Nashir, your mind was protected. You were dampened by your friend's talisman. This is different, Darien Lauchlin. How can you justify such a risk?"

Trembling, he used his arms to leverage himself off the ground, struggling to gain his feet. He staggered and had to catch himself on Azár's outstretched hand. The horizon veered sharply before stabilizing again. Darien put his hand out, trying to halt the motion of the world in front of him.

He said, "If I can shield my mind while drawing on the

Onslaught, I'll have an advantage no other mage in the world has ever had. No one would be expecting that. It almost worked…"

"You nearly sent your soul back to hell!" Azár snapped, anger infecting her tone.

"But I didn't." He turned away from her, glancing back toward the canyon. He took a step toward it. Then another.

She stalked after him, as if incensed by his resolve. "You want to try this thing again?!"

"Yes."

He paused next to the cliff's edge, motioning toward the dense wall of rock that spanned the gorge.

"That used to be the side of the mountain." He indicated the dark slopes across from them. Jagged ridgelines stabbed at the sky, piercing the ocean of clouds that swarmed overhead.

"It must have collapsed and blocked the river. If I can shift some of the rubble, even just a fraction, the weight of the water behind it should clear the rest." He nodded his head. "That's the old river bed. If I can force the water back into its proper course, the lake will drain itself."

Azár stood at his side with her hands on her hips. "You think to move all those rocks? There are too many. What you propose is impossible."

Suddenly dizzy, Darien dropped to a crouch. He closed his eyes and brought his hands up to his brow. His head throbbed in time to his pulse. "I'm eighth tier," he said wearily. "Such an act is not beyond me."

"Eighth tier…?" Azár stared down at him, looking dumbfounded.

"Aye."

She lowered herself down by his side, her face softening into a look of pity. She reached a hand out, setting it on his shoulder. "Why did you never tell me this before?"

Darien shrugged, lowering his hands. He kept his eyes averted. "I don't like to speak of it."

For a long moment, she gazed at him in silence. Finally, she whispered, "No wonder you were such a monster. You were mad."

He turned to look at her, wondering if she might be right. He sat back, propping himself with one arm. The cold breeze felt good on his damp skin. His eyes lingered on Azár's, exploring the depths of forgiveness there.

He licked his lips, trying to work up the nerve to apologize. "I want to talk to you about what happened—"

"Don't."

Darien nodded, glancing away. He drew in a deep sigh. "I *am* a monster, Azár. But you have my word: I'll never touch you again."

Her lip curled, drawing up like a dog's. "I don't want your promises." Her tone seethed with sadness and ice.

Darien felt defeated. His shoulders sagged, his body slouching. Not for the first time, he found himself questioning the necessity of his own existence. He was sick of this world, sick of his sad and sorry place in it. Each day seemed to reduce him to new depths of shame. He was weary of it all.

He asked, "What kind of reassurance can I give you?"

"I already told you."

He knew what she meant. She was talking about marriage again. Darien bowed his head; he couldn't give her what she wanted. In truth, he was surprise she still wanted him at all. Resigned, he pushed himself to his feet.

"Stay here."

He limped toward the edge of the cliff, reeling like a drunken man. He stood there, swaying, as the world rippled in front of his vision. He hated heights, hated cliffs. This one didn't bother him as much as others. Probably because he didn't care anymore whether he lived or died. Still, he could feel his feet start to itch. The palms of his hands grew clammy.

He closed his eyes and groped within. Keeping his mind closed against the vortex, he called on the Onslaught and let the Hellpower trickle in. This time, he let it fill him gradually, not seeking to hurry it. He could feel it dribbling through his pores, saturating him slowly. He stood there on the edge of the cliff, swaying, soaking it all in. Eventually, he was full. He could hold no more.

Darien opened his eyes.

The world was darker and tinged with green. His head and body no longer hurt. The wind no longer blew. Azár no longer existed or even mattered.

There was only the cliff in front of him and the rubble-wall of rock.

His eyes found the biggest boulder, one positioned like a keystone in the center of the massive wall of earth. He narrowed his eyes and focused his concentration on it. He felt the rock start to *shift*.

The boulder disappeared. Its sudden absence produced a small avalanche of debris that rained down into the depths of the gorge. Darien found another rock and *shifted* it, as well. The boulder was gone, leaving a large hole in the space where it had just been. The rubble around it gave way, filling in the gap.

Darien removed another great chunk of mountain. This time, a shudder ran through the entire dam. Rocks poured down into the gorge. A thin spray of water shot out from a crack, followed by another further up.

Darien directed his focus at the base of the obstruction, at a large swath of mounded rubble. He concentrated, his brow furrowing. The canyon itself started to vibrate. Then the whole world shuddered. There was a loud popping sound. More water sprayed out in shooting cones, bursting in quick succession all across the face of the dam. Rocks and rubble poured down into the gorge below.

There was a terrible, grinding sound. And then a deafening roar.

The entire dam gave way, consumed by a deluge of water. Rocks shot upward, flung high into the air in impossible trajectories. Water gushed through a narrow fissure that quickly widened, spilling out across the canyon before sloshing over the edge of the cliff.

A violent tremor knocked Darien off his feet. He rolled onto his knees, scrambling back away from the cliff's edge. Suddenly Azár was there beside him, shrieking his name and gripping him under the arms. She struggled to drag him backward as the roar of the flood drowned out everything else in the world. The ground jolted and buckled beneath them, threatening collapse.

Darien regained his feet, lurching as Azár dragged him forward. Behind them, the cliff gave away completely.

Azár screamed something, but Darien couldn't hear her over the roar of the deluge. She took his hand, pulling him forward. They climbed the rise of a hill then stopped, turning to look back.

The water of the lake had consumed the dam, obliterating any last trace of the obstruction. The River Nym raged into the canyon, rushing to reclaim its long-abandoned course. The lake drained quickly, its waters subsiding to reveal embankments of chalky gray. The roar of the water continued, relentless, the air dampened by spray.

"What you have done…!"

Darien could barely hear her voice over the surging roar of water. He released the Onslaught, allowing it to drain out of him. As he did, the world brightened just a bit. Still, the dim green of the netherworld lingered like an afterglow.

Azár gaped at him with a look of outright wonder mixed with revulsion.

Darien backed away from her, feeling soiled. He turned and walked to the top of the hill, brooding as he stared down at the receding lake. Across the valley, two soaring structures appeared, striking upward from the lake's churning surface. They had the look of something from antiquity, statues perhaps. Once finely wrought, now eroded and decayed.

"What are they?" he wondered aloud.

"They are the gates of ancient Vintgar," Azár answered, her voice barely audible over the raging thunder of the flood. "Darien Lauchlin…you have achieved the impossible. You have freed the past."

Darien looked at her, unable to feel even a small sense of accomplishment. Perhaps he had freed some small part of Malikar's history. But that act, in and of itself, was meaningless. Because Malikar's future was still very much uncertain.

Chapter Nine
A Single Blade

Kyel watched Meiran sipping tea at the table in Devlin Craig's quarters. She held the teacup in both hands, her slender fingers pyramided to support it. Her face was still pale and gaunt. A little grayish, especially under the eyes. She looked unwell. But at least she wasn't dead.

For that, Kyel was grateful…but also mystified.

Craig sat down on the bench beside Kyel, setting his cup down on the gouged and splintered table. Kyel's eyes went to the cup, noticing the steam rising off of it. The smell of coffee made his mouth water. He looked down at his own cup, filled with the same weak tea Meiran was drinking. He took a sip, trying not to make a face.

"The arrows were dipped in toxin," Meiran explained wearily. The cup in her hands trembled ever so slightly. "I healed the wounds, but I couldn't clear the poison from my blood. It worked too fast. I was out within seconds." She brought her teacup to her lips, closing her eyes as her hands trembled.

That explained why Kyel hadn't found any wounds on her, just rotting tissue. He thought it odd, though, that the toxin itself hadn't killed her. She'd gotten lucky. More than lucky.

Craig grunted. "That's why they left you for dead."

Meiran leaned forward, her hair swaying into her face. She pushed it back absently. "I still can't believe you healed me," she said to Kyel with a flat expression on her face. "You never had a talent for it. You must have come a long way since I left."

"Naia helped," Kyel admitted, feeling a sharp pang of sorrow.

Meiran said nothing, but took another sip of her tea. She hadn't reacted when he'd told her about Naia and Sareen. And about the Conclave. He really didn't know how Meiran was taking it all, whether she was angry or sad or anything in between. Come to think of it, she'd shown barely any emotion at all since she'd first woken up and cried her eyes dry against his shoulder. She was like a cloth that had been wrung out, all the substance within her drained.

"What can you tell us about the Servants?" Craig pressed. He leaned forward, the rickety bench shifting and groaning beneath his weight.

Meiran looked up, gazing at him through dark strands of hair. "There's a lot more depth to them than I ever expected. They're far more human than I ever thought they would be. So much more…but also so much less."

She stared down at the table as if studying the furrows in the wood. Her fingernails scratched at a nick on the surface. "I always thought they'd be nothing but soulless demons. Pure, perfect evil. But they're not. They're different. In a way, they are even more sinister.

"Quinlan Reis is a textbook example," she went on, her voice strengthening. "He seems utterly normal: polite, conversational. Sophisticated. His heart seems to be in the right place, at least on the surface. But deep inside, he's desperately flawed. I watched him strike out and kill an innocent woman without sparing her a second thought or a moment's regret. It was like watching him squash an insect."

Devlin Craig leaned forward, crossing his arms, his face deadly serious. "What about Darien? Is it the same with him?"

Meiran took another sip, her cup trembling in her fingers. Kyel's eyes followed the motion of her hand as she set it back down again. He could tell the question bothered her deeply.

"I'm afraid so." Her voice was stiff. Unemotional. "On the surface, he seems perfectly normal. He's the same man I remember. His personality hasn't changed one bit."

Her eyes shot up, locking on Craig. "But they've corrupted him in *significant* ways. He's entirely committed to their cause; he's very passionate about it. But he still holds a deep love for me and for the Rhen. He's conflicted. It's actually quite painful to watch. He doesn't understand. He doesn't see what he's become."

"And what exactly has he become?" Craig gazed at her steadily.

"Evil." Meiran's voice hissed through the shadows. "Darien wields the powers of hell. He raised a necrator from the dead right in front of me. He's planning to lead the legions of the Black Lands in an invasion of the Rhen. He believes it's all justified. The truth is, he terrifies me."

Kyel frowned, struggling to understand how any of that could be possible. "Well, they've obviously done something to him," he said. "But maybe he's still salvageable. Maybe we could help him, do something to help bring him back."

"He's beyond saving, Kyel. Believe me, I tried." Meiran shook her head wearily.

Craig's face was set in deep lines of concern. He leaned back on the bench, the legs creaking under his weight. "What's his rationale?"

Meiran took another sip of tea. The cup clinked against its saucer as she set it back down again. "He told me some vague story about the end of all magic. He says the Enemy depends on magic to grow their food in the absence of sunlight. He says they'll all die if they don't escape."

To Kyel, Darien's concerns sounded legitimate. It would certainly explain the way he was acting. It would be dangerous to dismiss such an apocalyptic warning. He asked, "What if it's true?"

Craig waved his hand in a dismissive gesture. "It doesn't matter if it's true. It wouldn't change our position. We still can't let them in."

Kyel planted his cup on the table, glancing up. "Why not? This changes everything. Don't you understand? If Darien's right, then they're not invaders—they're refugees."

Craig cast a long-suffering glance Meiran's way.

The prime warden brought her hands up, closing her eyes and massaging her temples. "We can't just admit a million hostiles into our midst," she explained to Kyel in overly-patient tones.

"Our responsibility is to our own people. We vowed to keep them safe. And that is exactly what we are going to do."

Kyel felt abashed. That was indeed the gist of the Acolyte's Oath: 'To serve the land and its people.' Of course, it didn't actually specify *which* land and *which* people he was supposed to be serving. Somehow, he doubted that oath had been devised to justify genocide.

He stood up from the table, feeling flustered. He paced away, letting the cup he was holding warm his hands. He chewed on his lip as he tried to sort out his feelings. It just didn't sound right. In his gut, he knew that Craig and Meiran were making the wrong decision.

"We can't just sentence an entire society to death by starvation," Kyel said at last. "We need to put a lot more thought into this. There must be some sort of compromise we can reach."

Meiran looked up at him with pity in her eyes. "Kyel, sometimes deciding what *not* to do is more important than deciding what *to* do. And, in this case, the answer is obvious. We must think about our own citizens who depend on us for protection. The people of the Black Lands chose to worship Xerys. They brought this fate upon themselves. I've seen them— they're savages. Barbaric. We cannot risk bringing such creatures into our midst. Look at me."

He looked at her, even though he didn't want to.

She said, "If we let them in, and then later find out we've been wrong about them, then it will be too late. They have the numbers and the mage-power to overwhelm the kingdoms. Our only hope is stopping them here in the pass."

Kyel knew better than to argue. He knew she was right...but she was also dead wrong. He turned away, breathing out a protracted sigh. He'd almost forgotten the way Meiran made him feel. She treated him like an ignorant child. He'd put up with it for two years.

"I'm very tired," she whispered, standing up from the table. "I'd like to go back now."

"I'll take you back," Kyel offered.

"No. You stay. I can find my own way."

She pulled the cowl of her cloak up over her head. It was thick gray wool, the kind worn by the soldiers of the keep. Not the white cloak of a prime warden. Meiran left her teacup behind, steadying herself in the doorway as she left the room. The door closed softly behind her.

Kyel settled into a chair opposite Craig. "What do you think?"

"It's a lot to take in." The commander took a stiff gulp of his drink, scowling as he plunked the cup back down on the table.

Kyel regarded him for a moment. Craig had always been a reasonable man. He decided to level with him. "Look. Darien was my friend. And he was your friend, too. I think we should trust him enough to talk to him, at least. We should hear his side of the story."

"No." Craig shook his head. "Darien *was* my friend. But I can't let that get in the way of my duty. And neither can you."

"Duty," Kyel echoed sourly, clutching his cup in both hands. "What if Darien's right? What if they really are just refugees? I don't care what Meiran says. If that's the case, then we can't just turn them away."

"They're not just refugees."

"How can you be sure?"

Craig looked at him hard. Then he pushed himself up from the table. "Come with me. I'll show you who they really are."

Kyel sprang up after him as the big man turned and crossed the room, jerking his cloak from a peg by the door and tossing it on. Kyel scrambled after him, following the commander out of the tower and into the keep's inner ward.

Outside, the courtyard was dark, the odor of wood smoke thickening the air. Fires lit all around the ward provided enough light in which to see. Gray-cloaked soldiers collected beside the flames, going about their business: repairing armor, fletching arrows, sharpening weapons. The whole fortress had a mechanized feel of well-oiled efficiency that Kyel could appreciate.

Craig led him through a portal to a spiraling staircase that wound down, corkscrewing, into the guts of the mountainside.

The stairs were steep, lit only by the occasional torch that fluttered weakly in the currents of air that rose from the depths. Kyel stopped to listen. It was quiet; there didn't seem to be anyone else about.

A low wailing sound drifted up from the darkness below.

Kyel's eyes shot to Craig. "What is that?"

The big warrior didn't answer. His nostrils flared with each drawn breath.

Guttural sounds of pain rolled toward them up the stairs. Craig led him downward in the direction of the noise as the air cooled around them. The torches flickered, the light inconsistent, casting long, wavering shadows. Another piercing cry echoed from below, louder this time. The anguish in it made Kyel's stomach twist into knots.

At last the stairs ended in a subbasement that had been turned into an impromptu dungeon. Metal cages lined the walls, the straw-strewn floor stained with blood. Everywhere he looked were chains and iron implements, along with a range of sinister devices. On one side of the room a large bronze kettle steamed over an open fire. The air had a thick odor to it, like the smell of a kitchen: full of wood smoke and burning grease. It almost smelled like roasting pork.

Walking forward, Kyel made out the shapes of three men. One was already dead, stretched out on a low table. It looked like he'd been hacked to death, that or hacked up after death—Kyel couldn't tell which. Another man, this one a white-haired soldier, was tending to a prisoner stretched out across the wall, this one still alive. The man was naked, brown arms and legs held spread-eagled by fetters attached to the wall. He moaned and thrashed, writhing in the bonds that held him.

Kyel stopped walking as it occurred to him what he was looking at. His eyes bounced from the cauldron to the dead man to the splayed prisoner in chains. It took him only a moment to put it all together.

"Gods' mercy…" Kyel whispered, the horror he felt seeping into his voice. He held his stomach, feeling like he was going to be sick.

The old soldier lifted a long-handled ladle from the kettle and raised it over the prisoner's naked body. The man started screaming, struggling frantically against his restraints. The soldier tilted the ladle slowly, dribbling a thin stream of liquid over the man's naked chest as the captive howled in agony. The old man set the ladle down and, using a fingernail, started picking at the flesh that bubbled up.

Kyel gagged and covered his mouth, the prisoner's shrieks echoing in his ears.

Craig walked over to the kettle and dipped the ladle into it. He gave it a good stir, then brought it up to his face, sniffing at the contents.

"Rendering lard?" he asked, grinning as he set the ladle back down in the pot.

"Not a lot of lard on this crop," the grim old-timer remarked. "Seems they get thinner by the batch. Must not be a lot of food left in the Black Lands."

Craig beckoned Kyel forward, but he didn't want to move. He remained rooted in place, too appalled to twitch a muscle. He couldn't stop staring at the poor captive, now hyperventilating and hanging slack in his chains, chest and shoulders a gory mess.

"Come on," Craig insisted, eyes commanding.

Grudgingly, Kyel moved toward him, keeping a good distance from the cauldron of boiling human lard. His eyes lingered on the captive's face, studying the man's bearded features with curiosity. He'd never seen a living man of the Enemy.

The prisoner's face twisted when he noticed Kyel approaching. His eyes widened in recognition, his struggles becoming frantic. He pumped his wrists against the manacles that held him until blood slicked his arms.

"You're torturing him." Kyel whirled on Craig, turning away from the grotesque display. He couldn't understand why the prisoner was more terrified by the sight of him than he'd been when his own flesh was being peeled away.

"Of course we're torturing him," Craig snapped, his face ruddy. "That's how we get information." He turned to the grizzled soldier who was standing by with ladle in hand. "Has he said anything else?"

"No, Sir. Nothing intelligible."

Craig's arm whipped out and caught the Enemy prisoner by the hair, wrenching his neck back against the wall. The man grunted, squeezing his eyes shut as slobber dribbled down his chin.

"What's your name?" Craig growled into his ear.

"Firat," the prisoner gasped. He cracked his lids open, eyes darting sideways at Kyel.

"Just Firat?"

"Firat son of Cozcun." The man's reddened eyes locked on Kyel and didn't budge. He was panting, chest and shoulders heaving as he tried to wriggle his head away from Craig. But the commander tightened his grip and pressed Firat back with the full bulk of his weight.

Craig leaned into him as if ready to plant a kiss on Firat's gasping mouth.

"Why are your forces massing?"

The man grimaced, twisting his face away. But Craig caught him beneath the chin, pinning his head back against the wall. *"Why?* We've made no acts of aggression!"

The prisoner said nothing, just groaned and squirmed. Craig wrenched him by the chin, turning his face toward Kyel.

"Do you know who this is?"

The man cowered, flinching away.

"Tell me, Firat, what would your people do if we let you into the Rhen? Would you lay down your arms and surrender?"

The man growled, eyes burning with furious zeal. From somewhere inside, he'd managed to conjure a last, desperate flare of resistance. He twisted his head out of Craig's grasp and rained spittle into the commander's face. Craig didn't flinch, just blinked the offensive fluid out of his eyes. He stepped back, crossing his gauntleted arms.

"We will arrive as conquerors!" Firat cried, lurching against the rusted chains that held him. "We will put your sons to the sword and enslave your daughters! Your cities will burn to ash, and your rivers will run with blood!"

Craig reached out and smacked the man's head against the wall. Firat went limp, thick blood running in globs from his nose. He slumped in his traces, blinking dumbly like a bludgeoned animal.

Craig turned back to Kyel. "As you can see, Firat is pretty specific about their intentions for us. Doesn't sound like they plan on negotiating." He wiped his eyes with the sleeve of his gambeson before turning back to his captive. "When are they coming?"

The man said nothing. He stared at Craig dully, eyes glassy and unfocused. He opened his swollen mouth, letting out a low moan.

Craig nodded toward Kyel. "This is Kyel Archer, Sixth Tier Sentinel of Aerysius. He has some questions for you."

The prisoner's face contorted in terror. *"No! No—please! I'll tell you what you wish—!"*

Craig grasped Firat behind the head and jerked him forward as far as his restraints would allow. He leaned forward until he was brow-to-brow with him. "I want to know when you're coming. I want to know who commands your armies. And I want to know numbers."

The prisoner thrashed against the granite strength of Craig's arm. Panic filled his eyes, rendering them wide and luminous. Sweat streaked his face and torso, along with the congealing juices of his butchered friend. "I will tell you! Just get him away!"

Craig cast a sidelong grin at Kyel. "The Grand Master will remain here until I'm satisfied with your answers. *Now answer my questions!"*

Firat shuddered. Eyes only for Kyel, he gasped, "We're waiting until all of the tribes can be gathered. A few more weeks…"

"All of your armies?" Craig demanded.

"Yes. Everyone. All must leave…"

"Everyone? You mean every man, woman, and child of the Black Lands?"

Firat nodded, then turned to glare at Craig. "Yes! Yes, everyone! Everyone must leave!"

Craig's hand squeezed a fistful of the man's hair, eliciting a scream. Kyel stood stunned, looking on in revulsion. He wanted to intervene. But he couldn't do anything but watch, transfixed by Craig's brutality.

"Who's in charge of your armies?" Craig demanded, grabbing Firat's flayed and blistered shoulders. *"Who?"*

The prisoner let out a strangled moan, clenching his fists in pain. "Byron Connel leads the legions of Bryn Calazar…and there is a new overlord, another Battlemage. He's rallying the legions of the Khazahar…"

"Do you know his name, this new Battlemage?"

Firat glanced fretfully at Kyel.

"His name, Firat!" Craig bellowed.

The man grimaced, glaring fiercely. "I do not know his name. But it is said he was once a Sentinel."

With a growl, Craig released him. Firat moaned a ragged gasp then sagged in his restraints.

Craig straightened and stood back, wiping his soiled hands on his gambeson. He nodded at the old-timer. "See what else you can get out of him. I think he looks hungry." He glanced down. "I don't think he needs his ball sack anymore. Why don't you fry it up and feed it to him."

"Aye, Force Commander."

As Firat began to scream, Craig's big hand grabbed Kyel by the nape of his cloak and swung him around, propelling him toward the door. Kyel lurched across the chamber, gagging as he passed the cauldron of boiling human fat. Firat's screams followed them out, all the way into the stairwell.

Back on the steps, Kyel jerked away from Craig, whirling to confront him. His heart pounded in his chest, his face heated by outrage. He felt like he was going to throw up, was actually surprised that he hadn't yet.

Firat's shrieks gurgled with agony before collapsing into muffled, strangled sobs.

"You all right?"

Kyel glanced up at Devlin Craig, eyes brimming with hatred. He shook his head as he righted himself, leaning with one elbow against the cold stone wall. "No, I'm not all right. That was despicable."

Craig just looked at him. "This is war, Archer. We do what we have to. Get used to it."

Kyel clenched his hands into fists, taking a step back away from him. His face burned with pent-up rage. He realized that he hated Devlin Craig. Hated him more than he'd ever hated anyone in his life. "He told you what you wanted to know. So why are you still torturing him?"

Craig shrugged. "Trust me, Firat's got a lot more stories to tell. Sheb will get them out of him."

Kyel just stared at the man hard and long, groping to understand how a person could be so callous. He'd been a Greystone soldier once himself. He remembered war being brutal. But this wasn't war—at least, it didn't have to be.

"What you're doing isn't right," Kyel maintained. "You should kill him cleanly."

Craig shook his head. "No. Information saves lives. That's the plain and simple truth. And the life of just one of my men is worth every second of Firat's pain. Do you have any idea what they do to our own captives?"

Kyel nodded, remembering the rumors. He could feel Craig's eyes boring into him, piercing through the shadows of the stairwell. He felt suddenly deflated. "I've heard."

Craig pressed on, "Every man here is under orders to never leave a living man behind for the Enemy. There's good reason for that. I'd do the same for you. I hope you'd do the same for me."

Kyel shook his head, spreading his arms in a gesture of futility. "I can't use my power to take a life…"

"But you can use your hands."

"I…" Kyel tried, but couldn't finish. He wasn't sure where the commander was going with this. All he knew was that he wasn't going to like it. He studied Craig's face resentfully.

"Here." The soldier stepped forward, plucking a knife from his belt and planting its hilt squarely in Kyel's outstretched palm.

Kyel flinched, almost dropping the weapon. But for some reason, he clung onto it. It was a long, thin-bladed dagger with an ebony hilt. It looked familiar, but he wasn't sure where he'd seen it before. He stared down at the weapon, face aghast in silent denial.

"I can't carry a blade," he said.

"Yes, you can. Your Oath doesn't prevent you from using a weapon. Only tradition."

He knew Craig was right; that's how Darien had justified keeping his sword. Only, Kyel had a lot of respect for the slippery slope Darien had thrown himself down. It had all started with a single blade…a blade he'd refused to give up.

"It's called a mercy knife." Craig nodded at the wicked-thin dagger in Kyel's hand. "Look, there's no easy way of putting this, so I'll just state it plainly. You don't want to be taken alive. Remember what they did to Darien? For you, it'd be a whole lot worse."

Kyel swallowed, squeezing his palm around the hilt of the dagger. It felt like an iron weight in his hand. He remembered watching Enemy soldiers hoisting Darien over a flaming pyre. He remembered the sounds of his screams.

"I don't understand," Kyel said. "Why would it be worse for me…?"

Craig placed a steadying hand on Kyel's shoulder. "Because with Darien, they were pressed for time. But they wouldn't be with you. Their mages can heal you while you burn. They can keep you alive for hours, perhaps days. I want you to think about that. Really think about it." He paused, giving Kyel a moment to do just that.

Kyel did. The numbness in his hands and feet spread up his arms, chilling his insides. In the dim silence of the stairwell, his own thundering pulse rumbled like thunder in his ears.

"Right here." Craig reached up, drawing two fingers across his neck under his left ear. "And here." He repeated the motion on the other side. "You'll bleed out in seconds. You'll go right into shock; it won't even hurt."

Firat's last, agonized scream echoed atrociously through the stairwell.

"Keep that dagger close," Craig whispered.

Chapter Ten
Vintgar

Tokashi Palace, The Black Lands

"Your petition was denied."

Darien paused in the action of pulling on a worn leather boot. He glanced up at Sayeed. "Why?"

The Zakai officer took a step toward the bed Darien was sitting on. He held his hat tucked in the crook of his arm. The expression on his bearded face was dour.

"The Omeyan Clan perished," he explained in a voice devoid of emotion. "You are allowed to claim the blood of your ancestors, but that claim alone does not suffice. You have no men of your own bloodline who will follow you."

Darien tugged the boot on over his heel then stood up from the bed. He reached for a linen shirt and wormed his arms into the sleeves. Then he wrapped the warbelt around his hips, fixing it in place.

"I have the Tanisars."

"The Tanisars are not blood of your blood."

Darien nodded. He fastened on his cloak with a silver brooch then reached up to tie back his hair.

"What are my options?"

Sayeed shifted his weight over his feet, screwing his face into a thoughtful grimace. He stood there for some time while Darien waited, gazing at him steadily. In the corner, the demon-dog scratched at an itch, its foot hammering on the floor. The coal-fire in the hearth crackled and popped.

"You should accept your Lightweaver's offer of marriage," Sayeed said. "Then you would have the Jenn Asyaadi behind you.

The Asyaadi have great respect among the tribes. Their blood is very ancient, and they have long controlled the Khazahar's trade routes."

Darien stood frozen, staring at the fire in the hearth. It cast an oily light that blurred across the walls of the bedchamber. At last he blinked as if waking from a trance. "Marriage is not an option."

Sayeed looked patently uncomfortable. A host of conflicted emotions ranged over his face, settling finally into a look of grave concern. He took another step forward, shifting his hat to his other hand. "May I speak frankly?"

"Of course."

Sayeed's tongue traced over his lips. He seemed to be searching for the right words. Or perhaps he already knew the words he wanted to say, but was reluctant to utter them.

"What your woman did to you was cruel," he said at last. "But it was also deserved."

Darien frowned. He hadn't expected to hear that. Neither did he agree; he had done nothing to deserve such treatment from Meiran. He'd given everything for her. All he'd ever wanted in return was a trace amount of understanding. Or compassion.

She'd given him neither.

Sayeed went on, "You betrayed every cause you ever championed. Including hers."

Darien felt as though he were a straw man with a straw soul, and the stuffing inside him had just been ripped out and thrown asunder. For it was true; Sayeed had a point. He had abandoned Meiran's cause and taken up another.

"But it's not your fault," the officer continued quickly. "You were ignorant. Your eyes were closed. And now that they are open, you cannot help but see things differently." He paused, his expression quite serious. "It is said that a wound that bleeds inwardly is the most dangerous of all. You have such a wound, Darien Nach'tier. I see you struggle with it. I fear what will happen if you don't find a cure."

He walked forward and placed a hand on Darien's arm. "Take my advice: forgive the woman who betrayed you, knowing that you also betrayed her. Then marry your Lightweaver."

Darien sidestepped Sayeed and retreated across the chamber. He couldn't help it. He was just as repelled by the man's proximity as he was by his advice. He didn't like to be touched.

Sayeed withdrew, understanding in his eyes. By now, the man was more than aware of Darien's peculiar idiosyncrasies. The people of Malikar needed much less personal space than he was accustomed to. It had taken Darien some time, but at last he'd convinced Sayeed of his need for distance.

"Are you ready?"

"Aye." Darien scooped up his sword from where it hung by his bedside, drawing the baldric on over his shoulder. It was the sword Meiran had given him. More than once, he'd come very close to throwing it in the lake. But each time he'd stopped himself just shy of committing the act. He couldn't bring himself to give the blade up; it was too much a part of him.

"Are you sure you want to do this?" Sayeed said as he cast open the door. "The caverns are still wet and very treacherous. We should send an expeditionary party down first."

"I'll risk it," Darien said. When he moved toward the door, the demon dog rose and made as if to follow him. But Darien raised his hand. The awful beast circled its cushion once then lay back down again. It stared up at him with its muzzle between its paws, looking dejected.

Once out in the corridor, Darien was surprised to find Azár there waiting for him. She stood beside his door next to the retinue of Zakai that followed him everywhere. Darien shot an accusatory look at Sayeed, who just shrugged in reply.

Raising his eyebrows, Darien asked, "Aren't the krill in need of your magelight?"

Azár had assumed the duties of a palace Lightweaver, so every few days she rotated in from the lightfields to tend to the true riches of Tokashi: the krill ponds beneath the fortress, beneath even the swirling energies of Tokashi's vortex. Deep down in the depths of the ice warrens existed enormous salt pools teeming with krill that could only be supported by a constant input of magelight. The krill were harvested and used in place of meat to feed the Tanisar corps. They were also exported for their weight in riches, which accounted for the enormous wealth the Tanisars had amassed.

Seeing Darien's irritation, Azár smirked, managing to look both arrogant and innocent.

"The ponds can go hours without light," she assured him, gazing defiantly into his face. She wore a single red ribbon draped across her brow that wound down through the length of her braid. A small stone dangled in the center of her forehead. Darien had seen the style before on some of the serving women. It lent a softness to her features he wasn't used to.

He asked, "Is there something you need?"

"I came to speak with you."

Darien indicated his retinue of Zakai. "We're on our way down to the chasm. I can speak with you upon our return."

Azár smiled as she shrugged. "I will go with you. We can speak along the way."

Darien felt the heat of frustration rise to his cheeks. He glared at Azár. Then he glared at Sayeed.

"As you like," he muttered, then turned and strode away down the corridor.

His men fell in behind, hurrying to catch up. He didn't turn to see whether or not Azár was following; he knew that she would. Sayeed hastened to match his pace, face stern, hand resting on the sword hilt at his waist. When their group reached the stairs, Darien relented and let the senior Zakai move ahead of him, the rest lingering behind. He followed after, Azár silently fuming as she fell in at his side.

The men lit torches, passing around a flaming rag soaked in lamp oil. They descended the staircase, the air becoming chill and moist as they moved farther into the subterranean glacier. Darien could see his breath like a fog before his face. He shivered in a way that had nothing to do with the cold; the chill of the air provoked memories he'd rather leave forgotten. They continued downward until the ice eventually gave way to rough, dark stone.

The stone below the glacier was weeping, the steps covered with oozing mud that leaked water in small, gushing streams.

They had arrived at a level of the warrens that had been submerged by the lake only days before.

The going was slow, the path murky and uneven. Darien struggled through spongy silt pebbled with rocks, slogging along after Sayeed and his men. The walls bled mud and slime down their surfaces. Water ran down the stairs, eroding the deposits of silt. Soon they were walking through what amounted to a rushing stream fed by frigid water from the glacier.

Ahead, the officers drew up and stood consulting in whispering echoes. Darien moved forward through the press of bodies, interested to find out what they'd discovered.

"What is it?"

Sayeed pointed at a small, circular indentation in the wall. Darien's eyebrows shot up at the sight of a small button. It had a glyph carved on it, one he knew well. Beads of sweat broke out across his brow despite the chill.

"Everyone, move back," he warned.

When the soldiers had yielded him room, he reached down and depressed the ancient switch. There was the slightest clicking noise followed by the sound of a mechanism moving somewhere within the wall. For a moment, he held his breath. When nothing happened, Darien sighed, feeling a heady surge of relief.

"That trap would have killed the lot of you," he said. "I'll lead the way from here."

"Darien."

Turning, he saw that Azár had come up silently beside him. She had drawn her shawl up over her head, her arms wrapped tightly around herself for warmth.

"You should let me go first." Her tone was much softer than he was used to hearing from her. "Most of the Lyceum's knowledge was lost. But not all. What remains has been passed down to me. I have experience with this type of device."

That surprised him. He hadn't known any of the Lyceum's vast troves of knowledge had been retained by the mages who were the descendants of that culture. As long as he'd known her, Azár had professed only ignorance of even the most basic knowledge of magecraft. He hoped she knew what she was doing.

But he deferred to her with a wave of his hand, motioning her to go first.

Azár walked forward with an almost regal grace, parting the group of Zakai who stood in front of them. Darien watched her for a moment, admiring the confidence she projected. Then he moved forward, following closely on her heels.

Azár led them down the mud-encrusted stairs, pausing every so often to depress some of the trigger switches, ignoring others. Some appeared to be nonfunctioning. Others would have resulted in deadly consequences if they'd been tripped. As Darien walked, he studied Azár carefully. He took note of the way she moved, trailing her fingers along the wall at her side. The deliberate placement of her feet among the rubble with never a misplaced stride.

She led them deeper into the warrens, shadows and silt collecting under their feet. The cold was relentless, clawing its way through his wet garments. Darien began to shiver despite his thick cloak.

Azár paused to disarm the next device they encountered. There was a small click in the wall. Then she turned to look back at Darien, eyes glinting with excitement. "Do you feel that? We must be nearing the eye of the vortex."

Darien didn't feel anything; with his mind walled away, he had no sense whatsoever of the magic field. Azár must have a rare talent to sense the field's currents while shielded. He hoped she was right; he was anxious to find out if all the risk he had taken to drain the lake was worth it.

The silt-slick stairs they trudged down eventually ended in a tunnel encased by mud. Water had collected on the floor, forming deep pools. Up ahead, a blue-green light filtered in through an opening in the rock. Darien squinted, wondering where that gush of cool light could be coming from.

Azár started forward, feet slogging through water and oozing muck. The claustrophobic space they were in opened up into a vast cavern, the path they were treading leading toward an arching stone bridge that spanned a gaping chasm. Chill air wafted up from far below, carrying a fresh riverine scent.

Darien moved quickly past Azár, out onto the arching span of the bridge. A wind seized his hair, rippling his cloak. Turquoise light streamed upward, saturating the cavern in a scintillating dance of color. The chasm was enormous, both continuing upward and cutting down into the depths. Darien walked to the edge of the bridge, to a low wall that was chipped away in places. He leaned over, staring down, seeking the source of the light.

Far below, the River Nym cut its way through the bottom of the chasm, its waters swift and turbulent. The glow that filled the cavern emanated from the river itself, filtering up through the air, reflecting off the water-polished rock. A breeze delivered the scent of the river, wild and fresh and teeming with life. Darien felt exultant. He'd never seen anything so beautiful in his life.

He turned to find Azár standing behind him, basking in a pool of summery magelight.

"The eye of the vortex," he breathed. "The river flows through the source."

"No." Azár's eyes were fixed on the Nym's swift currents. "The river is the source."

Darien frowned, suddenly troubled. That's not how the magic field worked. "Come on, let's get down there. I'll show you. At the center of the eye will be a Circle of Convergence. That's what we'll find. That river's just a river. Nothing more."

"It's beautiful," she whispered, gazing down into the turquoise wash of light.

So was she, Darien had to admit. He muttered, "Aye."

Azár took a step back away from the edge then turned and crossed the bridge to the other side. Darien followed her, anticipation speeding his stride. On the other side of the gorge, the path became encased by rock. Another mud-ruined stair took them downward. Water dripped from the ceiling, splashing on his head and wetting his hair. His feet sloshed through puddles of oozing mud.

They came to a point where the ceiling had partially collapsed. Large boulders and debris filled the narrow passage, blocking their path. Darien and Azár lingered behind as Sayeed's men labored to clear away the rubble. They formed a human chain, handing rocks and debris from one man to another, depositing them along the cave walls.

Feeling idle, Darien turned to Azár. "You said you wanted to speak with me?"

Her face darkened. "Later. Now isn't the time for it." She turned and moved to the opposite end of the passage, leaving him feeling awkward and alone.

When the path was clear, their small party forged ahead again. They came to a place where many corridors branched off their path, lightless, boring into the depths of the rock that surrounded them. Darien wondered where the passages led; the ancient fortress of Vintgar surrounded them, but there was no sign yet of its former grandeur, only of its decay.

The deeper they went, the more the tunnel became clogged with filth and debris. Eventually they came to another place where the ceiling had collapsed entirely. Sayeed's men strained against the wall of rock without success; it seemed as if the weight of the entire mountain bore down upon it.

Darien watched the men labor, nettled by frustration. At last, he'd had enough.

"Stand back," he ordered. Then he opened his mind to the Onslaught. The corridor darkened then flared a sinister shade of green. Darien was aware that his entire body blazed with an unnatural glow, exuding the Hellpower from his pores.

He concentrated, willing the debris to be gone. Nothing happened, so he concentrated harder. Suddenly, he felt the entire obstruction *shift*, just as he had *shifted* the boulders of the dam. The mountain above them rumbled, provoked by his meddling. The floor shook as pebbles rained down from the ceiling. The blockage ahead had disappeared completely, revealing a tiled mosaic that gleamed up at them from the floor.

Darien let go of the Onslaught and walked toward the spot where the rocks had just been, eyes fixated on the floor. He knelt down, running his hand across the vibrant tiles. They formed an elaborate pattern of wine and gold. It reminded him of an ornate tapestry, somehow preserved in ceramic and time.

"Is that…what this place once looked like?" Azar whispered,

stroking a tile.

Darien looked up at her. "It would seem."

He regained his feet, still marveling at the mosaic beneath his feet. Only then did he realize the stares that were aimed at him, the gaping disbelief on the faces of Sayeed's men. He spread his hands. "This is your heritage," he told them. "Perhaps someday Vintgar can be restored. But not today."

He motioned Azár to go ahead then followed after her, gazing down at his feet as he crossed the intricate web of tiles. They marched along another mud-strewn passage decorated in crumbling rock and oozing slime. The noise of the river was much louder now. The sound of its rushing current echoed through the darkness from somewhere close by. They came to another passage, one that sloped downward into black depths of shadow.

Reluctant to use magelight, Darien let the green glow of the netherworld light their path. The sloping corridor they followed led to the bottom of the caverns, opening into a wide space that bordered the gorge. They stood in a many-vaulted chamber lit by the river's vaporous glow. Ruined archways and crumbling corridors led off in all directions.

"Here," Darien said, closing his eyes. He tore down the barriers that protected his mind from the vortex and let the magic field come gushing in. He gasped, reveling in the sweet perfection of the field lines that converged in this place, here in the eye of the vortex. He sucked in the power, basking in euphoric bliss. When he opened his eyes, he saw that Azár's face had taken on a smile of elation.

He couldn't help himself; he sighed in relief, glad just to feel whole again. But the contentment he felt was short-lived. A feeling of cold purpose stole over him, reminding him of his business here. Darien turned back to his men, beckoning them forward.

"Stay close. The Circle of Convergence is this way," he said, and started off across the filth-covered chamber, splashing through puddles on the floor. He felt his way with his mind, following the smooth currents of energy.

He found Vintgar's Circle of Convergence in an adjoining chamber, on the other side of a collapsed archway. Darien stopped in the entrance to the hall, glancing around at the slime-encrusted walls, and taking in the shattered ceiling. A solid bank of mud encased the floor. They would have to dig down through layers of silt and fallen rock to unearth Vintgar's Circle.

Still, even through the layers of mud that covered it, he should be able to sense something of the Circle below. But that wasn't the case. The Circle of Convergence lay buried mere inches beneath his feet, but he could feel no connection to it at all.

It was not slumbering beneath all that mud.

It was dead.

He was sure of it. Darien bowed his head, letting the tragedy of the loss settle in. He needed the Circle, needed it desperately. He'd hoped to use it to disrupt the curse that infected the skies. Now that chance was gone. Gone forever.

"There's nothing here," he said at last, sorrow heavy in his voice. "Nothing for us, at least."

Azár nodded, a look of understanding in her eyes. Sayeed and his men started back toward the entrance of the hall, faces grim. Perhaps they sensed his mood. Or saw the burden of loss in his eyes. It didn't matter; they knew something had gone terribly wrong.

Darien allowed the light of the river to guide their way through the system of littered corridors. Even here, in the heart of ancient Vintgar, there was nothing of the past left to find. No furniture or artifacts had managed to survive. Everything was encased by mud or weathered away. The fortress of Vintgar had drowned under the Nym's displaced waters a thousand years ago. Nothing of its former grandeur remained.

"Lord, over here," one of the men called from behind.

Darien turned, starting toward the officer who beckoned him from the opening of a passage. He stopped in a doorway, his feet rooted to the floor.

He couldn't move. His eyes were locked on the center of a shattered room, where a pristine cross-vaulted arch rose majestically from the mud and slime. It glowed with a soft amber light that was both eerie and comforting. The arch appeared as though neither time nor floodwaters had dared touch it. Darien moved toward the artifact, drawn as if compelled. He stopped inches away, reaching out to run a hand down the rose-colored pillar. He could almost feel the charged power that surged within it.

"What do we do?" Azár asked, drawing up at his side. She was staring in awe at the transfer portal, an expression of wonder on her face.

Darien extended his hand in invitation. "We go through."

She looked at him with surprise in her eyes then eyed the portal skeptically. "What if it's broken?"

"Then I suppose we'll find out. But I don't think it is." Darien was sure of it; he could feel the stirring of power in the artifact. The lines of the magic field warped around it then disappeared smoothly within. Azár nodded, taking his hand.

Sayeed moved quickly, inserting himself in front of them. "No! Lord, let me go first. It is my life that should be risked; not yours."

Darien's first impulse was to deny him. But he found himself relenting. As mages, both he and Azár were irreplaceable. Sayeed was not, as much as Darien hated to admit it. There were many Zakai who would be willing and honored to take his place.

"Very well," Darien said and stepped back, letting go of Azár's hand.

"Thank you, Lord, for this honor." Sayeed bowed stiffly then moved into the center of the portal, positioning himself between the pillars that supported the cross-vaulted arch. He turned back around, his face set in lines of determination.

"What do I do?" he asked.

"Close your eyes," Darien advised. "Empty your mind and let the portal do the rest."

Sayeed nodded, closed his eyes, then took a step back, adjusting his position under the arch. There was a brief, brilliant gush of light. And then he was gone.

Darien moved quickly around the transfer portal. He hoped he wouldn't find Sayeed's body slathered across the rocks behind it.

He had no idea what the portal would do if not configured correctly. Suddenly, he was very glad Sayeed had volunteered. He could kick himself for almost risking Azár's life. Despite the cold, he began to sweat. The man should be back by now.

"What is he doing?" Azár grumbled.

"I don't know." Darien placed his hand on the stone of the portal without actually stepping inside. He closed his eyes and felt deep within the artifact. There was no resonance, no distortion of the energies that moved within it. Nothing seemed amiss.

A strong flash of light startled him, making him flinch back. Sayeed staggered out of the brilliant glare, face pale and covered in sweat. He bent forward, hands on his knees, catching his breath.

Darien felt more excited than concerned. "Where does it go?"

Sayeed drew himself up, still panting, his expression dour. "The portal leads to Bryn Calazar. Lord, your presence is requested immediately."

Darien felt his excitement wither. "By whom?"

Sayeed swallowed, managing to look even paler than he had before. "By Prime Warden Zavier Renquist."

Darien nodded somberly. After Byron Connel's visit, he had every reason to fear the wrath of the prime warden. He should have seen this coming.

"Wait here," he told Azár, and moved stiffly toward the portal.

She shook her head, inserting herself ahead of him. "If you go, then I go also." She offered out her hand.

Darien stopped, staring for a moment at her soft fingers. He glanced back up at her face, at the stubborn set of her jaw. At the firm resolve in her eyes. He knew better than to argue.

"As you like," he said, and took her hand in his.

Chapter Eleven
Blood Bond

Bryn Calazar, The Black Lands

D arien released Azár's hand and stepped away from the transfer portal, moving out of a blinding wash of light. He found himself in a vaulted chamber filled with many similar arches. He recognized the space immediately: the portal chamber in Bryn Calazar. All around him, black-mailed bodies fell to their knees then bent forward to the floor. Darien gazed at the sight, awed and shaken. This was an entirely different reception than he had experienced before.

"Arise," he said.

At his word, the mailed bodies returned to their feet, coming forward to form a tight cluster about him. His gaze leaped from helm to helm, the sight intimidating. This had once been the only image he had of a people he'd known only as the Enemy. Now he understood there were real people behind those helms: fathers, brothers, husbands, sons. He wished he could see their faces.

"Remove your helms," he ordered.

When they did, he realized that he'd been wrong. Darien stared in shock at the stern faces of the guards that surrounded him. More than a few were female. He hadn't expected that. He looked from face to face, making eye contact with each man and woman in the chamber. At last, he nodded, more than a little shaken.

How many women had he killed at Orien's Finger? He would never know the numbers. He knew it shouldn't matter. But it did. He sensed Azár moving to stand beside him as the guards replaced their helms.

A white-bearded man wearing the robes of a priest of Xerys appeared at the top of the steps. "Darien Nach'tier," he said in a raspy voice. "Your presence is requested."

Darien did his best not to cringe at the sound of the old man's voice. The words felt like a noose slipping around his neck. He could almost feel it tightening. He said to Azár, "You should wait here."

"Where you go, I go." Her tone brooked no argument.

Darien didn't want her accompanying him to this meeting with Renquist. He couldn't guarantee it would have a good ending. But he relented, knowing better not to protest. After all, it was his life, not hers, at risk.

The guards parted to let them pass as they made their way toward the stairs. The priest in crimson robes greeted them with a nod, saying nothing as he led them up the steps. The man's face was skeletal, his eyes sunken in their sockets. He shuffled as he walked, one leg obviously weaker than the other. They emerged from the stairs into a large, domed room with a Circle of Convergence set into the floor.

Darien halted, at once stunned and dismayed at the sight. It was larger than Aerysius' Greater Circle had been. Alas, this one was quiet. Staring harder at the patterns on the floor, he realized that the lines of power had been irrevocably warped. It wept, leaking magical energies like a sieve. Another Circle, lost to time.

Only, this loss was staggering.

He tore his eyes away from the distorted artifact that seemed to bleed power from its pores. Instead, he fixed his stare on the back of the red-robed priest who walked ahead of them. He followed the old man across the floor and into a hallway beyond. With a bow and a flourish of robes, the priest stepped aside, gesturing toward a wooden door.

Darien paused, considering the door. He was hesitant to open it; it was the only wooden door he had encountered in all the Black Lands, made of solid oak and bound by iron bands. He understood the vast wealth and power conveyed by that single fixture. He feared that door, feared what might await him on the other side of it.

He grasped the cold handle and depressed the latch. The door creaked open a fraction on its own. He pulled it the rest of the way, exposing a dim chamber within. Darien drew back and raised his hand, signaling Azár to let him enter first. He paused, collecting his nerves. Then he stepped forward into the room.

At the sight of Zavier Renquist, he dropped to his knees and bowed forward, pressing his head against the rugs as, beside him, Azár did the same. Closing his eyes, Darien engaged his other senses. Fragrant incense thickened the air, masking the odor of coal soot. There was the rustle of fabric from across the room. A soft, trickling noise. Then silence. Silence and agarwood and soft woven carpets. The combination provoked a nauseating wave of fear.

For a moment, he felt transported back to the tent where Renquist had manipulated him into submission. Or into hell; there really wasn't much difference. It all had the same unnerving feel.

"Arise and be heard."

That resonant voice chilled his blood to ice. It was distinctive, and singularly disturbing. Darien rose from the position of prostration, regaining his feet.

Resplendent in robes of deepest indigo, Zavier Renquist stood to greet them both. *"Sulimu kadreesh,"* he uttered, moving to clasp Darien in a close embrace.

"Akadreesh issulim." Darien shuddered at the proximity of the man. He didn't like anyone that close to him. Especially someone with the amount of power he sensed in Renquist. He'd never known another mage who commanded such strength and authority. By comparison, Darien felt like a mere pawn to be moved at will.

The prime warden released him and turned to Azár, who bent forward to kiss the hem of his robe. He extended his hand, inviting them to sit beside him on embroidered cushions arranged in an intimate circle upon the floor.

A serving boy came forward, carrying a bronze pot with an elongated spout. He produced a cup and poured a small amount of brown liquid into it. This, he handed to Renquist, who received the beverage without thanks. Azár was served next. The third cup went to Darien. He knew that the cups were poured in that order intentionally; Renquist was making certain that Darien was aware of his place.

He knew better than to decline the offer of drink; he valued his life. The odor of coffee filled his nostrils. He took a taste, finding the bitter flavor to his liking.

"Tell me," Renquist said, setting his cup down at his side, "how is your health?"

"I've been well, Prime Warden." Darien took another sip, savoring the taste. The coffee was strong but not overpowering. It was also very hot; the cup felt wonderful in his hands after the chill of Vintgar's ice warren.

Renquist nodded. "I hear you returned the River Nym to its proper course. That was no small feat. Tell me, Darien. How did you accomplish such a miracle?"

Darien winced internally at Renquist's choice of words. It was no miracle. His actions had been stupidly reckless. That or attempted suicide; he wasn't sure which.

"I found a way to use the Onslaught while shielding my mind from the vortex." He didn't bother to elaborate. He just hoped Renquist would let it go at that. He waited, gazing down into his cup at the patterned swirls of cream.

The prime warden seemed to accept his answer. Raising his own cup, he said, "And what is the state of Vintgar's Circle of Convergence?"

Darien thought of Bryn Calazar's dead Circle, feeling a pang of loss. "I'm sorry, Prime Warden. Vintgar's Circle was destroyed beyond repair."

"Perhaps. I will have it examined by someone more competent."

Darien paused in the action of raising his drink to his lips, shaken by the insult. He set the cup back down, a growing unease tightening his gut. The chamber seemed colder than it had just moments before.

Renquist continued, "You have fulfilled many of the tasks set out for you. In that respect, I am pleased. But there is still the matter of Nashir…" His voice trailed off into a festering silence.

Darien drew in a deep breath, fighting to steady his already rattled nerves. "I assume you've heard from Byron Connel."

"Yes. A message did arrive." The prime warden took a sip of his drink. "I was greatly troubled by the news. You shouldn't have been able to best Nashir; he had superior training and a thousand years more experience than you. I must admit…I can't help but find myself impressed." His eyes locked with Darien's. "I hear you raised a necrator. That is a rare talent. We may need you to produce more."

"I don't know what I did," Darien said quickly. "I don't think I could repeat it." He didn't remember much of the torture or its aftermath. It was not something he wanted to remember; he'd done his best to forget.

"You will try," Renquist directed. It was not a request.

"Aye, Prime Warden." Darien drained the last of his coffee, an attempt to hide the sickened look on his face. The cup was replenished as soon as he set it down.

"Lightweaver Azár." Renquist turned to the woman. "Are you satisfied with Darien's progress?"

Azár shot Darien a nervous glance. "I am, Prime Warden. He has proven a worthy ally. He has gathered many fine warriors behind him."

"And yet…" Renquist's gaze slid back to Darien. "I hear you are having difficulty uniting the tribes?"

Darien had to nod; there was no use trying to hide it. Renquist must have anticipated the challenges he would face. "I rule the Khazahar in name alone. I've the support of the Tanisars. But I've failed to gain the support of the tribes."

"Because of your blood."

"Aye. Because of my blood." It was hardly a secret.

The prime warden's stare drifted downward to Darien's waist. To the golden buckle of the warbelt fastened there. The prime warden's stare lingered on the buckle. "What an interesting piece of workmanship," he said finally. "Omeyan, unless I miss my guess?"

Darien closed his eyes, feeling the last of his hopes slip through his fingers. The room felt suddenly, oppressively cold. Perhaps Renquist had seen the warbelt on Quin. Or even on Braden Reis a thousand years before; whichever. It didn't matter. His own possession of the belt was inexplicable. And incriminating.

The game was up.

Renquist leaned forward, capturing his gaze. Very softly, he said, "Do you have something you wish to tell me, Darien?"

Cold beads of perspiration broke out on his brow. Immediately, Darien was transported back in time to the pavilion below Orien's Finger, to his first meeting with Renquist. When the demon had broken him with nothing more than the simple, crushing truth.

A trickle of sweat dribbled down his face, dropping to the floor. He wet his lips with his tongue. "Quinlan Reis left me this warbelt along with a note. He claims it belonged to one of my ancestors."

The gap of silence that followed his words seemed to drag on forever before finally wearing out. With the silence came the creeping feel of danger. Darien knew he was being judged. He also knew he may not survive the judgement. He was well aware of the price of betrayal.

"When was the last time you saw Quinlan Reis?"

There was no use being evasive. "I saw him when he brought Meiran to me in Qul."

Another gaping silence. Darien counted the seconds with the ebb and flow of his breath. Another drop of sweat leaked down his face.

"And where is Quinlan Reis now?"

"I sent him on to Athera's Crescent."

Another pause. Another drop of sweat. Darien kept his eyes focused on the bronze cup in Renquist's hand.

"Toward what end?"

"To find a way to resolve the curse over the Black Lands."

He shifted his weight. His fingertips twitched.

"And where is Sareen Qadir?"

Darien's breath froze in his throat. He hadn't thought of

Sareen.

"I don't know. I never saw her."

The warmth of the air seemed to bleed right out of the room.

"And where is Meiran now?"

"I don't know."

His breath turned to mist before his face.

"Darien."

He squeezed his eyes shut, unable to look the demon in the face.

"Do not lie to me, Darien. If you lie to me…I will know."

Which had to mean Renquist was a Sensitive…and he'd been reading Darien's emotions all along. The information clicked into place like the last piece of a wood knot. Darien froze, unable to breathe.

He sat in a room with the most dangerous creature in all the world's history. There was a reason why Renquist had gained that reputation. Darien struggled to find his nerve under the weight of realization. The man could sense anything he felt.

"I'll say this one more time." The prime warden's voice sliced through the air like the edge of a blade. "Where is Meiran now?"

Darien took a deep breath. "She sided with Nashir against me. If it wasn't for Quin, they'd have gotten their way. Meiran bolted after that. I've no idea where she went."

Renquist absorbed this information in silence. At last, he motioned for his drink to be replenished. Raising his cup, he commanded, "Return immediately to Tokashi Palace. Find a way to win the allegiance of the tribes. I want every last human transferred out of the Khazahar by the end of the week." His eyes filled with shadow and malice. "Now. You are going to stand up and walk out that door. *While you still have the ability.*"

Darien didn't hesitate. He swept to his feet, managing a stiff bow.

"Prime Warden," he breathed as he turned to leave. Before he reached the door, he heard Renquist utter:

"Lightweaver Azár. Please remain."

Darien pulled the door closed behind him. The corridor outside was empty. He leaned his back against the wall, closing his eyes as he struggled to control his pulse. His arms trembled at his sides.

He knew exactly how close he'd come.

He waited, staring at the floor, for an infinite period of time.

At last, the door to the chamber opened and Azár rejoined him in the hallway. She glanced at him with an expression that suggested everything but said nothing.

They traced their steps back the way they had come. Azár walked at his side, conspicuous in her silence. Back across the cold Circle of Convergence that writhed and wept like a dying thing. Down the stairs, into the chamber filled with portals and black-mailed bodies.

Azár gave him her hand. There was a brief flash and Bryn Calazar was gone.

Somehow, he was still alive.

Darien stepped out of the portal and turned to Azár, knowing he'd been left without a choice.

"Please join me for dinner tonight," he said.

She turned and studied his face. At last, she consented with a nod.

Darien buckled the Omeyan warbelt about his waist. Then he turned to face Sayeed. "Is there anything else I'll need?"

The Zakai officer frowned, face squirming through several layers of thought. He slowly shook his head. "Not at this time. All will be negotiated after." He took a step forward, fixing the lay of Darien's robe. He handed him an embroidered vest.

Darien pulled it on, avoiding the looking glass next to the bed. He already knew what the image would tell him: that he looked nothing like the man he remembered. His hair had grown longer, worn tied back in a single braid. The green robe and vest were unlike any style he'd ever considered wearing in the Rhen. Indeed, he could have never afforded such luxury. Other than his complexion, he looked every inch Malikari.

It felt like he'd left the Rhen behind completely. It didn't even feel a part of him anymore.

"Let's go."

Sayeed bowed and swept the door open. Darien strode out into a cluster of Zakai, who moved quickly to surround him. They accompanied him to the dining hall where, mercifully, he was allowed to enter alone.

A long wooden table awaited him there. He took a seat at the table's center, a footman moving forward to assist him. The servant's attentions made Darien uncomfortable; he still wasn't used to such treatment. It went against every grain of self-sufficiency he'd been trained to rely on.

"My thanks," he muttered as another servant set a fingerbowl down in front of him.

He sloshed his fingers around in the water, scooping some up in his palm to wipe over his face. He blotted his cheeks dry on an offered cloth. The bowl was removed, a celadon plate set before him in its place.

Then he waited.

A servant came to pour tea.

Another brought arak.

Darien took his time about draining them both.

He stared at the table, at the walls, at the blue-painted ceiling. He considered the workmanship of the beaten copper bowls in the center of the table. He studied the table's hardwood grain. He was about to stand up and leave when Azár entered, clothed in a gown with flowing sleeves, her hair wrapped in ribbons.

He'd never seen her in a gown. He almost forgot to stand.

"Thank you for coming," Darien said, rising awkwardly.

Azár looked at him sideways. Her expression was just as fierce as it had ever been. He motioned for her to take the seat opposite him as maids rushed to settle her in. She suffered their attentions much more gracefully than he had.

After the meal was served, Darien dismissed the servants with a wave of his hand.

They ate in silence. The kitchen staff had prepared a rich stew made from krill harvested from the ponds below the palace. Darien ate hungrily, relishing the taste. His body, starved for meat, had learned to crave the dish. It was seasoned with spice hot enough to make him break out in a sweat.

The silence became uncomfortable. Darien was conscious of every clink of silverware, of the sound of his own teeth working in his mouth. He tried to think of something to say, something to ease the tension in the room. But he couldn't force one word past his lips. He couldn't think of anything to say that would not betray his intentions.

Abruptly, Azár pushed back her plate, sitting up straight in her seat. "I'm not hungry."

She was glaring at him, he realized. He supposed he'd been an inconsiderate host. Darien swallowed the food in his mouth, bringing his napkin up to wipe his face. Moving purposefully, he pushed back his own plate. Azár's eyes were intense, probing, daring. Still, he couldn't speak. He just gazed back at her.

"Why did you invite me here?" she asked.

Darien sighed, knowing he couldn't put off his purpose any longer. He folded his napkin on the table, taking his time about it, using the space to summon his nerve.

"I don't know how to say this. So I'll just say it," he said, gazing down at his plate. "I don't wish to marry. It doesn't have anything to do with you. There's nothing wrong with you. It's just that…I lived my life already. Understand? There's nothing left of me to offer a woman. I'm empty."

He glanced up, searching her face. He expected to find it full of hurt and resentment. But Azár's expression hadn't changed. She sat motionless in her chair, eyebrows raised. Waiting for him to continue.

He cleared his throat, scooting forward in his seat. "So I'll not lie to you and tell you that I'm proposing marriage out of love. I'm not. I'm asking for your hand because it's the only option left to me." His gaze shot down to the table, fixing on a knot in the wood. He didn't want to look at her. He was too ashamed by his own audacity.

To his surprise, she didn't walk out. Instead, she leaned forward and took his hand. "I am not a woman of the Rhen. I understand what you are saying, and I'm not offended. Marriage is not about love. It is about commitment. Love comes and goes many times throughout the lifetimes of two people. It is the commitment that remains. If you wish to commit to me, Darien Nach'tier, then I will commit to you, as well."

He looked up to study her face. To his surprise, her expression had lost all of its ferocity. He was confused; he didn't understand. She should despise him for what he had said.

For some reason, she didn't.

He asked, "Are you certain?"

"Yes. I am certain." There was absolutely no doubt in her eyes. He couldn't understand it.

"You know what I am…and you've no problem with it?" He held her gaze firmly, looking for any trace of reluctance but finding none.

Her voice was adamant. "You are a demon. I know this…*and I don't care.*"

Darien couldn't fathom her reaction. It made no sense. "Why not?"

She shrugged and squeezed his hand. He stared down at her fingers, creamy brown, soft and delicate.

Azár said, "You made many wrong decisions in your past. For this, you are damned. But there is much *sharaq* in you. I have seen it. I will honor you as my husband. And I know you will honor me as your wife."

Darien found the nerve to look her in the eye. "Then I ask you formally: Azár ni Asu'am, will you marry me?"

"I will."

Uncomfortably, he squirmed in his seat. "Then I'll have the clerks prepare the marriage contract. I understand I need to provide you with a bride-gift. Feel free to write into the contract whatever it is you desire. If I have it, it will be yours."

She nodded, her eyes sliding to the side. "How soon will you want the contract signed?"

"As soon as possible." This was not about love. This was about war. He needed the legions of the Khazahar, and he needed them yesterday. Azár was only a means to an end, and she knew it.

Still, her thumb stroked his skin. Her fingers squeezed his. Then she released his hand and stood up.

"I will go prepare," she said and left the room.

Darien sat staring at the door, staring at her plate, staring at his hand, long after Azár had left. He tried to label his emotions, but found that he couldn't. The truth was, he had no idea what he was feeling. Or what he was supposed to be feeling.

Certainly not this.

Chapter Twelve
Of Sorrow and Ash

Ishara, The Black Lands

The prevailing wind blowing down from the Sagros Mountains was razor-sharp and gnawed at the bone like a pack of dogs. Naia shook her head in frustration at its power, pushing all of her weight against the brute force of it. The sting of the wind wrung tears from her eyes, sucked the breath right out of her lungs. Her fingers throbbed even in her thick cotton gloves. She held her cloak closed against her chest, clutching it tight. She had tried pulling her cowl forward to warm her head, but the fiendish wind just yanked it back off again. After a few attempts, she'd given up.

Battered and exhausted, Naia staggered to a stop.

She felt a hand on her back. The demon at her side was attempting to reassure her. It wasn't working.

"Come on!" Quinlan Reis shouted in her ear, tugging on her arm. "…a little further! We have to…" His voice faded out, suffocated by the hellish wind.

Naia didn't need to hear him to understand his point. They had to find shelter. The wind was just as wet as it was chill. It sucked the heat and energy out of her body, leaving her shivering and staggering.

She glanced at the sky, awestruck by the clouds that raced across the dark expanse, flickering and flaring with light. The clouds moved at an impossible speed, surging toward them from the vast horizon that loomed larger than the world. A ball of lightning silhouetted the jagged mountains in the distance. They looked like the black-toothed jaw of some predatory beast.

Another stab of lightning revealed a tall, cone-shaped peak just ahead, its flanks charred, its summit oozing rivers of blood.

Not blood, she realized. Lava.

Stooped and shaking, Naia followed Quinlan Reis in the direction of the volcano. They made camp in the lee of an ancient lava flow and prepared to wait out the wind. Naia sat in the dirt, hugging herself as her teeth clattered and her flesh shivered. Her companion dug out a fire pit and lit a small pile of coals. The heat of the flames was more than comforting; it was life-saving. Naia held her hands over the coal-fire as waves of exhaustion stole over her. The wind howled overhead, wailing like a wounded thing.

As her companion set about the business of cooking their meal, Naia curled up into a tight ball. She wrapped her cloak snugly around herself and fell asleep.

"Time to eat."

Naia opened her eyes, feeling rested and warm. She sat up, rubbing the crusted sleep from her eyes. For a moment she sat there considering Quinlan's profile in the flames. The flickering light of the coal-fire created a harsh rendering of his features, the flesh of his face shadowed and sunken under sharp cheekbones. His expression spoke volumes about nothing.

He leaned forward, offering out a piece of stale bread. Naia blinked in distaste.

"You missed dinner," he explained. "This is breakfast. Better eat this time."

Naia accepted the bread and took a bite, worrying it around in her mouth. She supposed she should be grateful. She swallowed the pasty lump, chasing it down with a sip of water that tasted like dirt. Unable to help it, she made a face.

The darkmage noticed her and smirked. "My apologies. Malikar has a sad lack of mountain springs. It's deplorable, I know. My fault, of course. Just like everything."

Naia forced a smile, unamused. She was becoming accustomed to the man's self-deprecating wit. It was quickly becoming just as stale as the bread in her hand. "The water is fine, Quinlan."

"Call me Quin."

He rose and shouldered his pack. Then he stomped out the fire, kicking dirt over it with his feet. Not that it mattered; there wasn't anything nearby to burn. The wastelands of Malikar were a sterile rockscape. There wasn't a trace of detritus in the soil. Even the riverbeds were far more sand than clay.

Naia pushed herself to her feet, grateful that the wind had died down. The hardpan that stretched before her was crystalline-calm. The clouds moved across the sky with far less urgency. Their shadows striped the desert below in ever-alternating patterns of black and gray. The expanse before them wavered, surreal.

"Well, we're almost there, at least," Quin said as he trekked off.

Naia followed a short distance after him. It wasn't long before they came to the end of the lava flow and skirted a tumbled array of sharp rocks before turning northward. A flat plain stretched ahead of them, broken by strange geometric patterns. Naia stopped, staring at the view, her mind groping to find an explanation for the unnatural terrain.

"What is it?" she asked.

Quinlan Reis turned back to her, swiping a sleeve across his brow. "What's left of Skara. An ancient city that was destroyed in the Desecration."

Naia's eyes scanned the ground ahead of them, at last recognizing the geometric shapes for crumbled walls and jagged ruins. There was not much left, really, only the footprints of what must have been a vast metropolis. The ruins stretched across the flat expanse to the distant foothills ahead. Not too far away, the remains of an ancient statue stuck out of the dark soil of the desert. It had once been a marble sculpture of a rearing horse, now forlorn and obsolete. Half the horse's head had crumbled away.

"How did an entire city perish?" Naia wondered out loud, feeling disturbed by the amount of death that must have occurred here. Her eyes scanned the ruins, her mind estimating casualties.

The demon beside her nodded at the large, conical peak leaking lava and belching great plumes of smoke. "The side of the mountain blew out. This entire region was consumed by mud and hot ash."

Naia shook her head, envisioning all the dead that had been left unattended. Left to rot, covered in debris. The image was sickening.

"How awful," she whispered. "I can't imagine what their deaths must have been like."

"Quick. They broiled where they stood."

Naia shot a glance at him, shocked by his indifference. The expression on the man's face was unreadable. She took a step away from him, suddenly uncomfortable.

"Why are we here?" she asked.

Quinlan Reis gestured to the rubble spread before them. "Because the people of Malikar have all turned away from the old gods. You won't find a temple of Death intact anywhere in the Black Lands. Except here."

Naia looked at the patterned terrain and then back at her companion. She frowned, not understanding what he was talking about. "How? This isn't even a ruin. Everything's been leveled down to the bare foundations."

Quin offered the same, sardonic grin he liked to wear so much. "Why don't you look again, darling." With that, he turned and walked away, over to a large, flat slab of stone poking out of the black wasteland. He jumped onto it and walked across to the exact center of the slab. There, he found an opening. With his foot, he scooted a wedge of sand over the edge, watching as it rained down into the space below.

Naia hadn't the faintest idea what the man was trying to demonstrate. Then it occurred to her. She sprinted toward him.

"Are you saying this is a roof?"

Quinlan Reis smiled. "So it would appear."

Immediately, the entire ruin took on entirely different dimensions. Once again, Naia's eyes wandered over the symmetrical patterns of the rubble. Only, this time, she didn't see bare foundations. She saw rooftops. Ancient Skara lay yet before them, intact, but submerged beneath the ground.

Her mind reeled in wonder. The possibilities…

"So the entire city lies beneath us?" she gasped as she scrambled up next to him on the stone rooftop.

The darkmage flashed her a grin. "By all accounts."

Naia turned slowly, her eyes tracing the lines of the buried city. "But how do we know which of these rooftops is the Temple of Death? There are far too many to just start digging down and looking into all of them."

Quinlan crouched, snatching off his hat and holding it over his knees. He looked up at her, his face suddenly weary. "As it happens, I lived in Skara for a time. I once knew my way around the city quite well."

There was a heavy weight of sadness in his voice. Someone he'd known had lived here, Naia surmised. Someone he'd cared for deeply. She almost felt empathy for the man. Then she remembered who he was. And what he was.

"So you know where the temple is?"

He nodded. "The Temple of Death in Skara was one of the great wonders of the ancient world. I could never forget it. No matter how much I'd like to." He bowed his head, looking a bit deflated. "It was in the civic center across from the palace. It shouldn't be hard to find."

With that, he rose and set his hat on his head. He walked to the edge of the slab and jumped down. Turning back, he offered out his hand. Naia accepted it, exploring the lines of Quinlan's face with her eyes.

She let him lead her up what must have been a broad avenue, now a wide road paved in ash and bordered by stone walls. A low rumble echoed in the distance, like the earth groaning under its own weight. She had no idea whether the sound came from thunder or the guts of the volcano. She glanced sideways at Quinlan. The darkmage didn't seem to notice or to care. He was walking with his gaze focused on the street ahead. He wore a melancholy expression, not seeming the least bit interested in the wonders buried beneath their feet.

"Who lived here?" Naia asked, attempting to draw him out in conversation.

He shot an irritated glance her way. Then he scowled. "It doesn't matter. She's dead." But his expression softened, and at last he relented. "There was a girl. We were both apprenticed to the same master who brought us here for study. The geology of the region is…unparalleled. And so was the metallurgy. We studied together and became quite close. But she ended up marrying someone else."

"What was her name?" Naia asked.

"Amani." The way he said it proved he loved her.

Naia bowed her head in commiseration. She could feel the pang of his grief. "I'm sorry. It always hurts when the person you love loves someone else more."

Quinlan Reis stopped walking. He turned around, anger and hurt infecting his eyes. Naia stopped too, wondering what she'd said that could have been so wrong.

"This is a completely different situation," he growled, making a futile sweep in the air with his hand. "It's not like you and Meiran; Darien didn't have to choose between the two of you. Amani didn't *choose* to be the wife of my brother—*he chose her.* And neither she nor I had any gods-damned say in the matter. There wasn't anything we could do."

Naia just looked at him. His words stung like a spear-thrust, hitting her in the heart.

"What are you saying?" she said, her voice quavering. "Did Darien choose Meiran over me?"

Quin looked flabbergasted. For a moment he just stared at her. Then he spread his hands broadly and shook his head. "What do you mean, choose? There was no choice to be made! He never even *mentioned* you."

Naia froze. She stood there looking at him stupidly, her mouth hanging slack. The hurt clenched her throat, heated her cheeks.

"I'm sorry," the darkmage said. "That was rude."

"No." Naia blinked the tears from her eyes. "Don't apologize. I needed to hear that." She tried to swallow the feelings back down where they came from. It hurt. Gods, it hurt. But she had other things to think about. Darien was the least of her problems. Apparently, he wasn't even her problem anymore.

"Quinlan," she began, but he cut her off.

"I told you. Call me Quin."

She nodded, swiping at the stubborn tears that refused to go away. "Quin. I'm sorry about what happened between you and Amani. You're right; it is an entirely different situation. You and your lover were torn apart. Darien and I...No. What am I saying? There never *was* a 'Darien and I.' I was just a fool."

She turned and took a step away—

—and tripped as a gaping hole loomed right in front of her feet.

Naia cried out, pinwheeling her arms and arching her back away from it. For an eternity, she teetered there on the edge. Then the hole reached up and sucked her in. She was falling.

A hand caught her cloak, jerking her back. Naia fell on her rear in the dirt and scrambled away from the edge.

Quin leaned forward, squinting as he peered into the dark opening in the ground. He knelt and picked up a rock that was lying half-buried in the sand. He held the rock over the shaft and dropped it in. There was a long delay before Naia heard the sound of the rock hitting stone. Quin straightened, adjusting his hat.

"Careful." He offered Naia a hand. "That would have been quite a drop."

Still shaking, Naia allowed the darkmage to pull her to her feet. She leaned over the hole as far as she dared, trembling fingers grasping Quin's hand. Down below, she could see only blackness.

"It's probably the interior of a building." Quin leaned in close to dust her off. His palms moved briskly over her shoulders and down her back. "You nearly fell through the roof. Which isn't the most practical of all entrances."

Naia was too shaken to appreciate his humor.

"Here." Quin patted her arm in reassurance. "Just hang onto me and watch your step."

He guided her wide of the cavity. Naia glanced behind,

distrusting it, worried that it might collapse and widen toward them. Her suspicion extended to the entire street, not trusting any of it. Any step she took could end in disaster. They could break through the fragile crust of a rooftop and fall to their deaths without warning.

She let Quin guide her down an ash-paved boulevard lined with the tops of block walls. The rooftops of ruins peeked out of the ground to either side, some taller than others. Some of the jutting masonry looked like it had been used recently to shelter travelers. There were no people about, though. No one lived in Skara. No one alive, at any rate.

They walked past fragmented ruins to the center of the sprawling maze. There, they came to what appeared to be a lake of gray powder. It was encircled by enormous slabs of stone thrust out of the ground at odd angles. Quin drew up in the center of the flat circle, turning slowly as his eyes scanned the wedge-shaped marble that surrounded them. With a grunt and a nod, he started toward a broad slab that sloped upward out of the dust.

He paused with one foot lifted on the rooftop where it rose from the sand. "This is it."

Naia looked up at the enormous structure that slanted away from them, hundreds of feet long and just as wide. It appeared seamless, as if formed from one singular chunk of marble. Which implied that it was wrought by magic. She had never seen anything of the like since leaving Aerysius.

"How do we get in?" she asked, despairing. The temple doors had to be several stories below the level of the roof; it would be impossible to dig through that amount of dirt.

Quin shrugged his pack off, setting it down on the ground. Then, squatting beside it, he proceeded to rummage through the contents. At last he produced a palm-sized copper cube with strange markings on every facet. He hefted it in his hand, appearing to study the object critically. Then he glanced sideways up at her, nodding in the direction of the ruins across the street.

"Go wait for me on the other side of that wall. Oh, and you might want to cover your head."

Naia frowned at him, wondering what the strange object could be. Something dangerous, if he wanted her that far away from it.

"What is it?"

The darkmage grinned. "Something extremely useful, under the circumstances."

Naia considered the innocent-looking cube and shrugged. If Quin thought something that small could move that much dirt, she wouldn't argue. But she was still curious; was it an artifact? Or something more sinister?

She turned and walked across the street, taking refuge on the other side of the block wall. Squatting, she gazed down at the silken dirt beneath her feet. Naia ran her fingers through it, making parallel furrows in the dust. The sand was light and soft, like fine powder. It shimmered with miniscule crystals, like twinkling stars in a matte-black sky. She lifted her hands and noticed the tiny minerals clinging to the fibers of her gloves. She rotated her hands, watching them glisten.

"Get down!"

Naia covered her head as Quin's body slammed into the ground beside her. Then a resonant *THOOMB!* sent a plume of dust straight up into the air, raining down on their heads like pelting hail. The clatter of pebbles bouncing off stone went on for several seconds before finally letting up.

Naia dropped her hands from her head and gaped at Quin, who gaped back at her. He took a peek over the top of the wall.

"Shall we go assess the damage?"

Naia could only nod as she stood up, finger-combing the dust out of her hair. The street was no longer smooth, but littered with chunks of marble and scattered debris. A crater had appeared next to the sprawling slab that was the roof of the Temple of Death. The hole was significantly deeper than Naia had imagined it would be. Quin's little cube had done a lot more damage than she'd anticipated.

But it was still just a crater; nothing more. The explosion hadn't managed to even crack the temple's exterior.

Quin fidgeted, chewing his lip in obvious frustration. He raked a sleeve across his brow. Then he made a vague gesture back the way they had come.

"One more time," he said. "And this time, *get down!*"

Naia didn't need to be told twice. As Quin jumped inside the crater with another cube in his hand, she ran back across the street and took up position behind the eroded wall. Only, this time, she lay with her body flush up against the stone, on her stomach in the dirt. She closed her eyes tight, knowing what was coming.

There was the sound of running footsteps. Then another THOOMB!—even louder this time. She heard Quin's body landing somewhere behind her, followed by the clattering noise of raining pebbles. Eventually, the torrent tapered off. For a moment, the ruined city was as silent as the dead it contained.

Naia rolled over and found Quin on his back, staring up at the sky. His face was covered in dust, blood dribbling from a cut over one eye. He blinked, and the air over him seemed to ripple. The blood and grime immediately disappeared. He rolled over and sprang to his feet.

"Are you all right?" Naia gasped.

"I'm dead." The darkmage shrugged as he bent over to dust his pants off. "So I suppose that makes me, by definition, not quite all right. Let's just say that I'm about as right as I'm ever going to get."

Naia folded her arms, glowering at his failed attempt at sarcasm although small part of her appreciated it. The world they walked through was dark enough.

"Well, now." He turned and strode back across the street. "Let's see if that made a dent."

Naia followed, noticing that the crater was now twice as wide as it had been before. Quin jumped down into the newly formed pit. Naia paused, looking down. The cavity was much deeper than it looked. And this time, the explosion had ripped a gash in the temple wall, scoring a larger hole out of what must have been a window.

Quin grinned up at her, beckoning her to join him.

Naia slid down the crumbling slope, catching his hand to steady herself. She paused to dump the pebbles out of her shoes, then straightened to examine the wall. Quin dropped to a crouch, running his hand over the marble façade of the temple. A bright glowing orb erupted beside her face. Naia flinched away from it before realizing that it was just a globe of magelight. She caught herself on Quin's shoulder, almost knocking him over.

"A bit jumpy, aren't we?"

"The word you're looking for is fearful," Naia corrected him. "And yes, I am. Mostly of you."

The darkmage cracked a grin. "Excellent. Then you won't try arguing with my next idea."

She stared at him then stared at the gaping hole. Her eyes widened slowly, and she started shaking her head.

"No."

"Yes."

Chapter Thirteen
Perfectly Damaged

Tokashi Palace, The Black Lands

Darien extended his arms out to his sides, holding the position awkwardly as Sayeed buttoned the sleeves of the black tunic they'd had tailored to fit him. The garment was unlike anything he'd ever felt before, stiff and heavily embroidered. Looped buttons ran from the high collar all the way down to the hem. Sayeed finished with his sleeves then strapped the Omeyan warbelt around his waist. Over the belt he wrapped a golden sash, through which he hung a long, curved dagger in a tasseled scabbard.

Sayeed retrieved a matching sword, bowing low as he held it up, presenting the blade. He bared a few inches of steel, exposing a single edge with three deep grooves. The hilt was wrapped in bronze wire and set with semiprecious stones that matched the stones on the scabbard. It was a handsome weapon that looked ornamental. But it bore the scars of battle. This blade had seen war.

"This is the sword carried by Khoresh Katim in the battle of Harmudi," Sayeed stated, sliding the elegant scimitar fully back before slipping it through the sash at Darien's waist.

He arranged a scarf over Darien's shoulders, saying, "First will be the ceremony. Afterward, there is the reception. It is then that the warlords of the Khazahar will declare their support for you."

Darien nodded, tugging at his collar, which was buttoned up so high he could scarcely breathe. He could feel his throat fighting against it every time he tried to swallow.

The Zakai officer drew away, considering his appearance

gravely. He issued a stiff nod of satisfaction. "Have I answered all your questions?"

"Aye."

Sayeed took Darien by the shoulders and pulled him close, pressing a kiss against his forehead. Darien suffered the touch, not liking it, but was too surprised to object. Sayeed bowed and stepped back, opening the chamber doors.

Setting his hand on the hilt of the scimitar, Darien strode out into the hall. There, a retinue of Zakai awaited them dressed in formal uniforms. Today they were far more than just his personal escort. Today, the Zakai stood in place of the family he no longer possessed.

Sayeed fell in at his side as they left the residential wing.

Darien was shocked to find the usually silent halls of Tokashi Palace teeming with people. At the sight of their party, a cry went up from the gathered onlookers. Drums and pipes began to play as shrill trilling noises rang off the walls. The crowd surged forward, people scrambling to reach out and touch him as he passed.

Sayeed had warned him about the custom. Something about luck, though Darien didn't understand it. He bowed his head as a wash of panic overcame him. The world lurched, suddenly unstable. He couldn't stand the proximity of so many faces, the feel of their hands on him. He closed his eyes and tried to trust Sayeed to guide him through the crowd. Fingers brushed his face, pawed at his clothes, slid over his hair. The noise of the crowd and the blare of instruments overwhelmed his senses.

"Are you well?" Sayeed whispered in his ear.

Darien nodded, swallowing his panic.

At last, they broke out of the thick of the crowd as his entourage led him onto a bridge that spanned the chasm above the river. There, Darien felt comfortable enough to open his eyes and look down. It was much cooler here, the air fed with chill from the ice caverns below. The bridge arched upward toward a canopy that had been erected for the occasion.

Great crowds gathered to line both sides of the river's chasm. Darien drew to a stop under the colorful fabric of the canopy, his eyes falling on the priest who awaited him in crimson robes.

A priest of Xerys.

He shouldn't have been surprised, but for some reason he was. Despite his reservations, Darien moved ahead of his retinue and strode forward to shake the cleric's hand. The gaunt and dark-haired man said nothing, looking confused by the gesture.

A loud, ululating noise erupted from all around the cavern, coming from every direction at once. Darien glanced down and saw the crowd parting like a wave. A lone figure emerged from the thick press of bodies, veiled in red, a red sash tied around her waist. Women in colorful robes guided her forward through glistening tendrils of magelight that gleamed like daybreak, escorting her onto the bridge.

Darien felt his mouth go dry as he watched Azár's procession. His grip on the sword hilt grew intense. He tried to get a glimpse of her face beneath the veil, but the thick red lace obscured her features. She came to a halt on the far side of the canopy, the priest of Xerys between them.

The priest turned away to light the flame of a single taper on an altar behind him. He then raised a pitcher and waited for Azár to present her hands. He poured a thin stream of water onto Azár's open palms, then did the same for Darien.

The solemn man took Darien's hands and led him forward until he was standing in front of his bride, a woman whose face he couldn't see, whose heart he didn't know. With the priest's guidance, he took her hand in his.

Skin so soft.

He traced his thumb over the back of her hand.

Words were spoken, but he wasn't listening. The contract was signed, first by his bride and then by himself. More words passed him by. The whole while, he was gazing down at Azár's hand, studying every fine detail of it.

An explosion of noise echoed through the cavern, swelling to a deafening thunder. Shaken, Darien at first didn't understand the reason for it. Only when Sayeed nudged him forward did he realize it was time to kiss his bride. Reaching up, he drew Azár's veil back over her head, revealing her face.

His breath clotted in his throat.

This was not the fierce woman he thought he was marrying. A soft beauty stared back at him with nervous eyes, unbound hair flowing down her back. Her red-stained lips trembled. Darien hesitated, unsure of himself. Then he leaned forward, kissing his bride on the forehead, just as Sayeed had instructed him to do.

The noise in the cavern crescendoed to a climax. Drums clattered and bagpipes skirled. Trills of celebration echoed off the walls of the ice chasm. Through it all, Azár somehow managed to smile. He found it comforting. Taking his bride by the arm, he led her down and off the bridge, following his retinue of Zakai.

The thunder of celebration followed them all the way to the Grand Hall of the palace, already teeming with color and noise and wondrous smells of food. Darien took a seat beside Azár in cushioned chairs on a raised dais. Men and women flooded in, dressed in regional costumes and bearing gifts.

One by one, the men of the clans stood and came forward. They mounted the stairs to the dais, where they fell to their knees before Darien and his bride. One by one, the warlords knelt and kissed the hem of Darien's robe, pledging their fealty. One by one, he accepted their allegiance with a nod. His fingers still clutched the hand of his Asyaadi bride who looked on but said nothing. After the last man rose from off the floor, the drums thundered back to life and the feasting began in earnest.

"It is time, Lord," Sayeed whispered in his ear.

Darien stood, Azár rising at his side as the guests rushed forward to link hands, forming a long tunnel to the door. Darien ducked, still holding Azár's hand as they moved beneath the span of arms, swords, and spears. The thunder of applause vibrated the walls even as the doors of the hall swung closed behind them. The guests returned to continue their celebration as the newlyweds retired to their wedding night.

Darien turned to Azár as uniformed Zakai swarmed around them in the hallway. "Are you well?" he asked her.

She nodded, uncharacteristically demure, flashing him a fragile smile.

He held her hand the whole way as the officers escorted them back to the Residence. Mercifully, they let him enter his own chambers alone with his bride. As the door closed behind them, the soldiers outside gave a loud, whooping shout.

Darien closed his eyes and sighed, thankful just to be alone.

Almost alone.

Obviously, he was not.

His nerves snapped tight like over-tuned harp strings.

There was a rustle of silk as Azár moved to stand in front of him. He felt her hand touch his cheek. He resisted the urge to draw away. Her fingertips stroked the whiskers of his face, tracing his jawline. Then her lips were on his, the slightest pressure of a kiss.

It was too much. He winced, taking a step back.

"You don't like to be touched," she said. It was not an observation. More like an acknowledgment of a boundary.

"No," he admitted. "Not anymore."

She reached out and took his hand in hers. "My poor husband," she whispered. Her kohl-darkened eyes slipped to the floor. "You are just as damaged as I."

He frowned in concern, his thoughts faltering. "What do you mean?"

Her gaze fixed on the ground, she informed him, "My master used me every day. Sometimes more than once a day. He hurt me badly. In many different ways."

Darien's nerves turned to water, then to ice. Then to fire. Anger consumed him until he burned and shook with rage. But there was nowhere to direct his wrath; Azár's abuser was already dead. Already right where he needed to be: burning in the depths of hell.

Where Darien's wrath would find him eventually.

His bride continued, "I told you I was not looking for love. Above all else, I need a man I can trust not to hurt me. I am sorry, my husband. That is why I chose you."

Darien shook his head, his mind grappling with this newfound reality. "I don't understand," he whispered, drawing back. "You're the one who kissed me. You said you wanted me…"

"I'm sorry. It was just a test. I had to know how you would react."

"But that time in the lightfields—"

"You made a promise to me. And you kept it. You and I are a perfect match, don't you see? You desire sex but are unwilling to risk your heart. I desire love but am unwilling to share my body. Together, we will learn from each other. We will conquer our fears. In the meantime, feel free to indulge in concubines." She placed a hand on his chest. "Just save your heart for me. Someday, I will come to collect it."

As Darien stood in shock, she turned and moved away, wandering deeper into their shared quarters. She glanced around, appraising the dim space.

"We will need another bed," she muttered.

Chapter Fourteen
The Goddess of Mercy

Skara, The Black Lands

"We're going down there." Quin gestured into the gaping blackness of the hole that the explosion had created in the side of the building.

Naia could feel her face paling, draining of its color. She leaned over to peer into the jagged crack in the temple's wall. Her gaze traveled only as far as the glow of Quin's magelight would allow. From what she knew of Death's temples, she could tell the hall below was part of the Inner Sanctum, a network of chambers secreted away from the public eye, where many of the temple's holiest rites were performed. Imposing columns, many stories tall, marched up the length of the room on both sides. A series of wrought-iron chandeliers were suspended from the ceiling, hung at intervals one after another until they disappeared into shadow.

Naia's palms tingled as she gazed down at the floor many stories below. Unless they could fly, they could never get down to it.

"It's too far…" she began, staring at the black circlets of the chandeliers that formed what looked like an aerial skipping path.

"I think we can drop from here down onto the top of that column." Quin nodded down at the ledge created by the flared lip of the column below, where it met with the lintel of the wall. The column was a lot closer to them than the ground, but still quite a fall. And a narrow target to aim for. Naia couldn't believe he was even suggesting it.

"Not without breaking bones," she disagreed. The tingling in her palms swelled to needling pinpricks.

"So what if we do break some bones? We can heal them."

Quin's wry tone was entirely too jovial for Naia's liking. She spared him a sharp glare of reproach, growling, "What if we break our necks?"

The darkmage shrugged. "Don't land on your neck." He added a belated grin.

The expression didn't help. Naia frowned as she examined the narrow ledge below them. She wasn't sure it could support their weight. But she didn't see any other way down to the floor, either. She looked around for another path down the wall, but didn't see any other option.

Naia sighed. "Say we do manage to make it down there without falling off. Then what?" She stared at Quin fiercely, challenging him to come up with a solution.

He complied. "I think I can sway that chandelier over. Then all we have to do is jump on."

Naia looked down at the light fixture. It was an enormous, black iron circlet bedecked with dozens of tapers. It hung suspended from the ceiling by a lengthy chain. Naia was uncertain whether the chain would break beneath their weight. Especially considering it had been hanging there for a thousand years.

"I don't believe I can do that." Her voice trembled in her throat. The pinpricks in her palms had devolved into cold, clammy numbness. She felt terribly dizzy.

Quin grinned and patted her on the shoulder. "It will be an adventure, but I think you can manage it. You seem nimble enough."

How could the infernal man be so optimistic? There was a very real chance both of them would fall to their deaths. Well, perhaps not both of them. Naia had to remind herself that Quin Reis was already dead. Which might explain his casual cheer in the face of near-certain disaster.

She said through clenched teeth, "Assuming our weight doesn't snap the chain right out of the ceiling, where do we go from there?"

Quin spread his hands as if the answer should be obvious. "Then we sway it over to the next chandelier. And then the next. And the next, all the way down the line."

Naia stared into the darkness that encased the far end of the hall. The glow of Quin's magelight didn't penetrate far enough to disrupt the shadows at that end. There could be anything down there. Or nothing.

"And what then?" Naia asked, still gaping into the dark.

The darkmage issued an exaggerated shrug. "We'll figure it out when we get there."

Naia arched an eyebrow. "You're not serious."

"I'm always serious. I seldom get taken seriously, but that's a topic for another conversation."

Naia shook her head, settling back against the side of the building. "I...I can't. Do. That. No." Her head-shaking became emphatic.

Quin patted her back and grinned. "Of course you can. There's nothing stopping you."

"Just common sense!"

"Overrated. Never got me out of trouble."

"Then what did?"

He appeared to consider that for a moment before admitting, "Usually murdering somebody."

Naia scoffed. "And that's supposed to make me feel comforted?"

"No. But you did ask." He reached up, adjusting his hat. There was a fiendish sparkle in his eye. "It's either this or we walk all the way back to Bryn Calazar and hire a ship. By the time we actually make it to Titherry, the war will be over, and you'll be dead. Then I suppose I can just retire to hell and rot for all eternity."

Naia sighed, glancing once more at the shadows. "Fine. Do you want to go first, or shall I?"

"Oh, I think I should go first," he said, standing up. He shrugged out of the straps of his leather pack, handing it down to her. "Here. Would you mind hanging onto this? You can toss it down to me later."

Naia accepted the pack, throwing it on over her shoulder next to her own. Before she could come to terms with the fact that they were actually going forward with this ludicrous plan, Quin was already seated on the edge of the hole. He hoisted his legs over then dropped down, clinging to the blocks with his hands. His head shot up from the other side like a gopher popping out of a hole.

"Kiss for luck?"

Before Naia could gasp her disapproval, he let go and disappeared.

There was a short span of silence. Followed by an echoing wail of pain.

Naia surged forward, leaning over the break in the wall to search the shadows below. Quin had landed on the ledge. He was tossing about like a turtle on its back, holding one knee against his chest, face twisted in pain. She could tell the moment he healed the injury, watching him sag visibly in relief. He sighed and collapsed back against the stone.

"Are you all right?" Naia called down to him.

"Never better." His voice wasn't as cheerful as before. He rolled into a sitting position then pushed himself erect, back flush against the wall. At least the ledge was wider than it had looked. Smiling up at her, Quin raised his arms. "My pack, if you please?"

Naia held it out over the wall, letting the pack sway over him before letting it go. Her aim was a little off. Still, Quin managed to snatch it out of the air with one hand.

Naia realized it was her turn to jump down to the ledge. Suddenly, she felt very pale and very clammy, and more than a little queasy. The world seemed off-kilter, the ground unstable. Her heart kicked up its pace, sprinting in her chest. She didn't care for heights. She cared even less for drops.

Swallowing, Naia paused to gather her dignity and her courage. She lifted her skirt and settled down on the crack in the wall, swinging her legs over. She made the mistake of looking down.

The floor of the temple was very far below. And the ledge was exceptionally small. Quin stood directly beneath her, holding his hands up as if preparing to catch her. Naia wasn't sure that was a good idea; she was likely to fall off and take him with her.

"A little to the left," he called up.

She scooted over. She could see him just between her feet.

"There! Now just kick off."

Just kick off, she thought. As if it were that easy.

It was.

She flung herself forward before indecision could stop her. The edge of the column came rushing up, and she smacked hard, face-down against the stone.

The next thing she knew, she was staring up, blinking, into Quin's grinning face. He was absent his hat, which was peculiar. A darkmage needed a dark hat, she figured, and thought he looked rather diminished without one. His curly hair hung tousled about his shoulders, lending him a feral appearance that seemed entirely out of character.

"Where's your hat?" she muttered. Her voice sounded weak and bleary. She didn't understand why.

"In my pack. How do you feel?"

She gazed down the length of her body. She was lying stretched out on the marble top of the column, her head pillowed in Quin's lap. It was dim and cold, the air thick with mildew and humidity. It smelled like rain.

"I feel...alive," she said. "You deserve a good kick. You almost got us killed!"

"But I didn't." The darkmage smiled. "And we're right where we need to be. See?" He gestured around at the expansive emptiness that surrounded them.

Naia sat up and gazed at the shadows of the hall, its walls and arcades awash in the glow of Quin's magelight that trailed like a red mist down the length of the hall. The far end of the chamber was no longer lost to shadow. There, two great statues of the goddess sat on enormous thrones, a thin waterfall spilling between them. Naia recognized the statues: the aspects of Mercy and Sacrifice, two faces of the goddess she knew well.

The floor of the hall was still so very far below. She had no idea how they were going to get down to it. Magelight erupted from the ancient rings of the chandeliers, drenching the hall in a greasy, blood-red light.

"Are you ready for the next hurdle?"

Quin climbed to his feet, shaking the dust off his pants. Without waiting for her answer, he reached out a hand toward the nearest chandelier. With a groan of protest, it bent toward him on its chain as if drawn by a magnet. The edge of the iron circlet came close to their stone perch...but not all the way. There was still a sizeable gap between the column and the fixture. They would have to jump. And it was a jump up, not down.

"Oh, no..." Naia gazed at the chandelier open-mouthed. "You're not thinking..." Of course he was. She shook her head, not bothering to complete the sentence. It was no use.

She stared harder at the chandelier, studying its structure in an attempt to understand how either of them could ever scale it. The fixture was composed of two iron rings that held candle cups, a smaller ring at the top, and a much wider ring below. Both rings were reinforced by iron crossbars. The chandelier was mounted to the ceiling by a long chain that hooked onto the smaller ring. Four more chains came down to stabilize the larger circlet on the bottom.

Quin looked at her with a reckless glint in his eyes.

"*No, don't—!*"

Without a word, he drew back against the wall and took a running leap. He caught the iron ring by his fingertips, the whole fixture lurching under his weight. Tapers rained down, tumbling to the floor stories below. The magelight flickered, dimming, on the verge of going out.

"Quin!" Naia screamed.

The chandelier recoiled, swaying away from the column as Quin scrambled to pull himself up over the rim. At last he hooked one leg over, clinging to the bar as the fixture swung in great arcs like the bob of a pendulum. He got another leg over, pulling himself upright. Below, the floor of the hall seemed to lurk hungrily.

To Naia's horror, Quin wasn't satisfied with his perch. He grasped one of the stabilizing chains and pulled himself to a standing position on the iron crossbar, reaching out toward her with his other hand. The chandelier swayed back toward the ledge and then stuck there, frozen at the extreme of its arc.

"Come on!" The look in Quin's eyes was just as insistent as his voice.

Naia knew there was no argument; she couldn't remain on the ledge forever. Neither could she retreat back up the wall. She wiped the sweat off her palms onto the bodice of her gown. Just to be sure, she wiped her palms again. Then, just as Quin had done, she took two steps back and pressed her body flat up against the wall. Naia stood there for a moment, breathing in shallow, rapid gasps, as the world spun around her. She took a failed step forward and stopped. She backed up again. Sagging, she groped for resolve.

"You won't fall. Just jump. I'll catch you."

Naia wished she could trust him. But he was a demon, and she couldn't.

She squeezed her eyes closed then opened them again. She glared fiercely at Quin. She wished he still had that stupid grin on his face, but he'd lost it somewhere along the way. Clenching her hands into fists, she ran and leaped from the top of the column. She plunged right past Quin's outstretched fingers and started screaming as she fell.

Her body jerked upward, as if snapped back by a rope. Quin's strong grip caught her wrist. She was hauled upward into his arms as she gasped and trembled in terror and disbelief.

"How did you do that?" she gulped.

"Darien fell from Aerysius and lived," he responded with a shrug. "If I knew for a fact I could do it again, I'd tell you to jump off and I'd float you right to the floor. Unfortunately, I'm not sure I could repeat it."

The chandelier swayed steadily to and fro. The chain groaned and creaked. Below them, the floor contorted in an unsteady motion.

Naia asked, "You don't know what you did?"

Quin shook his head. "No idea. Just happy as a daisy that it worked."

"A lark."

"What?" He looked confused.

"The phrase is, 'happy as a lark.'"

Quin gazed at her and smiled. "Well, I'm happy as a lark, then." His smile went back to where it came from. "I'm going to go first. Wait until I'm across, then follow behind me. Do what I do."

Naia shook her head. "No. Let me go first. If you fall, I don't want to be trapped up here."

He frowned as if unsure about that plan, but ended up nodding. "Fair enough. Drop down and hang from that bar, then go hand-over-hand."

She gathered her courage then did as he suggested, sitting down on the crossbar that supported the chandelier's outer ring. The bar wasn't very thick; she could get her hands around it. Which was good; the ring that held the candle cups was much thicker, and she doubted she could keep a good grip on it. She dropped down, her legs kicking as she swung from the bar.

Hand-over-hand, she made her way slowly down the length of the bar toward the outside edge as the fixture dipped lower, tilting beneath her weight. When she reached the outer ring, she stopped and looked back at Quin.

The chandelier righted itself. It began to sway, gently at first, picking up speed as it went. Then it paused and swung back the other direction. It stopped at the apex of its arc, the iron ring frozen above the next chandelier in line. The gap was too much. Terrified, Naia glanced back at Quin.

The next chandelier swung toward her until it rested up against the ring of the fixture she was riding. Naia breathed a sigh of relief and swung from one giant ring to the next. But as she grabbed on, the whole contraption lurched beneath her weight. Quin righted it, but not before it sent her heart leaping into her throat.

Naia sucked in a deep breath as the chandelier tilted back to level. Her hands were slick with sweat. She pulled them off one by one, wiping her palms dry on her gown. She made the mistake of looking down. The floor swam in shadow far below her dangling feet. She broke out in a sweat all over again.

Naia bit her lip in concentration and started forward again, hand-over-hand down the bar as the fixture tilted.

This time, the transition was easier. Quin had anticipated the weight redistribution. Naia paused, wiping her hands. She healed the blisters that were forming on her fingers and palms. Then, little by little, she edged along the bar and onto the next fixture. And the next. And the next. Six chandeliers in all.

Until she reached the far wall. And had no idea what to do next.

There was nowhere to go. Naia clung to the bar still stories above the floor. The only thing beneath her was the statue of Mercy seated upon her marble throne. But it was too much of a drop; even if she did make it, Naia felt sure she'd roll right off.

She glanced back at Quin in desperation.

"Just close your eyes and let go!" he shouted, still standing on the first chandelier. His voice rang off the walls, his face bathed in crimson magelight that made him look even more demonic than he was. "Either you'll make it, or you won't!"

"That's not very reassuring!"

"Don't think about it! Just let go!"

She sucked in a breath and gasped out a prayer. "Merciful goddess!"

She screamed as she fell. The slap of her body against stone knocked the scream right out of her. Then she was falling again.

Something jerked her to a stop. She hung in the air, her feet swinging beneath her.

Her head throbbed, and her stomach recoiled in a surge of nausea. She tried to concentrate, healing herself as best she could. Her vision went dim. A profound sense of weariness dragged her downward. She swung gently in the air, like a bird riding a tree branch on a breezy day.

"Wake up!" That was Quin shouting.

Naia dragged herself back to consciousness, blinking awake. She clawed her mind back into focus. Was she still hanging in the air?

"Open your eyes and look at me!" His voice sounded much

closer than before.

Naia looked up and saw him hanging overhead from the fixture right above her. He was clutching the outer circlet with both hands, looking down at her with his chin against his chest. His feet dangled uselessly, the toes of his boots pointed at the floor. The chandelier swung in a slow circle, the frame that held the candles wrenched at an unnatural angle.

Naia saw Quin's precarious situation and felt a swift jolt of fear. Then she saw what was holding her own body up, suspended in the air. The fear turned to a wave of panic that broke over her, ripping a scream from her throat.

The strap of her pack had somehow hooked on to the statue's upraised hand, caught on one delicate thumb. She hung suspended, still far above the floor. The hand of the goddess had saved her life. The hand of Mercy. The coincidence felt like a gut-punch. Guilt filled her face with heat that overwhelmed even her fear. She had abandoned her goddess two years before. Yet her goddess had not abandoned her.

She squirmed, kicking, until she managed to slide out of the straps that held her pack. She fell and hit the floor.

Naia rolled over on her side, scrunching her knees up to her chin. She rocked there back and forth, trembling and sobbing in relief and regret. She was barely aware when her pack lifted on its own, rising from the statue's hand to settle softly by her side.

"Naia!" Quin called down. He was still hanging from the acutely tilted fixture, taking turns flexing the fingers of first one hand then the next.

Naia staggered to her feet, craning her neck to look up at him. He looked pathetic up there, legs kicking as the contraption swayed and creaked, the chain groaning in a fatigued voice. She glanced from Quin to the statues of the aspects, at the water streaming thinly to a pool at the base of the thrones. The sound of the fall was a muted, sibilant drone.

Above, the chandelier Quin dangled from lurched and began to sway. Her eyes went wide as she saw what he was attempting. He was causing it to swing far enough to time his drop over the head of the nearest statue.

"Don't!" she shrieked up at him. If he missed, he'd drop all the way to the floor. The chandelier swayed all the way to the far wall with a contemptuous creak. It slowed with a grating noise, then swung back toward her again.

With a shout, Quin let go.

He dropped right onto the goddess' head, slapped hard, then slid down her front. His body tumbled past her outstretched hand, landing face-down in her lap. Naia rushed forward, plunging into the pool, splashing as she surged toward the statue's feet. She could see Quin's legs hanging over the marble knees. He didn't appear to be moving.

"Quin!" she called up at him.

A foot twitched. There came a low groan. Then:

"Why do I always end up in the laps of stone-cold women who won't spread their legs?"

Naia gasped, more in dismay than relief. Her hand flew to her mouth. "You dare blaspheme the goddess in her sacred hall?!"

Above her, the feet disappeared and Quin's face poked out, grinning down. "Doesn't feel very sacred. More like haunted and abandoned."

Hanging on to the statue's knees, he swung his legs over then dropped. He landed in the reflecting pool, staggering to catch his balance. He bent over, panting and swaying. Naia waded toward him, catching hold of his shoulders.

"Do you want me to heal you?"

He shook his head. "No. I've got it."

He closed his eyes, screwing his face into a grimace. A wave of energy passed over him, and he caught his breath. He wavered over his feet then straightened, hands going up to tug at his rumpled coat. He plunged his hand into his pack and retrieved his hat. He took his time about adjusting it. At last seeming satisfied, he spread his arms out at his sides.

"See? All just a grand adventure."

Naia looked at him. "I'm beginning to understand why you're dead."

Chapter Fifteen
The Beautiful Dead

Skara, The Black Lands

Naia slipped her pack on over her shoulders and waded through the shallow, murky pool in the direction of the waterfall. The spray was chill, the mist dampening the dusty air of the sanctum. The water poured from an opening high up on the wall between the two stone statues of the goddess. It plunged in a thin, veil-like stream between the hewn thrones. She couldn't tell if the feature had been created by man or by time. She supposed it didn't matter.

She turned and stared back toward the anterior of the hall. By the diffuse red glow of Quin's magelight, she could make out the tall doors that led to the temple's sanctuary. From her years of study and worship, she knew that was not the direction they needed to go. They would need to find a way deeper into the heart of the temple, where the most sacred of all mysteries was contained. There was no obvious exit from the sanctum, but that didn't surprise her. The Catacombs were one of Death's most closely-held secrets.

She looked back toward the statues of the goddess, feeling certain. "We must go through the waterfall." It wasn't a guess; she just knew.

Quin glanced up, a look of surprise on his face. The spray of the mist collected on his face in a dewy sheen. Almost reverently, he removed his hat.

Hiking her skirt up over her knees, Naia splashed forward through the frigid pool. She closed her eyes as she moved into the waterfall, clamping her jaw as the chill of the water washed over her head, wetting her hair and awakening every nerve in her body. Shaking and drenched, she stepped out on the other side and opened her eyes.

Darkness confronted her.

Teeth chattering, she cast a trail of magelight ahead, a brilliant azure glow that flowed like mist to illuminate a filthy corridor ahead. She heard the sound of splashing behind her and then Quin appeared at her side, soaked and shivering, hugging his hat against his chest. He looked at the magelight and stiffened, his eyes flashing back to her.

"I keep forgetting you inherited Darien's legacy," he said, looking suddenly somber. "What tier are you?"

"Third," Naia replied through chattering teeth. "Meiran inherited the other five."

"That's too bad," Quin said, voice brittle with scorn. "She doesn't deserve them."

Naia found herself silently agreeing. Quin had told her about Meiran's betrayal of Darien. She didn't hate the woman for it, but the contempt she felt was only a moment's reflection short of hate. Of course, she couldn't claim that she was more worthy of the legacy. By the ancient laws of Aerysius, she had forfeited her right to it when she'd forfeited her Oath. No matter how much she regretted that decision, it was something she could never take back.

Naia returned her attention to the corridor ahead. The ceiling had crumbled, creating a debris field at their feet. Tall, rusted candlesticks lay scattered across the floor at haphazard angles. A thick layer of ash coated everything. Naia trailed her fingers over the relentless gray of the wall, revealing the colorful design of the tile beneath. The corridor must have been beautiful at one time.

She lifted her wet skirt and stepped over the first tumbled candlestick, picking her way carefully across the mangled floor. At the far end of the passage were three imposing openings that led off in scattered directions: one to the left, one to the right, and another leading straight ahead. There were no doors; doors were unnecessary. No light could enter the passages beyond, and no shadow dared cross the thresholds. It was as if there was an indomitable barrier separating the light of the world from the velvet darkness beyond.

Naia stopped, turning back to her companion. "Quin. Look at me."

He did. His face was streaked with water that dribbled from his hair. His ancient eyes spoke of weariness and sorrow, wisdom and regret. Naia shivered harder, taken aback for a moment by the layers of depth in his eyes. He really was a demon, she realized. She would have to remember that...especially where they were going.

"On the other side of these openings is the Catacombs," she said with a fierceness that surprised her. "I must warn you: the living are forbidden to communicate with the dead."

A mirthless smile shadowed Quin's face. "I deduce that doesn't apply to me."

He was most likely correct. But she had no idea how to deal with Quin's peculiar circumstances, or how he might be affected by the Strictures. He was not alive, but nor was he a shade. He existed somewhere apart, a despoiled soul denied all hope of the Atrament.

Naia frowned. "Perhaps. But for you, there may be other dangers."

Quin folded his arms. "Such as...?"

"There are places within Death's Passage that are sacred to the goddess. A soul such as yours will be forbidden to trespass. Entering such a shrine would shred the fabric of your soul." There were few such shrines, but they did exist. And they were difficult to avoid, if they came across one.

Quin scowled reflectively. "I'd like to avoid any amount of soul-shredding if I possibly can."

Naia looked at him in sympathy. "I'm sorry. Some aspects of the Catacombs exist more in the Atrament than they do in this world. And, as you know, your soul is incompatible with the Atrament."

He chortled. "'Incompatible.' That's a diplomatic way of putting it."

Naia squeezed his arm, as if by pressure she could impart an appreciation of the danger he faced. "Speak to no one. Touch nothing. Go nowhere unless I say it's safe. Do you understand, Quinlan?"

Holding his hat in his hands, he executed a formal bow. "Madam, you have my word I'll behave. As much as I can, at any rate."

Somehow, Naia doubted that. Nevertheless, she nodded before turning back to the darker-than-black openings before them. Quin's sarcasm was quickly forgotten as she put her mind to the problem of selecting which path they should take.

Atrament, Oblivion, Netherworld.
Mercy, Sacrifice, Vengeance

"Skara's temple," she murmured, her brain working to decipher the code. "Which face of the goddess was displayed at the pinnacle of the dome?"

Quin appeared to be wrestling with an unpleasant memory. "The ugly one," he said finally. That would be the aspect of Sacrifice.

They would choose the Oblivion portal.

Not that the portal actually led to Oblivion, just as the portal on the right didn't lead to the netherworld. It was a mnemonic, a device used for aiding memory. The Catacombs existed apart from distance and time, though travel through them still took time and covered distance. The paradox was one of the temple's holy mysteries. She was determined to select the shortest route to their destination, even if it wasn't the straightest.

Her hand clenching Quin's wet sleeve, she guided him toward the looming entrance directly ahead. She could see nothing but perfect darkness on the other side of the doorway. No path. No light. It was like the world ended right there in front of them. She stepped across the threshold.

Death's Passage

The world wavered a bit around her then steadied. She was no longer in the gray corridor conquered by years and volcanic ash. Instead they had arrived in a mist-filled tunnel hewn from solid rock. Beside her, Quin sucked in a sharp, rattled breath.

She turned toward him. And winced when she saw him.

He positively glowed with a brilliant aura of sickening light. He was staring down at himself, rotating his arms slowly, a look of concern in his eyes. Naia knew immediately what the queer, putrid light represented. She'd seen such an aura before, on Darien. But it hadn't been anywhere near this vivid. Compared to the green brilliance surrounding Quin, Darien's aura had been a mere foreshadowing.

Quin's damnation was undeniable.

He raised a glowing hand before his face and said, "Well, this is certainly disconcerting."

Naia wished she had better tidings to offer. But she was used to being the bearer of ill news. "It is not an optimistic sign," she said, mustering all the tact and evasion of an anointed priestess of Death.

Quin dropped his hand, appearing resigned. "I don't suppose it is. Apparently, the goddess is well-aware of my transgressions."

Naia looked at him in sympathy. There was no glossing over the truth. "It means your soul is not destined for the Atrament," she told him directly. "It is destined for hell."

He shrugged, forcing a smile. "Hardly anything I wasn't aware of before." He raised his hands, using the aura to illuminate the wall next to the opening of a passage leading off. "Comes in rather handy, actually. Look here."

Naia peered around him and saw a set of markings etched into the wall. Quin leaned closer, examining them with keen interest. "Well now, I wonder what that means."

Naia took him by the arm, turning him away from the inscription. "It means you need to keep out," she said firmly. "That passage leads to a warded hall, and you're not welcome there. You could walk in there. But you'd never walk back out again."

"Interesting." Quin ran a hand back through his hair then set his wet hat on his head. "What's so important that it needs warding?"

There were some secrets a demon like Quin Reis should not know. Perhaps this was one of them. Or perhaps this was something he really should know. Naia decided on the latter. With a sigh, she informed him, "That passage leads to the Hall of the Masters. It is a shrine dedicated to the souls of mages who have passed on to the Atrament."

"I see. And since I'm damned…"

"You don't belong there, Quin. I'm sorry." She said it as gently as she could. Even so, it sounded harsh to her ears. "If you were to walk in there, you might make it halfway to the center of the room. Then the wards would be activated. The last thing you would see would be a brilliant flare of light as your soul incurred the wrath of the goddess…and then nothing. Forever."

Quin stared apathetically at the passage. "Doesn't sound entirely bad. I can certainly think of worse. I'm destined for worse, come to think of it."

"It would not be painful," Naia agreed. "But it would be very final."

Quin dismissed the assessment with a wave. "Anything's better than an eternity spent in hell. Perhaps it's an option I should remember for later."

Naia could only gaze at him, agreeing with him quietly in her heart. He didn't seem that awful of a person. She couldn't wish an eternity of suffering upon his soul, no matter what sins he had committed.

"Let's go," she prompted gently.

He turned and walked beside her down the dim corridor, soft mist swirling out of their path like a writhing mass of snakes. The air was sharply cold but not humid here. It had a stale, dry quality that smelled of dust and old decay. Naia scarcely noticed. She was used to the atmosphere of the place. She had spent years of her life within these passages. If anything, the odor was slightly nostalgic.

She led Quin out of the tunnel and into a vast chamber honeycombed with vaults that contained the remains of the dead. The walls stretched higher than she could see, until they disappeared, lost in distance and shadow. A cold breeze sweet with the stench of rot rustled her skirt. There was magelight here, glowing in the recesses of the vaults. She could make out the shrouded corpses in the lowest levels.

Quin made a face at the ripe odor, craning his neck to look up into the endless heights of the surrounding walls. Naia took him by the hand, leading him forward. They walked into what looked like a small city or a maze, past mausoleums and ancient sarcophagi, monuments and statues with faces of the deceased. They were on a street of sorts in a city of the dead. The stench of decomposition grew stronger, almost overwhelming. Quin covered his nose with the collar of his coat. He looked back at Naia with a look of apology.

She couldn't blame him. She remembered how it had been for her, so long ago. When she had first begun ministering to the dead. Before she'd become accustomed to the culture of decay.

They walked onto a bridge that spanned a river of what looked like black water. It wasn't water, Naia knew. But she wasn't about to tell Quin that. Not all cadavers ended up in the vaults. Not every corpse was worth the space. Or the effort. The black liquid below took care of the rest.

They reached the end of the bridge and exited the cavern, passing under a horseshoe arch decorated with iron filigree. The ever-present mist tumbled forward ahead of them, creating an illuminated path that split just ahead. One fork led to the next vast room of vaults. The other veered away toward chambers she was eager to avoid.

Quin stopped at the fork, looking at a side passage with speculation in his eyes. Naia didn't wait for him, knowing that was not a path he should tread. She walked quickly toward the curving passage ahead, calling back to him over her shoulder, "Hurry, it's this direction. We still have a long way to go."

She'd taken several steps before she realized he wasn't following. She stopped, turning to glance back with a feeling of trepidation. She could see the glow of his body clearly through the fog, moving toward the open doors.

"Quin," she called, starting after him. Her shrill voice rang strangely in the darkness, as if muffled or half-muted.

He paid no attention. She wasn't sure that he heard.

Naia hurried toward him, catching him by the shoulder and forcing him to turn around. "What are you doing?" she demanded. He had no business going past that door. She knew what was there; she could taste the danger like metal on her tongue.

Quin didn't answer. Instead, he shrugged out of her grasp and strode into the dim chamber, following an illuminated path of mist. Naia trailed behind him, unsure of what to do. He seemed determined to ignore her.

"Quin, stop. Please trust me. You don't want to go in there."

The hall they entered was empty, save for one columned structure at the far end: a mausoleum made of glistening white marble with veins of gold. The glowing mist led straight toward it like a signal beacon. Quin lurched toward the mausoleum as if compelled. He only stopped when he encountered the iron grate that guarded the entrance to the tomb.

He gripped the wrought iron bars and gave the grate a sharp tug. When it didn't give, he started wrenching at it, rattling the bars as if trying to rip them off their hinges. When the grate still refused to budge, he whirled back toward her, eyes burning with fury and frustration.

"How do you open this?"

"Why?" Naia demanded. "You don't understand what you're doing. Why do you want in there?"

"Because of that!" He pointed above the tomb's entrance, to a triangular slab of marble held up by fluted columns, where the word REIS was etched into the stone. Naia stared at the letters then stared at Quin, feeling deflated.

He looked at her with self-hating desperation in his eyes. "How do I open it?"

Sighing, she yielded to his need, though it went against her better judgment. She reached out and took hold of the grate, pressing the release mechanism on the back. With a throaty groan that sounded like a death rattle, the grate swung outward. Quin stood for a moment with his hand lingering on the marble of the doorway, staring into the dim shadows beyond. His face was stern and haunted. Solemn but resolute.

Naia felt a twinge of apprehension in her chest as she watched him take an echoing step inside, crossing onto the marble tiles of the floor. She moved to follow him, magelight trailing in beneath her feet. There wasn't much space within; it was a small room just big enough for two people, white marble walls to either side. Halfway up the wall in front of her, an anchored vase held a single white rose. She pressed her hand against the cool face of the marble, running her fingers over the etched words:

SEPHANA CLEMLEY
PRIME WARDEN OF AERYSIUS

The rose blossom looked perfectly fresh, as if it had been placed there just that morning. Naia reached out, touching the marble on the opposite wall. There, in letters carved boldly into the polished surface:

BRADEN REIS
FIRST OF THE SENTINELS

Reading that name, she felt a lump rise to her throat. She turned to look at Quin, wondering what he must be feeling. She knew from previous conversations with him that he had never come to terms with his brother's death. She supposed it might be good for him to confront his feelings about it. Grief had a purpose, after all. It was the first step of forgiveness, of letting go.

Quin stood next to her wrapped in his glowing aura of corrupted light, hat in hand, head bowed solemnly. The other hand rested against the wall of his brother's tomb. He was leaning on it heavily, staring downward at the ground. He stood there silently, reverently, alone with his loss.

At last he looked up and asked, "Is there a way to open it?"

Naia frowned, profoundly disturbed by the request. Opening tombs was something that simply wasn't done. It went far beyond disrespect, to a place that bordered on blasphemy. "Why would you want to open it?" she whispered, appalled.

"I want to see him." Quin's gaze was hard, his face resolved. He wasn't asking her permission.

Naia wasn't sure what to do. He was obviously distraught. She set a hand on his arm, seeking to comfort him. Or at least deter him. "Quin. Your brother has been dead for a thousand years."

He shook his head. "I don't care. I want to see him."

She had dealt with grief before; it was something she was used to. She had trained most of her life to deal with the circumstances surrounding death. Not just the care of the departed, but also tending to the wounds of loved ones left behind. But this went far beyond grief; she could see it in his eyes. This was something different. It wasn't grief. It was guilt.

She resorted to appealing to his morals. "It's not right to disturb the peace of the dead. It's disrespectful. And undignified."

Quin shot her a hostile glare. "Is that why you chose to wake Sareen? Because disturbing the dead is undignified? Don't patronize me—just tell me how to open it."

He turned and felt along the marble wall, at last locating one of the release mechanisms that would, if depressed, unlock his brother's crypt. Naia reached out and caught his hand.

"Please. Braden earned his rest."

But Quin was apparently disinterested in his brother's rest. He was drowning in guilt and shame. Quin's gaze seared through the filthy green aura that framed his face, a white-eyed look of wildness and reproach.

"Just tell me how to open this gods-damned box!"

Naia realized there was no use trying to dissuade him. She didn't understand his need but, then again, she didn't have to. Perhaps this would help him put the past in perspective. More likely, it would leave a permanent scar, like ripping open an old wound. She just hoped it didn't fester.

Naia reached up and turned his face toward her. Gazing into his eyes, she said very carefully, "Quin. I need you to understand something before we open this. It's important. I'm sure the temple worked very hard to insure your brother was well-preserved. But a thousand years is an awfully long time. He may not look anything like you remember."

He grimaced, growling through clenched teeth, "That's the problem—I can't remember! I don't remember what Braden looked like, and I promised I'd never forget! I gave him my word..." He swallowed, looking feeble.

Adamant, Naia shook her head. "This isn't the answer, Quin. I don't think your brother would want you to see him like this."

He jerked back from her. "Listen to me plainly: *I don't care.* Open it. Now."

Naia sighed, collecting herself. "If you insist." She leaned forward, depressing the twin mechanisms recessed on either side of the wall. There was the slightest clicking sound. Then the marble face of the crypt parted at the seams. Naia twisted the device, creating handles to slip her fingers through. She pulled, putting her back into it; the marble face was heavier than it looked. It folded down, the drawer of the crypt sliding effortlessly out of the wall.

Inside the drawer lay a body covered by a thin shroud.

Naia's breath caught in her throat. She knew who lay beneath that delicate fabric. The legend of Braden Reis overshadowed the accomplishments of any other mage in all of history. He was not only the founder of the Order of Sentinels; he was the one man who had stood opposed to Zavier Renquist.

She glanced at Quin, feeling terrible for him. And terrible for his brother. This was not the choice she would have favored for either of them. Or for the temple she had once held allegiance to.

She feared what lay beneath that cotton shroud.

Quin stared at the covered remains, his face fixed in a scowl of infinite sorrow. Solemnly, he reached down and fingered the fabric of the shroud. He whispered, "I want to see him."

Naia closed her eyes, a nervous wave of tension passing over her. She let out a lingering sigh. Then she took hold of the shroud's soft fabric and drew it back.

At her side, Quin made a quiet gasping sound.

She already knew what her action had uncovered. She didn't

have to look. She drew the fabric lower, folding it down. She smoothed it out with her hand. Only then did Naia open her eyes to gaze upon the remains.

Braden Reis was garbed in the indigo robes of the Lyceum, his hands folded neatly over his chest. Naia stared down at him for a long moment, afraid to move. Afraid to say anything. She was too frozen by dismay.

Quin whispered, "I don't understand…"

Naia did. The remains of Quin's brother had not been preserved. Instead, Braden Reis had been frozen in time. His flesh had been placed here scant minutes after death, probably before the body had even cooled. Here within the spelled wonder of the Catacombs, time had not been allowed to touch his flesh to work its ills. Whoever had tended his remains had done well by him. He was perfect in every way: the flush of life still touched his cheeks. His hands looked supple, the skin smooth and plump. He was a handsome man, far more so than his brother. There was a strength about him that even death could not deny.

Quin shook his head, drawing in a shuddering breath. "How is this possible?"

Feeling terrible for him, Naia took him by the hand. She said in a lowered voice, "The Temple has many holy mysteries. This is one. I'm sorry, but I'm not at liberty to elaborate."

Quin's eyes widened. Then they narrowed. "You knew!" he accused. "You knew he'd be like this! That's why you didn't want me to see him!"

Naia struggled to maintain her composure. It was difficult; there was so much she wanted to tell him. And so much she could not. "Quin. It's time. We've disturbed your brother's peace long enough."

"No." He shook his head, drawing back from her. "Wait. You can bring him back! Like you did to Sareen! You can bring him back, can't you?" His eyes were wide, glinting in desperation.

But Naia was already shaking her head, fending off the idea by waving her hands in front of him. "No! Quin, I can't bring him back."

"Why not?"

Because it was forbidden.

"I could heal his body," Naia confessed, avoiding his eyes. Instead she stared down into the face of his dead brother. "Maybe with prayer and supplication, we could convince the goddess to part the Veil of Death. But Braden was a mage, not a demon like Sareen. I have no way to heal the loss of his legacy. You know as well as I: once a person inherits the gift, it becomes inseparable from their life-force. We would be healing him just to watch him die all over again. I'm sorry, Quinlan. I truly am. You must say goodbye to your brother now. I'm going to wait outside."

She squeezed his arm then turned to slip past him. As she did, something in the drawer caught her eye. Something tucked beneath the shroud, only one silver glint visible to the eye. She knew instantly what it was. While Quin was focused on his brother's face, Naia scooped the silver necklace up in her hand and fled the mausoleum, head bowed, shoulders shaking, hands clasped in front of her. She ran forward through the glowing spill of mist without aim or direction. She didn't have a destination in mind; she just wanted to get away. She couldn't escape the image of Braden Reis. It followed her even as she fled.

Naia chanced a glance back over her shoulder, then paused and opened her hand. She held up the object she had stolen from the crypt: a silver medallion with a dull, black stone of many facets that hung from two silver bands. Just the sight of the Soulstone made her sick. She thrust it deeply into the pocket of her cloak, then turned to wait for Quin.

It was a reckoning long overdue; she sincerely hoped he'd found what he sought so desperately.

She had the troubled feeling that he hadn't.

Chapter Sixteen
Lessons in Patience

Pass of Lor-Gamorth, The Front

The wind howled under the door, fanning the candle's fragile flame. The shadows in the room flickered, first growing bolder then shrinking. The wind gusted again with a howl that sounded like the shriek of a dying animal. The candle's flame blazed to life, flaring for a split-second before dying.

Kyel stared at the cooling wick, willing the tiny flame back to life. It sprang up with a jubilant glow, as if excited to be reborn.

Kyel pushed away the text he'd been studying and grumbled, "I don't understand this passage at all. It says, 'a net preponderance of shadow is required to offset a net preponderance of light.' How is that bloody possible? Isn't shadow just the absence of light?"

"Let me see it." Meiran extended her hand without looking at him, engrossed in the scroll she'd been reading.

Kyel shoved the book toward her and watched as she turned to settle over it, one elbow on the table, palm supporting her head. Her eyes scanned slowly over the scrawled writing. Finally, she shook her head, shoving the text back in his direction. "I'm not a Sentinel. I know very little about the nature of light. What I do know is this: we don't have much time. So if you come across pages like this that you find yourself struggling with, just skip over them and move on to something else."

From the other end of the room, Cadmus cleared his throat. "Pardon, Prime Warden, but do you mind if I take a look at it?"

Meiran didn't glance up at him. "Go ahead."

Kyel got up and walked the book over to Cadmus, who donned a pair of spectacles then hunched over to read the passage. He pressed a finger to the page, trailing it beneath the lines of text as he read. When he was done, he looked up to consider Kyel over the frames of his lenses. "Well, it seems obvious to me. This type of shield forms from a web that absorbs or reflects weaponized light. Shadow, in this context, is merely referring to the web's capacity for absorption. Look, it says so right here." He tapped his finger on the page.

"Right." Kyel took the text back, snapping it closed without looking at it. "I'm sick and tired of energy transformations—they make my brain want to bleed!"

Cadmus shook his head. "You keep forgetting Nerid's Second Law."

Kyel tossed the book down on the table, throwing himself down in his seat. "Damn Nerid's Laws! If I want something to disappear, I'll bloody well make it disappear!"

"I've had enough." Meiran set the scroll she was reading down at her side, staring from face to face. "From both of you. Brother Cadmus, if you insist on continuing to interfere with Kyel's education, then have the grace to do so away from my presence. Kyel, patience is a skill that continues to elude you. I hear from the forgers that weaving mail is an excellent way to acquire patience. Go spend the rest of the day in the smithy."

Kyel gaped at her. "You're not serious?" There was a war coming. How could Meiran want him wasting his time when there was still so much to learn?

"I am. Consider this a demerit." Her tone brooked no argument. She picked the scroll back up, unrolling it in her hands.

Kyel stared back and forth between Meiran and Cadmus, blinking slowly. Then he whirled in disgust and careened through the door, slamming it behind him. He strode out of the tower into the inner ward, his black cloak billowing in the wind of his wake. He crossed the ward in a hurry, hot with anger. He was aware of the stares of the men on him, tracking his every motion. Everywhere he went, it was always the same.

A soldier guarding the cistern muttered the word "darkmage" and spat on the ground. Normally, Kyel would have ignored the insult. This time he stopped, spinning back toward the man. He grabbed the soldier by the collar and slammed him back against the wall.

"What's your name?" he demanded, not caring that half the yard had stopped to stare at him.

The bald soldier smirked, eyes laughing and daring him. "Go ahead. Do it. Show everyone what you're made of. It ain't gonna shock nobody."

"This is horse piss," Kyel gasped, leaning into the man's face. "I haven't done anything to you!"

"You're the Oathbreaker's little cunt. I was at Orien's Finger. I know what you mages really are."

"I am *not* Darien Lauchlin," Kyel growled. He released the man, forcing his sleeve back past his elbow and holding it up in front of him. "See? I've still got the chains of my Oath. I've never used my power to strike a man, and I never will."

The soldier scoffed, staring at the markings on Kyel's arm with a look of revulsion. "We'll see about that. We'll see what you do when the first spear comes at you and you piss your pants. 'Cause none of us here's gonna have your back. Most of us lost brothers or fathers at Orien's Finger. On the battlefield, you'll be on your own." He looked up into Kyel's face and sneered, chuckling softly. "You're gonna burn, boy. I and my mates, we're gonna watch."

Kyel stared at him, feeling the heat of anger scalding his cheeks. He didn't say anything; he was too shocked to respond. Instead he drew back, turned, and stalked away. He kept his stare fixed on the ground, knowing for certain that the eyes of every soldier in the courtyard were pinned on the embroidered star on his back.

Meiran stood up from her chair, crossed the room, then took the seat across the table from the temple watchdog who had managed to embed himself like a tick in their midst. His interference was starting to wear. She'd had just about enough.

The man looked up at her, a kindly smile on his face. He had gentle eyes, but his nose was bulbous and red with broken veins that extended onto his sagging cheeks. He was either too stupid or too smart to take her seriously. She suspected the latter.

Removing his spectacles with one hand, Cadmus rubbed his eyes and said to her, "I understand your frustration with my involvement, Prime Warden. But what we really need is a functional Sentinel, not soldiers with gaps in their mail coats."

"You and I must talk." Meiran leaned toward him with her elbows on the table. "I need the help of the temples, which is the only reason you're not straddling an ass back to Glen Farquist. You and I both know that the little 'agreement' you pulled over on Kyel means absolutely nothing. There *is* no more Aerysius; the office of prime warden was decapitated the day Emelda Lauchlin died. You have no authority whatsoever over Kyel or myself. I've only suffered your presence so far because I might be able to gain something by it."

The kindly smile didn't slip from his lips. Cadmus was simply sitting there, staring, blinking. He wore the same expression a parent would while patiently waiting a child to finish a tirade.

Meiran ignored him and went on, "You, on the other hand, have everything to lose. When the Reversal of the magic field happens, every one of your temple mysteries will become undone. Then everyone will know the truth: that your gods are made of tin, and your miracles are manufactured. What will you do when the only true power in the world comes from a hole in the ground and is wielded by demons hell-bent on destroying you?"

Cadmus' expression didn't crack. If anything, his smile broadened. "We need each other, Prime Warden," he said finally. "Our 'manufactured miracles,' as you call them, are the only chance you have of stopping Xerys' armies. You and Kyel are both crippled by your Oath and too self-righteous to acknowledge it. Without the aid of the temples, the Rhen will most assuredly fall."

His eyes took on a look of sympathy. "It pains me to say this, but I'm sure you already know: both you and Kyel are already dead. Your corpses just haven't finished twitching yet. When all is said and done, what kind of legacy do you wish to leave behind? If you cooperate with the temples, at least some small remnant of civilization will remain. If you don't…then the world will belong entirely to Xerys, to be forever remade in *His* image. I don't think you'd want that."

It was like someone had just drenched her with a bucket of ice-cold fury. Meiran felt physically numbed by the shock of it. For moments, she could do nothing more than just sit there, glaring at him contemptuously, hoping that somehow the violence in her eyes approached the wrath she felt inside.

"Why do we need your help?" she asked in a whispered hiss.

Cadmus shrugged and spread his hands, the patient smile returning to his pudgy face. "Because we are not Bound. And we have the power to bring them down."

Her wrath condensed, sharpening into threat. "Then I hope you have a plan."

His smile was oily and triumphant. "Don't worry, Prime Warden. We do."

Kyel dropped another circular piece of wire onto the anvil. He picked up a blacksmith's hammer and, taking careful aim, started pounding the wire ring. It took about ten solid hits before it was perfectly flat, the ends overlapping. He picked it up and threw the flattened ring into a bucket full of other flattened rings, just one among hundreds.

Another thirty thousand of those, and they may have enough for a mail shirt. Of course, that was all Kyel knew how to do. An actual blacksmith would have to do the punching and riveting and link the chains into the right pattern.

He picked up yet another circlet of precut wire. Ten or twelve solid hits on the anvil, and another flattened ring went into the bucket with a *clink*. He thrust his fingers into the can and picked up another wire.

"What the hell are you doing?"

Kyel turned to find Traver gawking at him from the doorway. He went ahead and pounded the next ring flat before plunking it in the bucket. "Hammering chain."

Traver strolled over, face distorted by an expression of incredulity. "What the bloody hell for? We've got blacksmiths to do that!"

Kyel shrugged, pounding out another ring. "I'm supposed to be learning patience." He tossed the finished ring into the bucket.

"And are you?"

Kyel turned toward him, massaging his right arm. "No." He sighed wearily.

He cast a dispirited glance at Traver, motioning to the bucket of flattened rings. Traver plunged his fingers in and picked up a handful. He nudged them around in his palm before tipping his hand and allowing them to spill back out.

"Doing that all day would make me desperately *im*patient," Traver said, running a hand through his hair. Then he grabbed Kyel by the arm, firmly steering him toward the door.

"Come along. Day's done already; you may as well come back tomorrow. How 'bout you join me for a drink?"

Kyel tossed the hammer down then followed the captain into the chill night air of the ward. The lights of bonfires danced from the corners of the yard, sparks zipping through the air like glowing fireflies. Halfway across the courtyard, he became aware of the stares he was collecting. Which brought back the memory of the soldier he'd confronted.

Kyel glared at the first sentry they came to, a bearded man guarding the tower's entrance. "What are you looking at?"

The soldier glared back at him, jaw clenched tight in a scowl of disgust.

Traver stepped forward, scant inches from the man's face. "He asked you a question, soldier. I think you'd better answer him."

The guard's hard eyes focused on Kyel. "I'm lookin' at a dead man, Captain." He spat on the ground, the glob landing between Kyel's feet.

Traver threw both hands out and slammed the man back

against the wall. Kyel caught hold of him, pulling him back. "It's fine, Traver! Leave him be!"

"It's not fine!" Traver ducked out of Kyel's grasp and shot forward, grabbing the soldier by a fistful of hair and bringing a fist back to throw a punch. The man didn't fight, but neither did he cower. He received the blow willingly, his head cracking back against the wall. He leaned forward, spitting out a tooth along with a drooling string of blood.

Traver gave him a last, good shove. "Report your ass to latrine duty!"

"Aye, Captain." The man saluted and strode briskly away, leaving his bloody tooth behind on the ground. Traver glared after him, looking fit to kill.

"It's not his fault." Kyel sighed, staring down at the tooth.

"What do you mean? You're the last damn Sentinel we have! You're the only thing between us and those demons out there— so they'd better start respecting that cloak on your back."

Kyel shook his head. "Respect has to be earned. I haven't done anything to earn it."

Traver nodded slowly. Then he turned, clapping Kyel on the back. "Come on. Let's get some mead in you." He guided Kyel into the tower, up to his own quarters on the third floor. There, he pulled Kyel up a chair and rummaged around in a wooden chest, pulling out a sack of mead. He poured them each a cup, brandishing his own in the air before throwing his head back and chugging it down.

"So how'd you make captain with only half a hand?" Kyel asked him, taking a sip of mead. He made a face. It was wretchedly strong, and he wasn't used to the taste of fermented honey.

"Well, I had seniority," Traver shrugged. "And it wasn't like I could go back to being a foot soldier. So Craig stuck me in the armory and helped me work myself up."

"So you have Royce's old job?" Kyel asked, trying another sip. This one went down harder than the last. He smacked his lips together, running his sleeve across his mouth.

Traver shook his head. "Nothing all that grand; I'm in charge of requisitions." He drained his cup and poured more. "So tell me…you've been getting a lot of that kind of treatment?"

Kyel took a heavy gulp and made a face as it went down. "It's not their fault. Ever since Orien's Finger, there's just no trust for mages. People fear what they don't understand."

"Aerysius wasn't destroyed that long ago," Traver pointed out. He dropped down on his cot, sliding his boots off and throwing them in the corner. "People should still remember what the Sentinels stood for."

They should, Kyel supposed. But they didn't. "All they remember is Darien," he said regretfully. "He didn't make it very easy for people to trust him."

"No. He sure didn't." Traver knocked back another swallow.

"I need to change that before the battle," Kyel said. For some reason, the mead was starting to taste a whole lot better. It was calming his nerves, making it easier to think, even as the magic field tapered off. What the soldier in the yard had said to him had shaken him up more than he'd realized. He needed the men to have his back. He had to be able to trust the soldiers defending him. But in order for that to happen, they'd have to trust him. It seemed like a paradox.

"Aye, you're going to need to work on that," Traver agreed. "You can't lead men who see you as a threat." He glanced sidelong at Kyel. "How long's it been since you've played a game of cards?"

Kyel couldn't help the grin that slipped to his face. "Too long, actually."

Traver immediately set his cup down and produced a pack from his pocket. His hands went to work shuffling, expertly sending the cards dancing between his fingers. His skills had improved considerably, Kyel realized, especially considering he was short two fingers. Traver sent the cards into a showering cascade then offered the pack for Kyel to split.

"All right. What do you got to bet?"

Kyel split the deck, then groped at his pockets, finding only a few coppers, a small rock, and a tiny ball of lint. Traver snatched up the rock, holding it in his palm with an expression of delight on his face.

"Isn't this the same damn rock you used to carry around?"

Kyel had to chuckle. "It is. I picked it up on the practice yard two years ago. It's my lucky rock. Although I'm not sure its luck has been working lately." The piece of white quartz had stood out at him from all the black rocks of the pass. He'd picked it up to remind himself of what hope looked like. He'd carried it with him ever since.

Traver tossed the stone back to him. "You need to keep that. Don't be gambling with it."

"So what, if you win it from me? You might need the luck more than I do."

"Oh, no!" Traver shook his head. "I wouldn't take your damn luck for all the gold in Chamsbrey. But I will take those coppers off you, so you'd better ante up."

"Are you sure?"

Devlin Craig let his hand fall to his side, still clutching the report. The old soldier named Kelbs gave a slight shrug. His face was as hard and cratered and cold as a winter in the pass. He had a no-nonsense way about him that suffered no stupidity.

"Those are the best estimates we've got, Commander."

Craig squeezed his hand, crumpling the strip of parchment. "Gods be damned."

"Don't blame the gods, Commander," Kelbs advised in a practiced monotone. "Blame our own damned lack of foresight. We should have seen this coming."

"You mean *I* should have seen this coming," Craig growled.

He trudged over to the table with its collection of maps strewn across it. He leaned over, planting both hands on the table. He examined the array of implements already spread out across the surface and took a deep breath. Then he started moving rocks and broadheads, repositioning them.

"They're draining all the Black Lands," he decided finally. "They're sending everything they've got against us."

To the two officers still lingering by the door, he said, "Send messengers to generals Blandford and Horthall. I want the Northern armies pitched at our rear. And I want men up on those ridges tomorrow, planting powder kegs and laying out charges. If they want to take the pass, we'll let them. But we'll make it their graveyard."

To the old sergeant, he directed, "Prioritize supply. We need provisions. And arrows—as many arrows as you can get. There shouldn't be one goose with a feather on its wings anywhere between here and Rothscard."

"Aye, Commander. How long do you think we have?"

Craig took one last glance at the maps, feeling fate kick him in the ass. "Not long enough."

Chapter Seventeen
Blood Feud

Tokashi Palace, The Black Lands

Darien awoke to soft rustling noises coming from the other side of the room. He cracked his eyes open just enough to gaze across the dim bedchamber. He could make out his wife's silhouette illuminated by the wan glow of an oil lamp. She was kneeling in the corner, rummaging around in the small chest he kept there. Darien watched her closely, not sure how he felt about the situation. He kept some very private tokens in that chest. She had no business going near it.

He sat up.

His movement caught her attention. Seeing him awake, Azár turned and smiled, making her way toward the bed. She knelt next to him. Her hair spilled freely down her back, unconstrained. Her eyes were wide and dark like a sea after sunset.

"It is time to wake, my husband," she said. "I was just finishing packing. I hope you don't mind, but I put a few of my own things in your chest."

"I don't mind," he responded, settling back into the deep pillows of the bed. That explained her invasion of his privacy, he supposed, although he still didn't like it. He rubbed his eyes, wishing she'd go away. He was naked beneath the blankets and feeling the usual morning urgency. The proximity of her soft skin wasn't helping the situation.

"I need my clothes," he grumbled.

She handed him his trousers. He struggled into them beneath the covers then walked stiffly into the adjoining bath. Bracing himself with a hand against the wall, he had to lean forward to angle his stream into the keyhole-shaped opening in the floor. When he returned to the bedchamber, Azár was still there, now sitting in the chair by the writing desk. He didn't understand why she remained; in the days since their wedding, she'd made a steady practice of avoiding him.

He found a fresh shirt and pulled it on, covering it with his new black cloak: a present from his wife. He bent over, pulling his boots on by the straps. She watched him the whole while, eyes tracking his every motion.

"Are you packed?" he asked her, more to break the tension than anything else.

"I am."

She had brought few belongings with her to the palace. Most of her physical wealth she carried on her person in the form of jewelry he'd given her as part of her bride-gift. But all the jewels in the world were worthless in comparison to the true wealth that Azár was rich in: the character and quality of her magelight. That was a princely treasure, worth more than any riches.

There was a knock at the door and Sayeed entered alone, bowing gracefully. He looked a little puzzled at finding Azár and Darien in the same room together. He'd been conspicuously restrained ever since the second bed had been hauled in and Darien's ghastly hound evicted to the stable.

Sayeed said, "Word has come from Bryn Calazar that the Kajiri portal is now available to us. We have only four days to empty the Khazahar of all its people."

Four days. That wasn't much time.

Thankfully, the tribes were gathered in the valley below; they'd been trickling in little by little since before the wedding feast. Still, the journey down into the ice caverns was difficult. It would also take time to move that many people through two transfer portals. First, a journey to Bryn Calazar, the hub that connected all the portals in the Black Lands. Then another transfer to Kajiri Flats, where Malikar's armies were staging. They would have to be precise about the logistics, or the evacuation could quickly degrade into disaster.

"Get the first twenty battalions through the portal," Darien said, buckling his warbelt. "Then the baggage. Then the civilians. Have the rest of the battalions bring up the rear."

Sayeed bowed his way out the door as a young girl entered with a breakfast tray. Darien helped himself to a piece of flatbread, absently offering a bowl of fruit to Azár. He tore off a bite, then set himself to the task of packing up the ink pots and parchment on the writing desk.

"You are quiet this morning," Azár said. "Why?"

Darien shrugged. "I'm bringing war against my own homeland. I still have friends there." He stooped to tuck the papers in his hand into the chest, checking the stoppers on the inkwells.

Azár finished chewing, her eyes studying him intensely. She asked, "And how does that make you feel?"

He turned to look at her. "It makes me feel sick." His voice carried more venom than he'd intended. He strove to modify his tone. "I don't understand why any of this is necessary. I'm still hoping that more reasonable minds will prevail."

She raised her eyebrows, plucking another plump grape off its stem. "More reasonable minds than Meiran?"

"That's what I meant." He put the ink pots into the chest and closed the lid.

She asked, "Do you still think it's possible to negotiate with them?"

"I don't know. I aim to try." He slid into the chair opposite her, one arm resting on the desk. Looking at her suspiciously, he probed, "And what about you? You're about to leave everything you've ever known behind. How does that make you feel?"

She shrugged dismissively, her face bland. "There is nothing that holds me here. I have seen the face of the sun. I've felt the warmth of it on my skin. I want to feel the sun again."

Darien understood. It was no more than she deserved. He said, "I'll give you the sun, Azár, if it's within my power."

Her kohl-lined eyes stared at him suspiciously. But then a dazzling smile dawned on her face, glowing brighter than any sun that he remembered.

"Then I know I will see it," she said. "Because there is nothing that is outside of your power."

He grimaced, finding the statement ironic.

"What?" she asked.

"That's just a lot of faith. I hope I can live up to it." He scooted his chair back, standing up. "Are you ready? We've a long road ahead of us."

She set the fruit down on her plate. Then she rose, drawing her scarf up over her head. It was bright turquoise, a color that complemented her skin tone perfectly.

Darien took one last look around the chamber, wondering if he'd miss it. He thought he would. It was the most luxurious quarters he'd ever had. He doubted he'd ever find better. He wasn't sure how much longer he even had left in this world. Not very much, he was afraid. It felt like time was speeding up, winding tighter like a spring about to snap.

He offered his arm to Azár, his innocent wife who was just as doomed as he was. He tried not to think about it, shoving the thought aside. He would save that worry for another time. It didn't matter, really. The Reversal was coming, and there wasn't a damned thing anyone could do about it. Especially not him.

Together, they walked away from the Residence enveloped by a cluster of Zakai. Two horses were led toward them, their hoofs *clop-clopping* on the tiles. Alongside his red stallion trotted the demon-hound, its nose to the floor, eyes like glowing green coals. At the sight of its master, the beast cocked its ears forward, its throat emitting a low purr. Or perhaps it was a growl; he really couldn't tell. The beast had been relegated to the stable ever since the wedding, much to the horses' dismay.

Darien helped Azár onto the mare that was part of her bride-gift, then waited as an officer held his own stirrup for him to mount. The Zakai led the horses forward by their tasseled bridles, the sounds of their hoofbeats echoing off the walls.

As the doors to the Residence closed behind them for the last time, Darien couldn't help but wonder if the sounds of their passage would be the last to ever ring in Tokashi's magnificent halls. They were leaving the Black Lands, possibly forever. Unless he could find a way to clear the curse over the skies, there would never be a reason to return.

Kajiri Flats, The Front

The horses didn't like the transfer portals.

Darien's stallion reared and nearly bolted, while Azár's mount put its head down and bucked like an unbroken colt. After the first transfer to Bryn Calazar, both horses balked, refusing to enter the second portal. Only after their heads had been wrapped in cloth did they relent and allow themselves to be led under the cross-vaulted arch.

There was an intense flash. And then Darien found himself stepping out onto the black dirt of a floodplain he'd only ever looked down upon from the pass above. Directly ahead loomed a familiar peak: the Spire of Orguleth. He'd only ever seen it from the other side. The peak on the left must be Maidenclaw, though it looked nothing maiden-like from this direction.

He unwrapped his horse's head and looked around with a growing mixture of wonder and dismay. He'd never seen so many tents. They stretched out toward the vast horizons in every direction, arranged in perfect rows. Each tent had a lantern that hung before it on a pole. Thousands of tents. Thousands of lanterns. Thousands upon thousands of men and women.

The dark plain that swallowed them resembled a night sky full of stars. Above, the clouds roiled as the clouds ever did, racing and crackling with uneasy energies deep within their depths. His horse snorted, bobbing its head and stamping a hoof.

A group of Tanisars moved forward, speaking in hushed voices to Sayeed. The Zakai officer turned to Darien, translating, "Our camp is to the south, Lord. Your tent has been made ready. However, your presence is requested in the command pavilion."

Darien nodded. "Please have my wife escorted to our tent."

"It will be as you say." The man bowed.

Azár glanced at Darien but said nothing; it was impossible to read her eyes. She gazed at him with absolute trust and didn't bother saying goodbye. Darien watched Sayeed's men swarm protectively around her, leading her mount away. He was grateful for the Zakai; a woman of Azár's beauty had no business in a military encampment.

That was his first thought. Then he remembered the women who served in Bryn Calazar's legions and was reminded of his wife's ferocious nature. Perhaps a military encampment was exactly where Azár was intended to be.

Sayeed led his horse forward as soldiers emerged from the tents to watch their small procession through the camp. It didn't take Darien long to realize that it was not a warm reception. Many of the men and women that lined their path looked at him with hatred in their eyes, some spitting on the ground as he passed. No one spoke a word; the camp was eerily quiet. But the anger of the soldiers didn't need a voice.

Sayeed looked at him and explained, "These are the legions of Maridur. Their numbers were decimated in the last invasion. They will have no love for you."

Darien nodded without saying a word. All along their route, men and women spat and turned their backs to him. He could almost smell the stench of their hatred. It sapped the energy from him, making him feel drained and weary. He understood their anger and contempt; he had killed thousands of their comrades. Their anger was justified.

At last they reached the command tent, a purple pavilion supported by many poles. It was the size of a small house, with flaps tied back to serve as the opening to a dim interior. Their party drew up in front of it. Darien left his stallion with Sayeed and started walking forward.

"Darien Nach'tier!"

He turned just in time to see a spear hurling toward him. It gored him right through, pinning him fast to a tent post.

He gaped in shock at the trembling shaft sticking out of him. The world was darkening quickly, like heated paper charring at the edges. His mind groped frantically for the magic field as his vision faded. He drew in the field as hard as he could, throwing it mindlessly at the pain. Then he started screaming as his flesh began to burn.

The last thing Darien saw was Sayeed standing in front of him, scimitar held high in a warding stance. Then he relaxed into darkness.

He was surprised that he woke at all.

Darien opened his eyes to find a familiar face staring down at him.

"Well, here we are again," said an equally familiar voice.

"And where is that?" he whispered hoarsely.

He was groggy, to the point that he couldn't make heads or tails of his surroundings. The woman leaning over him had dark brown skin and sleek ebony hair. She was elegant in an unusual way, beautiful without meaning to be.

He blinked a couple times, fumbling through hazy bleariness to remember her name. The woman placed a hand on his chest, closing her eyes. He could feel a faint stirring of power deep inside. She was another mage, and she was probing him, he realized.

"You are in my tent," she explained, smiling at him with her eyes. "I had your men bring you here so I could watch you while you recovered." Her smile slipped a bit. "You seem to have a hard time keeping yourself alive."

Her name finally came to him: Myria Anassis. He was surprised to see her there. He'd thought she was in Bryn Calazar with Renquist. With effort, he squirmed into a sitting position. "What happened?"

"As you can imagine, not all of Malikar's soldiers think highly of you. One man in particular decided that vengeance was more important than his own life. He lost his entire family at Orien's Finger. All five of his brothers. Do you understand the concept of blood feud?"

He did. Darien realized that he'd been a fool; he should have expected such an attack. "Thank you for saving me," he murmured.

Myria scoffed, trailing a hand down her waist-length hair. "You saved yourself. You burned the spear to ash and cauterized the wound. You were lucky; we couldn't have gotten to you in time."

He reached up, rubbing the place where the shaft had penetrated. There wasn't even a scar left. Myria had done a masterful job with the healing. He gazed at her in speculation, remembering the time she had healed him in Bryn Calazar, right after his arrival in the Black Lands. Then, she had propositioned him for sex. He'd rejected her at the time. The look in her eyes made him regret that decision.

She stood up. "Do you feel up to walking? Warden Connel would like a word with you. Well, more than a word. Frankly, I think he's quite pissed."

He still felt groggy, but figured he was up for a walk if he had to be. Darien pushed himself up off the pallet, rising stiffly. He looked down at his body, realizing he wasn't wearing much.

"Here's your trousers," Myria said, and tossed them to him. Her eyes lingered on his chest.

He caught the trousers and drew them on, lacing them up the front. Then he donned the tunic she handed him.

"And here's this." Myria offered him a chain hauberk. "Orders. You're not to go anywhere without at least a mail shirt. And I'm told you're to be fitted for a set of field plate."

Darien stared at the ring mail before accepting it with a shrug. He pulled it on over his head, tugging it down his chest. It was well-made, and not as heavy as it looked. He girded his belt over it then pulled on his boots, snatching his swords up off the ground.

"I hear you wed."

Darien glanced over his shoulder as he shoved the scimitar through his belt. "I did."

"Congratulations." Myria smiled in a friendly way, handing him his long sword. "I also hear the marriage remains unconsummated."

Darien paused in the action of shouldering his baldric. For a second he stood frozen. Then he straightened, turning away from her. "I suppose I'll have to speak to my men."

"Rumor flies swifter than the arrow," she assured him. "Don't blame your men, Darien. Blame your wife."

He turned to look back at her, searching her face.

"Don't worry," she commiserated, trailing a hand down the tent post that stood between them. "I understand a marriage of necessity. I had one of those myself once." She leaned forward, long hair swaying over her shoulders. "The offer I made is still open. If you ever get bored, well...you know where to find me."

Her words took him off-guard. Hadn't she just been congratulating him on his marriage? He stared at Myria, wondering what kind of city ancient Bryn Calazar must have been like. Obviously very different from Aerysius. She saw the look on his face and grinned, obviously happy to have unsettled him.

"Come on." She turned, beckoning for him to follow. "I'll show you to the command tent."

As soon as they stepped outside, Darien found himself confronted by two rows of Zakai who fell immediately to their knees. Sayeed walked toward him, head bowed, and fell to the black dirt at his feet. There was a small commotion as soldiers from the surrounding tents moved in closer to watch. Soon, Darien found himself surrounded by armed and spiteful men ringing him dangerously.

He was already grateful for the mail shirt.

His eyes scanned the crowd warily, at last coming to rest on a man who knelt behind the row of officers, his wrists and ankles bound. The man bled from his nose and an abrasion over his eye.

Head bowed, Sayeed offered Darien the hilt of his own sword. "I failed you, Lord. Please take my life."

Darien ignored him and walked instead to the prisoner bound on the ground. He recognized him now. It was the man who'd assaulted him with the spear.

He knelt in front of him. The warrior's dark eyes regarded him with fierce abhorrence before he tried to turn his face away. Darien reached out and caught his chin, denying him. He forced the man to look him in the eye.

"I understand I killed your brothers," he said.

The prisoner made a snarling noise and showered him with a rain of spittle. Darien wiped his face dry on his shirt sleeve. Then he leaned closer, as if daring the man to do it again.

"I understand anger," he said softly. "I understand vengeance. That's why you have to die."

Darien rose, summoning the magic field. He turned his back as the screams began. He strode toward Sayeed. He could hear the prisoner thrashing on the ground behind him, howls turning to shrieks as the anguish became unbearable. Darien paused, focusing his stare at the ground, listening to the gruesome sounds of death by implosion. The rhythm of the convulsions went on and on, finally expiring with a popping noise. When Darien turned to look back, what was left of the body was still twitching spastically.

The remaining soldiers had drawn back away from him a fair distance. He glared his anger at the gathered crowd, raising his voice. "Anyone else feel the need to settle a score? Let's get this over with *now.*"

Apparently, no one did.

When not a soul came forward to challenge him, he turned his wrath on the kneeling Zakai. "You failed me once. Never fail me again. *Now, get up.*"

He tugged at the magic field until energy clawed like blue flames over his body. The men sprang back away, fear wild in their eyes. Darien trudged forward, his very presence boring a hole right through the center of the crowd.

Myria followed, her face smug as she jogged forward. "You're creating a scene," she whispered when she caught up. "That mail shirt won't stop everything they can hurl at you."

"I don't care."

He stopped, scanning the dark plain ahead for sight of the pavilion, changing his course toward it. Seeing the hostile energies leaking out of him, soldiers moved back, scrambling out of his way. Darien let a wash of azure magelight erupt from the ground in front of him, trailing forward to light and clear his path. People saw it as a sign, backing away with their palms held up in a gesture against evil.

Darien released the magic field as he stopped before the pavilion. He ducked as he entered, thrusting back the tent flap.

The interior was dark and dappled with ruddy light. The scent of agarwood did a poor job of masking the stench of sweat and coal smoke. The tent was larger than it had looked from the outside, with multiple rooms cordoned off by hanging fabric, the floor carpeted by ornate rugs. To one side, a group of people were arguing heatedly over a table dominated by an oversized map. Darien couldn't help but stare at the two women among their number who seemed even more vocal in their military opinions than either of the men. One was pounding a fist on the map to elucidate her point.

"This way."

Myria pulled back the fabric of a partition and guided him into another, dimmer area. Darien ducked as he went in, straightening to find himself staring at Byron Connel. The Warden of Battlemages reclined on a long sofa positioned up against a wall of the tent. He leaned forward, setting a waterpipe down on the rug as he beckoned Darien to come forward.

Darien stiffened, wanting nothing more to do with the man. Memories of their last encounter still haunted his nightmares.

"There you are," the Battlemage said, standing up. He clasped Darien in a mercifully quick embrace then turned to kiss Myria on the cheek.

"I'll leave the two of you alone," she said, smiling at Darien as she turned away. Her hand trailed down his back.

Connel chuckled. "You had him long enough. It's my turn." He sat back down on the sofa and lifted the pipe, putting the mouthpiece to his lips. He waved his hand, indicating the seat across from him made from a bale of hay wrapped in cloth. Darien sat heavily, eyeing Myria through a gap in the partition.

Connel said, "I hear you've been trying to get yourself killed before the fighting starts."

Darien couldn't help but grin. "That wasn't my intention, actually."

"Yes, well, intentions are always worth their weight in gold, aren't they?" Connel took a heavy draw on the pipe.

Darien shrugged. "I suppose they are."

Connel set the pipe down, his face going grim. "Welcome to

the Front, Darien. Here's the situation: about half the population of Malikar wants you dead for what you did at Orien's Finger. The other half would rather see you tortured slowly over a long period of time. Which is unfortunate, because they're the ones tasked with keeping you alive on a battlefield. So you're already at a disadvantage."

Darien sighed. "I never figured it would be easy."

Connel narrowed his eyes. "It's not going to be. You'll be a target everywhere you go."

He passed him the waterpipe. Darien accepted it, drawing the smoke into his lungs. The tobacco went down smoothly, with a strong taste of fruitwood. It was decadent, unlike anything he'd ever experienced in the Rhen.

"So what do you suggest I do?"

Connel appeared to be pondering the question as he accepted the pipe back. He sat with his face screwed into a frown for a long moment, hand resting on his bearded chin. At last, he said, "We'll have to find a way to prove your loyalty very publicly."

Darien wasn't sure he liked the sound of that. His thoughts went to his ordeal in Bryn Calazar, when he'd been paraded like a beaten slave through the streets of the city.

"And how are we going to do that?"

"I don't know. I'll come up with something." Connel glanced back at him. "In the meantime, make yourself at home. Just be careful. We'll be settled here for about another week as the last of the stragglers find their way to us. Then we'll be heading south."

South. Into the Rhen.

Darien felt the strangled chill of that thought settle into him, penetrating deep into his bones. He'd known when he'd come here that war was on the imminent horizon. But sitting at the Front in a command tent made it seem that much more of a reality. Quietly, he asked, "Any plans for negotiation?"

Connel shrugged. "There's plans. Of course, you'd be a part of any negotiations that take place."

Darien wasn't certain if that was a good idea. After his last interaction with Meiran, he didn't think he was capable of talking anymore. He asked, "What's the status of Greystone Keep?"

"It's been rebuilt."

"In only *two years?*" It seemed inconceivable. The monarchies of the Rhen had ceased to support Greystone's defenses in previous years. Apparently, the last invasion had shaken them up enough to make them reevaluate their priorities.

Connel said, "They allocated the resources and dug in."

Darien was having a hard time envisioning it. The logistics seemed impossible. Whoever had coordinated that effort already had his respect, and then some. "Who's their new force commander?"

"A man named Devlin Craig."

Darien shot up straight in his seat. "Craig?" Hope flared like a beacon in the darkness. But it was brief. Devlin Craig had been his friend, but that had been under different circumstances. Like Meiran, Craig would be opposed to him now. He'd see him as a traitor.

"You know him?" asked Connel.

"Aye. I know him."

"Will he work with us?"

Darien shook his head, breathing out a heavy sigh. His eyes gazed at the waterpipe. "I don't think so. Although he might be willing to talk." If he could just get Craig to sit down at a table and hear him out…but no. He'd been unable to convince Meiran. What chance would he have with a man who'd forged a career defending the pass from the Enemy?

Connel leaned forward. "That's all for now. Go get some rest. You look like you need it. Oh, and congratulations on your nuptials."

Darien was taken aback that Connel already knew of his marriage to Azár. "My thanks," he muttered awkwardly, rising to his feet.

He swept the cloth partition aside, emerging into the main area of the command tent. The argument over the maps had wound down. The tent was quiet, filled with a slight haze of smoke that snaked through the slanted light from the lanterns. He turned toward the entrance but stopped as he spotted Myria seated on a cushion in the corner. She noticed him and rose, gliding over to stand in front of him.

"Leaving already?"

Darien nodded, feeling weary. "It's been a long day."

A mischievous grin sprang to her face. "We could make it a long night. I've got wine."

He blinked, shocked by her forwardness. He stared at her hard, taking her all in. Her smooth, dark skin, the sweet curve of her hips, the long drape of her hair. He had to admit, he found the offer enticing. The playfulness in her eyes sealed the deal.

"I suppose I could use a drink," he decided.

Myria's grin was triumphant. "Let's go out the back way," she urged. She scooped a conical helmet off the floor and handed it to him. "Here. Put this on."

Darien tugged the helm down over his head, figuring it wouldn't look too out of place in the context of their surroundings. He understood her intentions: the helm had a wide nose guard that would render him anonymous. He followed as Myria took him by the hand, guiding him out of the pavilion and into the darkness.

She led him across the bustling encampment that was oddly quiet for the amount of activity going on. None of the soldiers they passed paid him any mind; the helm did its job. The eyes of the men slipped right over him, past him, beyond him. They looked but didn't see; he was invisible.

In all his adult life, Darien couldn't remember one single day when he hadn't been the object of every stare. To be so completely inconspicuous was a bizarre feeling. A freeing feeling. No one noticed. No one cared.

Myria pushed back the cloth drape of her tent.

She made her way over to the far wall while he lingered in the entrance, struggling to remove his various armor and armaments, making a small pile of his things in the corner. She returned to present him with a cup of wine, which Darien accepted gladly. He stared down at the blood-red liquid in his hand. Then he raised the cup to his lips and let the wine slide down his throat. It did little to quench his thirst. He grimaced, handing it back.

Myria set the cup aside and drew him in for a kiss.

Darien stiffened, pulling back. "No."

"No?"

He shook his head. That wasn't what he wanted, not why he was here. He didn't want to be touched like that.

Myria peered at him until understanding dawned in her eyes. For a moment, she looked almost wary.

"No," she agreed.

Her fingers slipped to the blue sash at her waist, tugging at the knot. Her gown fell open, exposing long inches of firm, smooth skin. Darien stared, his eyes sucked into the gap between fabric and held there fast. Her hand stroked across his chest then altered its course, skimming downward.

She sank to her knees on the rugs in front of him, gazing upward into his eyes. Her slim brown fingers worked at the drawstring of his trousers, taking their time.

The lanterns dimmed around them, wavering, then went out. There was no light or love in the act that followed.

Chapter Eighteen
Isle of Winter

Isle of Titherry, The Rhen

Naia winced and squinted as brilliant light clawed away the darkness of the Catacombs. The screech of metal grinding against rusted metal shuddered down her nerves, making her clench her teeth as the doors of the shrine peeled open in front of them. They stood in a shard of garish blue light that widened with the yawning of the doors.

"I do believe we're underdressed for the occasion," Quin remarked, and started buttoning his coat.

Naia held her cloak closed against the searing chill that invaded the shrine's outer door. "What's the occasion?" she asked, shivering.

"Winter." Quin didn't appear particularly happy about it.

"What were you expecting?"

"Not winter." Quin jumped down off the marble foundation of the shrine, turning back to offer Naia a hand.

She landed in the snow and staggered a few steps, making crunching noises with her boots. She glanced around at a world clad all in white, pristine and radiant. The ground was covered in freshly fallen snow, the trees frosted with ice that shimmered beneath a cold sun. The air was crisp and deadly cold.

Naia's breath made a misty cloud before her face. She glanced at Quin in alarm.

"Have you ever been here before? Is this normal for this time of year?"

"No," he responded, glancing around with a concerned expression. "Only Harbingers were ever allowed here, even in my day. The entire island was off-limits."

Naia said, "I've never met a Harbinger before."

"Then you're not alone. No one but Harbingers meet other Harbingers. They've always been a secretive lot."

Snow frosted the landscape, unmarred by bird or animal tracks. A powdery field ranged away from them to the rolling mountains in the distance. A crystalline woodland bordered the foothills. Except for the small shrine behind them, there was little trace that civilization had ever existed here.

Naia listened to the great silence that surrounded them. "Where do we go?"

Quin didn't seem to know the answer to that. He stood with his hands on his hips, glancing nervously about. He worked his lips against his teeth.

"Athera's Crescent is somewhere high in the mountains. That's all I know."

His tone was dismal. Perhaps he was still grieving for his brother. Or perhaps their situation was far more dire than she'd feared. Naia stared at him, wondering if there was something he wasn't telling her.

She asked, "How much food do we have?"

"It's not food I'm concerned about." He turned slowly as he surveyed the stark landscape around them. "Something's not right. Don't you feel it?"

She did. Something was *off*. That's the best word she could think of to describe it. Like a bite of food that had just turned; that's what the world was like here. Not fresh. But not tainted, either. Just *off*.

"I think so," she whispered. "Do you see a road?"

"No." Quin shook his head. "But I bet it's over there."

He gestured across the snow-fed meadow to an archway half-buried in the distance. Naia agreed; the arch looked like a gateway to something.

"Let's go."

She started across the meadow, her feet crunching through the top layer of snow. Quin came along at her side, arms wrapped around himself, looking thoroughly miserable.

A wind kicked up, chilling them all the more. The sky didn't seem quite as bright as it had just a minute before. Naia couldn't see the sun through the gray haze that closed in over them, but she had the feeling that the day was winding down. Night would soon be following. Which was a daunting prospect, considering how cold it was already.

"We need to find shelter," she complained.

Quin nodded but didn't say anything. He seemed focused on where he was walking. They trudged on through murky grayness that smothered like a blanket. They found a straight path that ran along the edge of a wood that seemed grown from crystal.

Up ahead, there was an orb of diffuse, golden light.

"What's that?" Naia asked.

"Looks like a lamp." Quin frowned at the pallid glow that filtered toward them through the haze.

"What's a lamp doing all the way out here?"

He shrugged noncommittally as Naia tried to make sense of it. They were both shivering, and the cold was only getting colder. Naia's toes and fingers were already numb. They would have to find shelter soon.

They arrived at the base of a lamppost that stuck out of the snow. Its presence there was bizarre; utterly out of place. There was nothing else around. Nevertheless, it glowed with a defiant flame, its glass murky.

"Someone had to light it," she said.

"Not necessarily."

She didn't like the expression on Quin's face. He was considering the lamppost with a look of anxious dread. Whatever it was that was *off* about this place was sinister enough to frighten even a darkmage. Which made Naia doubly afraid.

She glanced back at the crystalline wood then turned back to the path ahead.

Then she turned and looked again.

"Is that…?"

She raised a trembling finger, pointing at a shadow set amidst the ice-frosted trees.

"A cottage," Quin agreed. He took a reluctant step toward it.

"Maybe whoever lives there will put us up for the night," Naia said hopefully, starting after him.

"And maybe they appreciate their solitude." Quin caught her arm, forcing her to stop.

Naia looked at him, torn. "Are we going to find out? Or shall we just stand here until we freeze to death?"

"I suggest a more cautious approach. Why don't you wait here while I go check it out?"

"No." Naia shook her head. "We go together. We're stronger together than we are apart."

Quin gave her an appraising look. "Are we? You freed yourself from the chain on your wrist. But did you also cast aside the indoctrination? In other words, are you comfortable killing someone if that's what it takes to survive?"

Naia looked at him through the mist of her breath. He was staring at her, face implacable, arms folded in front of him. Waiting for an answer.

"If that's what it takes," she agreed finally. She'd taken a life once already. And she knew she could do so again, if the situation called for it.

Quin seemed mollified. "Good. But I'm still going first. Count to twenty then follow me. At the first sign of any trouble, don't wait. Just run."

Naia nodded as a creeping white fog stole over them. Quin turned and walked into the thickening mist and was quickly shrouded from sight. The fog swallowed him whole, just as it gobbled up the rest of the world. Naia could see nothing but ubiquitous, unrelieved white. She heard his footsteps moving away from her, the sounds seeming more distant than they should.

She waited in the wan yellow glow of lamplight, counting, "One. Two. Three…" The lamp itself made the slightest hissing noise, almost inaudible, like the final gasp from a dying throat.

On twenty, Naia started after him. Her feet crunched on crispy snow that yielded beneath her weight, the noise strangely muffled by the fog. She couldn't see the cottage up ahead, so she walked to where she imagined it would be. When the wooden planks of steps appeared in front of her, she felt relieved.

Across a porch made of roughly-hewn boards, the cottage door was cracked open already. Naia pushed it open the rest of the way and slipped within. The interior was musty and dark. It had a dusty, abandoned feel. The floorboards creaked beneath her weight. The chill of winter lingered even here inside the cabin. The cold was relentless, going on forever.

Naia glanced around and saw Quin standing in a liquid pool of magelight. There was no one else in the one-room hovel. Only a bed and a table with a bench. A cupboard stuffed with plates and bowls was shoved into a corner. But no people.

A lantern sat on the table, uncorrupted by rust. Quin lit the wick with the power of his mind. By its faltering glow, he started rifling through the cupboard. He stooped down, leaning far into the cabinet as Naia approached behind, surveying the goings-on.

"Is there food?"

"A little," he said, shutting the doors and rising to his feet. He turned around, scanning the stark confines of the room. "Not much. Unless it's stored somewhere else." He walked over to the bed and picked up what looked like a nightshirt, holding it up in front of his face. The covers had been tidied, a patterned coverlet folded neatly at the foot. Naia ran a hand over the linen sheets. The straw of the mattress was fresh, not mildewed.

"Whoever lived here left in a hurry. They left everything behind." He tossed the nightshirt down in the corner.

"How long ago?" Naia asked. The cottage looked like it was dozing, waiting for its family to return home. Plates and cups were set out on the table beneath a thin layer of dust.

Quin took his glove off and ran his finger along the surface of a shelf beside the bed. He held it up before his face, rubbing the dust off with his thumb.

"A couple years, I'd say."

A spot of color caught Naia's attention. Bending down, she retrieved a comb from off the floor. It was made of bone and painted red. Long blonde hairs wove between the teeth.

"I wonder what happened," she whispered, setting the comb down on the table.

Quin moved behind the bed, inspecting the far corner. There, he hunkered down, prodding at something on the floor. With a grunt, he wedged open a door built right into the floorboards, exposing a flight of rickety steps leading down beneath the cottage.

Naia moved quickly to his side, bending over to see where the steps led.

"What do you see?" Quin asked.

"A root cellar, I think," she said, taking a step down.

"Stop. Let me go first," he insisted, moving around the opening in the floor. "I'm far more dark and rotten than anything that could possibly be lurking down there."

Naia didn't argue. She withdrew, letting him go ahead down the steps, following right behind. The stairs creaked and grumbled under her weight. Quin's magelight erupted into view like hot magma spilling down. He stepped off the last stair onto the straw-strewn floor of the cellar. Drawing to a halt, he raised his hand.

It was the look on his face, more than the gesture, that stopped her short. Naia turned slowly in the direction he was looking, toward the far wall of the cellar.

Two corpses sat frozen in the corner.

Naia gasped. Not because they were dead; that didn't bother her. What bothered her was *how* they had died. The agony frozen on their faces was horrific.

Naia moved past Quin, her mind already working. She knew that muscles relaxed upon death. Sometimes rigor mortis would produce facial expressions that were disturbing, but that was transient. Nothing like this. These people had died in agony and had frozen that way. The terror of their final moments was perfectly captured, perfectly preserved, never-ending.

A man and a woman, curled up in the corner, clutched tight in each other's arms. The man's hand was raised before his face, as if warding something off. His other arm cradled the woman against his chest. Her mouth looked stretched, her scream silent and eternal.

There were chains on both their wrists.

Naia turned away, filled with a bone-numbing sadness. She was used to the dead. There were times she preferred them to the living. But this was not such a case. Something awful had occurred here. Something hideous.

"What happened to them?" Quin asked, bending down to take a closer look at the dead man's face. His magelight cast his shadow on the wall, long and distorted in the blood-red light.

"Hard to say," Naia whispered. "I will need to examine them."

With his help, they laid the stiffened cadavers out on the cellar's earthen floor. She knelt over them, first the man, then the woman. Unbuttoning shirts, probing tissues with her mind and fingertips. There was no physical damage that she could find; all their vital organs were intact, just frozen.

Only their brains had melted.

Melted was the right word for it, she felt certain. It was as if their heads had been heated until everything inside had turned to liquid.

She tried pushing the man's up-thrust arm back down to his side, but it refused to budge. She knew some tricks that would tame an uncooperative limb, but she was hesitant to use them. These corpses were not destined for the hereafter. She left the arm as it was and stood up, dusting off her skirt.

She said, "I can only guess it was some type of regional surge of the magic field. What's strange is, the decomposition is not nearly as progressed as it should be. It's as if they've been frozen here since death."

"Maybe they have been," Quin said.

Naia frowned. "That doesn't make any sense. They must have died years ago. They would have thawed out over the summers."

"Unless summer never came." Quin rubbed the back of his neck, his gaunt face shadowed in thought.

Naia gazed at him, mouth open. "Are you saying the winter never lifted?"

"Look around." Quin spread his hands. "It's supposed to be the middle of spring. I don't see any signs of it. No thaw. No birds. No animals. It's still the depths of winter here."

Naia had to agree. Even here, this far to the south, spring

should have taken hold by now. But the trees were still clad in white, the snow still fresh upon the ground. He was right; spring had never come to the island.

"How is that possible?"

Quin shrugged. "I don't know. How is it possible that Malikar has no sunlight?"

"That's different, though."

"Not if they're related."

Naia supposed she'd have to give some thought to that. As Quin moved off into a corner of the cellar, she turned back to the corpses on the ground. She wished she could do something about the faces. She supposed she could. Kneeling down beside them, she rested her palm against the ghastly face of the woman. She reached out with her mind and massaged the tissues into submission. She closed their eyes, eased their gaping jaws, smoothed dead lips over teeth. With a little effort of will, she returned the man's outstretched arm back to his side.

Then she left them to each other.

Quin rose from the corner of the cellar, arms laden with roots. From somewhere, he managed to work up a half-hearted grin. "At least these tubers are still good."

Naia nodded without speaking.

"I'm in the mood for curried yams," he called over his shoulder. "What about you?"

The meal was enjoyable, despite Naia's reservations. The tubers, like the corpses, hadn't gone to everlasting rot. She was even starting to grow accustomed to Quin's peculiar style of cooking. The spices he used were good at disguising ingredients that had lasted long past their time.

After supper, Quin grew quiet, his face going solemn. He raked out the ashes in the hearth and built a fire without a word. Naia stretched out, basking in warmth and savoring the scent of wood smoke. Quin sat at the table, gazing at the lantern's glass chimney, hands clasped on the splintery wood. She thought she knew what was troubling him. It was troubling her, too.

Naia got up from the floor and moved to sit beside him on the bench. When he turned to look at her, she said, "I'm sorry about your brother. I can't imagine what you must feel. I wish I could do more."

Quin bowed his head.

"Braden's dead," he said simply. "Just like we'll all be soon." He shrugged. "He actually has it better than the rest of us. He'll never have to face the repercussions of what he brought about. I suppose I spared him that."

"*You* spared him?"

Quin nodded, grimacing. The lines around his eyes looked like furrows in a droughted field. "The artifact they used to execute him was my own creation. A medallion I called the Soulstone. I didn't create it with that purpose in mind...but nevertheless..." He rose from the table and crossed the floor toward the hearth. He settled down there next to the fire, kicking off his shoes.

"You can have the bed," he said, then said no more.

Naia reached into the pocket of her cloak, fingering the medallion on its silver band. Her mind and heart spun slowly in dizzying circles.

Naia awoke to the sound of shifting dirt.

She pushed the covers off, scrambling into her shoes and fastening her cloak. She paused long enough to look around the empty cabin. There was no sign of Quin. Only a constant scraping coming from outside. She moved to the door and, opening it, walked out into a heavy white mist that clung like sorrow over the woodland. The silence of the forest was expansive. Another grating noise came from behind her.

She turned to find Quin standing over two dark graves that looked to have been ripped right out of the snow, patting at a mound of wet earth with the blade of a shovel. He wiped his brow and looked up at her, thrusting the shovel into the ground.

Naia moved to stand beside him, staring down at the freshly-turned soil. The two graves made her feel almost heartbroken. But the sight of Quin disturbed her more. He had arisen well before dawn to care for the deceased. She had neglected her duty, so he'd done her work for her. Apparently, the demon had managed to scrounge up more compassion for the dead than she'd been able to herself.

He turned toward her with eyes darkened by remorse. He even had the courtesy to remove his hat. "You're the priestess. Why don't you say some words?"

Naia bowed her head, thinking herself unqualified. Nevertheless, she closed her eyes and raised her hands, palms spread as if beseeching. "May these souls know the peace and blessings of the goddess." It was a simple prayer said over simple graves. She opened her eyes and gazed down at the black scars in the snow.

"That's it?" Quin said. "I was expecting something a bit more profound."

Already moving away, Naia said, "I'm not a priestess anymore. And, even if I were, my temple would never condone planting the dead in the ground. There is no prayer for such a burial."

The darkmage looked perplexed. He tugged on his hat and wrenched the shovel out of the ground. "Why bother with the Catacombs? I've never understood that. My people always just covered our dead in a pile of dirt. Then they used the occasion as an excuse to drink and fuck."

"That sounds like a pagan custom," she said dismissively, ignoring his language. Such a practice sounded blasphemous. "Such burials were never endorsed by the temple, not even a thousand years ago. The Catacombs are necessary because we believe in the resurrection of the dead at the end of times. It is our temple's sacred duty to preserve the remains of those who are worthy."

That got his attention. "What resurrection? How?"

Naia shrugged, knowing that she'd said too much already. "It is one of the most holy mysteries. The Book of the Dead says only that we must prepare. It does not specify why."

Quin's lips curled into a sneer. "Sounds like a load of mystic horseshit to me."

Naia frowned at him. "Just because it hasn't happened yet

doesn't mean it's not going to."

"Well, let's hope it doesn't happen today. We have a very long road ahead of us." He snatched the shovel up and pitched it away from him. It speared into the snow, quivering at an angle.

They returned to the cottage and salvaged what they could. Blankets and warmer clothes were high on Naia's list. She found a wool coat that had once belonged to the dead woman. Quin provisioned himself with a scarf and mittens, along with fur-lined boots only slightly too big for his feet. They filled their packs with provisions from the cupboards and the root cellar.

Then they started out toward the mountains, which seemed to loom much larger than they had the previous day. They walked a straight path, keeping the ice-clad forest to their right. The fog eventually burned off, the sky turning a fierce azure blue, but the sun burned cold. The isle clung tenaciously to its winter cloak, refusing to yield.

A breeze blew through the branches overhead, which swayed and crackled, showering ice crystals all around. Naia glanced at Quin. He shook the ice off his hat and squared his shoulders under his pack. A gray fog rolled in.

They walked for hours in a world silenced by gloom and powdered by white. Eventually, they reached another forlorn lamppost surrounded by a yellowed glow of light. Naia reached out, running her hand down its frozen surface, wondering at its murky glow.

"Please say it's not just me who finds this curious?" she said to Quin. "We're on an island where everything is either frozen or dead. So who's left to employ a lamplighter?"

Quin gazed up at the mysterious fixture. He raised a gloved hand to his face, rubbing his eyes wearily. "Well, now that you mention it, yes, it is curious. But I'm not gullible enough to believe that these lamps are tended by anything other than magic."

With that, the lamp guttered and went out. Then it sprang back to life.

"They're artifacts," he explained. "No tending required. They sense the gloom and react accordingly. It's magelight. Not lamplight."

Naia saw it now, the subtle difference in the quality of the light. He was right; the lamp was artificial, manufactured. He was further correct in labeling her gullible. She felt chagrinned.

"This lamppost is here for a reason," Quin said. "It's a marker. I think we should turn this way."

He scraped at the snow with his boot, exposing a path that wandered away in the direction of the mountains. Naia hadn't realized they'd walked all the way across the valley and were now so near the foothills. Towering cliffs rose before them in granite majesty, cloaked in frost and crowned by fog.

They started down a path through a grove of white-barked trees that grew in perfect rows, casting long shadows at odd angles across the snow. At last they came to a wall of precipitous cliffs. The trail they followed led toward a split in the rock face, more like a deep crack than anything else. A narrow stair led up into the crack, continuing upward hundreds of steps before disappearing in the fog.

Another lamppost marked the entrance to the jagged stair.

Quin looked at Naia and gestured at the marker. "It appears we're supposed to climb."

And climb they did. The stairs were steep and unforgiving, rising with the mountainside as the walls of the crack narrowed overhead, becoming more like a chimney. The smell of wet rock and mold lingered heavy in the air. Naia let Quin toil ahead of her, his back bent under the weight of his pack. She placed her feet carefully, nervous about her footing. The stairs were, in places, slick with ice.

Naia slipped and caught herself with her hands. Fortunately, she didn't tumble down the mountainside. In a short span of time, the stairs were proving themselves the enemy she'd feared. Her knees ached, her lungs burned, and her back strained under the weight she carried. Still, the stairs continued relentlessly.

Ahead of her, Quin stopped and cast his pack down at his side. He planted his rear on the step ahead of her. He was breathing hard, his face flushed and beaded with sweat.

"Time to eat," he announced.

They ate right there on the steps. Above, a frozen waterfall glistened in the shadows, made of thousands of slender icicles. When they finally started moving again, the stair seemed somehow more precipitous. More fog drew over them, darker and colder than the last.

"How much longer, do you think?" Naia asked, shivering.

"I don't know." Quin sighed, gazing upward with a hand on his hat.

The stairs eventually had an end. They came at last to a place where the crack in the mountain twisted around then finally wore itself out. They had reached the top of the monolith. Ahead was a sprawling display of rolling white peaks that tumbled into the distance. An imposing castle loomed before them on the crest of a hill, rich walls reflecting the sun's rays. Light spilled from dozens of windows with a promise of welcome and warmth.

Naia felt a surge of relief upon sensing the end of their journey. She rushed toward the castle's drawbridge, but was jerked immediately to a halt by Quin. She whirled around, trying to pry her arm out of his iron grasp.

"Stop!" he rasped, his face sterner than she'd ever seen it. "Something's wrong. This isn't right!"

He wrenched her back behind him.

"What is it?" Naia peered around him at the castle, not seeing any reason to be afraid. Then, slowly, she understood what he meant. Her jaw dropped. She stared up the limestone walls in shock.

Unlike everything else around them, the castle was not caught in the perpetual throes of winter. It stood in a bright patch of sunlight, banners rippling in the air, its walls shining and pristine. As if winter's grip had never touched it.

"It's new…" Naia gasped.

"The castle is very old," corrected a low voice from behind them.

Naia whirled to confront a woman who looked like no other person she'd ever met in her life. A woman of skin surpassingly dark, her lips painted with a golden sheen. A series of white dots arched across her brow. She wore a blue turban with a large stone set in the middle of her forehead.

"My name is Tsula, daughter of Mundi," she said in a thickly accented voice. "Master of the Third Tier of the Lyceum of Bryn Calazar."

Quin winced, staring at the woman with an expression of incredulity. "That's not possible," he gasped. "The Lyceum was destroyed a thousand years ago. Even if everything here's frozen in time, it hasn't been frozen that long."

The woman turned and considered Quin with dead-cold eyes. "I am not frozen, Grand Master Quinlan Reis. I am, most fortunately, *thawed.*"

Chapter Nineteen
A Man of Wrath

Kajiri Flats, The Front

D arien rose and dressed in the musky warmth of Myria's tent. He pulled the mail coat on over his clothes and hung his small arsenal of weapons from his belt. The hauberk was heavy to wear, dragging at his shoulders. He felt sluggish beneath all that chain. He worked his arms back and forth, getting used to the feel of it. He glanced back over his shoulder.

Myria lay where he'd left her, the steady sounds of her breathing whispering through the quiet. The dark drape of her hair spilled like a waterfall over the covers. One of her slender fingers twitched in her sleep. He didn't bother waking her. He had nothing to say.

Tugging the helm down over his head, he left the tent, stepping out into darkness. He trudged through the camp past clusters of men going on about the business of warfare: stoking cookfires, sharpening weapons, fletching arrows with dried willow leaves. No one paid him any mind; there was no reason for them to.

He found his way to the command tent, looking for Sayeed. The encampment was enormous, like a vast, sprawling city, and he had no idea how to navigate it. He didn't even know where to find his own tent or his wife.

His *wife*. Just the word in his head made his lips twist into a scowl. He felt affection for Azár, but that was all. He admired her; she was clever and independent. She had summoned him from the dead, but that was the extent of her power over him. It was too bad; Meiran had cauterized his capacity to feel.

He thought of Arden and Meiran, two women with voracious

appetites for causing pain.

And then there was Myria, who sated his lust without requiring intimacy. She'd been accommodating to his particular needs, which was all he could ask. He'd done his best not to leave her wanting.

He found Sayeed and his retinue of Zakai resting in the lee of the command tent. They didn't see him coming, or at least didn't recognize him. A couple of officers glanced up casually, taking note of his passage, before glancing away. It was Sayeed who finally identified him, frowning at Darien's warbelt until recognition finally dawned on his face. His look of surprise was quickly replaced by a look of fury.

He surged to his feet, every movement sharpened by anger.

"Where have you been?"

The other Zakai followed him to their feet, confusion rampant on their faces. Darien removed the helm and slipped past Sayeed into the tent. The officer followed him in, lowering his voice as he whispered:

"How are we supposed to keep you safe if you elude our protection?"

Darien turned to fix the man with a sidelong glare, not liking his tone. "I had my reasons."

But Sayeed refused to be intimidated. He drew himself up, one hand on the hilt of his sword, returning Darien's glare right back at him. "I do not care what you do—or who you do it with—as long as it does not compromise your safety. But I must insist, *Lord,* in the future, that you trust our protection. And our discretion."

Darien shook his head, frustrated and furious. "Just get me to my tent."

But a voice from behind him stopped him short. "That didn't take very long. Myria must be losing her touch."

He turned to find Byron Connel standing in the gap between partitions. Darien felt his blood sour to vinegar in his veins. The man clapped him on the arm, amusement brightening his eyes. "I've got a favor to ask of you."

Darien wasn't in the mood for favors. "What is it?"

Connel laid a hand on his shoulder, steering him back into the dim interior of the tent. "I need you to scribe a note for me."

"What kind of note?"

"An invitation. To your old friends."

Darien's eyes narrowed, but he forced himself to keep walking anyway.

The note didn't take long to write. But it took a lot out of him, a lot more than he'd ever thought it would. Considering whose hands that scroll would eventually end up, Darien was starting to feel more and more like a traitor. It wasn't a feeling he was comfortable with.

He'd seen this day coming; from the very beginning, it had been inevitable. But that didn't mean he had to feel good about his part in it, or good about himself. He knew exactly what he was, had no delusions about it. He was not a man of honor. He was a man of wrath.

He indulged himself in a brooding melancholy as Sayeed and his men led him back through the encampment. He said nothing the entire way. Neither was a word spoken to him; the officers were still angry at him for slipping away. As he walked, Darien took careful note of the camp's landmarks, taking a survey of banners and numbers. It was quite an assortment of people they'd gathered, most not even regular military. A mixture of men and women, city folk and common villagers. There were small, dirty children running about the camp, laboring at chores just as hard as the adults. It was a sight unlike anything he'd ever seen before. A hard sight.

What surprised him most was the odor of the place. It didn't smell like any encampment he'd ever been in; there was no reek of filth or human waste. Wherever they'd dug the latrine pits, they were well away from the heart of the camp and well-tended. The efficiency and discipline of these people never ceased to impress him.

Sayeed led him to a large tent raised slightly apart from the rest of the camp, flying the blood-red standards of the Tanisar corps.

Darien removed his boots and stepped within, glancing around the dim interior. The space looked comfortable, even opulent, lit by hanging lanterns and oil lamps, the floor carpeted, the walls paneled with cloth. There was even furniture: a low table surrounded by seats and, behind a half-drawn partition, an over-stuffed bed. The posts of the tent were wrapped in spiraling ribbons, creating a chaotic splendor of color.

He moved further into the space, drawn toward the bed's promise of comfort. In the dim light of the lanterns, Darien undressed and crawled beneath the covers. He extinguished the lanterns with a thought and closed his eyes, letting complete darkness settle in.

A rustling sound made him start.

The mattress shifted as Azár lay down alongside him, her body naked and pressing close against his.

Darien froze, unsure of what to do. Never once had he ever shared a bed with his wife, nor anything more than just a kiss. Her hand stroked his shoulder, sliding down his arm. He closed his eyes and suffered the feel of it.

"I lay with Myria," he said.

The hand stopped moving.

"Good."

That wasn't the answer he'd been expecting. On the floor, magelight bloomed and spread in glowing azure pools, running over the carpets like a blazing stream. Darien rolled over, taking in Azár's face in the writhing blue light. He gazed at her steadily, contemplating her non-expression, feeling dread sink deep into his heart.

He sighed. "I think you need your own tent."

"No." She shook her head. "That is not the answer."

"Then what is?"

She gazed at him with that same, indifferent stare that yielded nothing.

"We must build trust between the two of us," she said at last. "We are alike, you and I. We have both been hurt, and are both afraid of pain. But we will be needing each other very much, very soon. And we do not have much time."

She was right. About all of it. Only, he had no idea where to begin. "So, what do you propose?"

Her stare ticked upward toward the patterned roof of the tent. Her soft fingertips brushed his skin.

"Kiss me, Darien."

A cold weight gripped his chest. He couldn't move.

So she kissed him, instead. Slowly at first, her fingertips tracing the whiskered line of his jaw. He closed his eyes, his muscles going tense. The kiss became deeper, more adamant. Her hair fell forward, filling his nostrils with the fresh scent of her. He could feel her soft skin pressed against his.

She pulled back. "Is this affecting you?"

"Aye," he admitted. "But probably not in the way you'd like." His body was stirring, awakening, very aware of her presence and disposition. He was reminded of Myria's practiced touch.

Azár gazed down at him, her disappointment evident. He couldn't blame her; she deserved more. Far more.

"Hold me." Resigned, she collapsed against him.

He couldn't deny her. He wrapped his arms around her and drew her close. She lay there cradled against his chest, staring straight ahead into nothing. She felt so small, so fragile in his arms. He wondered how she could possibly survive the firestorm that was surely coming.

Then he remembered that she wouldn't.

The Reversal was coming. And there was nothing he could do to stop it.

Something inside Darien clicked. Deep down inside, that realization brought about a subtle but significant change.

He held her tighter.

He pressed a kiss against her hair then closed his eyes, letting the magelight fade softly into darkness.

Chapter Twenty
Rabid

Pass of Lor-Gamorth, The Front

Raindrops splattered the stone pavement as thunder rumbled overhead. The musty smell of rain and wet masonry lay heavy on the air. It was cold. Kyel rubbed his aching fingers, trying to work some heat back into them. The continual darkness was already miserable enough; the damp weather made it intolerable. Rain soaked his cloak, streamed down his face. He paid little heed to the groups of roving soldiers that patrolled the fortress, backs stooped, necks bent under the oppressive weight of the endless gloom. It was stretching too long. It was starting to wear on all of them.

He looked to Cadmus and Meiran, who were standing by his side. He caught just a glimpse of Meiran's face beneath the shadows of her cowl. She looked pale. To Kyel, she'd seemed frail of late. Perhaps he'd done of poor job of burning the poisons from her system. Or perhaps it was something else, the threat of war taking its toll. He didn't know. She was quiet, quieter than she'd ever been. She barely spoke to him of late, and when she did, her tone was usually biting.

A stab of lightning glared white off the stones of the tower as a rumble of thunder rattled his bones. Kyel ducked through the tower's entrance, waiting for Meiran, then made his way in silence as he blinked away the after-glow. By the time they reached Craig's quarters, only a few motes still danced across his vision. That strike had been close. He could still smell the sharp stench of charged air.

Meiran reached up and rapped hard on the force commander's

door. The door clanked and then groaned, shivering open. Kyel moved in and glanced around, noticing the table in the far corner with its scattered maps and haphazard trinkets. A melted candle with pearls of wax leaking down its sides provided meager light.

Commander Craig beckoned them in, shutting the door behind them.

"What is it?" Meiran asked, drawing back her cowl as she moved deeper into the room.

Craig raised his hand, offering out a scroll. Kyel saw that the wax seal had already been broken. "Our presence is requested at a parley tomorrow," Craig said. "It's signed by Darien."

Meiran took the scroll from his hand, unfurling it slowly, as if wary it would bite. Her eyes scanned over the page, her expression darkening. "It's his signature," she confirmed, handing it back.

"I know." Craig tossed the summons down on the table, peering deeply into Meiran's face. "Are you sure you're up for this?"

Meiran locked eyes on him. Her pale, smooth features tightened like a compressed spring. "Yes. Whatever it takes." Her voice was dull like lead.

"No second thoughts?"

"None."

Kyel glanced back and forth between the two of them, an unsettling feeling of trepidation creeping under his skin. He didn't like where this was going, what this was coming to. He was starting to wonder if they would even give Darien a chance to negotiate.

Craig cast a piercing look at Cadmus. "What about your part?"

The cleric squared his shoulders, clasping his pudgy hands in front of him. "I've summoned a priest to assist us. He should be arriving sometime in the night."

Kyel frowned. A priest? What need had they of a priest? Surely they could use a blessing, but this seemed extreme. Unless they were preparing for annihilation. Even then, a clerical blessing wouldn't matter much. But Craig just nodded, distilling this new information with a glower. He turned to Kyel.

"I want you with us tomorrow," he said. "You know him best."

Kyel shook his head, moving away from Craig toward the wall. He turned around, leaning with his back up against the uneven stones, crossing his arms. "That would be Meiran, not me. I don't know him at all anymore."

Craig disagreed. "You were there with him at the end. You watched him turn."

"Meiran met with him," Kyel argued. "Of all of us, she knows him best—"

"That's not the same," Meiran insisted, moving forward. She clasped Kyel's hand, gazing intently into his eyes. "He only showed me what he *wanted* me to see. But you actually know him, Kyel, the way he is now. Better than any of us."

Kyel supposed she might be right. He drew in a deep breath and let it out slowly with a shrug. "I suppose I could..."

Craig nodded. "Report to the armory. Get yourself fitted with some gear. You're the only Sentinel we have, and we'll be needing you alive."

Kyel started across the floor but paused and glanced back. He saw that neither Meiran nor Cadmus were following him toward the door. They stood paused by the map table, watching him go. Seeing the looks on their faces, he had a strangling feeling. Like he was being purposefully sent away.

Darien had sent him away, too. To protect him.

This didn't feel anything like that.

He could still feel their eyes on his back as he pulled the door closed behind him.

He walked across the courtyard to the armory, where he procured a padded gambeson. The armorers had him try it on right there in front of them to make sure it fit. He left the armory and found his way to his own quarters, ignoring the pointed stares that followed him everywhere he went.

That night, he had a hard time sleeping. The rain rattled the roof above his bed, splattering and clawing at the window. The door leaked something fierce; cold air whistled under it as the wind ripped and howled through the corridors outside. The small fire in the hearth fed little warmth into the place. The wind chased the heat away as quickly as it was made.

Kyel tossed and turned on his straw-stuffed mattress. All night long, his dreams eluded him. He finally fell asleep sometime very late, or perhaps very early; he couldn't tell. He woke up cold and sad and more than a little bit afraid.

He sat up on the edge of the bed, running his hands through his hair. Perspiration beaded on his brow even though he sat shivering. He raked at the sweat with his cloak, shaking his head to clear his thoughts. It didn't make sense. He didn't understand what he was feeling. Or whether he should trust it.

The pavilion had been raised on the rise of a low hill, against the backdrop of Orguleth's bell-shaped dome. Kyel checked his horse, drawing back on the reins. The gelding snorted and stamped, nervous about being so far from home. At his side, Craig sat astride a brown destrier, a white cloth held in his chain-gloved hand. Meiran rode alongside the priest summoned by Cadmus. The priest had been introduced to Kyel as Brother Desco, a quiet and oily man whose stare tended to linger in one spot far longer than was appropriate. He'd arrived late in the night with a supply caravan up from Wolden. Kyel wasn't even certain which temple Brother Desco was ordained to. He'd taken an instant dislike to the man.

Ahead, armored figures emerged from the pavilion.

Kyel remained on his horse as a group of mailed soldiers approached their position. They all wore helms, so he couldn't make out faces. It took him a moment to realize that the approaching party carried no weapons. Craig raised his arm, holding up the white fabric in his hand for all to see. The Enemy soldiers halted in front of them, helmed faces regarding them. Then their ranks opened, parting fluidly.

A lone man moved forward through the tight press of armor and bodies.

Kyel felt his face go slack as he recognized who it was. Cold ice encaged his heart, numbing his limbs until all he could do was sit his horse and stare.

Darien Lauchlin strode toward them with a dangerous grace, his face cold and terrifying. He was garbed all in black, in a style as foreign as his features. He was surrounded by the same cloak of confidence Kyel remembered so well.

Darien's gaze locked on Meiran and stuck there.

Kyel swallowed, unable to move. Unable to react. He shot a sidelong glance at Craig, seeking reassurance. But the look on the commander's face was anything but reassuring. Kyel reached within, latching on to the magic field. He drew at it slowly, taking comfort in its feel.

Darien stopped in front of them, his eyes moving from Meiran to Kyel to Craig.

"Thank you for coming," he said.

His voice was not harsh. The familiar sound of it startled Kyel from his thoughts, sent his head roiling in a turbulent mixture of emotions. It took him instantly back. Back to his pledge to Darien in the pass, back to his trial in the vortex, back to the sinister chamber that housed the Well of Tears. He remembered the master who had never doubted him, not even once. Darien had always trusted him, even when he couldn't trust himself.

He stared hard at the demon standing before him, and felt afraid.

Darien Lauchlin turned to Craig. "I have nothing to say to Meiran. I'll speak with you and Kyel alone. No one else." He cast a significant glare at the priest, who favored him with a slight nod, as if from one adversary to another.

Craig sat frozen on his horse, arm still holding the long strip of white cloth. At last, he gave the slightest nod. "Very well."

He draped the banner over his saddle and swung down from his horse's back. He turned to Meiran and the priest as Kyel followed him to the ground. "Wait here. This won't take long."

Kyel wasn't sure he believed that. Looking at that dark pavilion, he rather thought it had been erected for a purpose far more substantial than a minutes-long dialogue. He considered the small retinue of black-mailed guards, uncertain that he trusted them.

Then he looked at Darien, not certain he trusted him, either.

A bleak feeling crawled under Kyel's skin. This could be a trap, he realized. By the look on Craig's face, he could tell the commander had arrived at that thought ahead of him.

Darien turned, gesturing for them to follow as he showed them his back and strode toward the tent. Kyel followed him through the guard of plate-mailed bodies, his eyes trained on the sway of Darien's cloak. The mage's hair was longer, the cloak different, the whiskers on his face overgrown. But there was no mistaking that graceful confidence the man projected with every stride. It was Darien's signature.

He held open the flap of the tent, allowing them to enter. Once inside, Kyel stood still, letting his eyes adjust to the dimness of the interior. The pavilion was lit by a subtle amber light, the glow of lanterns set about on a floor draped with rugs. There were a few cushions thrown down for them to sit on; that was all. Save for the shadows, the tent was empty.

Darien sat cross-legged in the center of the room, resting his arms upon his knees. Kyel took one of the cushions across from him, seating himself awkwardly. Craig sat down beside him, adjusting and readjusting his posture several times. He looked patently uncomfortable.

At last, Darien nodded at Kyel. "It's good to see you. How have you been?"

His voice was rich and warm, exactly as Kyel remembered it.

"As well as can be expected," he managed, unsure of what to say. He didn't trust the man in front of him. Darien didn't look like a demon, like the monster Meiran had described. But neither did he look like himself. He had changed. Calmer, steadier, more focused. Much more sure of himself. Yet, the shadows Kyel remembered still haunted his eyes.

"I'm thirsty," Craig said. "What have you got to drink?"

Darien spread his hands. The thick sleeves of his robe fell back to reveal a tangle of red scars on his wrists. Kyel remembered them well. The sight of them made him want to retch.

"I'm sorry," Darien said. "Among my people, it's considered inappropriate to share cups with our enemies."

Devlin Craig scoffed. *"Your people.* Are you serious?"

Darien's expression didn't change. He remained impassive, staring at Craig levelly. "I am very serious. This is the path I've chosen. These are my people now."

Craig scowled. He thrust a hand into his pocket and produced a metal flask. Removing the stopper, he took a healthy drink from it. He took his time about stoppering it back up again, setting it down carefully.

"What the hell are you doing?" he asked. "I see you sitting there with my own eyes, and I still can't believe it."

Darien stared at him for a lingering moment. Then he said very quietly, "I assume Meiran's told you about the Reversal of the magic field that is coming."

"That you *say* is coming, aye. She did." Craig's face conveyed his doubts. Kyel still wasn't sure whether or not he believed it.

"It *is* coming," Darien insisted. "And when it does come, every person living north of the Shadowspears is going to starve unless you let us in. I can't let that happen. Condemning an entire nation to death goes against every fiber of my conscience."

"You swore your soul to Xerys. Apparently that didn't go against the fibers of your conscience."

Darien only shrugged, casually dismissing the insult. "I did what I had to do. You've got Meiran back because of it. I have no regrets."

"Well, I have plenty. Starting with saving your life."

Darien glanced down, seeming to be taking a moment to collect himself. When he looked back up again, his face was full of resolve. "I asked you here because both of you were once my friends. I'm hoping that together we can forge a peace between our two nations before this escalates into something awful. I'm here to save lives, as many lives as I can. I don't want to spill one drop of blood that I don't have to."

Craig's eyes turned as hard as tempered steel. "I don't mind spilling blood."

The comment took Kyel aback. He didn't know why the man

was acting so unreasonably. He figured they should hear what Darien had come all this way to offer. Especially with so much at stake.

"There are over a million people in the Black Lands," Darien said evenly. "That's an awful lot of blood to have on your hands."

Craig just shrugged. "It won't be on my hands. We didn't blacken the skies over Caladorn. It was Renquist and the rest of your kind who chose to dance with the devil instead of doing the right thing. Renquist sold his people out. Why don't you go talk to him about blood."

"Renquist was trying to save civilization as we know it," Darien said. "Both our societies depend on a magical infrastructure that's still in place today. Our entire way of life is threatened by the Reversal. Someday soon, the world you wake to is going to be very different than the one you know today. And then it will be your problem to deal with."

Kyel thought about that, wondering if he was right. He'd seen it, the magical infrastructure Darien was referring to. The hot water in Rothscard's pipes, the city lanterns that looked so much like captive magelight. Aqueducts that shuttled water uphill. The way Cadmus could communicate with the High Priest even at a distance. The troves of knowledge in Om's libraries, the vast warren of the Catacombs. That was just the beginning, he knew. He envisioned a sprawling network of magically-enhanced technologies that were so taken for granted that most people weren't even aware of their existence.

"It sounds like we're going to have a lot of work on our hands," Craig said. "The last thing we'll need's a million more mouths to feed."

Darien leaned forward, his eyes intense. "Food isn't going to be the problem. The Rhen has enough arable land to go around. Cities like Rothscard and Auberdale are going to be the hardest hit when the infrastructure collapses. What you're going to need is a larger labor pool. We can provide that."

Craig sneered. "How do we know this Reversal's even real? That this isn't just some ploy to slip your forces past our defenses?"

Warily, Darien said, "My offer to Meiran still stands."

"And what offer is that?"

"I said I'd surrender myself to you as a guarantee of trust."

For the first time since the beginning of the conversation, Darien looked less than arrogant. He licked his lips, fidgeting with a flap of leather on his belt.

Craig glowered. "You want to bring a million people through my pass. It's going to take a hell of a lot more than that to gain my trust. If what you say is true, then you're running out of options. I'd say it's time to start discussing the terms of your unconditional surrender."

Darien's eyes hardened. He looked suddenly very much like a demon. "Believe me: we are far from out of options. Our legions outnumber your own, and our Battlemages can stop your hearts and level your walls. And then there's the very simple fact that every member of our population will fight to the death *because that's all they've got left.*"

Craig stared at him, unblinking.

When he didn't respond, Darien went on, "We don't want a war. All we want is to survive."

"At our expense," snapped Craig. He blew out a sigh, glancing at Kyel. Kyel didn't know what to say. He understood the very real danger in Darien's threats. He also understood the underlying plea for help. He wasn't sure Craig did.

"All right, Darien. Let's talk terms." The commander planted a finger on the rugs in front of him. "You want more than just safe passage. You want land and homes and the means of making ends meet. And all that's going to have to come from somewhere—so *where?* I don't know of any farmers eager to hand over their harvests to—."

Darien cut him off. "We need passage, Craig. Sooner. Not later. Before the light goes out and famine decides our fate for us. There's something you have to understand. We're coming, and there's nothing you can do to stop us. Either you let us in willingly, or we'll march right over your bones."

Craig took a slow sip from his flask. Then he stoppered it and set the container down at his side. "These are my terms. You want to end this without a fight? Then we demand nothing less than your unconditional surrender. You disarm and leave your armor and armaments behind. You submit yourselves to our rule of law. Every mage, commander, and senior officer becomes our prisoners of war. We'll let the rest of your population through the pass one fraction at a time. If there's any sign of treachery, we'll slit all your throats and seal the pass."

The more he talked, the darker Darien's expression became. He was shaking his head long before Craig came to the end of his demands. "You can't have every mage," he said. "Our Lightweavers are useless on a battlefield, and they're all condemned, besides. They'll not spend the rest of their lives in a Greystone dungeon. You can have me and Myria. But that's all."

"There's Eight Servants, Darien. You're offering us only two. That's not near enough."

Darien glared defiantly at Craig. "I told you. We're coming, one way or another. I offered myself and Myria as a token of trust. This is the last offer I make before I walk out of this tent and tell half a million men to burn you to the ground and grind your bones to dust."

Craig's eyes studied Darien's face without blinking. He reached for his flask and drained the last of its contents down his gullet. He set the container down hard, as if emphasizing a point.

He rose to his feet. "Tomorrow evening in the canyon," he said abruptly as Kyel and Darien rose after him. "You will formally surrender your arms, colors, and hostages. If I get one whiff of treachery, the deal's off."

Darien stared at him long and hard before finally nodding. He extended his hand.

Craig sealed the agreement with a handshake.

"I want to speak with Kyel," Darien said. "Alone."

Craig nodded his permission and ducked out of the tent.

Kyel turned to face his former master, finding the harshness gone from Darien's face. Suddenly, he looked just like the man Kyel used to know. For a moment, he was caught off-guard. He didn't know what to say.

Darien took a step toward him, real concern on his face. "Tell me truly. How've you been?"

Kyel almost answered him with the truth, but stopped himself short. The truth was unpleasant, and Darien already knew it anyway.

So he spread his hands in exasperation, demanding, "That's all you've got to say?"

Darien sighed, shaking his head. "What else can I say? I can't say I'm sorry, because I'm not. I can't say I wish things were different, because no amount of wishing will ever change anything. You'll be dead soon. And I'll be the one who killed you. That's a fact."

Kyel could see the pain of guilt in his eyes. This was not a monster, Kyel realized. Darien might be a demon, but he was not demonic.

"I'm the one who put on the Soulstone," Kyel reminded him. "You didn't force me to do it."

Something about what he said had an effect on Darien. A gloom settled over him. Reaching out, he placed a hand on Kyel's shoulder. "For whatever it's worth, I'm very proud of you," he said sincerely. Then he pulled back, looking away.

"Are you evil, Darien?"

The man paused. He glanced back at Kyel wearily. "My actions speak for themselves. I most certainly am evil. But my people are not. Don't confuse that distinction. The people of Malikar are not the Enemy."

"Then who is?"

Darien stared at him, eyes pleading. Pleading for what, Kyel couldn't fathom.

"We're the enemy," Darien said at last. "You, me, Meiran, Naia…us mages, with all our contemptible power. It's our power that makes us weak. It gnaws at us. Robs us of the strength of our humanity. Deep down inside, we're all just children playing with fire, thinking we can control it. Thinking we can contain it. We can't.

"I am sorry about one thing," he said as he turned away. "I'm sorry that I ever dragged you into any of this."

He left through the back of the pavilion, leaving Kyel feeling confused and melancholy. He hadn't realized how much he'd missed his former master. And now he felt even more conflicted than before. He understood Darien. He understood him better than he understood Craig.

He left the tent and made his way toward the horses picketed outside, his black cloak fluttering behind him. He kept his gaze lowered to the ground, refusing to look at Meiran even though he could feel her eyes on him. When he reached his horse, he released it from the tether and swung his leg up over the saddle. Then he kicked the beast forward, following on the heels of Craig's mount. The captain didn't stop until they were well away on the other side of the ridge. There, he drew up, swinging around.

"You're right," Craig said to Meiran. "They twisted him. They twisted him good. He's gone rabid."

Meiran nodded in agreement, her eyes filled with sorrow and understanding.

"What do we do?" Kyel asked.

Craig glanced down, his face darkening. "There's only one thing to be done with a rabid animal. We have to put him down."

Kyel looked away, feeling his gut wrench.

"You did good back there," Craig continued, nodding at Kyel. "It was the look on your face that gained his trust more than anything."

Kyel's eyes shot up, his heart staggering as he realized what the man was saying without actually saying it. He realized he'd been used.

From the back of his horse, Brother Desco cracked a festering grin.

Chapter Twenty-One
Harbinger of Destiny

Isle of Titherry, The Rhen

Quin awoke, shivering violently.

His eyelids snapped open to blue-black nothingness. It was cold. The kind of cold that seeped into the flesh, prickling like a thousand icy needles. He didn't know where the cold came from, only that it consumed him. He couldn't feel his hands, his feet, his fingers—like they didn't even belong to him. He wasn't in charge of them anymore. Someone else was shaking them, shaking *him*. He could feel his whole body trembling as if some invisible stranger were trying to jostle him awake.

"W-w-waa…do you w-want?"

The effort of forcing the words past his frozen lips was almost beyond him. His jaw was clattering so hard he almost couldn't understand himself. He bit his tongue trying to fight out the last syllable.

"You know what I want."

He recognized that voice. He'd heard it before. Many times, come to think of it. This wasn't the first time she'd been here. He'd denied her before, countless times. Countless denials. Before slipping back into numb nothingness. But something was different this time. There was an urgency in her voice that hadn't been there before, all the other times. He wondered why it was there now.

"I…c-can't…help you…"

His words stumbled over his shuddering jaw as his teeth tried to clatter their way into his brain. He blinked several times, finally succeeding in clearing his vision enough to make out the woman standing over him, staring down. Her face was stern, her cat-like eyes dazzlingly black, as deep and vibrant as the shadows that surrounded her. Her skin glistened with what looked like golden dewdrops.

She stared at him, her gaze implacable. "I was frozen in this very room for a thousand years. I know what it's like. I won't let it happen to me again."

She waved her hand, and at once ice crystals formed and started groping up his legs, spreading upward from the frozen floor. They entwined about his calves, twisting like a thorn bush as they crept over his knees and groped at his thighs. Quin didn't want them going any further. His mind strained for the magic field, for the Hellpower, for anything he could use to fend them off.

There was nothing but the cold and the spreading tendrils of ice.

He glanced to the side and was appalled at what he saw. There, leaning against the wall beside him, was Naia. Her face was white, her long lashes frozen closed. Her hair, iced over and plastered to her face. Her hands, clawed into stiffened knots in front of her.

She was frozen solid. Like the mages in the cabin.

"N-naia…" he moaned.

The woman above him had no mercy. She said, "When the Reversal hits, she would die anyway. It is better this way."

"No…"

"There is nothing in the world that will prevent it. She will die no matter what you choose. On the other hand, there are many lives that will be saved if you choose to assist me."

He believed her. He didn't know why, but he did. His teeth chattered harder. The ice inside of him clawed deeper, threatening his heart. The frozen vines twined about his hips, his groin, constricting.

"I'll h-help you…"

There was a crackling sound as the creeping ice receded back down his legs. The frozen tendrils didn't melt; they un*grew*, writhing and unbranching until they were once again part of the glassy floor. Quin gasped in pain as hot blood gushed back into his legs. The warmth spread throughout his torso, into his shoulders and arms, flushing his cheeks. Pain followed like scalding water boiling his blood.

He gaped up at the woman's staring face, marveling as he felt his body come back awake. His shivering stopped, his muscles relaxing. He looked over to where Naia sat rigid, just as pale and frozen as before. The thaw hadn't reached her.

"Come," the woman commanded, extending a two-toned hand with long, tapering fingers.

Quin gazed at that hand, blinking at the memories it evoked. It had been a very long time since he'd seen a person with skin that color.

The sight of that beautiful hand made him want to weep.

He reached up and clenched her fingers.

"Do you swear?" she demanded.

"I swear."

"Very well." She pulled him ungracefully to his feet.

He turned immediately back for Naia. In two steps he was by her side, kneeling down, taking her clenched fingers in his hands. They were rock-solid. Ice crystals shimmered in her frozen hair. She was alive in there, somewhere. He could feel it. She wasn't dead. But he had no way of reaching her. Quin cupped her cold face with his hands. Her skin was stiff but soft. Frozen, just like the rest of her. He stroked her cheek with a finger.

"Let her be." The harsh voice behind him stopped him short. "Trust me; it is better this way."

Anger like red heat suffused his vision, clenching his throat. He glared back up at the woman as if trying to sear her with rage. She remained indifferent, her stare penetrating. Drowning in hopelessness, Quin leaned down and pressed a kiss against Naia's cold forehead.

Then he rose to his feet and moved away. He was shaking again, and this time not from cold. Naia was a lovely woman, and this was a cruel mistake. He swallowed a hard lump of anger in his throat as the door to the cold room swung shut behind him, sealing her in. The lock clicked, making him flinch. He cast a glare of reproach at his stern companion.

The mysterious woman awaited him in the corridor, appraising him with an indomitable gaze. Her dark face shimmered with gold, some type of powder, he suspected. She turned her back on him and preceded him down the hallway. He followed her up a rise of flagstone steps into a sprawling room that dominated the entire bottom floor of the castle. It was warm, even summery. Radiant light streamed in through windows set high above.

Quin glanced over the room, which was filled with rugs and furniture arranged in intimate clusters. Hundreds of people could have easily filled this hall and never felt pinched for space. Many hearths girthed the chamber, promising warmth and comfort to prospective visitors. It was a space designed for the specific purpose of bringing many people together.

Eerily, they were alone.

The unoccupied chamber resounded with emptiness. It stank of dust and abandonment. Even the light coming in from the windows seemed bereft of energy. Quin paused, arching an eyebrow as his eyes scanned the hall.

"Obviously, not all is as it should be," his guide answered his unspoken question. "Come."

She started forward past clusters of chairs and couches, striding over to a door recessed in the far wall. She pulled it open, ushering him within.

He moved through a tinkling clatter of beads that hung in the doorway, parting them with his hand. He stepped into a dim, confined space that screamed color from every wall. Quin stood still, staring around, letting his eyes wander over the variety of tapestries and decorative items laid out on shelves or dangling from the ceiling. Some of the patterned textures he recognized. He turned back to the woman in front of him, finally understanding.

"You're from Aeridor," he observed.

"I am. Aeridor as it was a thousand years ago."

She smoothed her silken robes and settled into a chair, beckoning for him to take the one opposite. He did, running his hand over the woven texture of the chair's fabric that echoed the colorful patterns of his memories. It occurred to him that no other room like this probably existed anywhere in the entire world. It was a saddening thought.

"What was your name again?"

"I am Tsula daughter of Mundi," she reminded him.

"Why are you here, Tsula?" He shifted nervously in the chair, reaching up to adjust his hat. The room was warm, and he could feel prickles of sweat breaking out on his forehead.

The woman folded her hands in her lap and stared at him flatly. "I am here because I have no choice. As are you."

His gaze wandered over the cluttered, claustrophobic space. Tsula's bed was tucked into a corner, piled high with blankets. Tables littered with knick-knacks defined the small space. Chests and slender cabinets of polished wood, candles and oil lamps, aglow with wavering flames. And a fragile scent lingered in the air, putting him at ease.

"You're a Harbinger?" he asked.

"Yes."

"And just how old are you?"

"As old as you are, Quinlan Reis. Like you, I was born before the Desecration."

Reaching to the table at her side, she removed the lid from a woven basket and produced a loaf of bread. She broke off a piece, setting it on a plate. This, she offered to Quin.

He didn't have to think twice. He snatched the plate from her hand, stuffing his cheeks full. There was no oil to dip the bread in; it was dry. But even still, it was one of the best things he'd ever tasted in his life. He was literally starving, he realized. When the bread was gone, he licked his finger and dabbed up every crumb on the plate before setting it aside.

He glanced up to find Tsula watching him.

"That was delectable," he said at last. "Your baking staff should be commended."

He looked around, wondering what other food could be stored in the room's various baskets.

"We are alone in the castle."

"So it seems. Forgive me for my prying ways, but…where does your food come from?"

"The food comes from the cold rooms down below. When I am hungry, I simply thaw, cook, and eat." She rose and picked up Quin's plate, clearing it away to a basket by the door. Quin stared after it, wishing she'd offer him more. But instead, Tsula returned to her chair.

From the small table at her side, she picked up a pair of jaw-like tongs and used them to hold a small clump of charcoal over a candle's flame. The charcoal eventually grayed, the smell of it filling the air. Tsula set the smoldering lump in a small copper brazier that looked very much like a wine goblet. On top of the charcoal she placed chips of wood. They began curling and smoldering with a rich odor that quickly filled the room.

"I'm sure you have many questions," she said, setting the tongs down and turning back to Quin. "You may ask."

"Why, how very gracious of you."

Quin closed his eyes and breathed in deeply, his emotions stirred by the vivid odor. Flickers of reveries traced his closed eyelids, along with the profound sentiments that accompanied them. A sharp pang of loss stabbed his chest, making him stiffen in his seat.

"It's been a thousand years since I last smelled the scent of agarwood," he said at last. "It evokes such powerful memories. Some beautiful. Some despicable. It leaves me feeling…quite conflicted."

"Good," Tsula said. "Conflicted is exactly the state you should be in."

Quin opened his eyes and looked over to her. At her side, the smoke from the small brazier drifted upward in a thin trail toward the ceiling. Tsula stared back at him without expression.

"What do you want from me?" Quin asked.

"I am going to ask for your help in bringing about the end of the only world you've ever known."

She said it as easily as if asking him to carry water for her. She reached for a tea pot beside her chair and poured two cups, one for him and one for herself.

Quin accepted the cup and brought it to his lips, never taking his eyes off her.

He said, "Pardon me if I seem skeptical, but the last time someone asked me to help bring about the end of the world, things didn't work out so very well."

"That is because you were only halfway committed to your cause."

He cocked an eyebrow. "Oh, is that why Caladorn ended in darkness and ash? And all this time, I've been thinking it was because I helped open a gateway to hell."

Tsula set her tea down and raised her hand. "Hear me out. Let me tell you my story."

"By all means." Quin took a long, loud slurp of tea, watching her reaction over the cup's brim. But Tsula didn't react. Instead, she simply waited for him to set his cup down before continuing.

"A thousand years ago, I was the Warden of Harbingers. When the Reversal came, I was here in this castle, operating Athera's Crescent at the very moment the magic field reversed itself over the isle. That's how I came to be frozen."

"I don't understand," Quin admitted. The field hadn't fully reversed. And, if it had, Tsula would have been dead, not simply frozen.

"Of course you don't understand," she snapped. "Athera's Crescent is the largest and most sophisticated artifact ever to exist in the history of the world. You would need to know something about its workings to understand anything I have to say."

Quin grimaced. "I *am* an Arcanist, you know. I do know some things."

"But you are not a Harbinger," she pointed out.

"No. Not a Harbinger." He rolled his eyes and gestured with a flourish. "By all means. Proceed."

She nodded. "Athera's Crescent is like a bowl, collecting rivers of information from every corner of the world." She cupped her hands in demonstration. "Any use of the field—any disturbance anywhere in the world—sends echoes throughout the entire magic field like ripples in a pond. These variations are collected and analyzed here by Harbingers. Or at least they were—before every last Harbinger was killed."

"How were they killed?" Quin took a loud slurp of tea.

"Athera's Crescent requires a tremendous amount of power in order to operate. It harvests this power by siphoning field energy away from specific locations across the world. Places you know of as vortexes. The power of a vortex is harvested by its Circle of Convergence and then delivered here through a series of conduits."

Quin frowned. That was new information. He'd never heard anything like it before, and it was jarring that he hadn't. "So…you are saying that Athera's Crescent is the reason why every vortex in the world exists?"

If that were true, he couldn't fathom why he hadn't learned of it long ago. Perhaps it was some secret of the Order of Harbingers; every order had them. But a secret of that magnitude…

Tsula nodded. "That's right. A vortex is simply a whirlpool created by harvesting a magical reservoir. When the Lyceum's Circle of Convergence was destroyed, that cut off a significant supply of power to the Crescent. Fortunately, there was enough power coming in from the other vortexes to sustain it. At least, there was…until Aerysius fell."

"What happened then?" his voice was a mere whisper.

"When Aerysius was destroyed, its conduit was severed. After that, there simply wasn't enough power to sustain the Crescent. The Harbingers did everything they could to try to redirect power back to it. They even resorted to tampering with the vortex here on Titherry, altering it so that it sucked the heat right out of the air, converting it into flux. Their plan didn't work. All they succeeded in doing was destroying themselves in the process. It was too much, all at once. It created a surge that killed every last mage on the isle."

Quin nodded, thinking of the frozen corpses they had discovered in the root cellar. "So that explains the cold. But that doesn't explain you. Why is it that you thawed out while everything else froze solid?"

Tsula lifted the tongs and used them to flick some of the blackened ashes off the charcoal. She then added fresh chips of agarwood.

"I was frozen by magic," she explained. "When the power failed, so did my containment."

That made sense. Quin breathed in the heady odor of incense, the smoke becoming quite thick in the small chamber. "Well, that's fortunate. At least there is one surviving Harbinger left in the world."

"No, Quinlan Reis. That is most *un*fortunate," Tsula corrected him.

Quin frowned. "And why is that?"

"Because it has become my duty to rid the world of magic."

He blinked as her words sank in. He folded his hands in his lap. His eyes traveled from her face to the swirling tendrils of smoke that rose from the burner.

"Well, I do hope you've got something stronger to drink around here," he muttered finally, setting the tea aside.

Tsula stared at him with those eyes that only accused and never forgave. She rose and made her way toward a cupboard set against the wall. From within, she produced a golden flask. With a glance at Quin, she poured the liquor into a cup, then began adding water from a pitcher. He raised his hand quickly.

"Stop."

She righted the pitcher, handing the cup to Quin. He gazed down at the milky color of the arak, contemplating it for a moment.

"Here's to apocalypse," he murmured. Then he tilted his head back and tossed it down. The liquor burned his throat, the strong spices awakening his senses. When it hit his belly, it lit a warmth that shot excitement through every nerve. It had been a long time since he'd taken a drink.

He offered the cup back to Tsula, motioning for more. She refilled it with a scowl, this time without any attempt to dilute it. Quin savored the taste. He closed his eyes, swirling it about on his tongue before swallowing it down.

"You have no idea how good this feels," he said. Then he

drained the rest, setting the cup upside down on the small table at his side. "No, thank you," he said when Tsula went to refill it.

"So why do you feel the need to end all magic?" he asked, still with his eyes closed. "Isn't that sort of like biting the hand that feeds you?"

"Not when that hand is responsible for the oppression of half the world's population," the woman said, settling back into her chair.

"And by oppression, you mean...?"

"I speak of the curse that blackens both Caladorn and Aeridor. I have seen it through the mirror of Athera's Crescent. I've seen what it's done. To your people...and to mine."

"I wasn't aware that the curse had affected Aeridor."

"Aeridor was consumed by darkness. But unlike Caladorn, we had no mages to provide us with light. No lightfields. My people starved to death long ago, trapped on a continent with no light and no means of escape."

Quin hung his head. His memories of Aeridor were dim. Palaces sprouting from jungle, covered in flowering vines. Fountains and reflecting pools, manicured gardens and acres of lawn where exotic creatures roamed and grazed.

Lost to darkness because of him.

His mouth went dry. The effects of the arak evaporated from his mind. The once-fragrant incense now smoldered, reduced to char and ash.

"That's why I came here," he muttered. "To find a way to break the curse. There must be a way to do it."

The woman stared at him with those merciless eyes. Hands clasped in her lap, she told him, "Athera's Crescent must be brought back fully online. Then, we will search for that way together."

Quin nodded. It wasn't a nod of agreement. More like resignation. "What do you need?"

Tsula sat forward, her eyes claiming him entirely. "I need an Arcanist. Someone with the skills and knowledge that were lost a thousand years ago when the Lyceum burned to the ground. In short...I need you."

"What do you need me to do?"

"I need you to repair the conduits that were severed when Aerysius fell to dust and rubble."

Quin reached down and fingered the stoneware cup. He didn't turn it over. He just let the pads of his fingers trail over its cold smoothness. His gaze wandered to Tsula's hands, hands that looked so familiar. Amani had been born in Aeridor. Her mother had been a prominent mage from the Empire. Amani had favored her mother in both looks and grace. Quin stared at Tsula's lovely hands with bittersweet sorrow.

"I'll need my tools," he said finally. "And I'll need Naia."

"Why do you need the girl?"

"Moral support." Quin picked up the empty cup, turning it back over.

"No."

"Why not?" Leaning forward, he plucked the pitcher off the table and poured the undiluted liquor into his cup. Keeping his eyes fixed on hers, he took a long, savoring gulp.

The look on the woman's face was contemptuous. "Because. The world needs you to perform this service. A service which, if successful, will kill every last mage that still exists, including the girl. I can't risk having your emotions conflicted."

Quin cocked a cynical eyebrow. "Didn't you say conflicted was exactly the state I should be in?"

Tsula's eyes hardened to stone. "I misspoke."

"Why should I help you at all?" Quin tossed back more of the potent liquor. "Call me deranged, but I happen to like the world exactly the way it is. Mages and all."

The smoldering glare she leveled at him was venomous. But with the liquor to fortify his courage, Quin didn't heed the warning in her eyes.

"Because," Tsula snapped as she rose from her chair. "Destroying the magic field is the only way to free the skies over Caladorn. And over Aeridor. This is your duty, Quinlan Reis. You brought about the curse because of your inability to face the consequences of your actions. For a thousand years, the world has suffered those consequences for you. No longer. You are the last Arcanist this world knows, and I am the last Harbinger. Together, the two of us will endeavor to repair that which you tore asunder."

Quin stared up at her as he drained the last of his cup.

"Not without Naia."

Chapter Twenty-Two
Surrender

Pass of Lor-Gamorth, The Front

Darien stood looking up at the dark and jagged ridgeline. A light breeze ruffled his hair and chilled his skin. The gloom of the stark landscape seemed more oppressive than it had just moments before. He glanced at the clouds, frowning at the faint traces of light that flickered there. He was tired of darkness, tired of the constant melancholy that filled his soul.

He wanted to see the sun again. Even if it was just one last time.

The crunch of Connel's boots alerted him to the man's presence at his back. He didn't turn around, just stood gazing upward at the devastation in the sky.

"You did well," the darkmage remarked. "I know how hard that had to be for you."

Darien nodded. It had been hard, much harder than he'd expected. He wasn't sure which had been worse: having to look in Meiran's eyes or admitting to Kyel his shame. In a way, he was responsible for them both. Craig, too. Their friendships were casualties of his own self-destruction.

"I don't trust the commander," Connel said.

Darien nodded. He didn't, either; he knew better. Devlin Craig had been a disciple of Garret Proctor, just as Darien had been himself. Craig knew how to wrest opportunity from desperation.

"He knows exactly what he's doing," Connel went on. "The new keep's positioned in the center of a node."

"I know. I'm the one who told him about it." Darien's eyes

followed the craggy slopes of the Shadowspears. Somewhere up there, lost in the choking mass of cloudcover, was the new keep, a fortress his eyes had never once looked upon. Built right over the spot where Arden Hannah had tried to burn him at the stake. Where Devlin Craig had saved his life from the flames.

He breathed a sigh. "But the node actually works to our advantage. Craig's mages will be impotent, but we'll still have access to the Onslaught. They won't be expecting that."

"If you use the Onslaught, that will void the truce you just negotiated."

Darien looked at him. "If I use the Onslaught, they'll have voided it already."

The man nodded thoughtfully then started walking back toward the pavilion. Darien fell in step with him, matching his pace.

Connel said, "I wish you hadn't surrendered our officers. We can't afford that kind of loss."

"We won't have to." Darien ducked as he parted the flap of the tent. "Order every senior officer to find an infantryman with their same height and build. Have them trade uniforms and weapons."

A look of appreciation grew on Connel's face. "You're good at this."

"That's why I defeated your armies."

"No." Connel shook his head. His smile disappeared. "You defeated me because I overestimated you. I assumed that just because you were a Sentinel, that you wouldn't be morally depraved. I was wrong. You're willing to sink to depths that I'd never imagine."

Darien stared at him, returning glare for glare. Then he turned and stalked out of the tent.

Kajiri Flats, The Front

Darien took his time about riding back to camp. He wasn't in a hurry. His mood was just as bleak as the horizon. He let his horse pick out its own trail, head lowered, foraging fruitlessly in the barren soil. It was late in the day when he finally rode into the outskirts of the encampment, helm pulled down to hide his face. He thought about paying a visit to Myria but reconsidered. He made for his own tent, instead.

He tossed the reins of his horse to a foot soldier and moved into the tent, tugging off his helm. He unfastened the brooch that held his cloak, letting the heavy garment fall from his body.

Azár burst through the tent's partition, nearly startling him off his feet.

His wife's face was red with anger. She held her hands clawed into fists, her eyes narrowed like slivered coals. He'd never seen her so enraged. The hostility on her face made him take a step back in retreat.

"There is talk that my husband intends to abandon our cause and return to the side of our adversaries! Is this true?"

Darien was surprised that word of the parley could have reached the camp ahead of him. He'd been hoping to break the news to Azár himself. What bothered him most was the distorted version of his agreement that had gotten back to her ears. It made him fear what the men under his command must think.

"It's not true," he answered coolly. He walked past her toward a jug of wine set out on a table. He didn't bother with a cup. He upended the jug and let the cool liquid spill into his mouth, drinking it down in thirsty gulps.

"Then tell me, what is the truth?"

Darien set the jug back down. He lowered his gaze to the table's surface. It wasn't made of wood. Something like slate. He poked his fingernail into a crack, musing at the texture. Without looking at her, he explained, "I volunteered to become their hostage—Myria and myself, actually. To guarantee we'll honor the terms of the truce I struck with their commander. It was the only way they'd agree to let us enter the pass uncontested."

Her eyes widened. "They will kill you," she whispered.

"No." He shook his head. "That would violate the terms of the agreement." He raised the jug and took another gulp of wine. Then another. The magic field wavered for just a second. He set the jug back down with a heavy *clunk*.

Azár moved toward him. She wore a blood-red shirt with flowing sleeves, her hair collected in a single braid. She looked just as fierce as the first day he'd met her. She reached up and took his face in her hands, gazing piercingly into his eyes.

"My people have a saying: 'Be a thousand times more wary of your friends than of your enemies.' This is because your friends know best how to harm you."

To Darien, the proverb sounded wise. He couldn't argue with the logic. "I'll be wary," he said to assure her.

Azár's gaze lingered on his face. Finally, she drew back, whirling away. She snatched the jug off the table and poured herself a cup. Then she lay back on one of the sofas arranged along the tent's perimeter, stretching out her legs.

"I am concerned for you," she said, glancing up at him. "When do you intend to surrender to these people?"

"On the morrow." He placed his hand around the handle of the jug but didn't lift it. Instead, he traced his fingers along its cool, engraved surface. The copper jug commanded his attention. It was far easier to look at than his wife's anxious face.

"So, we have only tonight, then." Regret cooled her tone.

He nodded, still engrossed in the textured handle.

"Have you managed to find any feelings for me yet?"

His eyes shot up. She was staring at him expectantly, he saw. Waiting for him to reply. "I feel something," he forced himself to admit. "I'm not sure how deep it goes."

"But you do feel something?"

He nodded, not certain what his own feelings even were. Grief, sorrow, guilt...one of those, or more likely a combination. Nothing good. Certainly not what she wanted.

Azár sat up, setting the wine cup down by her side. Her eyes drilled into him, as if trying to bore a hole right through his skin. She rose to her feet and stalked toward him, her stare wandering downward, taking in all of him. She circled slowly, her fingers trailing over his shirt. Darien tensed, her touch sending electric shivers through his skin.

She came to a halt in front of him.

"My husband is a handsome man," she said at last. She reached up and pulled at the thong that held his hair, allowing the dark strands to spill down his back.

She leaned in, studying his expression. Then she said firmly, "You will do as I say and only as I say. You will stop if I say stop."

He nodded, understanding the need. "Aye. I will."

"Kiss me."

He closed his eyes and complied. He brushed his lips against hers, not quite a kiss. Then he drew back, frowning deeply.

"Lower your guard," she whispered.

He realized that she wasn't asking any more of him than she was willing to give of herself. Somehow, that made things easier. He brought a hand up to her face, caressing her soft skin. Then he gathered her in and kissed her hungrily.

The sunless morning came too soon.

Darien wasn't ready for it.

He rolled out of bed, leaving Azár slumbering with her lips parted slightly, the expression on her face for once tranquil. He found his clothes and pulled them on. But then he took them right back off again. Instead, he went to his chest and rummaged around, producing the same pair of black breeches and cotton shirt he'd worn on the day he'd died. It somehow seemed fitting. He'd abandoned the Rhen and his former life wearing those clothes. It seemed appropriate that he should return in them. He donned his cloak and broke his fast with a piece of bread and a handful of dates.

The whole while he chewed, he stared at Azár's sleeping face, contemplating her broodingly. It wasn't that he regretted the act they had shared; he didn't. But it did complicate matters. It made what he had to do that much more difficult. It was one thing, walking into uncertainty, when he'd felt his wife was cold and distant. It was completely different, knowing that he left someone behind who genuinely cared for him.

He would have to make provisions, he realized, for the chance he didn't return. Overnight, Azár's security had become a new priority, one he hadn't taken into his calculations before.

He frowned, studying her soft beauty as he munched down the last bits of bread and washed it down with a glass of wine. Then he rose, wiping his mouth, and bent down before the bed. He leaned over and kissed Azár on the cheek. She didn't stir. He could hear the peace in her soft breath. He could see it written on her face. It made him glad.

Straightening, he donned his boots and made his way out of the tent. As he emerged, the thanacryst rose to its feet with an enormous yawn. It stretched, first its front legs, then the rear, then stood staring at him with expectant, sinister eyes.

Darien raised his hand, signaling the demon-hound to remain. He didn't know what the thing would do when the camp moved on. The beast seemed to not mind Azár. He hoped it would follow her. So far, it hadn't shown any inclination to use her as a food source.

Darien frowned, suddenly worried. He'd never questioned the wisdom of keeping the creature. It had always proved a loyal companion. Now he found himself doubting his own judgement.

"Stay here," he told it, knowing full well it probably wouldn't obey. He decided to try anyway. "Protect Azár." The thing continued to gaze at him. He turned away. The hound settled back down again into the dirt, its nose between its massive paws.

Darien trudged away toward the heart of the camp, aware of the sound of footsteps jogging to catch up with him. He turned to find himself flanked by Sayeed and his nephew Iskender, a clot of Zakai hurrying in their wake. He noticed that Sayeed and his nephew had traded uniforms. He was glad to see that his commands were being heeded, especially by his own men.

"Lord, I must tell you that I am opposed to this plan," Sayeed growled in a voice lowered so that none of the other men could hear.

"Your opinion is noted," Darien said. He had no intention of getting sucked into an argument. He walked over to where the horses were picketed and, stooping, pulled at the knot to free his own.

"I don't think you understand. They cannot be trusted —"

"Sayeed," Darien said, laying a hand on the man's arm. "I want you to keep my wife safe. Stand by her side, no matter what. Don't come looking for me."

"Lord—"

"No matter what," Darien insisted. "Be in the vanguard when they open up the pass. Get her through as quickly as you can."

Sayeed looked ready to argue. But instead, he effected a stiff and formal bow.

"Yes, Lord."

Darien considered this man who had stood at his side through so many battles. Not physical battles. But the inner kind that mattered more and hurt harder. He finally realized the depth of his appreciation for him.

"Don't call me 'Lord,'" Darien corrected him on impulse. "Call me 'Brother.'"

Sayeed looked stunned. He stood there for a moment with his face going slack, the color draining from his copper skin. "My Lord…"

Darien shook his head. Sayeed was the one man Darien knew he could trust. He had grown tired of the formal distance demanded by the Tanisars' rigid code of honor. Damn formality. What he needed was a friend, not another subordinate.

"Go in peace, Brother," he stated gruffly.

Sayeed swept forward and clasped him in a rigid embrace, nearly pulling him off his feet. He kissed Darien on both cheeks. Darien returned the gesture as best he could, trying not to seem as awkward as he felt.

"May the peace of the gods be with you," Sayeed said, patting his back. Then he pulled away, collecting himself.

Darien climbed onto the back of his horse as Iskender mounted the spare. Zakai trotting along at their sides, they rode through the camp as onlookers came running to line their path. War drums thundered, men stood shaking spears and swords at the sight of their approach.

To Darien's surprise, the hatred of the men for him seemed to have cooled overnight. A fiery outcry swelled from the heart of the encampment. They rode through dirt streets lined by howling warriors, finally reaching a large crowd gathered in the assembly area in front of the command tent.

There, Darien dismounted, leading his horse to where Byron Connel stood at Myria's side, ranks of uniformed officers gathered behind them. Darien surveyed the assemblage, taking a moment to realize what he was looking at. These were the men the officers had traded roles with, gathered now to accompany him into the pass. Darien's gaze swept over their faces. Not a man looked as though he didn't belong. The officers had chosen their replacements well.

He drew up in front of Connel and Myria, the Battlemage nodding a terse greeting. Myria regarded him with an expression of amusement. She was wearing a short, brightly patterned tunic over trousers, a broad shawl draped over one shoulder.

"So, here's the man who sealed my fate with a handshake," she said.

Darien knew he owed her an apology, or, at the very least, some reassurance. "If everything goes as planned, we'll be guests of the commander for a week." It was an attempt to sooth her nerves.

It didn't work.

Myria cocked a perfectly arched eyebrow in his direction, looking skeptical. "And how often do things go as you plan, Darien?"

He couldn't help but smile. "Not often," he admitted.

Myria nodded, her face smug. "And what happens when they don't?"

"Then I improvise." He gestured toward the mountains. "They built Greystone Keep within a node. Their mages won't have access to the magic field. But we'll still be able to use the Onslaught."

"We can't heal ourselves with the Onslaught."

"Then we'd best not get injured."

Sincere doubt shadowed her expression. He couldn't blame her. Darien turned to Connel, nodding his head in the direction of the gathered men. "Is this everyone?"

"It is," Connel said, stepping forward. "Volunteers, one and all. Their lives are in your hands. Better pray your friend doesn't see fit to double-cross you."

Darien couldn't guarantee it. If Devlin Craig was bent on treachery, then there was precious little he could do to prevent it.

Connel clapped his shoulder. "Go in peace."

Darien returned the gesture then climbed astride his horse. The stallion danced sideways with a nervous snort and a jingle of tack. Darien gathered the tasseled reins in his hands, bringing the animal back under control.

Iskender jumped lithely down from the mare and held the stirrup for Myria. She mounted gracefully, clucking her horse forward while Sayeed's nephew joined the group of foot soldiers.

Byron Connel gave a nod.

The low, throaty moan of a war horn rose over the field, sliding up dismally through the octaves. At the sound of it, the men started forward, marching to a syncopated meter tapped out on a single drum.

Darien urged his horse forward at a walk, Myria at his side, as over a thousand men formed up in a great column behind him. He turned his horse toward Orguleth, toward the Pass of Lor-Gamorth, his eyes taking in the flanks of the Shadowspears. Roiling cloudcover obscured the tops of the mountains. The flickering lights in the clouds beckoned him onward.

The horn cry rose again, the sound more ominous than before. The drum tapped out its fatalistic cadence.

Darien glanced back at Connel to find that the man had already turned and was walking away, hands clasped behind his back. Myria rode to his left, head bowed. Two standard bearers trailed at their sides, one holding the red emblem of the Tanisars, the other the green field of Bryn Calazar's legions.

They marched forward, toward destiny or death. He didn't know which. One path led to sunlight, the other to eternal darkness.

Darien stared up at the mountains, feeling a terrible sense of foreboding.

It took hours to march the distance between the staging grounds and the alluvial fan that formed the wide mouth of the pass. By the time they started up into the canyon, it was already late in the day. The soldiers walked with their backs straight, showing no signs of fatigue. The drum continued tapping out its relentless beat.

At the mouth of the canyon, Darien pulled back on the reins and raised a hand, commanding a halt. Behind him, silence reigned over the columns behind him as the men stopped and stood motionless in perfect ranks. A slight breeze chased his cloak and ruffled his stallion's mane.

Ahead, the fog that shrouded the pass parted just enough that he could make out the dark outlines of palisades. Fog and shadows obscured the air, but at last he saw the strength of Craig's army. His scouts had already warned him about the numbers.

Still, it was an intimidating sight to behold. Ahead, an army numbering in the tens of thousands stood guarding the wide bottom of the pass, lining the walls of the canyon, continuing up the slopes.

Beneath him, Darien's horse stamped nervously. A strong odor on the air made his eyes widen: the scent of wood smoke. Orange fires glowed from behind the fortifications, following the path of the river up as it snaked into the Shadowspears. In all his time in the Black Lands, Darien had never once smelled the odor of burning wood. The smell conjured an intense wave of anxiety sharpened by a sense of dread.

Movement ahead caught his attention.

A group of riders had broken away from the main host and was approaching his position. Darien kept a tight rein on his horse, letting the party approach. There were about twenty men, all mounted. Two rode in the fore, the others following in a single, spread-out file. Every man held a hornbow at his side.

Devlin Craig stopped his horse yet fifty paces away, Meiran drawing up next to him on a silver gelding. Craig's men came up behind, forming a line as if taking up position to advance.

Holding Craig's eyes warily, Darien dismounted. He glanced at Myria, nodding for her to follow suit. Then he turned, signaling his men to stay back.

Darien and Myria walked side by side toward the awaiting Greystone entourage, leading their horses behind them. It was a long, sobering walk across the canyon floor, painful in many ways. Darien could feel the eyes of his men lingering on his back, as well as the suspicious glare of Devlin Craig. Meiran's bitter stare tracked his every movement.

It had been right here, in this very canyon, where the Enemy had dealt a deathblow to Greystone's infantry under Darien's command. That defeat had been counted as a victory, even though the graves had outnumbered the living. Now Darien returned to the same site, the same defeat.

Only, this time, he was the Enemy.

His gaze wandered over the faces ahead of him. There was a sadness in Meiran's eyes that he hadn't expected to see. The look on her face, on Kyel's face, made everything that much more difficult.

He halted as soldiers jogged forward to relieve them of their horses.

He turned to Craig. Darien stood for a moment, staring into the eyes of his old friend, searching there for some trace of compassion. There was none.

He said formally, "Force Commander Devlin Craig. I present to you myself, Grand Master Myria Anassis, and the commanding officers of the combined legions of Malikar. We are here to surrender unconditionally and throw ourselves upon your mercy."

Before Craig could respond, Darien reached up and drew the leather baldric off his shoulder, offering out his scabbarded sword. Devlin Craig accepted the blade solemnly then handed the weapon to the officers at his side. Meiran's eyes left Darien to follow the retreat of the sword that had once been her gift to him.

When it was done, Craig nodded. "Tell your men to ground their arms."

Darien called back over his shoulder, "Ground arms!"

Behind him, the first line of men stepped forward and dropped their arms and armor down on the black dirt of the canyon floor. They then turned as one and were ushered away toward the canyon wall by Greystone soldiers. There, they were made to kneel, hands on their heads. The next rank of men stepped forward and did the same, dropping their arms and shields in a growing mass of weaponry. Then the next rank, until row after row of kneeling men collected along the canyon's walls.

Darien watched until the last of his men knelt at the mercy of Craig's soldiers. Gray-cloaked sentries walked up and down the lines, binding wrists, patting down bodies. The entire process of surrender would take some time; it was only just beginning.

In front of him, Craig plunged a fist into a pocket, producing two small vials of liquid. He moved forward, holding the vials in his hand. One he handed to Myria. The other he offered to Darien.

"Drink."

Darien received the vial warily, holding it up and noting the small amount of dark liquid it contained. "What's this?"

"It'll put you out," Craig answered.

Darien nodded, understanding. He felt a sinking feeling in his gut. He glanced back up at Craig. "Will I wake?"

"You'll wake."

It didn't sound like a lie. That didn't mean it wasn't. He felt drenched in fear; his plan hadn't accounted for this. Darien lifted the vial and drained the contents in one swallow. The mixture had a bitter taste. It made his mouth go instantly dry.

He dropped the vial on the ground.

He could feel it hit his stomach. A warmth ignited in his belly, spreading quickly to his limbs. His skin felt suddenly cold. The magic field quivered, then drained completely away.

At his side, he heard Myria groan. She wavered, staggering. He reached out to grasp her.

His arm was captured by a soldier who pinned him from behind. The man shouted something at him, but in his confusion, he couldn't make out the words. Another man slapped Darien in the face. He swayed, blinking, perspiration streaming from his forehead.

A skeletal man clad in gray robes stepped forward, peering into his face. A priest, Darien realized. He gaped into the man's face, his confusion rampant. What need had they for a priest? The man smiled odiously. Then he took Darien's hands one at a time, snapping something around his wrists.

He looked down, seeing heavy black manacles with strange markings that flickered and began to glow.

Darien's eyes went wide as he felt the Hellpower die inside him. Panicking, he fought against the manacles' power. But it was no good; his mind was ebbing, drifting away. He sank to his knees. The world faded even as he fought its fading. It didn't matter. In the end, the drug won out.

The last sound he heard was Myria's weeping.

Chapter Twenty-Three
Fatally Flawed

Isle of Titherry, The Rhen

Quin knelt down beside Naia's frozen form. She was covered with a thick coating of frost, her hair brittle with ice. Her fingers remained clenched like gnarled stone in front of her face. He placed a hand on her arm. Cold. Damn cold; so cold it hurt. He shot a glare up at Tsula.

"Move back," she warned, then struck out with the raw force of her power.

There was a sizzling sound, and steam rose from the floor, from the walls, from Naia herself. It made the air of the room hot and moist. Immediately, Naia relaxed and toppled over, spilling limply across the floor of the ice cellar.

Quin lunged to catch her, but not in time. Naia's head hit the ground with a hollow *thunk*. He scooped her up, cradling her head against his chest. Her skin was still gray, but brightening even as he looked at her. He patted her cheek a few times lightly, then harder. He stopped only when he felt her body spasm and quiver.

Naia's face twisted into a gruesome expression. Then her eyes burst wide open, deep black and unfocused. She sat up rigid.

"Watch out!" she screamed.

Quin hugged her close, not knowing what else to do. He ran his hand through her wet hair as her body trembled against his chest. She was sobbing, he realized. He wasn't sure if it was from shock, pain, or terror. Or a twisted combination of all three. He touched her cool hand, seeking to reassure her.

"Look at me," he said.

She did, tilting her head back enough to peer feverishly into his eyes. Her cheeks were splotchy red, her pupils large and round, staring through him instead of at him.

"What? Where?"

He could barely make out the words through the force of her chattering teeth. He released her hand, cupping her face as he glared up at Tsula.

"You're going to be fine," he assured Naia. His eyes shot hatred at the woman towering over him with arms crossed, face a mask of brutal calm.

"So cold!" Naia's jaw trembled against his chest.

Quin struggled out of his coat. Still clutching her against him, he wrapped her in the fabric, tucking it tightly around her body. He took her hands into his own and rubbed them briskly.

"Bring her along," the Harbinger commanded, backing out of the room.

Naia still trembled in his arms, her eyes staring dimly up at him. Quin wasn't even sure if she knew who he was. She wasn't up to walking, that was for certain. So he scooped her up, lifting her shuddering body off the ground.

There was a metallic clink as something fell out of her clothes. He looked down. And just about dropped her.

There, on the ground by his feet, lay the Soulstone medallion. Quin stared down at it, blinking dumbly, as his brain slowly registered its presence there in the cellar. It had fallen out of Naia's pocket. The stone was dull and black, like a faceted lump of damnation. Quin found himself holding his breath. To him, that sinister stone was the most terrifying thing in all the world.

He knelt, supporting Naia's weight on his knee, then stooped to snatch the medallion off the ground and replaced it in Naia's pocket.

"Bring her this way," Tsula said.

He followed the woman down the corridor and up a flight of stairs. Naia's weight was slight; there wasn't much to the woman. Her body still trembled from the cold, but not near as violently. When he looked down at her face, she was gazing up at him with dim awareness in her eyes.

Tsula led them down a long corridor lit by yellow magelight. Many doors lined the hallway. She picked one, seemingly at random, indicating they should enter with a jerk of her head.

"She can remain here."

Quin ducked past her into what looked like some sort of living quarters. He bent to deposit Naia in a chair as he scanned the room for blankets. He found a bed shoved up against a wall, piled high with covers. He picked them up in a bundle, surprised to find that the blankets had a freshly-laundered smell. He layered them over Naia.

"Let's get you warm," he said.

Then he looked up, noticing Tsula lingering in the doorway, watching him without expression. He stood and flung the door closed. Her hand shot out and stopped it, jolting the door back open. She stared at him blandly.

"Come to me in the morning," she commanded. "I'll show you where to begin your work."

With a chilling stare, she pulled the door soundly closed behind her as she left.

"Who is she?"

Quin turned back to Naia, pausing to tuck a corner of the blanket in beneath her chin. Her skin still felt cool to the touch. He answered, "I think she's the best chance we have."

Naia's head inclined toward the door. "Do you mind elaborating?"

"Actually, I do mind," Quin said. "Right now, all I care about is getting you warm."

Quin rose and glanced around the room, taking in their surroundings. They were in some sort of guest room, it seemed. There was a bed and a chair, along with a small writing desk in the corner. Against the far wall was a wood-burning stove with an iron crock set atop it. Curious, Quin strode over to the stove and took in the ancient-looking kettle.

"I'll be damned," he muttered, dipping his finger into the fine sand that filled the inside of the kettle. He leaned over and opened the door of the stove, happy to find it filled with a good supply of tinder. With a thought, he conjured up a flame. The stove sprang to life, instantly warming the cool air of the room. And the sand in the kettle.

Quin searched the room's interior until he found a small copper cup with a long handle. To his delight, there was a pitcher already filled with water and a coffee grinder. He wasted no time, grinding up coffee and pouring the grounds straight into the copper pot. As an afterthought, he reached into his pocket and added a pinch of spice. He then thrust the pot into the heated sand.

Naia sat up, watching him closely as Quin waited for the coffee to come to a boil. When it did, he spooned some of the froth into two cups and returned the pot back to the sand. When it was done, he divided the rest of the coffee between the cups, handing one to Naia.

"Drink," he commanded her.

Naia lifted the small cup to her lips and immediately made a face. "Ah! That's strong!"

"But it's warm," Quin insisted. "Drink it." He scooped his own cup into his hand, plopping down on the bed. He closed his eyes and took a sip, savoring the taste.

He glanced up at Naia with a grin. "You like it, don't you?"

She took another sip, at last returning his smile. "I suppose I'm getting used to your spices."

"Life is never bland when I'm around." He saluted her with his cup, then took another taste. Like the smell of Tsula's incense, the flavor of the spiced coffee took his mind back in time.

Naia asked, "What happened, Quin? Who is that woman?"

"Tsula's a Harbinger," he responded with a shrug. "She says she's been frozen here since my time. She wants me to fix Athera's Crescent for her."

"But...?"

"She wants to destroy the magic field."

Naia's face filled with concern. "Can that be done?"

"Apparently so." Quin took another sip of his coffee.

"How are we going to stop her?" Naia's face was quite serious. The coffee in her hand went untouched.

That was a good question, indeed. Quin had no idea what the answer could be. "I'm not certain that we want to stop her. It's possible it's the only way to break the curse."

Naia leaned forward, pulling the covers up around her. Her hair was still wet, falling in wavy ringlets around her face. In the poor lighting of the room, it looked almost black.

"What are you going to do?"

"I'm going to repair the Crescent," Quin decided. "And then I'll use it."

"What can I do to help?"

"You can keep me alive."

She frowned. "What do you mean?"

Quin set his cup down on a table beside the bed. He scooted back, leaning up against the wall. "My profession can be exceptionally hazardous," he explained. "That's why there were never many Arcanists in the world. The better you are, the higher your risk. The good ones always ended up dead, usually sooner rather than later. Challenging projects are always risky. Especially something like Athera's Crescent; none of the mages who built it survived the process."

Naia looked down, her expression grim. She took a slow sip of her coffee. Lowering her cup, she said without looking at him, "Thank you, Quin. This is very good."

"Just one of the many services I provide," he said with a wan smile. "You should get some sleep. I'll see you in the morning."

He rose from the bed and started toward the door. But a thought tugged at his mind, forcing him to turn back around. He extended his hand toward Naia. "Give me the Soulstone."

The startled look on her face was satisfying to see.

"Why do you want it?"

"Because I made it," he snapped. He wiggled his fingers. "Now, give it here."

Naia's mouth dropped open. *"You...?"*

Quin nodded, quirking a brow and flexing his fingers.

She gave a long, protracted sigh, then fished the medallion out of her pocket and handed it over to him. He closed his fingers around the dark stone, squeezing it tightly. Then, with a curt nod, he left the room, closing the door behind him.

Once in the hallway, he clutched the Soulstone against his chest. The corridor was lined with rough-hewn doors, the same as the one behind him. He didn't know where else to go, so he tried the door across from Naia's, finding it unlocked. It opened into another guest room much the same as the one he'd left. It took only a glance and a second of concentration before every candle and lantern in the room was ablaze, the room's woodfire stove awake and radiating heat.

Quin sank down in a chair at the writing desk, tossing the Soulstone down on the desk's smooth surface. In the light of the room, the medallion didn't look like a stone at all, but more like a dull chunk of coal. The silver bands of the collar were far more lustrous, glowing a liquid white in the candlelight. He spread the collar out on the surface of the desk, positioning the medallion upside-down.

Quin reached up and slipped his hat off his head, tossing it aside. He stared down at the Soulstone medallion, then gave a dispirited sigh. The last time he'd seen the artifact, it was lying beside the corpse of his dead brother. The Soulstone had been used to kill Braden. And Amani; Renquist had issued the order to execute his own daughter. Not to mention Darien, who'd been coerced into fastening the medallion around his own neck.

Three torturous deaths. All his own fault. When he'd created the Soulstone, Quin had overlooked the flaw that prevented the smooth transfer of power through the well-stone. He hadn't realized that one of the crystals was misaligned, creating resistance, but not enough to nullify the artifact. Instead, the Soulstone's victims were subjected to agonizing deaths, tortured as long as they had the strength and will to fight.

Quin stared down at the dull black stone, despising it utterly. So much suffering. All because he'd rushed the job and had the arrogance to think that his work didn't need double-checking. He resisted the urge to throw the damn thing against the wall. But he knew the Soulstone couldn't be destroyed like that. Besides, it offered him a singular opportunity that he desperately needed.

It had been a thousand years since he'd last engineered anything. His skills needed honing.

"Ah, hell," he muttered, running a hand back through the sweat-slick curls of his hair.

He reached into his pack and withdrew a tool roll. With delicate regard, Quin rolled it out on the desk in front of him, eyes scanning over the many implements of his craft that he'd collected throughout his lifetime. They were old, just like him. Some were much older. Small hammers and delicate probing instruments, wedges and corkscrewing drill bits, all with intricately worked handles, some bone, some wood or even ivory. Some were ancient. Some he'd made himself. Each separate tool was tucked into its own little sleeve in the leather roll.

He ran his hands over the tools reverently. It had been a very long time, indeed. Reaching into the rightmost pocket, he wriggled out a pair of wire spectacles with a swing lens loupe. He put them on, the vision of his right eye immediately blurring. He pushed the lens back and lifted the Soulstone up in front of his face. He clicked down a different lens, nudging it into place. One of the stone's dark facets popped into detail. He clicked down another lens, squinting as his eye adjusted to the depth of field.

At first, he could make out nothing. He moved the stone in and out until at last the individual crystals were revealed to him. He scanned the latticework: backward, forward, moving in and out through the layers. At last, he saw it: the one cuboidal crystal that was aligned different from all the others in the pattern.

He'd found the flaw.

He had never viewed it before. Not with his own eyes. He'd known it was there, but had never had the opportunity to see for himself that tiny imperfection. It seemed so innocent: one subtle, almost undetectable, crystal.

It had inflicted so much damage, so much pain.

Quin fumbled with the tool roll, extracting a copper probe. He held it up to the dark surface of the Soulstone and, focusing his concentration, willed the probe to sink inside. He watched it descend through the lattice of crystals as they bobbed out of the way of the moving tip. Until the probe was nudged up against the single crystal that was misaligned.

With the slightest dribble of magic, Quin focused all his will into that one crystal through the instrument in his hand. He watched it slowly rotate into position, sliding into place. He held his breath. When the crystal settled fully into the pattern, he let out a protracted sigh.

The flaw was fixed. Only, the crystal above had been pushed out of alignment.

Quin scooted his spectacles up and rubbed his eyes. He knew it wouldn't be that simple. Nothing was. Propping his elbow on the desk, he squinted harder and sank the probe back into the stone to reconfigure the next crystal in the pattern, pushing it back into position. Which knocked aside the next crystal above it.

A bead of sweat dripped from his forehead, dropping onto the desk. Quin wiped his face with his sleeve. Then he forced his mind to concentrate as he gazed into the deep black depths of the Soulstone, pushing the next crystal back into place. And the next. And the next, as the hours sped by and the nighttime waned...

Quin jolted awake at the sound of a piercing scream.

"What?!" he shouted, dropping the instrument he was holding as he jerked his head up off the desk. He stared blearily into Naia's ghost-pale face. Her eyes were wide, her mouth gaping at him in horror.

He wiped the slobber from the corner of his mouth, righting himself in his seat. His eyes scanned over the room, desperately seeking the source of the threat. But there was just Naia and himself. They were alone.

He frowned up at her with a vacuous look on his face.

"You're...alive...?" she gasped, taking a step toward him.

Quin frowned even harder. "Well, not precisely alive, but I take it that's not your point. By the way...why do you ask?"

She shook her head slowly, her hair swaying into her face. She pointed to the desk. Glancing down, he saw the Soulstone. And almost screamed himself.

The medallion was glowing red, full of a lively, scintillating light.

Full of a mage's gift.

"Who…?" Naia gasped. Then her face wrinkled in a look of disgust. *"Did you kill Tsula?"*

"No!"

"Then who?"

Quin ignored the question, scooping the Soulstone up in his hand. He donned the wire spectacles, flipping quickly through the lenses, staring deep into the perfect latticework of glowing crystals. Somehow, it was fully charged. Each crystal vibrated with radiant energy.

"Then why is it glowing? What's filling it?" Naia demanded

"The air," Quin gasped, not quite believing it himself. It wasn't possible…but it was the only explanation. It couldn't have sucked the gift out of him. He was not a living mage. He had no gift left in him.

"How?" Naia pressed.

"I don't know." Quin shook his head. "I was working on it last night. Just tinkering. I was trying to fix the flaw. I must have done something…"

He squinted harder, staring into the glowing depths of the jewel, at the charged crystals pulsating with life. There was no sign of the flaw. Every crystal was perfectly aligned. He'd made certain of that before falling asleep.

"I wonder…" he whispered. Removing the spectacles, he set them down on the desktop. Then, before he could change his mind, he wrapped the silver bands of the collar around his neck. With a click, the clasp snapped closed.

"No!" Naia lurched forward.

The stunning power that surged into him took his breath away. Quin's muscles locked rigid, his back arching in the chair as a gush of energy flooded through every fiber of his being. It was like a lightning strike that hit every nerve, a torrent of colors and sounds and feelings. The power was exhilarating, thrilling him completely.

The flow of energy stopped, his body going limp. He sat back in the chair, panting, sweating, every muscle quivering. He could still fill it, the stirring of power that moved within, pulsating quietly in the back of his mind. Greater and more fulfilling than ever he remembered. And it hadn't hurt one bit.

"What did you do…?" Naia gasped.

Quin reached up behind his neck, opening the silver clasp. The Soulstone, now dark, slid down his chest into his lap. He fingered it, nudging the medallion slightly. He looked up at Naia. Then he closed his eyes.

With his mind, he tugged at the magic field. Not through the Onslaught. This time, he touched it directly. He let it seep into him, feeling its soothing cadence, the rhythmic pulse of power he had known all his life. He did the simplest thing he could think of: he willed a mist of magelight into being.

The sound of Naia's gasp told him that his attempt had been successful. When he opened his eyes, he was surrounded by a mist of glaring white light. Quin flinched, pushing his seat back. He rose to stand, argent strands of mist weaving between his feet. He gaped down at it, unable to explain the nature of the color. Before, his signature had been dark red, the hue of spilled blood. The color of the legacy he'd inherited from his predecessor.

But this…

He looked down at the Soulstone in his hand as the explanation became clear to him. The gift inside him now wasn't the same legacy he'd inherited from his master. It wasn't even a legacy, not something handed down. It was the beginning of something *new*. Staring down at the Soulstone, Quin gave a mirthless laugh.

"What is it? What happened?" Naia demanded, confusion paling her face.

"I have the gift in me again," Quin said with a euphoric grin. "I feel it inside me. Ha! *Do you know what this means?"*

"No. I don't." She shook her head.

Quin whirled toward her, clutching the medallion against his chest. "It means I don't need the Hellpower anymore! I can reach through to the magic field *on my own!*" His eyes widened as the implications sank in. "Naia...*I'm alive.*"

Chapter Twenty-Four
Cruel Choices

Pass of Lor-Gamorth, The Front

K yel stared at the long line of prisoners being escorted into the practice yard below Greystone Keep. There, the captured men were lined up in rows and made to kneel, their hands secured behind their backs. Crackling bonfires blazed at the edges of the yard, casting a contortionist's dance of light across the faces of the captives.

Kyel couldn't help but stare, disturbed by the silence the warriors observed, even in the face of defeat. No one spoke a word. Their faces were grim and stern, staring straight ahead. Their expressions never wavered, even as more gray-cloaked soldiers poured into the yard.

At an order from a captain, one of the prisoners was dragged forward and forced to his knees in front of a wooden block. There were many blocks along the wall of the practice yard, Kyel realized. They'd appeared there overnight without him realizing.

A Greystone soldier came forward, hoisting a massive sword.

"What's this?" Kyel gasped to Meiran. "This isn't part of the agreement!"

The prime warden cast a troubled stare his way. "The agreement has been modified."

The burly soldier brought the weapon around, laying the blade across the prisoner's neck. He adjusted his grip. Then he lifted the sword up and brought it swiftly down. The corpse slumped sideways to the ground. The executioner kicked the severed head away.

No one moved. Not one man made so much as a sound. The

prisoners knelt in perfect lines across the yard, heads held high, backs straight. Four more men were dragged forward to their deaths.

Kyel turned away from the gruesome scene. There were a thousand captives. Did they intend to behead them all? He heard the dull *thud* of a sword striking off another head. Then another.

"Why are you doing this?" he demanded.

Meiran's face was sad but resolute. She was still pale, dark circles lingering beneath her eyes. He suspected they arose from lack of sleep over the decisions she'd been forced to make. Decisions he'd not been party to. He understood why. He would never have condoned any of this.

"We can't take any chances," she said evenly. She held her hands clasped in front of her, taking in the grisly scene. She flinched slightly as another sword reaped its harvest of blood.

Kyel couldn't watch; he kept his back to it all. *"Why?"* he demanded. "They surrendered. They came willingly!"

Her eyes shot toward him. *"Why* did they come willingly? Have you asked yourself that? Why would they surrender? Why take such a chance? Because they had a plan, that's why—a plan that we foiled."

Another thump, this one followed by an agonized scream. One of the headsmen had missed his mark. Kyel closed his eyes against the impulse to turn and take in the carnage. Another dull *thud* ended the victim's pain.

"So you're just going to kill them all?" Kyel spun away from her, casting a frantic glance back down the rows of prisoners awaiting their turns to die. No one begged for mercy or wailed against their fortune. It was the eeriest sight he'd ever seen, these soldiers patiently awaiting calamity, watching their own impending fate enacted over and over before their eyes.

Then he thought of the people of the Black Lands whose very existence depended on this broken treaty. Kyel's stomach soured, his joints stiffening. His heart staggered under the weight of guilt. He'd been a fool. He should have seen this coming.

"What about Darien?" he whispered, though he thought he already knew the answer. One look in Meiran's eyes confirmed it.

"He's too dangerous."

He couldn't keep the shock off his face. Meiran saw it and offered him a look of sympathy.

"I'm sorry, Kyel. It pains me, too."

He looked at her as if she were a stranger, unable to understand how she could so betray a man she had once loved. A man who had sacrificed his soul to save her own. It went beyond dishonor. Kyel peered into her eyes, trying to get a sense of the emotions living there. Meiran's eyes reflected the flames of the bonfires. But there was sadness there, as well. She had not made this decision lightly. But neither did she regret it.

"They are demons, Kyel," she reminded him. "We're just sending them back to where they came from. That's all. They don't belong here."

The logic of her words was lost on him. He wanted no part of it. "So this was all just a trap from the beginning?" He waved his arm in the direction of the prisoners being slaughtered behind him. "What about the rest of their people? What about the children?"

"They're the Enemy," Meiran pronounced.

Kyel stared at her, horrified. How could she justify any of this? He couldn't believe she could be so callous, that any of them could. It went against every principle of honor he'd ever been taught. "How can you...? *We gave them our word!*"

Meiran looked at him in pity. "Kyel. You're the last Sentinel we have left. What do you suppose our chances were before this? We had no choice."

"No," he disagreed. "We *did* have a choice—but you just made the wrong one!"

With that, he turned and stormed away, leaving Meiran to reap the fruits of her deception.

Darien's body shivered, but not from cold. His arms trembled violently, quaking the chains that held them. He couldn't help it. It was an effect of the drug they'd given him. His eyes stared blearily into the shadows, making very little out of nothing. Another harsh chill wracked his muscles. He clenched his fists against the awful feel of it.

"I'm sorry…"

He recognized the voice that whispered toward him through the darkness. It spoke to him from the past, from out of his memory. The sound of that voice was comforting. He struggled to force his eyes open, but his lids were heavy and kept sliding closed again. Blinking, he fought to put a face with the voice. But the features were blurry, unrefined. He couldn't keep focus. Behind, a torch dripped buttery light into the shadows. He heard another soft noise echoing toward him from the darkness, like the sound of distant weeping.

He squinted, peering, his body quaking in shuddering spasms. He squinted harder, willing the features in front of him to resolve. They finally squirmed into a blurry image of Kyel Archer's distorted face. His former acolyte sat in a chair beside him, hands clutched together in his lap. The look in Kyel's eyes spoke volumes of shame.

"What?" Darien shivered through clenched teeth. They had him tied down to a table of some kind. He was in a dungeon. The infernal manacles the priest had placed on him still encircled his wrists, cutting him off from the Onslaught.

Cutting him off from hope.

"They're going to burn you," Kyel said, his face pale.

Anger gripped Darien. He'd suspected treachery, but nothing this decisive. His mind leapt immediately to the men he'd brought with him.

Kyel went on, "I tried talking them out of it. They won't listen."

"What about the treaty?" Darien whispered hoarsely, struggling in vain against the arcane shackles that held the Onslaught in check. He pumped his wrists against them until his flesh tore open.

"There's no treaty. It was all just a trap. I didn't know—" Kyel's voice lurched. "I didn't know. I'm sorry…"

Darien's mind struggled to grapple with the implications. The men he'd surrendered, the armies that followed in their wake. The clans. His people…his wife. Nothing was safe. Everything was in jeopardy. And his one asset, the Onslaught, was denied him. He trembled harder.

"My men—"

Kyel shook his head. "All dead. Every last one of them."

Darien squeezed his eyes shut against the fury brought on by that knowledge. He wrenched against the manacles until blood flowed freely down his hands. He had to get out, had to warn them—

"Kyel. I need you to help me—"

"I can't." Kyel shook his head, eyes filling with regret.

Darien gasped for breath, shuddering as he fought against the death grip of the iron bands. *"Just get these damned things off me!"*

"I can't. I'm sorry, Darien. I have to go now."

He wanted to scream. Thousands of lives depended on him. Tens of thousands. If he could just get out of the dungeon—

"Kyel…"

"I'm sorry." His former acolyte rose from his chair and, reaching down, patted Darien's arm.

Darien locked eyes with him, capturing him and holding him there. "You can stop this! Kyel, you can stop it!"

Kyel shook his head. "I can't."

"You swore an oath to defend this land *and its people!"*

"That's what I'm doing."

"It's not!" Darien shouted, choking on desperation. "You're the last of us, Kyel! You can't pick sides—you don't have that luxury! These are *people!* People of this land who *need* you! Who are going to *die* without you! Think, Kyel! *You've got to be stronger than those chains!"*

Kyel glanced down at the emblems on his wrists. He took a deep, lingering, breath. He seemed to be struggling with his conscience. When he looked back up again, his eyes were moist. "I'm sorry, Darien. I wish I could help you." He turned and left, his long strides carrying him swiftly out of the room.

Darien sagged in his restraints. The last of his hope faded with the sound of Kyel's footsteps. He would get no clemency from

Devlin Craig.

"Myria!" he yelled at the ceiling, wondering if she was even still alive.

"I'm here, Darien." Her voice sounded just as dismal as his own.

He craned his head to the side, looking back over his shoulder. They had her in an iron cage across the room from him. She stood watching him, gripping the bars. She caught his eyes and shared a look that told him everything there was to say. Darien looked away, grimacing. He could do nothing for her. He'd condemned them both.

Silence lingered in the dungeon. Silence and shadow. For a long time, he lay there, just listening. The flickering flames of the torches snaked their dance, holding back the darkness by only a fraction. Eventually, the drug cleared enough from his system that his body stopped shivering. He lay there in the darkness, listening to the quiet sounds made by Myria in her cage. It sounded to him as if she'd accepted her fate, just as he had. There was nothing else either of them could do.

He heard the echoing sounds of footsteps approaching from the corridor outside.

Darien stared across the room into the blackness of the doorway. Craig entered the dungeon followed by the priest. They paused in the doorway as Myria fled to the other side of her cage, pressing her body back against the iron bars. The sight of Devlin Craig made Darien stiffen. His bloodied hands clenched into fists. He seethed with feelings he didn't understand: a fierce mixture of hatred and sorrow, desperation and fury, all churning together in a quagmire of emotion.

Craig glanced at the priest. "I want a word with him, first."

"Of course." The oily-haired man flashed a wan smile, stepping to the side.

Darien finally recognized the unfamiliar gray robes: this was a priest of Deshari, the Goddess of Grief. The people of the Rhen considered Xerys evil. But in Darien's opinion, the goddess Deshari was far more deserving of their terror. Deshari's adherents embraced pain, yearned for heartache and trauma.

They viewed agony as a catalyst of transformation.

It was a despicable cult. Their practices went beyond the immoral, and for no clear benefit to society. He considered Deshari far worse than Xerys, the same way a murderer was different from an executioner. At least his own dark god seemed justified for the evils He perpetrated. For the worshippers of Deshari, evil was both ends and means.

The gray-robed priest peered at him, an eager smile on his lips. In his eyes lingered a promise of pain.

Craig started forward, glancing at Myria as he rounded the corner of her cage. He strode up to the table Darien was strapped to, pausing to linger at his side. Seeing the look on his old friend's face spiked Darien's rage.

"Spare my people, Craig." It took everything he had just to get the words out. To swallow his anger and embrace humility. There was nothing else to do.

Devlin Craig gazed down at him with eyes that contained a mixture of disgust and pity. He shook his head in obvious confusion. "They're not your people, Darien."

He could tell by Craig's face that he didn't understand. He thought him unbalanced, perhaps even insane.

"They *are*," Darien insisted. "I wasn't born to them. But that doesn't make it any different. Please. Listen to me. They're good people. They're not the Enemy you think they are. They don't deserve this —"

But Craig cut him off, already shaking his head before Darien was finished. "It's not for me to decide. I'm just a soldier. I do what I'm told. And right now, I've been told to carry out your execution."

Darien sagged in his bonds, overcome by a feeling of hopelessness. He had failed before, many times in his life. But this was different. The stakes were too high.

"I'm sorry." Craig looked as though he was sincere. "I don't have a choice." He looked to the side, avoiding Darien's eyes. "So I'll let you decide. Do you want us to kill you first? Spare you the pain of watching her burn?" He nodded back over his shoulder at Myria's cage. "Or would you rather spare her?"

It was a cruel choice. Darien clenched his fists in rage. *"Gods damn you,"* he growled.

"I'm sure they will. Who first, Darien?"

No amount of begging would change Craig's mind. Darien realized that he only had one choice left to make. He closed his eyes and made it. He decided to spare Myria.

"Her first."

"All right." Craig nodded at the priest, who had been watching the exchange.

A sick smile formed on the man's lips. He reached long, bony fingers into the deep pocket of his robe, withdrawing a flask that contained a clear liquid. He turned to Myria, who stood clutching the bars of her cage.

The priest said something under his breath that Darien couldn't hear. Then he doused Myria thoroughly with the liquid from the flask. She lurched backward with a cry, fleeing to the corner of her cage as the priest backed away, laying down a trail of liquid all the way to the center of the room.

Myria stood clutching herself, shaking, her hair and clothes dripping. She began to hyperventilate, her breath coming in sharp, choking gasps.

Darien could only stare in horror, too sickened to react.

The priest walked over to the wall and fetched a torch down from its holder. Seeing the flame, Myria's sharp gasps turned to shrieks. She brought her hands up in terror, covering her face.

The priest lowered the torch to the ground. A trail of flame sprang into being, racing across the floor toward the cage. The flames leaped onto Myria, engulfing her instantly. Her screams filled the room as she staggered, ablaze. She fell to her knees, writhing and shrieking as the flames enveloped her completely.

Darien stared, transfixed by the shocking horror of the scene. Myria's flesh turned black then started to gray. She burned for minutes, her screams finally coming to a pitiful end. Still, the crackling of the flames persisted. The awful smell of roasting flesh thickened the air of the dungeon. Soon, Myria was reduced to a charred, featureless lump that sizzled and smoked.

Darien trembled in revulsion, praying that she was finally

beyond pain.

There was a long gap of silence in the chamber, broken only by the sound of his own shuddering breath.

Craig laid a hand on Darien's arm. "You were once my friend," he said. "I hope your soul finds peace."

Darien looked up at him, unable to respond.

Craig walked away, his long cloak swaying in his wake. He strode to the center of the room, head bowed, as the priest of Deshari moved forward.

The repugnant man fussed over Darien, making sure his bonds were secure, all the while staring at him with a ghastly eagerness in his eyes. Darien cringed away from the man, repulsed. The priest produced another flask and held it over him.

He uttered, "May the flames redefine you. This is your moment of pause before your soul breaks wide open. I want you to know…I envy you this opportunity. Relax. Embrace your transformation."

Darien shivered, appalled by the man's hungering gaze, the anxious yearning to see him burn. He closed his eyes as the priest upended the vial over him, drenching his face and hair, dousing his clothes. Then the man backed away, laying down a trail of accelerant across the floor.

Darien gagged at the reek of lamp oil, the fumes burning his throat and wringing water from his eyes. His heart lurched as the panic set in. He fought against his restraints, lashing his fists against the manacles, not caring if he broke every bone in his hands. His mind flailed desperately for the Onslaught, to no avail.

The priest of Deshari grabbed another torch down off the wall, its flame crackling in a stir of air as he walked back toward the center of the room. Darien's eyes followed the torch's flame, his body trembling in misery.

Devlin Craig looked away.

The priest stopped in the center of the room and slowly lowered the torch toward the trail of accelerant.

Something struck him from behind.

The priest was hurled off his feet, the torch tumbling from his grasp. His body slapped hard against the floor and lay there, a gray-fletched shaft protruding from his back.

The torch rolled across the floor toward the trail of oil.

Devlin Craig sprang toward the door, drawing his blade. Another arrow drove deep into his neck. He reached up, fumbling at the shaft as his knees buckled under him. He slumped to the ground, dropping his sword.

Kyel Archer lowered the longbow in his hands. He cast the weapon on the ground, a look of revulsion on his face. His eyes snapped back and forth between the priest and Devlin Craig, who lay thrashing about on the floor, pawing at the arrow embedded in his neck as he fought for breath.

Kyel ran forward, kicking the torch away. He knelt beside the body of the priest and searched frantically through the man's robes, at last springing back up with a ring of keys in his hands.

Darien almost wept at the site of him. Kyel was filthy and ragged, trembling as he crammed the keys one at a time into the manacles. The arcane restraints fell away, releasing the gushing torrent of the Onslaught. Darien groaned as he felt it rage into him, filling his mind with terrible ecstasy.

Kyel ripped off the rest of the restraints. Darien sat up, weak and almost too shaky to stand. He had to brace himself against Kyel to get his feet under him. He took a lurching step forward. The smell of lamp oil was strong on his skin, wetting his hair and saturating his clothes. The fumes choked his throat. He seared it away with the taint of the Onslaught.

Kneeling, he dropped to Craig's side and lifted his old friend up off the floor. Craig was still alive, wheezing and gurgling, his hand worrying at the shaft buried deep in his throat. There was little blood; it hadn't pierced the artery. Craig's panicked eyes scoured Darien's face, his mouth open and gasping.

Darien couldn't heal him.

"Close your eyes," he said.

Craig complied.

He died instantly, going limp as blood streamed from his nostrils. His shuddering stopped, his suffering ended. Darien felt no pity for him. He laid Craig out across the floor and rose, turning back to Kyel.

"What did you do to him?" Kyel whispered.

"I gave him mercy." Darien stepped over the corpse, moving toward the door.

"How…?"

"With the Hellpower."

Darien stopped in the doorway, extending his hand. Kyel stared at him wide-eyed, his mouth hanging slack.

"Come with me, Kyel."

"No." The young mage shook his head, taking a step back away. Darien could see the disgust on his face.

He pressed, "I need your help. I don't know the way out of here."

"I can't," Kyel gasped, edging backward another step. His eyes drifted to the corpses on the floor then flicked back to Darien's face.

Darien took a step after him, holding his gaze steady, his hand still outstretched. "You know we're in the right. That's why you did what you did. Come with me. I need you. *We* need you."

But Kyel shook his head. "I can't. These are *my* people. And I'm their Sentinel."

Hearing that, Darien went cold. He didn't want to kill Kyel. But he also couldn't leave such a threat behind. He closed his eyes, summoning resolve.

Darien reached within. The Hellpower was there: morbidly euphoric, darkly vibrant, beckoning. He gathered it in and probed deep inside Kyel, finding the nerves that drove his heart.

"You're going to kill me," Kyel realized.

Sinan son of Semal. Alton son of Orhan. Devrim son of Enver…

He opened his eyes.

"No," Darien whispered. He pointed at the cage where Myria's corpse lay charcoaled on the floor. *"Get in."*

Kyel looked like he was going to be sick. But he obeyed. With fumbling hands, he found the right key and unlocked the door. He straddled the grotesque remains and locked the cage door behind him.

"Throw me the keys."

Kyel did, tossing them down on the floor. They slid across the stones, coming to a rest beside Craig's body. Kyel retreated to the far end of the cage, where he dropped to a crouch, covering his face with his hands.

The cold gleam of metal attracted Darien's attention. He moved toward it, realizing they'd piled his things in a corner against the wall. He shouldered his blade's leather harness and fastened his cloak. Then he turned, eyes sweeping over the carnage in the chamber.

"Narghul," he whispered, his blood turning to liquid ice.

Two necrators rose from pools of shadow, twining upward from the floor.

Darien stared at the pair of lethal shades, grimly satisfied. He turned and strode from the chamber, his dark servants gliding behind in his wake.

Chapter Twenty-Five
Hapselon's Amulet

Isle of Titherry, The Rhen

A glance down at the Soulstone revealed what he'd already suspected. The dull black stone stirred with a fleck of radiance deep inside where the flaw had been. Quin held it up between them, dangling it in front of Naia's face. The cold necklace swayed in front of her, the bands of the collar catching the light, while the stone sucked it in like a black maw of darkness.

Except for that one rose-colored fleck.

"Look," Quin said. "It's charging again. It's drawing a new legacy right out of the air."

She leaned forward, peering deeply into the stone. Slowly, Naia's eyes widened. "How is it doing that?"

"Because that's where all legacies go when mages die without a successor...And it's where they all came from in the first place."

"I don't understand."

Quin shot her a quizzical look.

Naia took a step back then sat down on the bed. She crossed her arms in front of her chest. "I'm afraid there is a tremendous gap in my knowledge. Please remember I never received a formal education."

Quin lowered the Soulstone, dropping it down on the desk. He sank into his own seat, splaying his legs in a sloppy posture. "You've never read the *Praymayana?*"

When she shook her head, Quin nodded slowly. He was aware Naia had only spent two years in training, and in those two years had learned little more than the essentials. She was ignorant of all the foundational knowledge that a mage's training was typically built on. She knew what she was doing—generally—but had absolutely no idea why things worked or how they worked. It boggled his mind that she could be even half as effective as she was.

He took a steadying breath, summoning the magelight he'd created. It gathered around him, dancing in misty filaments. The soothing surge of the power within him raised goosebumps on his flesh. He closed his eyes, savoring the sweet bliss.

"I feel whole…" he whispered with a smile. It had been so long. Awash in the magic field, he could fill it moving through him of its own accord, without any external prompting.

"The *Praymayana* is an epic poem that dates back thousands of years before my time," he began, opening his eyes. "It chronicles the adventures of an ancient sage named Hapselon who thought he could climb to the top of the world and steal the fire of Om, thereby becoming a god himself. Unfortunately, due to his hubris, Hapselon neglected to realize that Om's fire would engulf him rather than granting him the godly powers he desired. As he lay dying, the goddess Isap took pity on him and healed his wounds. But Hapselon tricked her. As soon as he was healed, Hapselon took Isap captive and threatened to throw her off the top of the world unless Om granted him the powers of a god.

"So Om granted his wish. He placed upon Hapselon's neck an amulet that caused the magic field to feed Hapselon with so much power that the sage went mad. He was cursed, you see. His mortal mind couldn't handle the power of the gods. Hapselon ran raving down from the top of the world, reduced to a mindless lunatic. Everyone he touched was infected with the power of the amulet and received a small portion of godly power. In the end, after spreading the gift to thousands of people, Hapselon was diminished to just an empty husk, a withered and pathetic creature, drained of the power the gods had granted him. He finally died, passing from this world into Isap's domain, his soul to be tormented throughout eternity. His punishment was to watch generations of mages born and die, enjoying and then passing on the gift that should have been his, and his alone."

Naia nodded slightly. "What a tragic story. Like so many holy mysteries, its inception is most likely rooted in the truth."

"Perhaps." Quin shrugged. "I doubt there was ever any man named Hapselon and, even if there was, he certainly never climbed to the top of the world. But I do believe that some artifact like Hapselon's amulet did indeed exist, and that the gifts of the first mages were absorbed by it from the magic field itself. That myth was what inspired me to create this." He reached out and fingered the Soulstone, running his fingers across its dull black surface.

A voice spoke at them from the door. "You're awake. Good."

Quin startled, jerking his hand back away from the talisman. He turned to find Tsula standing behind them in the doorway, gazing at them with her arms crossed. Like always, her expression was devoid of emotion.

"There is food for you in the kitchens," she informed them. "After you break your fast, I'll show you where to gain access to the conduits." With that she turned and departed, the sounds of her footsteps fading down the hallway.

Naia turned to Quin. "Do you trust her?"

He lifted his hat and raked a hand back through his hair. "No."

"Why not?"

"Because she was going to leave you frozen." He shrugged. "Regardless of her objectives, that's going too far. If I had a copper to wager, I'd wager she's afraid of you."

"But why?" Naia leaned forward, her hair spilling over her shoulders like a wash of molten bronze.

"I have no idea," Quin admitted. It was indeed quite a mystery. He wished he could unravel that tangled skein, but had no idea where to begin. He stood up. "Well, let's hope this breakfast isn't poisoned. Shall we?" He motioned toward the door.

Naia nodded, stepping into the hallway. He pocketed the Soulstone and followed her out. Taking her by the arm, he directed her down the corridor, away from the sprawl of the castle's living quarters. He had no idea where the kitchens were situated; Tsula hadn't given him a tour. But he had a good idea where they should be, somewhere around or beneath the castle's great hall.

They found their way down a flight of stairs. At the bottom, the steps opened up on a sunny courtyard lined with a series of kitchen stalls. There were many, enough to provide food service for the entire castle. All empty, of course. All deserted. No smoke rose from the chimneys. The hearths were cold.

"Not much in the way of options," Quin complained as they strode through the courtyard. He glanced up, noticing that it was a pleasant, sun-filled day. At least, it was on the castle grounds. He had no doubt the rest of the isle was still gripped in the cold embrace of winter. He could hear the sound of bird-song in the distance, the rustle of wind through the branches of trees. The warmth of daylight felt good on his shoulders.

"Where's the food?" Naia wondered.

Quin guided her toward one of the kitchen stalls. It looked unused, though not unclean. In fact, there was no dirt anywhere. He ran a finger over the surface of a carving board. No dust. He frowned at that; Tsula had been frozen in time, but not the rest of the castle. Supposedly. He was beginning to wonder at that. So far, he'd seen no servants. So who dusted the counters? Who swept out the floors?

"This makes no sense," he said.

"Look." Naia pointed across the kitchen to another counter. There, arranged neatly in baskets, were pieces of flatbread and large rounds of cheese. There was even a basket of fruit. Quin and Naia exchanged glances.

"Was that there before?" Naia asked as she walked over and lifted an apple in her hand.

"I hadn't noticed it," Quin said.

Naia inspected the apple, turning it slowly, then bit into it with a loud crunch. She chewed cautiously. "Good."

That's all Quin needed. He helped himself to the bread, tearing off a large bite and cramming it into his mouth. Then he grabbed up a few slices along with some cheese, balancing a couple of apples in the crook of his arm. Jumping up to sit on the counter, he eagerly stuffed food into his mouth as fast as he could chew it. It had been a while since he'd eaten a hearty meal.

Naia hopped up beside him. She sat there eating hungrily, swinging her legs and looking around, gazing at the oven, the hanging kettles, the clean-swept floor. Anything but him. Quin watched her out of the corner of his eye.

The silence between them resounded.

Quin tore off a strip of bread and said, "Do you mind if I ask you a question?"

Naia looked at him. "Not at all."

Quin tore the bread in half, popping a bite in his mouth. "Do you still have feelings for Darien?"

The sound of her chewing stopped. Her legs paused in their swinging. Naia sat beside him perfectly still as the awkwardness between them turned into tension. Quin closed his eyes, cursing himself, already regretting the question.

"Why do you ask?" she said.

Quin swallowed the lump of bread in his mouth. It didn't go down very well. "Just curious," he muttered.

Naia shrugged. Then she took a bite of cheese. "I haven't really thought about it." Her legs resumed their swaying motion as the silence settled back between them. Apparently, she considered the subject dropped.

But Quin didn't want to drop it. He decided to press the issue. "He doesn't love you, you know." This time, he turned to look at her and didn't look away. He watched the emotions range over her face.

"Yes. I know."

He nodded. He tore off another strip of bread and started chewing. He gazed at the floor, at a little chip in the tiles. A breeze came up, pushing a leaf into the kitchen stall, scooting it across the floor toward them. It was an oak leaf. He realized he hadn't seen any oaks in a while.

"I didn't mean to offend," he murmured into the gaping silence that stretched between them.

"Then what did you mean?" Her voice was blunt with irritation. Her legs had stopped swinging again.

"I..." He shrugged. "I suppose I just don't want to see you

hurt."

Naia jumped down from the counter. She turned to face him. "My feelings are my own," she told him in a firm voice. "I've known for a long time that Darien doesn't love me. Nevertheless, I chose to care for him. It was my choice. I felt very strongly he was in the right, so I followed him, and I was there for him...even when it hurt. But he doesn't need me anymore."

Quin stared into her sad, dark eyes and could only nod.

"And that's fine with me," Naia went on. "I spent a large part of my life being what other people needed me to be. My father needed me to be a priestess, his successor. So that's what I became. I never paused to ask myself if it was what I wanted. I made my father very proud; that's all that mattered to me. But then I found a person who needed me more. So I left my father and went with Darien...and I became what he needed me to be."

Quin gazed at her, watching her face as she worked her way through all the emotions bubbling to the surface. He felt sorry for her. "Naia," he said. "I think the important question is...what do *you* want?"

She raised her chin. She put her hand out, pushing back her sleeve to reveal the red scars where the marks of her Oath had once been. "I have failed at literally everything I have ever attempted," she said. Tears streaked down her cheeks.

Quin reached out and caught her arm, wrapping his fingers around the markings on her wrist. "No," he insisted, leaning forward. "You've only failed at trying to be something you weren't meant to be. So tell me. Who is Naia? What does she want?"

"I don't know..." her voice faded away, her eyes filling with hurt.

Quin released his grip on her arm, tucking her sleeve back down to cover the welts. Then he leaned in close. "Look at me."

She did.

Staring into Naia's dark eyes, Quin told her, "You need to decide who you are and what you stand for. Until you do, you aren't much good to anybody. That's why you've always failed."

He sat back, his eyes becoming quite serious. "But I can't let you fail this time. This is too important. I need your help, Naia."

She gazed at him with incomprehension in her eyes. He reached out, stroking a wayward strand of hair away from her face. "I need you to help me destroy the curse over the Black Lands. And you won't be able to do that without a strong sense of self. Somehow, in the very near future, you're going to have to figure out who you really are."

Chapter Twenty-Six
Feast of Souls

Pass of Lor-Gamorth, The Front

Darien left the dungeon behind, following the flights of stairs upward. He couldn't get the awful stench of charred Myria out of his nostrils. He couldn't get the look in Kyel's eyes out of his head; he was infected by both. He braced his hand against the wall and vomited, spilling his guts onto the stairs. Then he wiped his mouth and kept going.

At the top of the stairs, he staggered through a doorway into the open courtyard of the keep. He cast a bleary glance around. He felt overwhelmed. He wasn't sure what to focus on; he couldn't separate what was important from what was not. Scores of soldiers swarmed the yard in a flurry of activity. Darien drew back against the wall, stepping into shadow. He stood there panting, fighting to catch his breath.

He was vaguely aware of the gray-cloaked man who noticed him. The soldier went immediately for his sword, crying an alarm. It was too much at once; the man was just a blur. Frantic, Darien pulled at the Onslaught and sent it hurling out of him like a terrible spear of damnation.

The soldier howled a cry of mortal anguish, his muscles locked rigid. He collapsed forward, flesh smoldering and popping as he died. The necrators swept in to swarm the corpse, feasting off the soul.

Darien stared at the gruesome sight, quietly satisfied. The confusion that had addled him fell away, leaving only a calm sense of clarity.

Another soldier attacked. Darien drew his blade and blocked

the first strike. He pulled his arms up, swinging the pommel out, and took the man down with the short edge of his blade. The necrators wasted no time.

He lowered the sword and backed away, stumbling over the first corpse. Shouts rang out from all across the ward. An arrow streaked down from the fortress, lodging in the dirt next to him. Darien glanced at the half-built tower and saw that Greystone archers were taking up positions at the arrow slits.

He tried summoning a shield to defend himself, but it didn't work. The Onslaught couldn't be used like that; it was strictly an offensive weapon. He could do nothing to protect himself from injury. All it would take was one well-placed arrow to bring him down.

With that thought in mind, Darien recalled the necrators and sprinted back toward the palisade. More soldiers ran forward to meet him, forming a line of spears and interlocked shields, blocking the only exit from the yard. Darien stood for a moment in indecision.

He took a step back.

Then he lashed out at them savagely.

The wall of soldiers collapsed, melting into a vile-smelling mass that steamed and gurgled in the chill night air. The necrators glided eagerly forward. Darien gripped his stomach, unable to tear his eyes away from the sight. He stood frozen, hit with the sudden awareness of what he was capable of. Figuring out how far he was willing to take it.

A dark thought occurred to him, sicker than all the ones he'd already had.

"*Narghul,*" he whispered.

More sinister shades rose from the hummock of melted flesh. As Darien sheathed his blade and fled through the portal, eight necrators drifted after him. *It takes twenty deaths to raise a necrator,* he'd heard once. He'd already done it with far less.

Outside the ward, he encountered more stairs. But as soon as his foot touched the first step, the wood broke beneath him. He fell through, catching himself with his hands as his legs dangled under him. He glanced down at the forest of sharpened stakes that awaited him below.

Darien grimaced, using all his strength to pull his body up through the broken cage of the stair. He rolled sideways, extracting his legs. Pushing himself to his feet, he eyeballed the trap warily. He saw that the stairs followed a particular pattern: alternating wood and stone. It was exactly the sort of device Devlin Craig would have devised. He cursed himself for not noticing the pattern immediately. He'd almost paid for his distraction with his life. He started down again, stepping over the wood and walking only on stone, his demonic companions gliding smoothly behind.

The stairs ended at a raised portcullis that marked the entrance to a long tunnel lit by torchlight. Darien grabbed a torch off the wall, holding it as he strode through the darkness. Eerie shadows swarmed around him, none more sinister than the shades trailing at his back. When he reached the end of the tunnel, he flung the torch to the ground. It continued to burn, its flame rippling in a gust of wind blowing up the mountainside. The savage wind caught his cloak, billowing it out.

Two guards saw him and started forward, spears leveled at his chest. They died horribly, the price for their vigilance. While the necrators feasted, Darien brought down a third man, who dropped and slid to a stop in front of him. Another two fell where they stood, their corpses smoldering.

Darien glanced down at himself to find his body saturated with the Onslaught. It leaked out of him like a green aura, just like the one he remembered from the Catacombs. But he knew better what it meant now. The aura wasn't a symptom of his damnation. It was a mark of grace, a flaring symbol of his god's vengeful wrath.

A soldier running up the steps stopped in his tracks and stood staring at Darien, his sword arm wilting. He turned and fled. One of the necrators glided after the man, overtaking him swiftly. The soldier writhed on the ground, shrieking as his soul was devoured.

Darien stepped over the corpse and started toward the stairs that led down the face of the mountain. Below, he could see a serpentine trail of lights snaking through the bottom of the pass. It could only be one thing: the hosts of Malikar escaping the Black Lands through the canyon. He stared at the long, drawn-out column as cold fear clutched his heart.

Craig's treaty had been a trap. Not just for him, but for them all. He realized then how thoroughly he'd been betrayed.

A war horn sounded from behind him in the fortress. The cry was answered by another, somewhere in the faint distance across the pass.

Darien drew up, his hand reaching reflexively for his blade. He waited, listening, panting for air. A glacial stillness gripped the pass. There was silence. Then another horn brayed across the black distance.

There was a low, deep-throated rumble.

A series of explosions burst out of the side of the mountain opposite him, disgorging thick clouds of hurling debris. The ridgelines buckled, fracturing. Then they gave way completely. Avalanches of snow and tumbling rock collapsed into the pass with a deafening roar that shook the air.

The thunder ended and silence reigned, the entire profile of the mountainscape forever changed. Thick clouds of dust rose from the bottom of the pass, choking off his view of the devastation.

Darien froze, panting, numbed by raw emotion. He gaped slack-jawed down into the bottom of the pass, searching the rubble for signs of survivors. Visions of fallen Aerysius filled his mind. At first it was all he could see. He chased the images away and concentrated on the tragedy below. Clouds of dust rose from the gaping maw of the canyon, bathing the mountainside in gray.

The entire world was gray.

Everything that mattered to him had been down there.

He stood blinking, the ache of loss slowly settling in. He hadn't loved his wife as he should have. He'd taken her for granted. And now she was gone.

Darien sheathed his sword. He staggered down the hillside, slipping and stumbling, until he burst through the invisible barrier that marked the edge of the node. He fell to his knees, rocked by the sudden presence of the magic field.

He threw his head back, gasping for breath as the magic field slammed into him, pulsing like a living thing. The necrators hovered as he knelt there, drowning in the field's soothing bliss. He sucked it all in, every drop he could stand, until his body bled with energy and his soul cried in pain.

Shaking, he heaved himself up from the ground, fighting to stand on legs that were desperately weak. He started down the hill again, stumbling down the stairs until he reached the main trail that descended into the canyon. If there were more soldiers about, he didn't see them. Perhaps they had fled. Perhaps he had killed them already. He didn't care. The world was gray and Azár was dead.

In the bottom of the pass, the dust was still settling. He couldn't tell if anything moved down there. There was nothing to see. In the riverbed below, there was nothing but silence. And a long, echoing sense of horror. He followed the trail down, hope leaching away a little more with every step. He knew it would take him at least an hour to follow the trail down off the mountain. And he feared what he would find.

The sound of hoofbeats behind him made him turn. A group of riders were approaching from the direction of the keep. Even from a distance, Darien could tell they were heavily armored. He stopped and gathered the magic field around him until blue energies crackled over his body.

More hoofbeats approached from the opposite direction.

He turned, sensing the danger.

Darien tugged at the magic field, summoning a pool of magelight at his feet. The approaching riders drew up in front of him, reining their horses in. From behind, an equal number blocked his retreat. Most held hornbows trained on him. A few men bared swords. Some leveled crossbows at his chest. Horses whinnied and tossed their heads, eyes rolling nervously.

Darien stood his ground, assessing the situation. He sought the eyes of the men, gauging their resolve. His gaze leaped from face to face, grimly studying each. He didn't make a move for the hilt of his sword. He knew he didn't need it.

"Ride away," he warned.

No one moved.

Darien turned and started walking in the direction he'd been heading, keeping his eyes trained on the path in front of him. Behind, he heard the twang of a single bowstring.

The arrow never hit.

He didn't look back at the firestorm that erupted behind him, consuming both men and beasts. But he heard their screams, which seemed to go on far longer than they should have. Lightning struck down from the sky, summoned by the terrible wrath of his power. He fed off its electric energy, letting it invigorate him, supplementing his strength. Then he hurled it like an explosive javelin toward the group of cavalry in front of him.

This time, the screams didn't last long. He bared his sword as he strode through the inferno, but there were no enemies left to fight. A lone horse galloped past him, stirrups bouncing, its mane and tail streaming flame.

He sheathed his blade and raised his hand, dismissing the necrators.

The burning stallion reared, screaming its terror and pain. Then it stopped, appearing suddenly, inexplicably calm. It turned and sprinted back to him.

Darien reached out and caught the horse's reins. He closed his eyes and smothered the flames, healing the burns and the memories. He stroked the animal's fur, soothing the gelding with his mind. Then he climbed onto the horse's back and urged it forward. The beast leapt onto the trail, galloping with all its heart and courage toward the bottom of the pass.

He let the horse run until it tired, healed it, then let it run some more. He did that again and again, exhausting himself as much as his mount. Even at that pace, the descent into the canyon took some time. And it was unsustainable.

Eventually, the horse dropped dead beneath him.

Darien jumped clear as the gelding stumbled and rolled, coming to a rest on its side. Darien stood over it, gazing down, swaying over his feet. He turned slowly around, staggering, taking his bearings as best he could.

By the time he reached the bottom of the canyon, much of the dust had already settled. It was possible to see the devastation that had been wrought. All along the neck of the pass that extended toward the Black Lands, explosive charges had been used to bring down the side of the mountain. The entire canyon floor was filled with fresh mounds of earth. Huge chunks of stone barred the passage.

In the canyon, no one stirred. The river itself had been drowned by the rubble.

An echoing stillness hung over the pass, thundering with presence.

Darien jumped down onto the fresh-spilt earth, knowing that he walked upon a grave. They were all there, beneath his feet. The people he'd sworn to protect. The wife he'd sworn to cherish. He dropped to his knees, plunging his hands into the soil as deep as they'd go. There was only dirt to cling to. He clawed his fingers through the soil, feeling sharp rocks gouge his skin. It didn't matter; the world was gray. And Azár lay dead somewhere beneath his feet.

Eventually, he rose and wandered in the general direction of the Black Lands. As he walked, his eyes scoured the rubble, hoping in vain. But there was nothing to justify such hope; in the bottom of the pass there was no movement, no stirring of life. Nothing left to save.

He stumbled forward, picking out a treacherous path over loose rocks and jagged debris. Finally, he came to the edge of the great scree. He staggered down the slope, sliding over crumbling earth and, to his relief, encountered people.

A group of men digging in the dirt glanced up and, seeing him, dropped their shovels and bared their swords. Shaking from exhaustion, Darien raised his hands, uncertain what to do. They were Malikari soldiers: Southerners, by the uniforms. They didn't recognize him, but why should they? All they saw was an enemy.

"Demas narghul masaad," he said in their language.

The men drew up, but didn't lower their blades. They exchanged outraged glances. One growled something that

Darien couldn't understand, then advanced. The others rushed forward behind him.

An arrow sliced through the air, just missing Darien's head. It buried itself in the chest of the first man, taking him to the ground.

Darien whirled to find a Greystone archer standing behind him on the lip of the scree. He didn't stop to think. He just acted. The man exploded in a shower of gore that rained down all around them. A hand tumbled through the air, falling to the ground at Darien's feet.

The Malikari soldiers faltered, looking at Darien with wide, terrified eyes. The man with the arrow in him moaned and thrashed upon the ground. Darien knelt at the warrior's side. He placed a hand on the man's heaving chest, getting a sense of the wound. The soldier gritted his teeth as Darien drew the arrow from his ribs. Then he healed the wound before the man could bleed out.

The others looked on, slowly lowering their weapons. At last, the soldiers surrounding him sheathed their blades. Darien looked from one face to the other, finally gesturing at the towering wall of rock behind them.

"How many?" he demanded.

The soldiers looked like they didn't understand.

He repeated the question in Venthic.

"Na qabir," one of the men growled. *Too many.*

Darien sagged, understanding. He gestured in vain at a shovel on the ground. "Are you finding anyone alive?"

The man looked at him then glanced down at the sleeping body of his injured comrade. He strode forward and took Darien by the arm, pulling him away.

Darien allowed the man to guide him down the riverbed, away from the killing ground. He followed the soldier without question, slogging through mucky filth.

They trudged past bodies covered in thick layers of blood and dust. Some had obviously been struck when the mountain fell. Others looked to have either been suffocated or drowned. It was hard to say. The soldier he followed skirted a pond that used to be part of the watercourse. A small child lay dead on the far side of it, face down in the mud.

Darien thought of his own son, who had died in his arms.

Then he thought of Azár.

He swallowed against a tight ball of grief. He had ordered Sayeed to get his wife through first.

He paused over the body of the child, then dropped to a crouch. Setting a hand on the boy's back, he confirmed what he already knew. There was nothing he could do. Everything had a limit, even him. The gods had seen fit to give him the power to bring death. But those same gods had denied him the power to bring life.

"Come."

He glanced up at the soldier, who motioned brusquely for him to follow. Darien heaved himself up off the ground, leaving the child where he lay. They wandered further down the riverway, past mounds of piled bodies.

Eventually, they came to a bend in the canyon where many people had gathered, most of them casualties. Men and women had been laid out in rows along the canyon walls, while others tended the injured. More victims were being carried in, as the dead were dragged away.

Darien looked around the site, at the number of wounded, and felt despair. He had already overextended himself. He didn't have much left to give. He looked at his guide, who beckoned him toward the injured.

Darien nodded wearily, and walked to the nearest victim. He knelt at the man's side, probing his body as the harsh soldier glared down at his back. He closed his eyes, resigned. He would heal as many as he could. It was all he could do. He would heal until he collapsed.

He tugged at the magic field, filling his mind, emptying his thoughts, and began.

He had no idea how long he'd been asleep. Darien awoke naked and comfortable on a soft mattress, a mass of thick covers pulled over his body. He didn't want to open his eyes. He wanted to just keep sleeping. The covers were soft, the mattress warm and comforting. He felt a light touch, a hand stroking back his hair. Darien opened his eyes and gazed upward, frozen by the vision that confronted him.

"I thought you were dead," he whispered.

Seeing him awake, Azár smiled. "I thought you were, too."

Chapter Twenty-Seven
Shahin Son of Marthax

Isle of Titherry, The Rhen

Naia gazed at Quin, considering his features. He was very obviously not a man of the Rhen. His bronze complexion and thick black hair seemed exotic to her. And yet, strangely, there were many things about Quin that didn't seem foreign at all.

"How did you come by your name?" she asked, jumping down from the counter she'd been sitting on.

Quin turned to glance up at her as he swept his pack up off the floor. "What do you mean?"

Naia shrugged, moving out of the kitchen stall. "Quinlan is a Rhenic name. You weren't born in the Rhen…So how did you come by it?"

Quin took her arm, guiding her out of the stall and back toward the entrance to the courtyard. Sunlight streamed down from a clear sky as leaves twirled from the branches above them. The walls of the castle gleamed in the light, making her squint. So much sun…on an isle encased by winter.

"Quinlan Reis was the name they gave me at the Lyceum. It wasn't my birth name."

Naia frowned at him. "What was wrong with your birth name?"

Quin thrust his hands into his pockets, explaining, "It was just something that was in fashion at the time. My brother and I were born to a nomadic culture, you see. When we were brought to the Lyceum, they gave us new names. Rhenic names."

Naia frowned harder, studying Quin's face. "That makes no

sense. I thought the Lyceum was more advanced than Aerysius?"

"Oh, it was, definitely," Quin agreed. "Have no doubt! But Southern culture was something of a style that swept through Northern society for a time. Southern dress, Southern ways…Southern names. It was just something that people did, especially in the larger cities. Surnames became very popular, even though we'd never used them before. It was a way of distinguishing civil society from the 'unwashed masses' of the interior. Which was ironic, really. The people of the cities hated the nomads and their ways, but they also envied them. I think they realized, deep down inside, that it was a better way to live, both physically and spiritually. And yet they detested them just the same. It was all rather perplexing and contrived."

They reached a large door that led into the interior of the castle. Quin shoved it open with his hand, swinging it inward.

"What was your given name?" Naia asked. "Before they changed it?"

"Shahin. Shahin son of Marthax." Quin held the door open for her.

Naia smiled, liking the sound of the name. She looked Quin over closely. He looked nothing like a man of the Rhen. He didn't look like a man named Quin, she decided.

"What?" he demanded, seeming put off by her attention.

"Shahin," Naia repeated, feeling the sound of the name on her tongue. She smiled. "I like it. It suits you better."

Quin shook his head, looking regretful he had told her. "No. It's been too long. I'm not that person anymore. You see, they didn't just change my name. They took everything from me. They changed me into someone else entirely. Now I'm just Quinlan Reis. That's it. Nothing more."

The way he said it saddened Naia. It was as though he felt reduced by his Rhenic name. Or not worthy of the name his own father had bestowed upon him. The longer she knew Quin, the more she realized how broken he was. She'd never met another man who so utterly despised himself.

"Very well, then. Quin." Naia tried to smile, but couldn't make it work. The expression faltered on her face then drifted away.

Quin opened another door, standing to the side and ushering her past. They entered a spacious hall carpeted by patterned rugs, the stone walls relieved by bright streaks of woven tapestries. There was an odor to the place, like must or old neglect.

Movement from across the room caught her eye. Naia looked over to see Tsula emerging from a narrow side-corridor. The woman wore a striking robe of emerald green with a matching headwrap. She glided toward them through clusters of furniture and stopped in front of them, hands on her hips, surveying them down the length of her nose. Naia found it hard to suffer that stare, resisting the impulse to cringe away from it.

"Are you ready to begin your work?" the woman inquired of Quin, who responded only with a nod. Her eyes flicked toward Naia. "Is she going with you?"

Quin nodded again. "I told you: I need her for moral support."

Naia stood in silence, watching the conversation as much as listening to it. She considered herself fairly adept at gauging a person's emotions by the look on their face, and Tsula's was practically shouting. Naia sensed the Harbinger held a deep disdain for her. She couldn't imagine why.

"You're not an Arcanist," Quin snapped. "I don't expect you to understand."

The remark prompted Tsula to arch a quizzical eyebrow in Quin's direction. Beneath it, her gaze slid sideways to fix on Naia. At last, she issued a curt nod.

"Then let us go." She turned her back on them and retraced her steps across the room.

Naia wasn't sure what to make of the confrontation. She stood there until she felt Quin's fingers lace through her own, prompting her forward. His face was rigid with anger. He said nothing as they followed Tsula out of the hall and onto a wide balcony.

Warm sunlight slanted down on them, glaring off the stone sides of the castle. Naia had to squint, shielding her eyes with her hand. Ahead of them, Tsula paused beside a curving balustrade that edged the balcony. A breeze washed over them, fluttering Naia's hair. Despite the warmth of the sunlight, the mountain air was cold. Tsula made a sweeping gesture with her hand, inviting them to join her. Naia moved forward alongside Quin, feeling almost hesitant.

They stopped before the balustrade and looked over.

Naia's fingers tightened reflexively on Quin's. She forgot to breathe for a moment, so staggered was she by the view. Athera's Crescent stretched before her, consuming the entire valley below. It was enormous, like a concave basin of polished silver that spanned the bowl-shaped valley from mountaintop to mountaintop. Its metallic sheen seemed more liquid than solid, running in soft currents like quicksilver.

Except for the places that were dark.

Huge fragments like jagged shards of broken glass fractured the Crescent, places where the liquid texture ran black with emptiness. The Crescent was broken, Naia realized. Broken in fundamental ways. The quicksilver surface of the dish roiled with vitality, its surface dappled with energies that swarmed across it, activating other currents...Until one of the dark fragments broke the pattern. Then the dance of energy ground to a halt.

Quin dropped Naia's hand and swept his hat off his head, running a hand back through his hair, his expression vacuous. At last, he turned to Tsula with a look of gaping disbelief, gesturing downward with his hat.

"You expect me to repair *that?*"

The woman's eyebrows raised. "If you can." Her expression didn't change. "If you cannot, then the entire world is surely doomed."

Quin stood there, hat in hand, eyes studying the Crescent in frantic thought. His upper lip gave a slight twitch. At last he blinked and muttered, "Well, this is one honey of a pickle." Then he replaced his hat back on his head and adjusted the brim. He looked down at his boots. Then he glanced back up at Tsula.

"Where are the conduits?"

The fire in his eyes and the resolve in his voice filled Naia with a warm surge of pride. She realized she had faith in this man, though she didn't know why. He was quietly confident, unassuming. Nevertheless, she felt certain that if anyone could repair the Crescent, it was Quin.

"This way." Tsula turned and walked past them, making her way toward the corner of the balcony. Quin followed her, leading Naia by the hand toward a broad staircase that led down from the castle into the bowl-shaped valley.

Naia paused at the top of the steps, her hand lingering on the rough stone of the balustrade. Quin paused, his eyes following hers. There was one single flight of steps all the way down into the mouth of an enormous cave that gaped up at them from below. Many smaller caves opened up to either side.

"Lava tubes?" Quin wondered aloud. He held his hat against a sudden gust of air that whipped at them from the Crescent. There, in the shadow of the mountain, it was much colder than on the balcony. The wind carried with it an arctic chill.

"That is the entrance to the conduits," Tsula said without looking back, never pausing in her stride. Her long gown billowed behind her as she descended the relentless flight of stairs, hand trailing along the stone bannister.

Naia followed at Quin's side as the woman led them down the mountain, hugging herself against the bite of the cold. Every so often, she glanced down at Athera's Crescent, which glowed metallically beneath them like a living thing. Its features swirled and churned around the places of fractured darkness.

A shadow fell over them, the air turning chill. Naia looked up, seeing that their path had been swallowed by the jagged mouth of the cave. Goosebumps broke out across her skin. She hugged her cloak more firmly around her. A glowing white mist bloomed beneath Quin's feet, wandering ahead of them to light their way.

Up ahead, the stairs leveled out into a ramp that descended into the depths of the cavern. Quin's magelight confronted the shadows, overwhelming them. It lit the walls of the cavern before them, casting distorted streaks of light. The cave narrowed, the ceiling closing in over their heads. A narrow stream converged on their path, carving its course alongside their trail, ever downward into the depths of the earth. The sound of its trickling was the only noise in the world, other than the sounds of their own footfalls.

Abruptly, Tsula drew to a halt. She turned back around. Her eyes moved slowly from Naia to Quin.

"I will accompany you no further," she said. "Up ahead, the cavern forks. You must stay to the right. It will take you down to a chamber where you can access the conduits."

"What am I supposed to do down there?" Quin asked.

The woman shrugged dismissively. "Either fail or succeed. What will be is already written, Grand Master Quinlan."

Quin made a face. "In other words, you don't have the faintest idea what I'm supposed to do."

Tsula was unruffled by the comment. "I am a Harbinger, Quinlan Reis. I interpret readings from the Crescent. It is not my job to tinker with the bowels of it."

Quin smirked and reached out to take Naia's hand. "Very well then. Madam." He touched his hat in Tsula's direction. "I guess I'll go tinker with some bowels."

He started forward, brushing past the woman. Naia started after him but stopped, releasing Quin's hand. She turned around.

"Why do you fear me?" she asked the Harbinger.

Tsula looked at her with a sobering expression. "I do not fear you. I merely despise what you are."

"Why? What do you think I am?"

"Surely you must know."

"No. I do not." Naia clasped her hands in front of her. She glanced at Quin, who had paused and was waiting for her.

"You are a chimera," Tsula pronounced, eyes narrowing in accusation.

Naia had never heard the term before. She had no idea what it meant. "A what?"

"A portent of disaster," the woman clarified.

"Why would you say such a thing?"

"Because I know what you are, and what you've been. And what you may become." Tsula stared at her with flat black eyes that held no mercy.

"Don't say another word." Quin walked forward, one finger raised in warning. He glared at Tsula with danger in his eyes.

The woman turned to look at him. She gazed at him in

contemptuous silence as he lingered with his finger held in front of her face. Under her breath, she muttered, "Peace be with you, Quinlan Reis." She swept past him, her long gown rustling as she made her way back the way they had come.

When she was gone, Naia turned to Quin. "What did she mean? About what might I become?"

Quin lowered his finger, still glaring after the woman. "I don't know, and I don't want to know. Neither do you," he snapped. He adjusted his hat. "She's a Harbinger. Her job is to sort through occurrences and possibilities. I don't know what she's seen, but whatever it is, it doesn't have to happen. She's not an oracle; she can't foretell the future."

Naia peered at him. "Is that not what a Harbinger does?"

Quin's smoldering glare flicked back in Tsula's direction. He paced away, hands in his pockets, then paced back, taking a swipe at the ground with his foot. "No. All she can do is forecast the likelihood of events. And I'm not sure how effectively she can do that, with the Crescent as broken as it is."

Naia considered his words. She couldn't help but think that there was something Quin was holding back. "What is a chimera?"

He glanced back down the slope of the cavern, his eyes bypassing her. "Another myth like Hapselon," he said. "A mismatched creature made up of the parts of many different beasts. A hybrid, of sorts."

"A hybrid," Naia said, her eyes widening in understanding. Suddenly, it made so much sense. "I'm a mage, and I'm also a priestess. Isn't that what she meant?" It had to be. It was the perfect explanation. Only...how did Tsula know? When Quin didn't say anything, Naia continued, "People keep telling me it's a dangerous thing. I'm still wondering why."

Quin looked at her then. Really looked at her, as if seeing her for the first time. Slowly, his eyes filled with wonder. "You *are* a dangerous thing," he assured her. "Have no doubt."

Naia couldn't help but smile. There was no mistaking the look of admiration in his eyes.

He blinked and took a step away. "Shall we, then?" He

extended his hand toward her. She eyed his hand, then looked up and considered his face. He was a demon. He was broken. He was also the most genuine human being she had ever met in her life.

She accepted his hand and walked beside him ever deeper into the cavern. The small stream of water trickled alongside their path, a fog of steam hovering over its surface. Quin's magelight lit the way ahead, his hand guiding her forward at his side.

They came to a fork in the cave, the one Tsula had warned them about. Naia glanced warily between the two dark holes in the volcanic rock that lurked ahead of them like the open maws of a hydra. Quin's magelight didn't penetrate very deep into either shaft. Both looked equally sinister.

Quin steered her toward the opening on the right. This tube was tighter than the last had been, so narrow they couldn't walk abreast. Naia followed Quin as his magelight lit their path. The cave's ceiling was so low they had to walk stooped over. Quin led her onward, downward, still holding her hand.

The darkness and the closeness became oppressive. And the silence. That bothered her most of all. It made her feel like she was back in the warrens below Aerysius. She didn't want to think of that.

Her companion didn't seem the least troubled by their surroundings. She stared at him, musing, "Is there anything you're frightened of?"

He didn't look at her. "There is."

Naia frowned. "What is it?"

He stopped, his hand releasing hers. He took a deep breath and held it in. Then he released it with a sigh. "I was a spy," he admitted. "An assassin, actually. It's not something I'm proud of. It's just who I was, who they trained me to be. I've done things..." He shook his head with a scowl. "I'm not an honorable man, Naia. There's a special place in hell for people like me." He looked away without finishing the thought.

She couldn't blame him.

He took her hand again, his grip tighter than before. "Let's go. We're almost there."

They walked forward. The sides of the passage became gnarled, rough and irregular. Naia reached out and traced the wall with her hand. It felt odd. It wasn't rock, she realized. It felt more like bark.

"What is it?" she gasped. "It looks like tree roots."

Quin stopped and knelt down, releasing her hand. He set both palms to the side of the passage, caressing the chitinous growth that encrusted the rock, winding along the side of their path.

"This is one of the conduits," he said, looking up at her. He scooted sideways, following the vine-like growth with his hands. Then he rose, motioning for Naia to follow as he moved forward down the passage, reinvigorated by purpose.

Naia followed as the lava tube twisted around, finally opening into a chamber filled with thread-like filaments. Naia stopped at the entrance, glancing around. The cave was aglow with a shimmering spider's web that seemed to ripple with every pulse of the magic field. All around, glowing fibers converged and twisted, interweaving in a luminous dance of color that lit the cavern.

"We'll set up here," Quin said, nodding to himself and licking his lips. He swung his pack down off his shoulder and hunkered over it. He rifled through its contents, at last producing his roll of tools, which he untied and spread out in front of him. He moved his hands over the assortment of objects, pausing now and again, lingering over some, before finally selecting an instrument.

He held up what looked like a gold necklace set with a crystal pendant. Only, instead of clasps, both ends of the chain were fastened to sharpened probes. He held one probe in each hand as his eyes scanned the chamber, taking in the glowing fibers that surrounded them.

"What is this place?" Naia whispered, her own eyes sweeping over the cavern.

"It's a nodal chamber," Quin said, running his hand along the root-like growth they had followed in the lava tube. The conduit unraveled into dozens of glowing fibers which in turn spread out into hundreds of gossamer filaments that crisscrossed the chamber.

"Where does it go?" Naia's eyes traced the conduit back toward the dark passage it had come from.

"All the way to Aerysius," Quin said. "Some come from Bryn Calazar…and all the rest of the world's vortexes. They siphon power from the Circles of Convergence and deliver it here to the Crescent. They also feed it with information from all over the world."

Naia caressed the skin of the large coil of fibers. It felt like the hard shell of an insect. She retracted her hand. "Do they run beneath the ocean?"

Quin shrugged, donning his spectacles. He held the necklace-like instrument up before him with both hands. "Something like the Catacombs, I suspect. It's got to be spelled."

He leaned forward, probing the large braid of filaments closest to him. The instrument's crystal came to life and began to glow. Appearing satisfied, Quin moved to another large braid, carefully probing it the same as he had the last.

Naia followed him at a distance. "What are they?"

Quin stood up, turning toward another bundle of glowing fibers. "This is what's known as a hyphal artifact. It's not carved or forged; it's grown. Think of it like a fungus made of thousands of tiny hairs, each hair capable of drawing tremendous amounts of power and information."

He moved down the vine-like bundle, sticking his probes deep into the chitinous flesh of the conduit. This time, the crystal failed to glow. Frowning, Quin rocked the probe back and forth, feeling deep inside the braided strand. Still, the stone failed to react.

"Here." He held the dull crystal up for Naia to see. "This is broken." He moved to the side, turning to probe another bundle of fibers. "And this one, too."

He glanced up at her. "These conduits have been severed from their Circles of Convergence. That's why Athera's Crescent is failing."

"Can you fix them?"

He licked his lips, shaking his head in an expression of

uncertainty. "I'm not a hyphal architect; this isn't my area of expertise. So I really don't have a good idea of what I'm doing." He took a deep breath. "That being said...I have to try. So there's a very good chance I'm going to kill myself."

The statement sounded like his usual dry sarcasm. It took Naia a moment to realize that it wasn't.

"You're not serious," she said. The old pain came back, the same grief she had felt when Darien had left her behind in the chamber of the Well of Tears.

Quin slid the spectacles from his face, setting them aside. He reached up and rubbed his eyes. Then he looked at her, his face earnest. "I'm going to have to form a link with the conduit to repair the damage," he explained. "The problem is, the moment I fix it, the surge of power is probably going to kill me."

She stared at him in dismay. "No, Quin."

He put up a hand. "Naia, you can bring me back. The way you did with Sareen."

Naia was already shaking her head. "There's no guarantee—"

Quin's expression hardened. "I have to do this." Before she could protest, he rose to his feet. "You can bring me back. I know you can. That's why Tsula is so afraid of you."

"I can't—" Naia felt tears of frustration gathering in her eyes. They stung, hot and caustic, like the corrosive feelings eating her up inside.

Quin clenched his jaw, his eyes moving over her face. He reached up and clutched her arms. "You *can*. You're the chimera, Naia. Both priestess and mage. You didn't abandon your goddess; she just chose you for a greater purpose."

"Quin—"

He took a deep breath, eyes sad but resolute. "Just try. That's all you can do. If you can't...then I forgive you."

He released her and backed away. Despite the cold of the cavern, a trickle of sweat streaked down his face. With one last glance over his shoulder, he turned and knelt back down beside the conduit.

Her emotions numb, Naia pressed her back up against the wall. She felt like she was still in Aerysius, in the chamber of the Well of Tears. Watching Darien turn his back and leave her behind forever. Nothing had changed since then. She was still there; she'd never left.

Tears spilled down her face.

She watched Quin lean forward, reaching deep into the conduit like reaching into the innards of a body. He felt around in there for a minute. Then he stopped, motionless. He closed his eyes and bowed his head. His shoulders relaxed, his breathing slowed, becoming deep and regular. He sat like that for minutes, slouched, as if in a trance. Ever so slowly, he began to glow.

Argent light erupted from his body, saturating the chamber. Naia squinted, raising her hands against the brilliance of it. Beneath Quin's fingers, the dark conduit gave the slightest flicker of life. Then another. Soon, it pulsed like a living heartbeat. Quin's face wrinkled with concentration as the glow surrounding him strobed with the rhythm of the conduit, awakening every fiber in the braided strand. Sweat dribbled down his brow, dribbling from his nose and chin. His lips twisted, first in concentration. And then in pain. The light of the conduit swelled, the glow radiating from Quin swelled with it.

Too late, Naia realized why he wasn't moving. His body was locked rigid, his muscles paralyzed by the torrent of energy streaming through the conduit. Streaming into him. The light in the chamber became dazzling. Jaw clenched, Quin began to shake and groan, his body convulsing even as he maintained his grip on the lethal fibers of energy.

There was a brilliant flash.

Naia screamed, throwing her arms up to ward her face. When she opened her eyes, her vision swam with black motes that swirled in front of her. Her eyes stung, full of tears. Dizzy, she collapsed to a crouch, feeling around at the ground with her hands. She scrambled forward on all fours, desperately searching, her vision too distorted to see.

Her hand grasped a wad of fabric.

Scrubbing at her eyes, Naia struggled to see. She could make out only patches of light and shadow. She used her fingers instead, exploring the fabric of Quin's coat. He was lying next to her, face-down. Struggling, she rolled him over and pressed her hands against his chest, delving inside him with her mind.

Only emptiness echoed back.

Biting her lip, she probed deeper. Deep into the lifeless tissues, exploring, desperate to ascertain the type and amount of injury his ruined body had sustained. She wasted no time. Squeezing her eyes shut, she delved his flesh with all the brute diligence she could muster. She doubted if all she could do for him would come close to being enough. He'd taken so much damage.

She didn't know what to repair first. She started working furiously, first on the lifeless muscles of Quin's heart. But it was impossible. No matter what she did, she couldn't get his heart to beat. She went back and retraced her work, reexamining repairs she had already made...all for nothing.

She tossed her head back, biting her lip in frustration. Minutes passed. Sweat ran down her face. Beneath her fingers, Quin's body was still and silent. She pounded on his chest with her fists, more in anger then out of any delusion the action would help. It didn't.

Nothing did.

She probed every organ, every tissue. All were perfect; there was nothing wrong with him. Nothing left to heal. Quin's body was whole; only his soul had fled. And, no matter what she did, it wasn't coming back.

She collapsed over him and wept. She cried until there were no more tears left. Then she sat up, wiping her spilled grief off her face. She struggled to stand, blinking against the brilliant light that filled the chamber, so much stronger than it had been before. Quin had repaired the conduits before the power surge had killed him. They pulsated with a rhythmic, ethereal glow.

She knew that she should leave. There was nothing more she could do for him.

The priestess inside her wanted to turn back, to give him the proper care he deserved. To prepare his soul for its journey. But then she realized where that journey would lead him. Naia jerked to a halt, her heart wrenching. Quin wasn't destined for the Atrament. If she left his body there on the floor, his soul would never know peace.

She couldn't leave him like that.

She returned to his side.

One last time, she prodded Quin's dead heart with the power of her mind, coaxing it back to life. The heart muscle shivered and lurched in his chest. It staggered forward, settling into the semblance of a natural rhythm. Quin's staring eyes slid closed and didn't open again. His chest moved, but he didn't awaken.

At first, Naia thought it was a victory. Then she realized that it wasn't. She couldn't part the Veil of Death.

Only Xerys could help His Servant now.

Naia bowed her head and prayed for Quin's dark god to show him mercy.

No. His name wasn't Quin. It was Shahin. Shahin son of Marthax.

She leaned back against the cave wall, hugging her legs against her chest. She sat there for a long time, silently observing the rise and fall of his chest, watching his breath stir the whiskers on his face. Hours later, she fell asleep.

Naia stirred, wakening slowly. She pulled herself upright and rubbed her eyes, blinking at the brilliant light that filled the chamber. As her vision swam into focus, she realized Quin's body wasn't where she'd left it. She stood up, glancing around.

"Naia."

She whirled, flinching back before she recognized him. Quin caught her up in his arms, hugging her fiercely. Then he pulled back enough to stare into her face.

"You really are the loveliest sight I've ever seen in my whole damn life," he said.

Then he kissed her.

And she kissed him back.

Chapter Twenty-Eight
The Path of Compassion

Pass of Lor-Gamorth, The Front

Kyel crouched on the floor of the iron cage, his back pressed up against the unyielding bars. He'd been there for hours, staring down at the blackened, distorted shape that had once been Myria Anassis. No matter how hard he tried, he couldn't stop looking. The grisly remains were morbidly fascinating; it was strange how her fingers were preserved in such detail: every feature sculpted as if from black marble. He could see every crease, every fingernail, each perfectly formed and perfectly blackened. Her face had been distorted into a hideous thing, a ghastly mask of horror that gaped at him eyelessly.

The smell was sickening. The dungeon reeked of charred human.

Kyel looked to where Devlin Craig lay fallen. The commander's face was turned slightly toward him, staring with an unfocused, endless gaze into the shadows of the ceiling. A gray-fletched arrow pierced his neck, the same kind that stuck out from the back of the dead priest.

Kyel's gaze retreated to his hands, pondering them. The same hands that had nocked the arrows to the bowstring. He'd loosed them both without a second thought. It had seemed like the right thing to do.

Now he knew what a terrible choice he'd made.

The chain on his wrist was still in place, he noticed with relief. He hadn't broken his Oath of Harmony; he hadn't killed with his gift. But the conviction that held him to that Oath had eroded. He could feel it. It was like an infection, spreading like a malignancy under his skin. That was the reason why mages were forbidden weapons in the first place. Power was a temptation under the best of circumstances. Under the worst of circumstances, it was a temptation almost impossible to deny.

Holding that bow had felt so natural, so right. He'd stood there in the doorway for minutes, watching as Myria burned. When the priest had raised his torch again, Kyel had reacted. He hadn't been able to stand by and do nothing.

He'd sided with a Servant of Xerys. He'd killed his senior officer. And then he'd regretted it all a scant moment later, when he'd seen Darien finish off Craig without hesitation or remorse. And then raise the necrators. Kyel had realized he'd made a grave mistake.

Darien *was* evil. So was Craig. So was the priest. And so was Meiran. They were all evil, each in their own way. For whatever their respective reason, each had abandoned the path of compassion.

He heard a sound: the muffled echo of footsteps approaching from the corridor. Kyel stared warily at the doorway until Traver's face appeared. The man stopped between strides, staring in shock at Craig's mangled body. With a shout, he shot forward to kneel at his commander's side.

Kyel drew his knees up to his chest, tucking his head, too ashamed to look. He sat there for silent minutes, drowning in shame as Traver grieved. He only looked up when he heard the sound of footsteps approaching his cage.

"What the bloody hell happened?" Traver's voice was hoarse.

Kyel couldn't look at him. "Don't ask. Just get the keys. On the floor by Craig."

Traver looked at him sideways then glanced down at the charcoaled mass on the floor of the cage. His expression crumpled into something halfway between disgust and disbelief. He made a raspy, gagging noise way back in his throat, bringing his hand up to his mouth. Then he turned and picked his way slowly over to the body of his commander. He returned to the cage, holding his breath against the stench as he fumbled with the lock.

Kyel rose and stepped over the blackened Myria-husk, anxious to be as far away from it as he could get. He slipped out the door as soon as Traver got it open. Once outside, he bolted toward the exit, wanting nothing more than to escape the dungeon and never look back. He forced himself to stop, turning to wait for Traver.

The captain didn't follow immediately. Instead, he went back to kneel at Craig's side, bowing his head in respect. He unfastened his cloak and pulled it off his shoulders, then draped it like a shroud over the corpse. He knelt there a moment in silence. When he stood back up, Traver had a look in his eyes that Kyel had never seen before.

"Darien did this?" Traver didn't sound like he believed it. He glanced at the longbow on the floor.

Kyel didn't respond. He dropped his eyes to the ground, staring as if mesmerized by the patterns of the stonework.

Traver strode up to him, squeezing Kyel by the arm. "This is bad," he said. "But there's worse up top. You need to come see it."

Kyel nodded, too ashamed to respond. He knew Traver suspected he'd murdered Craig. The captain didn't have any proof to support his hunch, but the suspicion was there, written in his eyes. Kyel followed Traver out of the dungeon and onto the stairs, walking in silence all the way to the surface. They emerged from the stairwell into the fire-fed shadows of the courtyard.

Kyel stopped and glanced around in an attempt to get his bearings. The ward was roiling with soldiers and smoke, the garish flames of bonfires casting tortured streaks across the ground. The scene was chaotic, a turmoil of commotion. There was a lot of dead, he realized. The bodies of the fallen littered the inner ward, blood winding through channels in the cobbles. In some places, the dead were piled up on top of each other.

A gruesome corpse lay only paces from his feet. The face was locked in a rigid scream, the skin blistered and oozing. Kyel recognized the man: it was the soldier who had called him a darkmage to his face. He couldn't guess the cause of death, but he could tell it had been awful. Kyel took a step back away from the corpse. Then another.

"Kyel!"

He turned to find Meiran rushing toward him, Cadmus following as fast as his portly carriage would allow. She looked relieved to see him. "Where have you been?" she demanded, looking him over as if assessing him for injury.

Traver said warily, "I found him in the dungeon. Craig's dead. So's the priest." He shifted his weight nervously over his feet, glancing sideways at Kyel.

Meiran's face went slack. She looked from Traver to Kyel. "Are you injured?"

Kyel shook his head, looking out at the mass of bodies sprawled before him like a personal vision of hell prepared just for him. "No."

Meiran looked at Traver, demanding, "What happened?"

"Darien escaped and carved his way out of here." Traver sounded more frustrated than upset. "It's not pretty." He pointed to where gray-cloaked men were dragging corpses toward the edge of the yard, laying them out along the wall.

"Darien did this?" Kyel whispered in dismay, eyes raking over the carnage. It sunk into him then: this was all his fault. If he hadn't killed Craig and the priest, then these men would still be alive. Their deaths were on him. Aghast, he turned his back on the grisly scene, covering his mouth as he resisted the urge to vomit.

"What about the woman?" Meiran asked.

"She's dead. They burned her," Kyel responded woodenly, glancing at the nearest clump of bodies. Some of them appeared melted, as if doused with acid. Some were still smoldering.

Traver said, "I thought the magic field didn't work here. How did Darien do any of this?"

Meiran looked around, surveying the extent of the damage that surrounded her. "This wasn't the magic field that did this. Darien used the Onslaught. Maybe when he killed the priest…"

Kyel continued his relentless study of his boots as her voice trailed off.

Traver threw his hands up. "That's it, then. I can't keep either of you safe. You're both powerless here, but apparently they can come and go as they please. And after what we just did to the pass, you can expect they're going to retaliate."

"What did we do to the pass?" Kyel looked up at Traver in concern.

"We blew the powder and brought half the mountain down on top of them."

Kyel stared at the man. Then his eyes shot toward the dark ridgelines in the distance. Alarmingly, the view was very different than he remembered. The number of casualties…

Kyel spun away. He couldn't look at Traver. Darien's people had been evacuating through the canyon. He wondered how many had been buried. How many civilians. He felt betrayed. He'd given his word to Darien that his people would be safe. He'd never thought Traver or Craig would go that far, stoop to such depths of dishonor. He'd underestimated them.

"How many…?" he whispered.

"At least eight thousand casualties. More if we're lucky."

Lucky? Kyel closed his eyes as the number seeped in. He felt a numbness in his belly that clawed at his heart. So much evil. He gazed around at the corpses of the fallen. There was no right side. No good choice. It was all wrong, from every perspective. He felt sick that he'd ever been a part of any of it.

"Prime Warden, we need to get you both off the mountain," Traver said quickly. "Before they come for us."

Meiran shook her head, her face resolute. "No. We'll stand with you. But not here. Take us someplace outside the node. Somewhere we'll have a good view of the approaches."

Kyel stared after the corpses being dragged across the yard, wondering how Meiran could think they could make any bit of difference. If Darien could do this…Kyel knew there was no way they could defend against that kind of power. That kind of malice.

"I'll take you to the old keep," Traver announced. "It's far enough back behind our lines, you should be reasonably protected. Any difference you can make, well…I'd sure appreciate it."

Darien threw back the tent flap and emerged into the shadows of day. Seeing him, a score of men sitting around a coal-fire clambered to their feet. One of them was Sayeed, and the look on his face was painful to see. It rekindled the rage inside Darien, along with a profound sense of shame. He'd led Sayeed to believe that his nephew would be safely returned. He'd been wrong about that, just as he'd been wrong about everything. Darien knew that he alone was to blame.

"I'm sorry," he said. There was nothing else to say.

The Zakai officer let out a beleaguered sigh and shook his head. "Their hands are stained with blood, not yours. You are not to blame for their treachery."

Darien couldn't accept that. It was too easy; it gave none of the responsibility back to him. "I should have anticipated this. It's my fault."

"It was their fate," Sayeed insisted, laying a hand on Darien's shoulder. "Don't trouble your heart, Brother."

Hearing the man label him 'brother,' even in the face of his failure, brought Darien to new depths of shame. Anger and guilt burned together in his chest, scorching a hole right through him. "I promise you, Sayeed: Iskender will be avenged. I'll boil their blood and scatter their ashes on the winds."

Sayeed stared at him hard, a mercurial expression in his eyes. At last, he said, "There is a saying: 'Anger begins with madness, but ends in regret.'"

"Not this time," Darien disagreed. "This time, my anger has no end."

He heard a scraping noise behind him and turned to find Byron Connel standing amongst the cluster of men. The Battlemage strode up, clasped him roughly by the arm, and jerked Darien back in the direction of his tent. Darien didn't have a choice about going along with him. He glanced back at Sayeed as Connel propelled him through the flap.

Inside, Connel ripped off his shoes one at a time and threw

them into a corner. Seeing him, Azár ducked through the partition. Connel sat down heavily on the floor, gesturing for Darien to follow. He seated himself across from the man.

Azár came back in with a tray in her hands, her eyes flashing in alarm. Wordlessly, she served tea. Connel lifted his cup to his lips without a word of gratitude as Azár seated herself at Darien's side. She was keeping her gaze lowered, Darien realized. For some reason, that incensed him.

He reached up and took his wife's face in his hand. Purposefully, he lifted her chin until she was staring unblinking into his eyes. A proud smile touched her lips. With renewed confidence, she turned to stare openly at Connel.

The darkmage didn't seem to notice the interaction. Either that or he didn't care. He sat gazing down into his cup as if seeking there for insight. Without looking up, he said, "Did you really mean what you said out there?"

Darien frowned, not certain what he was referring to. Then it occurred to him: Connel had walked up just when he was avowing vendetta to Sayeed. "Every word," he said, and meant it.

"Good." Connel's eyes snapped up to lock on his own. "Because I'm going to give you the chance to scatter all the ashes you want."

Darien set his cup down, his interest piqued. "Go on."

Connel obliged him. "We're going to hit them hard. I want you and your Tanisars to spearhead the assault. Your mission will be to penetrate their lines and encircle the keep. We'll come behind you and mop up anything that's left. You're going to need to create as much shock and terror as you can. Strike enough fear into their hearts, and they'll collapse before you. Can you do that?"

"Aye." The hunger in his voice made Azár turn to stare at him.

To Darien, the plan sounded exhilarating. It was exactly the thing he needed, exactly what he craved. He wanted to plunge his sword deep into the heart of his enemy. He wanted to repay them pain for pain. He couldn't help but smile, the thrill of anticipation making his blood burn hot.

Connel set his cup down on the rugs. "Get your forces ready," he commanded, rising to his feet. "They'll be expecting us to be licking our wounds. They won't be expecting an attack."

Darien followed him to his feet, assuring him, "I'll scatter those ashes for you."

The Battlemage nodded. "I'll see you in the Rhen, Darien. Or I'll see you in hell. Whichever comes first for us."

Darien watched him leave as Azár pushed herself up off the ground. She stood gazing at him darkly, her expression resentful. She wasn't the type to stay behind and wait. He couldn't blame her.

He asked, "Would you be willing to stand and fight at my side?"

Azár's eyes widened, her cheeks flush with excitement. She gazed at him with open gratitude on her face. "I would be honored to fight at the side of my husband," she said solemnly.

Darien smiled, feeling a vast swelling of pride. "Good. Because I know exactly how to use you."

Lightning flared as their horses rounded a bend in the mountain's side. A chill gust of wind came up from the direction of the Black Lands, beating at Kyel's back. It was the same oppressive wind he remembered from the first time he'd ever looked upon the pass. Not much had changed. This was still the closest to hell he'd ever been.

He could see the foundations of the old keep above on the ridge. It was a sad and eerie sight that looked as charred and pathetic as Myria's corpse had. Below, they had a sweeping view of the canyon, and all the way out to the plains beyond. From this elevation, the landscape looked enormous, unfolding before them like a great black heaven dotted with pinpoints of light. Kyel pointed downward, uncertain what he was looking at.

"What's all that?" he asked.

Traver nodded in the direction of the grasslands. "The combined armies of Southwark and Chamsbrey."

Kyel's brow furrowed in confusion. "When did they arrive?"

"Yesterday."

He glanced back and forth between Traver, Cadmus, and Meiran, his gut tightening. "Why wasn't I told?"

"Because you're too honest, Kyel," Meiran snapped, reining in her mare and turning back to look at him pointedly.

"What does that mean?" He didn't like the look on her face, or the accusation in her voice.

"It means you wear your feelings on your face. We couldn't share our plans with you. Otherwise, we would have never gained Darien's trust. He'd have seen right through you in a heartbeat."

"So you left me in the dark on purpose." Kyel shook his head, feeling almost sorry for her. The betrayal he felt almost seemed to justify his actions back in the dungeon. Almost, but not quite. Nothing could justify that.

Meiran turned her horse, starting up the trail toward the old keep. Kyel kicked his mount forward, coming up beside her. "I'm your Sentinel, Meiran. You can't just keep me in ignorance."

"If you want to be treated like a Sentinel, then start acting like one," she snapped.

He made no attempt to mask the anger and resentment her words provoked. He'd been trying so hard for so long. But he felt hindered at every turn. Mostly by Meiran…sometimes by Cadmus. Usually by both. He was tired of the blame. Tired of the ridicule. Especially by people he felt he could no longer respect.

"I've tried, Meiran," he said. "But I've been having a hard time understanding some of the decisions you've been making lately."

The prime warden stopped her horse and cast a withering stare his way. "You don't need to understand. You don't even have to agree. All you need to do is *exactly what you're told.* Can you handle that, Grand Master?"

Kyel gritted his teeth. "Aye."

He looked at Traver, who glanced away. Then he looked at Cadmus, who returned his gaze steadily and sadly. Kyel sagged in his saddle, feeling conflicted. He'd half a mind to turn his horse around and ride back down the mountain. Only, he had no idea where he would go. He felt lost and without direction. He was embroiled in a conflict, and he didn't agree with either side.

They dismounted and led the horses the rest of the way up the slope to the ruins. The wind whipped up again, battering Kyel's cloak as he brought up the rear of their procession. Forks of lightning revealed the broken structure that awaited them. Not much was left, Kyel saw. Only two walls of the keep remained standing. The tower had collapsed entirely, now only a pile of rubble.

The wind exhaled a great, exhausted sigh.

By the time they gained the keep's ruins, Kyel's hands trembled with cold and fury. He took one last glimpse behind then followed Traver around a crumbled wall. There, he gazed down into a wide hole in the ground, what had once been the basement of the fortress. Now mostly filled in with broken rock and glistening black shafts of charred wood.

They tied the horses up along the gutted wall and made camp in a corner protected by the wind. There was no roof, no floor. Just dirt and charred embers, crumbled stone and bitter memories.

Glancing around, Kyel grumbled to no one in particular, "What good can we do here?"

Traver didn't look at him. In fact, he was making a conspicuous study of not looking at him.

Meiran did, though. She fixed him with the same, insufferable expression. "We'll do whatever we *can* do, Kyel. Defensive shielding, creating diversions, healing the wounded—whatever the moment calls for."

Kyel wondered at the wisdom of that. Their new position wasn't very defensible, and the open basement could be easily overrun. He doubted it would be wise to draw attention to their location.

They carved a firepit from the ashes and made camp around it. Cadmus rummaged through his pack, finally producing a loaf of bread and a sack of jerky, passing it around. Traver took a good-sized hunk of meat and tore off a bite with his teeth. He poked at the fire with a stick, his face hardened. He hadn't said a word since they had gained the fortress. He threw the stick down in the fire.

"I'm going to go scout around," he announced, his face grimly set. He flung his gray cloak back over his shoulder. He stabbed a glance at Kyel. "Why don't you come with me?"

"All right."

Kyel stood up, dusting his hands. He didn't like the way Traver was acting. He glanced at Meiran and, at a nod from her, started after Traver. He followed the captain out of the lee of the crumbled wall and into the infernal wind. Traver turned back, taking a quick measure of him, then motioned for Kyel to follow. They found a trail that wound around through the wreckage then cut down toward the backside of the ruin.

The wind faded as they moved behind the protection of an outcrop. Kyel walked behind Traver, taking his time about navigating the narrow path leading down the steep embankment. There, almost at the cliff's edge, was a large boulder that Kyel remembered well. He used to sit upon that rock often, just to think. Every crack and grain of its texture was familiar to him.

"I remember this place," Kyel said, reaching out to touch the worn surface of the boulder. "I used to come here with Darien."

Traver turned toward him, and Kyel saw that the hardness hadn't left his eyes. If anything, it had crystalized. Kyel drew his hand back, alarmed. He glanced at the cliff. Then he looked back at Traver, unsure of his intentions.

"I need to ask you something," Traver said, his voice more serious than Kyel had ever heard it.

"What?" Kyel sank down onto the rock, ice clawing at his chest. He thought he knew what Traver was going to say.

Traver dropped to a crouch in front of him, until he was at eye level with Kyel. He leaned forward with a hand on the pommel of his sword. "Back in the dungeon...I noticed something that struck me as odd," he said slowly.

Kyel's eyes lingered on Traver's hand. He felt a sudden, ghastly chill. The rock scarp beside them seemed altogether too close.

Peering into Kyel's eyes, Traver asked him directly, "Where did Darien Lauchlin get a longbow?"

Kyel swallowed, looking down. The world stabilized, its motion jarring to a halt. And then it condensed, contracting until the only thing left was the condemnation in Traver's stare. Kyel couldn't move. He kept his eyes fixed on Traver's hand.

"Why'd you do it?" Traver asked, picking up a fist-sized rock. He turned it over in his hands, eyes coldly examining it.

"Because they shouldn't have to die in darkness!" Kyel spat, leaping up. It was an open admission of guilt, but he didn't care anymore. He'd had enough. He wasn't the one in the wrong here. Out of all of them, he was the only one in the right.

"I disagree," Traver growled, and hurled the rock.

An explosion of sparks erupted across Kyel's vision, glittering bright.

Chapter Twenty-Nine
Xerys' Shadow

Pass of Lor-Gamorth, The Front

The demons on the wind howled like ravenous dogs, shrieking and gnashing, ripping up the topsoil and flinging it at the Spire of Orguleth. At the mountain's base, thousands of soldiers stood, overwhelming the plain, their backs to the wind, faces to their fate. At the end of the march, there would be a dawn. For most, it would be the first dawn they'd ever looked upon. For others, it would be the last. It didn't matter; the wind wailed at them all indifferently.

Darien pulled himself across the saddle of his mount as the vicious gusts tried to tear him back off again. He moved with difficulty, unused to the enameled cuirass Connel had given him. Azár mounted her own horse, armored in a similar style of plate. She glanced over at him and smiled. A proud smile, full of dark promise for their enemies.

Darien heard a low growl, distinct from the wind. Looking down, he noticed that the thanacryst had wandered out from the lee of the tent where it had been sheltering from the wind. The demon-dog paused next to him, eyes fixated on the mountains, its hackles rising. A great glob of slobber drooled from its mouth, and its eyes gleamed like hell-born embers.

The call of a war horn rose above the wind, moaning like a tortured spirit. Darien tightened the strap of his helm beneath his chin. Then he gathered the reins of his stallion and directed it forward with the pressure of his legs. The horse snorted, jerking its head, then moved forward in a swaying gait. The combined legions of Malikar advanced behind him up the incline that led into the Pass of Lor-Gamorth.

Kyel groaned, biting back the pain in his head and the bile in his throat. His eyes slit open just a crack. It was all he could manage. Through a fog of misery, he saw Meiran leaning over him. Her face looked drawn, her expression like soured wine.

"Don't try to use the magic field," she cautioned in her usual monotone. "You have a head injury."

Kyel tried to blink his vision back into focus. He gazed up at her mutely, fumbling to comprehend his situation. He was lying on his side, hands and feet trussed like a hog awaiting slaughter. Just the thought of using the magic field made his stomach rebel with a pang of nausea.

"What's going on?" he murmured, his voice just as blurry as the rest of the world.

His gaze shifted to Traver, who stood on the other side of Meiran with his hands on his hips. The look of accusation in his old friend's eyes was painful to witness. Kyel suddenly remembered the rock. And why Traver had used it on him.

Meiran said, "You admitted to being a traitor. And a murderer."

That's right. He'd killed both Craig and the priest. Kyel supposed that did make him a traitor and a murderer. Funny how he didn't feel like either.

"Then why am I still alive?" Soon, his head would be clear enough to touch the magic field again. Then all the bonds they'd tied him with wouldn't matter. He couldn't understand why they hadn't killed him already.

Meiran folded her arms, bending down until her face was scant inches from his own. "Because their army is on the march, and they're coming here to destroy us. Despite my better judgement, *we need you.*"

Kyel's head throbbed, as much from the logic of that argument as from the injury.

"Let them through, Meiran" he said. "That way, no one needs to die. It's what you agreed to in the first place."

Meiran stood up, dusting herself off. She wore a disgusted look on her face. "They're out for blood, now. They won't just pass us by."

"And who's fault is that?"

The look in her eyes was caustic enough to corrode his confidence. Kyel closed his eyes as a fresh surge of nausea tightened his stomach. The world spun, and for a moment he thought he was going to be sick. But he spat the bile out of his mouth and swallowed the rest back down again.

He looked miserably up at Meiran. "I don't understand you. You've abandoned all sense of decency. You're just as bad as Darien. Honestly, I don't see any difference between the two of you. You've both been to hell, and you've both come back changed. Maybe there's something to that."

Meiran's face went slack, her paleness fading into whiteness. But her eyes remained hard. She whispered, "You think *I'm* the one who's corrupted?"

"I think you both are."

Meiran glanced to Cadmus, who was squatting on the other side of the dying fire. She turned back to Kyel. "It doesn't matter what you believe. I'm still the prime warden, and I'm giving you a choice. Defend me with your life. Help me get down off this mountain. Or die now on your friend's sword."

That wasn't much of an option. Kyel saw Traver's hand moving toward the hilt of his blade. His gaze traveled upward to the man's face. He saw his own fate meted out in blood in Traver's eyes.

Kyel sighed, resigned. "I'll defend you with my life. As much as my Oath will allow."

Meiran looked grimly satisfied. She said, "That chain on your wrist is the only reason you're still alive. Don't lose it. The moment that chain comes off, I'll give the order to have you slain."

Kyel nodded; he expected no less.

Meiran said to Traver, "Release him."

Kyel went rigid as both Meiran and Traver knelt beside him, one sawing through the ropes that held him, the other laying hands on his chest. Kyel stiffened, knowing exactly what was coming. But knowing didn't make it any better.

The shock of Meiran's healing swept over him, dragging him down like the suction of a whirlpool. He gasped, feeling his consciousness twist away.

The climb into the pass was slow and grueling, infinitely tedious. Rain slanted down like icy needles, buffeted by the wind. The collapse of the mountainside had buried the canyon and its approaches, which made progress even more difficult. Connel had ordered a battalion of engineers to precede them, forging a new trail and clearing debris from their path, until they reached a shallow lake that had formed behind the blockage in the stream. The walls of the canyon were too steep to bypass the lake; they would have to cross it.

Darien stared down from the top of a rock scarp at the narrow lake below, not liking the looks of the situation. The stream that fed the canyon had been blocked by the landslide. With no outlet, the water was collecting, forming a long and narrow lake that was altogether treacherous. The east edge of the lake lapped against a sheer rock precipice. The other side was overlooked by a series of low bluffs where his intuition told him Greystone archers would be stationed.

Darien didn't see any bowmen. But that didn't mean they weren't there.

He didn't trust it. The lake was a natural killing zone, a place where any advancing force would be slowed to a crawl, its defensive options limited. If Craig were still alive, he wouldn't let such an opportunity for slaughter slip him by. And even though Craig was dead, Darien guessed that his orders were still being followed. They hadn't had the time or talent to come up with something better.

Darien ordered a halt well back from the lake, out of bowshot. There was not enough room to erect tents, so he had his men camp right there on the top of the rubble, building cookfires to huddle around. If his men were going to fight, then they would fight rested, with their bodies warm and their bellies full.

"They must see us coming." Azár nodded in the direction of the cliffs above the lake, her eyes dark and shadowed with worry. "Why do we stop here and give them time to prepare?"

"Because I want them to see us coming," Darien answered, removing his helm. He pointed at the cliffs ahead with a chain-gloved hand. "I want them to watch us fill this canyon and get a good sense of our numbers."

Azár nodded, seeming to understand his intent. "Our numbers will strike fear into their hearts. Their ranks will crumble before us."

"Aye," Darien agreed. "That's the idea."

The look of excitement on Azár's face surprised him. He'd always known she was fierce; he'd admired that. But he hadn't foreseen how alive she would become at the prospect of battle.

"We will feed them their fear," she whispered.

"That will be your job. The light you'll weave will fill them with terror."

Azár's smile grew proud and ferocious. Never had Darien seen a woman more intensely beautiful than his wife was at that moment. He turned and walked away to where his officers stood gathered, the demon-hound stalking at his side. He caught Sayeed's attention with a wave of his hand, beckoning the man over.

"We'll maintain position here for a few hours," Darien instructed. "Tell the men to sharpen their tent posts at both ends. Double the fires. Burn every coal brick, if that's what it takes. I want it to look like we've got at least twice our true number."

Sayeed stared at him in incomprehension. "What do we do when we run out of coal?"

"It won't matter. After the morrow, we'll be in the Rhen. And then there'll be plenty of villages to burn."

Sayeed squeezed Darien's arm. Then he strode away to relay orders to the other officers.

Darien pulled off his gloves and turned to survey the column behind him, admiring the discipline of his men as they went about the process of setting up camp. Before arriving in the

Black Lands, he never would have imagined such efficiency possible. He looked about in awe of the people he led, of the wife he'd married, of the fortunes that fate had brought him. For the first time in years, he felt worthwhile.

He realized that this must be his purpose, the reason why he had been spared when Aerysius fell, why he'd cast off the chains of his bondage. Why he had pledged his soul to two dark gods and put the Soulstone on his neck. All that had happened for a reason.

Because these people deserved to see the sun.

And Darien was determined to give it to them.

The night wore on infinitely, the way nights do before a battle. Darien had a hard time staying asleep. He kept jerking awake, gasping for air and drenched in sweat. His mind worked furiously, sifting through strategies and weighing contingencies. Minimizing casualties and maximizing assets. He knew there was no way to predict how the battle would go; the best he could do was prepare and anticipate. But battles had a way of taking on a life of their own, and that bothered him. He didn't like anything outside his control.

Darien finally gave up on sleep and rose well before the rest of the camp. He ate a quick meal then set out, intending to take one last survey of the lake and the battlefield ahead. He wore his cloak over his black cuirass. With the helm on his head, he was indistinguishable from any other officer in Bryn Calazar's legions.

No one recognized him, which was good. He walked away from the camp, following the gentle rise of the slope above the lake. Scanning the cliffs ahead, he saw no fires. But he wasn't fooled; he knew they were there. Darien knew it because that's what he would have done. And he felt certain that's what Craig would have done, too.

He marveled that he felt no compassion for the Greystone soldiers he had once fought beside, as if his death had erased all ties to his former homeland. Craig's betrayal certainly had. Men he'd once considered brothers, he now held beneath his contempt. He didn't understand the people he'd been born to, didn't want to try to understand them.

He just wanted them dead.

The fires were doused, the Tanisars formed up in a long, drawn-out column, awaiting the order to advance. Helm tucked in the crook of his arm, Darien walked with Azár toward the clump of officers standing on a long, flat ledge. Azár was wearing her armor, carrying her helm. Darien's hand rested on the hilt of the scimitar given to him by Sayeed. The blade once held by Khoresh Katim, the only conqueror to ever successfully unite all of Caladorn.

The air was frigid, and his metal armor felt like a layer of ice. It sapped the heat right out of him, even through the thick padding he wore beneath it. Every breath formed a cloud before his face. Fingering the hilt of Katim's sword, Darien moved into the center of the cluster of officers. He swept his gaze over them, looking into the face of each man individually. He felt a twinge of anticipation, the feeling that the future was finally forming up into something tangible. The promise of sunlight ahead didn't seem quite as surreal as it had the day before.

To the officers standing 'round him, he said, "We'll have to advance right up the center, through the middle of the lake. It's not deep, but it'll be slow going. Expect an ambush. They'll have archers stationed above you on those cliffs." He pointed at the bluffs above the water.

He continued, "There's only a thousand of us. But every one of our soldiers is worth three of theirs. Pick the fastest men and women you have. They'll need to gain the far shore as quickly as they can. They'll be under heavy fire the whole way, so tell them to keep their shields up and their heads down. Our objective is to gain and hold the shoreline. Then we'll wait for the main force to relieve us."

He turned to Azár, who stood looking up at him with a noncommittal expression. He told her, "I want you riding at my side. I'll weave shadow as we cross the lake; I want them fighting blind. You can't dodge a blade if you can't see it coming. When we reach the shoreline, that's when I'll need your light."

Azár's eyes smiled at him, proud and eager.

Darien donned his helm and mounted his armored stallion, nudging his horse toward the files of men. Azár followed on her own mare as the officers dispersed to their respective commands. He directed his mount to the front of the column, where he drew up and waited.

When the battalion was formed up behind him, Darien drew Katim's sword. He held it over his head then brought it down decisively. The column behind him advanced. Darien kept his horse in check, allowing the warriors to pass him by as he called on the fury of the magic field, weaving shadow to cloak their intent. After the first battalion had past, he urged his mount forward, Azár at his side. The shadow he wove roiled over them like a blanket of coal-soot, covering them all in stifling darkness that muted even sound.

The infantry made their way down the rock scarp formed by the slide, then waded into the murky lake. The men moved through the water without a sound, holding their shields and weapons over their heads. Darien sent his stallion forward, wading into water almost up to its belly. Sayeed waded beside Azár's horse. A totality of silence travelled with them. No one spoke. There was no rustle of armaments or jingle of tack.

Nevertheless, a shout rang down from the heights. It was followed by the infinite quiet that only comes before the storm. Darien closed his eyes, bracing. He concentrated, thickening the shadows above Azár until they became a palpable barrier.

A whisper hissed through the darkness.

He couldn't see the arrow-cloud, so he let it descend upon them. Immediately, the silence of the canyon was assaulted by a raining clatter. Arrows clanged off shields, plunked against helms, rebounded off steel. Darien's cuirass rattled, battered by the volley coming down around him, as more arrows clanked against his stallion's armor. A man to the left of him grunted and went down, a clothyard shaft protruding from a gap between plates. Arrows collected on the surface of the water, floating like driftwood. The men around him surged forward, scrambling to reach the shoreline.

Another hiss, followed by the clamor of broadheads. There was a pause. Then more arrows came down in a constant hail as the archers began loosing their shafts at will. Darien gathered in his web of shadows further, tightening them densely around Azár while leaving his own men exposed. He heard groans and screams as more soldiers fell under the relentless barrage. But Azár remained safe, which was all that mattered. The life of one Lightweaver was worth more than a thousand warriors.

Ahead of him, the first ranks reached the shore. They were met by another cloud of arrows, this one coming from groups of bowmen stationed dead ahead against the canyon wall. At close range, the gray-fletched shafts were more effective. Instead of just plunking off armor, they began to penetrate. Screams and groans erupted all along the ranks as men began to fall with frequency. Bodies collected along the shore of the lake, creating stumbling blocks for the soldiers coming behind. Darien's horse tripped over a corpse half-submerged in the shallows, but it regained its footing quickly, surging toward the shore.

More men slumped and fell ahead of him. Darien tightened his cloak of shadows, unable to do more. Men sprinted past, rushing forward to pound the sharpened stakes they carried into the mud, creating a slanting thicket of spikes hidden by their numbers. More men screamed and fell as others set about the punishing job of resharpening the stakes after they'd been hammered in.

The barrage of arrows suddenly ceased.

Darien glanced up, knowing the reason. His body tensed in expectation.

A swelling thunder echoed off the canyon walls as a wedge of cavalry careened toward them. More Tanisars crowded the bank, a constant stream arriving from behind. The numbers amassing on the shoreline swelled, jostling the front ranks forward and pushing them toward the oncoming charge.

Darien raised his hands, reaching out from within and taking hold of the lines of power that swirled through the canyon. He drew it all in, every drop he could stand, until he was filled to the point of saturation and power bled from his body. Dropping the shadow-shield, he hurled everything he had at the incoming riders.

Horses staggered and fell, rolling as their riders flew from their backs. A few of the chargers made it as far as the front ranks, hurling onto the sharpened stakes as his own men sprang back. Animals screamed and died, spitted on shafts. Some turned and bolted back in the direction they'd come, foiling the momentum of the charge. Soon the entire beach was a gruesome tumult of confusion.

Ahead of him, Darien saw a line of Greystone infantry brandish their weapons. With a mighty warcry, they charged across the trampled beach, hoisting swords and pikes, maces and crossbows.

"Now," Darien said.

All around, Azár's magelight bloomed like glistening ribbons of dawn, so bright it made his eyes water. The golden warmth swelled, consuming the darkness in a wash of tortuous brilliance. Within it, Darien's own magelight spread forward like a molten river of bluest lava.

"Hold here!" he yelled to Sayeed and Azár as he kicked his mount through the blinding spill of light.

He could do no more with the magic field; he was already saturated to capacity and feeling the strain. So he called upon the Onslaught, sucking it into him with violent fury. Then he lashed out with everything he had, using Azár's brilliant magelight as a catalyst.

The resulting firestorm surpassed anything he could have imagined.

The screams were almost as terrible as the stench that followed. Only a few men survived long enough to engage the Tanisars. Some hit the ground, tumbling, then rose, fighting to bring their weapons up. They staggered a couple of steps before exploding. Others erupted into flame, some melting into the ground. The lucky ones just folded over and died.

The fresh corpses dissolved, searing the ground where they lay. Man-like shadows bloomed in their place. A host of necrators glided forward, disoriented. They were newborn and weak, yet uncertain of their duty. Darien looked upon his creations with a cold feeling of pride.

The Tanisars around him charged, taking advantage of the chaos. With a thundering cry, hundreds of warriors ran forward, weapons raised. The assault careened right into the center of the Greystone retreat, then continued forward as more soldiers poured through, widening the rupture.

Then the necrators swarmed in to finish off the rest.

Darien's horse reared, spooked by the presence of the shades. He was flung to the ground, the wind knocked out of him. He lay there panting as he watched his stallion bolt away. A Greystone foot-\ soldier saw him down and raised an iron mallet to finish him off. Before the man could swing, he was hurling backward, exploding while still in the air.

Darien hauled himself to his feet, summoning the remainder of the necrators under his command: a frightful army, if ever there was one. They ranged ahead of his mortal forces, questing, seeking, terrorizing. Soldiers screamed and fled, abandoning their duties and their comrades. Those brave enough to stand their ground met terrible ends.

He followed after his creations through the blinding glare of Azár's magelight. He trudged forward, using the Onslaught to punch a wedge through a group of foot soldiers. The men shrieked as they burned, the sound of their agony grimly satisfying.

Darien continued forward into the thick of the melee, tossing would-be adversaries back away from him carelessly. Arrows and weapons didn't touch him; they were no match for the wrath of the Onslaught that surrounded him like a lethal aura. His opponents slumped to the ground or simply burned where they stood.

A squad of infantry broke out of the enemy line to assault him directly, howling and with weapons raised as they sprinted toward him. Darien closed his eyes. When he opened them again, the men were boneless globs, and he was glowing with a terrible green light.

Darien staggered back, faltering. The strain of handling the vast amounts of power he'd drawn was taking its toll. He took a lurching step forward and felt an arrow plunk against his armor. Another shaft found its way through a gap between plates.

He cried out, driven to his knees by the searing fire that erupted from his shoulder. He gritted his teeth and tugged on the arrow's shaft, wrestling the chiseled barb out from under his collar bone. Reeling from pain and on the verge of passing out, he squeezed his eyes closed and healed the injury.

He caught himself with an outstretched hand as the mending swept over him. Eventually, the world stabilized. Somehow, he managed to stay awake. Darien picked himself up off the ground, clenching his jaw against the terrible weariness that was the price of the healing. He staggered, shambling like a drunken man. The heavy armor bore down on his shoulders, pressing down on him like a giant hand trying to squash him into the grave.

Seeing his struggles, his men swept forward and formed a defensive ring around him. It wasn't necessary. Every gray-cloaked soldier that broke toward him slumped to the ground, where they lay twitching and bleeding and melting into the dirt. The more he walked, the more exhausted he became, until he staggered with every step.

A foot soldier wrapped an arm around him, supporting him as Darien sagged to the ground. He couldn't bear the weight of the armor any longer. He reached up and unlocked the rivets that held his cuirass together, letting the plates slide apart. With the Tanisar's help, he shed the heavy steel, groaning with relief when the weight was finally off him. He sat there for a moment just panting, trying desperately to catch his breath.

"Brother, are you injured?"

Suddenly, Sayeed was there, kneeling at his side. He caught Darien by the shoulders, a look of intense concern on his bearded face. Behind him came Azár, glowing with radiance brighter than the sun. The world looked smeared, like someone had swiped a cloth across wet canvas.

Darien shook his head to clear his vision. He wiped his face with his sleeve, which came away stained. Sweat and blood streamed from his brow. He felt disoriented. He glanced around, at last realizing that the fighting around him had worn itself out.

Behind Sayeed, what was left of the Greystone defenders knelt at the feet of black-mailed guards. Scattered corpses littered the landscape like fallen logs, in some places collected into heaps. Shadowy necrators roamed the battlefield, diligent in their business.

"The canyon is ours," Sayeed reported, and clapped him on the arm with a grin.

Darien stared up at him, too exhausted to smile back. He nodded instead, closing his eyes in relief.

Chapter Thirty
Battlemage

Pass of Lor-Gamorth, The Front

D arien turned at the sound of hoofbeats to find Byron Connel riding toward them along the shoreline. His courser swayed in its gait, lathered sides crusted with mud. The Battlemage reined in and dismounted, his blue robes flowing out from under an enameled breastplate. He wielded the silver talisman Thar'gon in his hand. The weapon glowed with an eldritch light, drenching Connel in a halo of radiance. He strode over to where Darien sat resting between Azár and Sayeed. Looking down, he nodded a greeting.

"That was well-executed," he said, cold eyes shifting to the grisly terrain. "We'll mop up what's left. Use the momentum we've gained to take the keep."

Sayeed glanced down at Darien, raising his eyebrows in concern. Darien shook his head and spread his fingers in a gesture of negation.

Connel mounted and rode away, awash in the argent brilliance of his weapon. Darien let his eyes follow the horse and rider across the battlefield until both were lost from sight. Then he turned to Sayeed.

"I'm tired," he admitted. "But I'm not used up. Connel's right; we need to press our advantage."

"The keep is inside a node," Azár protested, her hand on the dagger at her belt.

Darien nodded. "Aye, it is. But I've the Hellpower." He rose to his feet, working his arms to test his shoulder. It moved freely without pain, but he could still feel the effects of the healing. He tried not to let his exhaustion show on his face.

"I want you to stay here," he told Azár. "You won't be of any use up there."

But his wife lifted her chin, narrowing her eyes. She slid the dagger from its sheath, holding it up in front of him. "I fight at your side," she reminded him. "Where you go, I go."

He pulled her against his chest, dagger and all, then released her just as quickly. He motioned to his officers to gather around.

"We'll continue on to the keep," he told them. "It'll be a frontal assault straight into the teeth of their fortifications. I know of some of the traps they've rigged, so I'll go ahead of you." To Azár, he cautioned, "I won't be able to heal. The Onslaught doesn't work like that."

"Then don't get hurt."

Sayeed moved forward to help Darien back into the cuirass he'd shed. The weight of the plate immediately bore down on him. He felt a deep-seated weariness that only sleep would mend.

He gave one last glance at the fallen corpses that patterned the ground around him, most wearing gray cloaks. It occurred to him that he felt not even a scrap of compassion for the fallen. He found that odd; these men had once been under his command. Yet the only feeling he could muster was a growing sense of vindication. He stepped over the first corpse that lay sprawled in his path, the remains of a young pikeman who would move no more.

Someone brought him a captured horse, a nervous brown destrier that was rightfully skittish of him. With a word, Darien dismissed his entourage of necrators. The absence of the shades calmed the gelding somewhat, enough to tolerate him on its back. Pulling Azár up behind him, Darien gathered the reins in his hand. He grasped a fistful of the horse's mane and kicked it forward.

By the time they reached the fortress, the wind had died. The whole world seemed to be holding its breath in anticipation of the inevitable.

Darien took a good, hard look at the keep and scowled, estimating the losses they would sustain trying to penetrate its defenses. He'd already fought his way out of there, so he knew he could fight his way back in. He just dreaded doing so. He already wore enough blood on him. It coated his armor and slathered the parts of his face not shielded by his helm. He was still exhausted. And he didn't look forward to the tests he would face within those walls. Kyel might be in there somewhere. And Meiran. He wasn't sure he could bring himself to kill either one of them.

The very thought of Meiran turned his blood to ice. Her image in his mind twisted something already broken inside him. It drove all rational thought away, until all he could see was red. Darien took a deep breath and hung his head. Then he glared back up at the fortress with new resolve.

"Brother."

He looked down to find Sayeed standing alongside his mount. The officer nodded in the direction of the slopes below the fortress. Darien followed his gaze, spotting a group of men who had emerged from the dark entrance to the keep, really just a hole in the mountainside. They looked like men of rank. One of them bore a white cloth in his hand, a token of truce. To Darien's relief, he didn't see Kyel among them.

Sayeed said, "They may be wishing to discuss surrender."

Darien was not disposed to discuss surrender. Perhaps the men approaching him could tell his frame of mind; they had a nervous look about them. One man tugged at his collar as he walked. Another fidgeted with his uniform. Every face looked strained and battle-weary.

"No quarter," Darien said, his gaze tracking the approaching men. "Leave two witnesses alive to report what they've seen here. No mercy to the rest. They die here, and they die brutally. Restraint now will only cost us later."

Sayeed nodded his agreement. Then he turned and relayed Darien's orders in the language of the clans. His men raised a warcry, shaking their weapons in the air. Upon hearing it, the Greystone officers turned and fled back in the direction of the tunnel.

"Visea," Darien whispered.

Five necrators melted into existence and swept forward up the steps. From within the tunnel came frantic echoes of horror. The commotion faded quickly into a haunting silence.

Darien thrust his arm up, gripping his gloved hand into a fist. Then he brought it down.

With a cry, the Tanisar ranks burst forward, breaking like a tidal wave of wrath upon the slopes of the mountainside. Darien allowed the soldiers to charge past him. He waited, watching as his men were halted at the entrance of the fortress by the fall of an iron gate.

He dismounted stiffly and stood leaning against his horse. Azár slipped to his side, considering him with a look of concern. "This is the edge of the node," she said, reaching out and catching his hand. "Stay here, my husband. Do not enter within."

He shook his head. "I'll be fine. I want you to wait here." He stroked a thumb across her soft fingers.

"I will not—" she started to protest.

"You're more than my Lightweaver," he said. "You're my light." Then he kissed her. For the first time, he felt his wife soften in his arms, the feral tension draining out of her.

He closed his eyes and reached deep inside her, pinching something there. He caught Azár as she slumped unconscious against his chest. Darien looked to Sayeed, who stared at him with a face frozen in shock.

"Take the horse," he commanded. "Get her back down the mountain. *Now.*"

Sayeed effected a curt bow then sprang onto the back of the warhorse. Darien lifted Azár up to him, making sure she was secure in the officer's grasp. Then he slapped the horse's rump, sending it forward down the slope. He turned and mounted the steps to the keep.

Above, he could hear the sound of screams and the battering of arrows against armor as his men took fire from the arrow loops above. His assaulting force had been stopped by the sealed gate that blocked the entrance to the fortress. Without a battering ram, they could go no further.

"Stand back," he warned the Tanisars.

The men complied, backing out of his way.

Darien closed his eyes, letting the Hellpower fill him until he could feel it wriggling inside every bone, worming beneath his skin. Then he opened his eyes and hurled it all back out of him in a blast of sickening energy directed at the gate. The iron gate turned at first red and then yellow, finally heating to white before it started to slump. The whole thing melted to liquid that ran in a viscous, spreading pool down the steps toward him. Darien willed the molten iron to cool. And it did. It hardened into a cascade of gleaming metal, its leading edge a handspan away from his feet.

He didn't hesitate. He stepped forward onto it.

"Lord!" one of the officers called from behind him.

Darien turned, glancing back over his shoulder at the man, who jogged up to him and bowed.

"Give us the honor of going ahead of you!" the man gasped, his eyes wide and full of battle-rage.

Darien understood. It was a matter of *sharaq*. He nodded at the officer. "You may have the honor."

He stood on the steps, catching his breath as a regiment of Tanisars swept past him over the cooling slag that had once been the gate of the fortress. He waited until the last man entered the tunnel, then donned his helm and started after them.

A deafening thunder ripped the air. Then the shockwave hit, hurling Darien backward off his feet as the entire fortress exploded in a shower of souls and stone.

Kyel jolted awake to an intense feeling of wrongness.

He moaned, groggy, tossing his head from side to side. Blinking, he willed the world back into focus. The spinning of the universe gradually slowed. His head felt better, not so much like a gourd with all its guts scraped out of it. That was the first thought he had. The second thought made him sit bolt upright.

He scrambled to his feet. Meiran was standing with her back

to him against a crumbled wall, staring out into the darkness that, for some reason, seemed less infinite than usual. In the distance, there was light. A violent, raging glow that painted her face and gleamed like blood crystals in her eyes. He took a step toward her, demanding, "What happened?"

The prime warden glanced back at him, one hand on the charred wall, her face condemning. "We brought the keep down on top of them."

Kyel felt a shiver of abject cold steel over him. He backed away from her, away from Traver's reproachful glare and Cadmus' downturned gaze. Edging backward up the dirt path, he fled the footprints of the ruin. He stopped on a lip of charred rock that was once the foundation of the fortress. He turned and gazed out across the wide ravine.

Fires burned where the new keep had once stood, their flames choked by smoke and dust. The entire stronghold had been reduced to rubble. Kyel stood there numb, gazing out upon a scene of devastation that was partially his own making.

"A lot of good people died today, Kyel." Traver's harsh words lashed out at him like a whip. Kyel jerked around to face him.

"And you blame me." He broke out in a sweat.

"I do."

Kyel clenched his hands into trembling fists. He whirled on Meiran, his eyes narrowing in cold rage. "All this could have been prevented if you'd just honored your given word. No one had to die!"

He glared back and forth between Meiran, Traver, and the fires. The graveness of their situation was starting to creep up on him. There was an entire Enemy army down there. And soon it would be marching in their direction.

"What do we do?"

"We need to go," Traver growled, gripping the pommel of his sword with his one good hand. "We can make it out of the pass by morning. Are we bringing him with us?" he asked Meiran, jerking his head at Kyel.

Meiran considered Kyel gravely, as if weighing his fate with her eyes. "Yes," she sighed finally. She started up the path toward him. But she jolted to a halt, gaping at something behind him.

Kyel whirled around. It took him precious seconds to realize what he was looking at. And precious more to react. He reached out with his mind, throwing up a golden shield between Meiran and the red-bearded darkmage striding toward them through the fog of smoke.

Traver drew his sword and stepped between them.

"*NO!*" Kyel shouted.

The demon didn't pause in his stride, but raised his spiked morning star over his head. He brought it down in a curving arc.

The weapon didn't connect. Yet Traver sailed backward, flung through the air as if hit by the brunt force of a hurricane. He hit the ground with a sickening noise.

Kyel gaped at the sight of Traver jerking spastically, his head leaking brains and blood onto the rocks.

The shock alone almost stunned him into inaction. But somehow, Kyel kept the golden shield up as he stood his ground between Meiran and the approaching demon. Behind him, he could hear Cadmus retching his dinner onto the ground.

The blue-robed darkmage halted in front of them, raising his accursed weapon. His eyes burned fierce, his body aglow with the argent light of the talisman. His brutal eyes locked on Kyel with a presence that was numbing in its strength.

"*Surrender.*"

Kyel couldn't react. He was paralyzed by the demon's gaze, gripped in ice-cold shackles of terror. Out of the corner of his eye, he saw Traver still twitching on the ground. He opened his mouth, but that was the best he could do. He couldn't force a single word past his lips.

The demon took a threatening step toward him, his gaze commanding. "Drop. Your. Shield."

Kyel swallowed, finally realizing who it was that confronted him: Byron Connel, ancient Warden of Battlemages. The same man who had single-handedly decimated Caladorn's armies.

In Connel's eyes, Kyel saw the promise of his own death.

There was no reason to fight, he realized. He'd already lost. He didn't have the skills or the strength to defend against Connel's power. Nevertheless, he maintained the wavering, golden shield. He'd given Meiran his word that he'd protect her with his life.

The only thing he could do was die for her.

It was the best he could do. It was all he could do.

"Kyel…" Meiran moaned.

He held the demon's stare, clenching his jaw, and waited for the death blow to fall.

Byron Connel nodded slightly. Then he struck.

An iron fist of air slapped Kyel in the face, picking him up and flinging him to the ground. An explosion of light shocked his vision as his head struck the rocks. Somehow, he retained enough of himself to realize that he'd dropped his shield. Frantic, he rolled over just in time to see Connel disappear.

And reappear in front of Meiran.

She opened her mouth to scream but only blood came out.

Kyel lurched to his feet, clawing the dagger Craig had given him out of its scabbard as Meiran crumbled to the ground. He stared down at her face as she lay dying, gasping her last breaths through a mouthful of blood.

The darkmage whirled toward him, weapon raised.

Kyel lunged forward, plunging the dagger hilt-deep into Byron Connel's right eye.

The demon staggered, dropping his silver weapon on the rocks. He fell to his knees. Then he bowed forward to the ground, driving the dagger even deeper into his brain.

Kyel stood, gasping, numbed by shock. Shaking, he dropped to a crouch at Meiran's side, scooping her up in his arms. He sent a frantic probe into her that returned only nothingness. He threw his head back, strangling a howl.

Power surged into him, locking his muscles tight. Too late, Kyel realized what it was. He tried, but he couldn't let go. All he could do was scream as five tiers of violent power slammed into him from Meiran's corpse.

His body convulsed, his breath wrung out of him as the energies quaked his mind, wracking his brain in a firestorm of sensations. Lights exploded across his vision, a violent shower of sparks accompanied by a stabbing thrust of pain. He threw his head back and screamed his throat raw. He kept on screaming until the violent torrent of energies finally subsided, and he was left weak and shivering, dripping with sweat and drowning in tears. When it was over, Kyel collapsed on top of Meiran's limp body, spent and wrung-out. He was panting, shaking, terrified, appalled...all at the same time.

He let Meiran go, covering his face as he sucked a shuddering breath into trembling lungs. He tried to grasp the implications of what had just happened, but was beyond the capacity for coherent thought. He picked up a rock, the closest thing within reach, and flung it away from him as hard as he could, chasing after it with a howl. Then he reached for the hilt of Connel's weapon, looking for anything else to throw.

He brought the silver morning star up, drawing it back over his shoulder. He was going to hurl it off the side of the mountain like the rock. But something stopped him.

Kyel knelt on the ground, gasping, trembling, gazing at the spiked talisman in his hand. It commanded his attention, captivating him entirely.

A soothing warmth settled over him, calming his nerves and comforting his mind. Kyel let out a sigh, infused with a sense of strength and power he'd never known before. His hands stopped shaking.

All the feelings of terror eased away.

In their place, Kyel felt only a growing sense of wonder.

To Be Continued...

Preview of

Darkfall

The
Rhenwars Saga

Chapter One
Dawnbreak

Pass of Lor-Gamorth, The Front

Not all fires burn hot. The fires in Darien's heart raged like a cataclysm of ice, consuming everything he was, everything he'd been. All that he'd ever hoped to be.

He stood at the edge of the Black Lands, at the furthest extremity of the Rhen. A place where the sea of darkness behind him lapped against the promise of sunlight. As he gazed out across rolling foothills garbed in shadow, he realized the only thing left ahead of him was an end. He wasn't sure what that end would entail, or what it would look like. He only knew it would be final. And he looked forward to that finality.

Winding behind him through the pass snaked a ragtag collection of survivors. Survivors who had, for a thousand years, forged an existence beneath the oppression of everlasting night. He wondered how they would endure under the glaring judgment of the sun. The thought bothered him, crippling his mind until it ground to a halt. He put the question aside, focusing instead on the vast, dark emptiness below, a plain that stretched to the distant horizon, broader than eternity. And the spatters of light that glowed like fireflies, creeping out across the sprawling night.

The campfires of two armies awaited them below.

Darien sat down on a boulder. He looked up into the brilliant face of a full moon gliding toward the zenith of the sky, a sky more wondrous than any he remembered. No longer did the savage clouds rage and rush toward the horizon. High above stretched a starry grandeur he'd failed to appreciate until those pinpoint lights had flickered out, shadowed by the cursed darkness that plagued the world he'd left behind.

Below, the glow of campfires danced and taunted, beckoning like a siren's song. He knew better than to heed that tempting call. It was what his enemy wanted: to lure them out from the protective walls of the canyon, to rush blindly into defeat. The Rhen's commanders had chosen their positions with slaughter in mind. Darien couldn't usher his own forces onto the plain without sacrificing the whole of his vanguard. Perhaps most of his army. Looking down, he could easily envision the mounded corpses that would collect and obstruct the mouth of the pass. They would be forced to scale that gruesome wall. Then the enemy archers could pick them off at will. It wouldn't even be a fight. It would be a massacre.

No, a sortie into the thick of the encampment was not an option. Without a miracle, they were pinned.

Perhaps he could provide that miracle.

The gravelly sounds of footsteps approached from behind. Darien didn't need to look to know that it was Sayeed; he had the distinct sound of the man's stride memorized. No other could replicate it; Darien would know the difference. When the officer drew up behind him, he turned and gazed up into the bearded face of his friend, his brother. The careworn look in Sayeed's eyes should have given Darien pause. But it didn't. He turned back around, looking out across the plain, considering the myriad campfires and their dire implications.

Sayeed bowed. "They have combined the armies of two nations into a single defensive force," he reported. "They have positioned bowmen and infantry to guard the mouth of the pass."

"What do you need?" Darien sat gazing downward at the plain, long hair stirring in the breeze.

There was a crunching noise as Sayeed shifted his weight. "We need a way of punching through their front ranks. Of creating a breach."

Darien nodded. He'd been thinking the same thing.

"I'll do it," he decided. With a sigh, he pushed himself up off the rock and turned to face his senior officer. The man instantly threw his hands up as if trying to ward him off. "No, Brother. It is too dangerous—"

Darien shook his head, already moving past him. "No. It's not."

Sayeed rushed to catch up, but before he could protest further, Darien said, "I'll push their line back away from the mouth of the pass. Send the infantry in after me. For every man that falls, have another ready to replace him."

He expected the Zakai officer to protest, but to his surprise, Sayeed didn't respond. He fell in beside Darien, matching him stride for stride as they descended the trail toward the bottom of the pass. To where his forces huddled in the cold without enough fuel to build fires of their own. With empty bellies and determined minds, and a tenacious faith that remained unfaltering.

They reached the trail that meandered along the river bottom. On this side of the mountain divide, the flagging river trickled downhill toward the plain ahead. They followed the path along the watercourse past lines of hunkering soldiers, toward the forefront of the ranks. There Darien paused, gazing out through the narrow gap in the cliffs that formed the gateway to the Rhen. A gateway that now stood barred by forty thousand soldiers eager to deliver them to their deaths.

He pulled on his threadbare gloves, flexing his fingers. He drew the scimitar he wore at his waist, offering it to Sayeed, who received the blade gravely with both hands. Then he turned and, squaring his shoulders, walked toward his fate.

"Husband."

Darien stopped with a sigh, closing his eyes. He didn't turn around. Instead, he bowed his head in defeat, waiting as Azár approached from behind.

"You promised. Never again." Her voice was as cold and flat as lead.

"So I did."

He turned and looked at her. Azár stood with her hands at her sides, her expression resentful. She had every right to be angry. He had betrayed his wife's trust and left her behind. It had been for her protection, but that hardly mattered. She'd made it abundantly clear that he would never repeat the mistake.

Darien had been born and raised a fighting man. He knew when he was beaten.

"Very well," he said. "I've been meaning to teach you some lessons. Perhaps now's the time for it."

He offered his hand. Azár stepped forward and took it, gazing upward into his face. The look in her eyes was fierce, daunting.

"Where you go, I go," she reminded him.

Darien nodded, internalizing her words. Turning back toward the mouth of the pass, he started forward, hand in hand with his wife.

"Lord! Your armor!" Sayeed rushed forward.

Darien waved him away. "I don't need it. Have the infantry ready. This won't take long."

Behind him, the men were already rising to their feet, reaching for their weapons. He could feel their stares on his back. He ignored them and kept walking. He raised his wife's soft hand to his lips, pressing a kiss against her skin.

"Feel through me," he directed her. "You'll have only a short while, and there's an awful lot to learn. Besides, I might need your help."

Azár looked at him and smiled, her eyes brimming with pride. "You won't need my help. My husband is the most dangerous man ever to walk the world."

"No," Darien said softly, surely. "I'm not."

Hoyte Griswalt shivered in the cold. The small fire he'd built wasn't nearly enough to overcome the wintry chill that stiffened his joints and numbed his bones. His breath clouded the air before his face, his toes aching like open sores in his boots. It wasn't supposed to be this cold, not so far north or this late in the season. He understood weather; he'd plowed a field far more years than he'd taken coin to serve in the royal army. Weather was something he considered himself attuned to, something predictable most of the time. But this weather... it wasn't natural. Hoyte could swear there was something wrong with the wind. Or wrong with the world.

He leaned forward to warm his fingers over the dying coals of the fire, careful not to stress the longbow lying across his lap. He grimaced as feeling shot back into his hands along with a bone-throbbing ache. The fingerless gloves he wore did precious little good. He rubbed his hands together and brought his palms up to his face, blowing warmth into them.

"Fuck, it's cold," said Moss. He was sitting across the fire from Hoyte, hunched forward with a tattered blanket slung over his shoulders, warming his hands.

Hoyte envied Moss that blanket, just as he envied the man's thick beard. His own cheeks would only sprout a few patches of sparse whiskers, a family trait that never failed to rankle him. His boyish face had gotten him teased aplenty in his youth. It was more of a curse now. A right good beard like Moss sported would go a long way toward warming his face. He reached up, running aching fingers over the pathetic growth on his chin.

"Damn fuckin' cold," Pinkston agreed, and spat into the fire. The glob of spittle hissed when it hit the coals. It was one of Pinkston's many talents. He could spit further than any man in their company, and with acute precision every time. He was also the best bowman Hoyte knew. He had arms like an oak, and a calm steadiness Hoyte envied more than Moss's blanket.

"How long do you think we're gonna sit here?" Flem asked, worrying at a strip of jerky with perfect yellow teeth. He was the only man Hoyte knew with straight teeth. Even if the two front ones were big enough to remind him of a jackrabbit's grin. Flem finally tore off a bite, his jaw working slowly in a circular motion, popping as he chewed. Hoyte hated that sound. A man's jaw shouldn't pop like that. It wasn't right.

"We'll sit here however long it takes." Hoyte picked up a thatch of dry grass from a pile behind him and tossed it into the fire. The flames flared up for a moment with a puff of white smoke.

"Why'd you fuckin' do that?" Pinkston said, sitting up. "You know I fuckin' hate it."

Hoyte shrugged. He couldn't care less what Pinkston hated. He thought about tossing another handful of grass just to piss him off. Instead he turned to Moss and said, "Any more of those beans left?"

"Naw. All that's left's a few strips of meat."

"I'll take it, then. Give here."

"Tastes like dog," Flem warned, still chewing his mouthful like a cud, jaw popping with every bite.

Hoyte shot him a glare, leaning forward to snatch the leathery strip from Moss's hand. He tore off a bite and started chewing.

"I'm gonna take a piss," Pinkston said and stood up. He dusted off his pants then started walking away from the glow of the campfire. Hoyte listened to the sound of his footsteps trudging away.

The footsteps stopped abruptly.

"The fuck is that?"

Moss and Flem rose, clutching their bows. Hoyte frowned, wondering if it was worth getting up. He supposed it might be. With a groan, he pushed his stiff body up off the ground, his joints cracking like Flem's jaw. He worked his shoulders, trying to stretch some of the stiffness out of them. Holding his bow at his side, he walked over to where Pinkston stood staring out toward the prairie with a slack mouth. He followed the man's gaze into the shadowy night. He didn't see a damn thing.

"What?"

Pinkston raised a gloved hand, pointing in the direction of the mountains. *That.*

Moss and Flem drew up next to them, Flem swallowing his meat noisily. Hoyte stared across the grassland, which glowed like a silver sea under the full moon. Ahead, the foothills of the Shadowspears rolled away toward a jagged wall of darkness. The mountains towered over them as if holding up the sky. Hoyte's eyes traced the slopes of the foothills before focusing on the prairie. At the forms moving toward them through the night.

"What the hell?"

A man and a woman walked through the tall grass, holding hands as if out for a moonlight stroll. A stroll through a kill zone, with trebuchets and catapults trained on them.

"The fuck," observed Moss.

He exchanged a flummoxed glance with Pinkston, who shrugged hugely, shaking his head. All around, soldiers surged to their feet, fumbled for their weapons. Hoyte calmly looped his bowstring around the notch at the end of the shaft. Then he withdrew a handful of clothyard arrows, thrusting them into the ground at his feet.

"Ready your bows!" the captain bellowed from behind them.

Hoyte grabbed an arrow and raised his bow, angling it upward as his eyes fixed on the approaching man and woman. Neither wore armor, and they didn't appear to be armed.

What the hell?

"Hold!"

Hoyte froze, eyes fixed on the two people closing the gap of prairie toward their ranks. No, they weren't people, he chided himself. They were the Enemy.

"Emissaries?" Moss guessed.

Hoyte figured he might be right, though neither held a token of parlay. It was possible they had come to negotiate. Apparently, the generals felt the same. Hoyte awaited the order to loose his shaft, but it didn't come.

The ranks bowed inward and opened up, admitting the man and woman into their midst. Archers swiveled to track their advance. Hoyte growled, realizing he now stood with his missile aimed at the company of bowmen across the gap. If the envoys proved treacherous, he was more likely to hit his own men than either of his marks. It was a bad situation, and he didn't like it.

"Hold!" the order came again.

Pinkston cursed under his breath, bow sagging at his side. Hoyte glared sidelong at him. "What?"

"It's him," Pinkston gasped, his eyes going wide. "Oh, gods, it's fucking him!"

"Who the fuck's *'him?'*" Moss demanded.

Hoyte felt his bowels loosen as he realized what Pinkston was trying to tell them. *"Lauchlin?"*

Pinkston stood there, head bobbing on his neck. Then he jerked into action, nocking an arrow as Hoyte had done. Flem stood there dumbly, his bow hanging slack at his waist.

"Draw!"

The shout confirmed Hoyte's worst fear. His eyes narrowed at the black-haired demon that had inserted himself into their midst. The man was still walking, deep inside their spreading ranks, holding the hand of a small woman whose eyes blazed with eager flames. Hoyte drew his bowstring back.

"Loose!"

Hoyte let the bowstring sing. Above, the moon disappeared as a cloud of arrows shot up into the sky. Hoyte had another arrow nocked before the cloud reached the apex of its flight. He let it fly as the first grouping of arrows rained down on its target—

—and shattered in a whiplash blast of air.

Screams and shouts drowned out bellowing orders as the ranks collapsed backwards. Hoyte stooped to snatch up his remaining arrows, backing away as quickly as he could. From every side, men jostled and bumped against him in their eagerness to retreat.

A raging firestorm erupted behind them, followed by the awful sound of screams. Hoyte glanced behind to see an inferno gushing toward them from the center of the camp.

The men at his back scrambled forward in terror, shoving Hoyte against the men in front of him. Pinned on all sides, Hoyte dropped his bow and used his elbows to batter his way through the frantic mob. He glanced about desperately for Moss and Pinkston, but they were lost in the surging mass.

Another firestorm exploded only a short distance away. Hoyte felt the heat of it sear his face. Men and parts of men shot high into the air, raining down on those still fighting to escape. The roaring of flames drowned out the sound of screams, as more explosions erupted all around, guts and gore and severed limbs pelting down like battering hail.

Hoyte fought to keep his feet, terror driving him away from the exploding horror. He was shoved, punched, clawed, squeezed, and bludgeoned at every step. He fought his way forward, every inch of ground seeming a mile as men on every side tried to push past or climb over the struggling mass ahead. Hoyte stumbled over corpses that lay trampled beneath the rage of feet. Soon he couldn't move. He couldn't breathe. The weight of soldiers around him crushed his arms against his ribs.

Hoyte would have howled in pain, but he couldn't suck enough air into his lungs to do it. He felt his ribs cracking. His legs gave out from under him. He should have fallen, but he was held upright by the sheer force of the surging masses.

A roiling furnace blasted him full in the face, ripping him out of the crowd and flinging him backward and up. He hit the ground hard, screaming in shock and pain. His arms scrambled feebly as he tried to lift himself up, but he couldn't get any traction with his legs.

He fought to raise his head from the ground and looked down at his body. At first, he couldn't understand what he was seeing. Then came understanding, along with horror. The last thing Hoyte saw as his vision dimmed was his charred backbone protruding from under his ribs, where his middle used to be.

To Be Continued...

Glossary

acolyte: apprentice mage who has passed the Trial of Consideration and sworn the acolyte's oath.

Acolyte's Oath: first vow taken by every acolyte of Aerysius to serve the land and its people, symbolized by a chain-like marking on the left wrist.

Aerysius: ancient city where the Masters of Aerysius once dwelt. Destroyed when Aiden Lauchlin unsealed the Well of Tears.

Alt: God of the Wilds.

Amani: daughter of Zavier Renquist and wife of Braden Reis who was executed for treason against the Assembly of the Lyceum. *(deceased)*

Amberlie: town in the Vale below Aerysius.

Anassis, Myria: ancient Querer of the Lyceum, now a Servant of Xerys.

Archer, Gilroy: son of Kyel and Amelia Archer.

Archer, Kyel: sixth tier grand master of the Order of Sentinels.

Arman, Nashir: ancient Battlemage and Servant of Xerys *(deceased).*

Arms Guild: institution for the study of blademastery. Also called the School of Arms.

artifact: heirloom of power that has been imbued with magical characters or properties.

Asyaadi Clan: group of kinsfolk who live in the village of Qul in the Black Lands.

Athera: Goddess of Magic.

Athera's Crescent: Mysterious and ancient artifact on the Isle of Titherry.

Atrament: the realm of Death, ruled by the goddess Isap.

Auberdale: capital city of Chamsbrey.

Azár ni Suam: Lightweaver of the Asyaadi Clan.

Battle of Meridan: infamous battle in which the Enemy was turned back in large part due to the efforts of the Sentinels.

Battlemage: ancient order of mages who accompanied armies into battle before the Oath of Harmony.

Black Lands: what was once Caladorn, now the desecrated home of the Enemy.

blademaster: title awarded to graduates of the School of Arms, or Arms Guild.

Black Solstice: The battle that ended the Fifth Invasion, when Darien Lauchlin destroyed the legions of the Enemy.

Bloodquest: ancient rite of vengeance condoned by the goddess Isap for righteous causes.

Bluecloaks: slang for the Rothscard City Guard.

Book of the Dead: ancient text wherein the Strictures of Death are inscribed.

Bound: describes a mage who has sworn the Oath of Harmony.

Bryn Calazar: ancient capital of Caladorn.

Cadmus: Voice of the High Priest of Wisdom.

Caladorn: fallen nation to the north, now known as the Black Lands.

caravansary: in the Black Lands, a large courtyard with attached rooms built for the purposes of accommodating caravans resting overnight.

Catacombs: place of burial that exists partly in the Atrament.

Cerulean Plains: large grassland region in the North of the Rhen.

Chamsbrey: Northern kingdom ruled by Godfrey Faukravar.

Circles of Convergence: ancient foci of magic designed to draw on the vast power of a vortex.

clan: in the Black Lands, a kin-based group of close, interrelated families.

Clemley, Sephana: ancient Prime Warden of Aerysius and lover of Braden Reis. *(deceased)*

Conclave: Council formed by the vicars of the Holy Temples that decides religious policy.

Connel, Byron: ancient Battlemage of the Lyceum, now a Servant of Xerys.

Craghorns: mountains that border the Vale of Amberlie.

Craig, Devlin: Force Commander of Greystone Keep.

Curse, the: term used to describe the darkening of the skies and earth of the Black Lands, as well as for the unusual weather patterns and electrical storms experienced in the region.

dampen: to shield a mage from sensing the magic field.

damper: an object that has the ability to dampen a mage from sensing the magic field.

darkmage: a mage who has abandoned moral principles.

Death's Passage: *see* **Catacombs**.

Desecration, the: the apocalyptic event that destroyed Caladorn by blackening the skies and the earth.

Deshari: Goddess of Grief.

Desco: priest of Deshari.

Dreia: Goddess of the Vine.

Eight, the: the Eight Servants of Xerys.

Emmery: Northern kingdom of the Rhen.

Emmery Palace: the queen's palace in Rothscard.

Enana: Goddess of the Hearth.

Enemy, the: collective name for the inhabitants of the Black Lands.

eye: area at the heart of a vortex where the lines of the magic field run almost parallel.

Faukravar, Godfrey: King of Chamsbrey.

field lines: currents of the magic field.

First Sentinel, the: *see* **Braden Reis**.

Front, the: area bordering the Black Lands.

gateway: portal to the netherworld.

Ghost Waste, the: desert in the Black Lands where the Spirits of the Wild are said to roam. Formerly known as the Dhural Uplands.

Glen Farquist: holy city in the Valley of the Gods.

Goddess of the Eternal Requiem: statue of an aspect of the Goddess of Death; her face of Righteous Vengeance.

Grand Master: any Master of the forth tier or higher.

Great Schism: separation between the Assemblies of mages and the ruling bodies of the temples.

Greystone Keep: legendary fortress in the Pass of Lor-Gamorth that fell during the Fifth Invasion.

Hall of the Watchers: Fallen stronghold of the mages of Aerysius, where existed Aerysius' Circle of Convergence.

Hannah, Arden: ancient Querer and former Servant of Xerys. *(deceased)*

Hellpower: *see* **Onslaught**.

High Priest: title of the religious leader of one of the ten Holy Temples.

hyphal artifact: an artifact that is grown instead of wrought.

Ironguard Pass: passage from the Black Lands into the Rhen created by Aiden Lauchlin.

Isap: Goddess of Death.

Ishara: border town in the Black Lands, in the region once known as Skara.

Isle of Titherry: Isle off the coast of the Rhen where exists the artifact known as Athera's Crescent.

Jenn: nomadic people of the Cerulean Plains, remnants of an ancient Caladornian horse culture.

Kateem, Khoresh: infamous Emperor who united all of Caladorn under a singular rule before the Desecration.

Khazahar Desert: arid region in the Black Lands that was once an expansive grassland.

Krane, Cyrus: ancient Prime Warden of Aerysius, now a Servant of Xerys.

Larson, Traver: captain at Greystone Keep, friend of Kyel Archer.

Lauchlin, Aidan: firstborn son of Gerald and Emelda Lauchlin who unsealed the Well of Tears. Brother of Darien Lauchlin. *(deceased)*

Lauchlin, Darien: former eighth-tier Sentinel and Prime Warden of Aerysius, now a Servant of Xerys.

Lauchlin, Emelda: former Prime Warden of Aerysius. *(deceased)*

Lauchlin, Gerald: father of Aidan and Darien Lauchlin, forth tier Grand Master of the Order of Sentinels. Executed by ritual immolation during the Battle of Meridan. *(deceased)*

lightfields: in the Black Lands, places where food is grown using light produced by mages called Lightweavers.

Lightweaver: in the Black Lands, mages who have the ability to produce a color of magelight that mimics the full spectrum of the sun.

Lyceum: ancient stronghold of the Masters of Bryn Calazar.

Mage's Oath: *see* Oath of Harmony.

magelight: magical illumination that can be summoned by a mage that takes on the signature color of the mage's magical legacy.

magic field: source of magical energy that runs in lines of power over the earth.

Maidenclaw: one of the two mountains that mark the entrance to the Black Lands.

Malikar: modern name of the nation that was once Caladorn.

Master: any mage; more specifically, a mage of the first through third tiers.

Meridan: *see* **Battle of Meridan.**

nach'tier: Venthic word for darkmage.

Natural Law: law that governs the workings of the universe that can be strained by the application of magic, but never broken.

necrator: demonic creature that renders a mage powerless in its presence.

Netherworld: realm of Xerys, God of Chaos.

node: place where the lines of the magic field come together in parallel direction but opposite in energy and cancel out.

Norengail, Romana: Queen of Emmery.

North, the: the Northern kingdoms of the Rhen, including Emmery, Chamsbrey and Lynnley.

Nym: ancient river in the Black Lands once considered sacred.

Oath of Harmony: oath taken by every Master of Aerysius to do no harm, symbolized by a chain-like marking on the right wrist.

Oblivion: outcome for a soul who is denied entry into both the Atrament and the Netherworld, which results in the complete destruction of that soul and the denial of eternity.

Om: God of Wisdom.

Onslaught: the corrupt power of the netherworld, also known as the Hellfire.

orders: different schools of magic among the Masters of Aerysius and the Lyceum of Bryn Calazar.

Orguleth: one of the two mountains that mark the entrance to the Black Lands. Also called the Spire of Orguleth.

Orien Oathbreaker: infamous Grand Master who used the Circle of Convergence on Orien's Finger to turn back the Third Invasion almost single-handedly.

Orien's Finger: crag on the edge of the Cerulean Plains where Orien Oathbreaker made his stand and where Darien Lauchlin turned back the Fifth Invasion. Formerly known as Xerys' Pedestal.

Pass of Lor-Gamorth: pass through the Shadowspear Mountains that guards the border of the Black Lands.

Penthos, Luther: High Priest of the Temple of Death.

potential: the ability in a person to sense the magic field.

Prime Warden: leaders of the Assembly of the Hall of either Aerysius or the Lyceum.

Proctor, Garret: legendary Force Commander of Greystone Keep *(deceased)*.

Qadir, Sareen: ancient Querer and one the Eight Servants of Xerys *(deceased)*.

Qul: village in the Khazahar Desert in the Black Lands, home of Azár.

Raising: Rite of Transference, during which an acolyte inherits the legacy of power from another mage.

Rakkah: the final test of an apprentice Battlemage

Reis, Braden: ancient Caladornian Battlemage who was executed for treason against the Assembly of the Lyceum. Founder of the Oath of Harmony and the Order of Sentinels. *(deceased)*

Reis, Quinlan: ancient Arcanist and brother of Braden Reis. One of the Eight Servants of Xerys.

Renquist, Zavier: ancient prime warden of the Lyceum, now a Servant of Xerys.

Rhen: name of the collective kingdoms south of the Black Lands.

Rhenic: common language spoken throughout the kingdoms of the Rhen.

Rothscard: capital city of Emmery.

School of Arms: *see* **Arms Guild**.

Sayeed son of Alborz: Zakai of the Tanisar corps at Tokashi Palace.

Seleni, Naia: former priestess of Death, now a third-tier Master of the Order of Querers.

sensitive: ability in some people to detect the emotions of others. Not dependent on the magic field, and not limited to mages.

Sentinels: order of mages chartered with the defense of the Rhen.

Shadowspears: mountains that separate the Black Lands from the Rhen.

saturation: Battlemage tactic of overloading with magical power in anticipation of creating an enormous discharge of force.

sharaq: ancient system of honor code of the Black Lands.

Silver Star: symbol of the Masters of Aerysius and the Lyceum, indicative of the focus lines of the Circles of Convergence.

Skara: ancient city in the Black Lands that was destroyed during the Desecration.

Soulstone: ancient artifact created by Quinlan Reis as a storage receptacle for a dying mage's legacy.

South, the: Southern kingdoms of the Rhen, including Creston, Gandrish, and Farley.

Strictures of Death: laws of Death.

Swain, Nigel: Prince Consort of Emmery, husband of Queen Romana and Guild blademaster.

Tanisar corps: legions of highly disciplined elite infantry units of the Khazahar.

temples: various sects of worship. Each temple is devoted to a particular deity of the pantheon.

thanacryst: demonic creature that feeds off a mage's legacy.

Thar'gon: magical talisman carried by Byron Connel that is the symbol of the Warden of Battlemages of the Lyceum.

thar'tier: word for Battlemage in Venthic, the language of the Enemy.

tier: additive progression of levels of power among Masters. The higher a Master's tier, the greater that person's ability to strain the limits of Natural Law.

Tokashi Palace: fortress in the north of the Black Lands.

transfer portal: ancient system of artifacts capable of transferring a person to various locations.

Transference: process by which an acolyte inherits the legacy of power from another mage, resulting in the death of the Master who gives up his or her ability.

Tsula daughter of Mundi: the last Harbinger.

Unbinding: the act of forswearing the Oath of Harmony.

Vale of Amberlie: long, narrow valley in the North of the Rhen.

Valley of the Gods: valley where exists the holy city of Glen Farquist.

Venthic: the language of the Enemy.

Vintgar: ancient ice fortress and source of the River Nym.

vortex: cyclone of power where the lines of the magic field superimpose and become vastly intense.

Well of Tears: well that unlocks the gateway to the netherworld.

Withersby, Meiran: Prime Warden of Aerysius.

Wolden: town in the Kingdom of Emmery.

Xerys: God of Chaos and Lord of the Netherworld.

Zakai: officers of the Tanisar corps that form their own distinctive social class.

Zanikar: magical sword and artifact created by Quinlan Reis.

Zephia: Goddess of the Winds.

The Eight Orders of Mages

Order of Arcanists: order of mages chartered with the study and creation of artifacts and heirlooms of power.

Order of Architects: order of mages chartered with the construction of magical infrastructure.

Order of Chancellors: order of mages chartered with the governance of the Assembly.

Order of Empiricists: order of mages chartered with the theoretical study of the magic field, its laws and principles.

Order of Harbingers: order of mages chartered with maintaining watch over Athera's Crescent.

Order of Naturalists: order of mages chartered with the study of Natural Law.

Order of Querers: order of mages chartered with practical applications of the magic field.

Order of Sentinels: order of mages chartered with watching over and protecting the Rhen in a manner consistent with the Oath of Harmony.

Acknowledgements

I would like to thank Kyra Halland, Andrew McVittie, S.D. Howarth, and Daniel Crabbe for being terrific beta readers. I would also like to thank Morgan Smith for her excellent editorial advice. And special thanks to my family for putting up with me.

www.ingramcontent.com/pod-product-compliance
Lightning Source LLC
Chambersburg PA
CBHW030658120726
47905CB00001B/266